ELLA'S WINGS

ELLA'S WINGS

A Story of Survival

MICHAEL WINSTEAD

ISBN 9780999242124

Cover design by Vally Sharpe

PRAISE FOR WINSTEAD'S NOVELS

By turns thrilling and moving, Ella's Wings is an ideal companion to the Ultimate Verdict series, taking readers deeply into the world of one whose life is forever altered by a terrorist attack. Riveting and emotionally complex, Ella's Wings will keep you turning the pages . . .
Joanne O'Sullivan, author Between Two Skies

For lovers of crime novels and courtroom drama, *Ultimate Verdict* by Michael Winstead delivers an exciting story that moves along without getting stuck in legal humdrum, builds up suspense and intensity, and makes us think hard and feel deeply while we turn the pages. Highly recommended! – *TheColumbiaReview.com*

Winstead excels at weaving philosophical questions of good and evil into realistic legal, professional and human conflicts . . . The plot is rich with creative twists and blind turns, leading to a satisfying (and surprising) conclusion . . .
Avrahim Azrieli, Author Deborah Rising

Ultimate Tribunal is an action-packed story that will be loved by people who enjoy suspense and legal thrillers. Laced with intrigue, yet thought-provoking, Michael Winstead's second novel successfully combines an excellent plot with a fascinating glimpse into courts and the criminal justice system. – *Susan Keefe, TheColumbiaReview.com*

ACKNOWLEDGMENTS

On this grand journey of being a husband, father, and lawyer, this novel took 23 years to finish. Its maturation was interrupted by my publication of three other novels. In some ways, *Ella's Wings* is my third child, and as parents know, the raising is not always easy. I say this as apology to those who assisted in this story's development, for over these two decades, I have inevitably forgotten some valuable contributions.

To my wife Candace, who is always my first reader, I could not have done any of this without you. You are the love of my life, who came to me late, but I know you will be by my side when the last word of the last chapter of the final book is written.

My gratitude to editor Joanne O'Sullivan, who recognized Ella's missing pieces and helped me guide Ella through the trials and tribulations of tragedy and a newly discovered life.

Vally Sharpe of United Writers Press created several drafts of the cover, enduring my suggestions and arrows before landing on an intriguing book cover that graphically captures Ella's story.

My thanks also to Hannah Larrew of Spellbound Public Relations for her wise counsel in the ways of marketing and digital publishing.

This book is dedicated to all the innocent victims of terrorism, whose names and lives should never be forgotten.

A portion of the book proceeds will be donated to victim relief funds.

PROLOGUE

Every year, more than 10,000 people worldwide are killed in terrorist attacks. The number of injured is much higher. News stories often report death tolls and details of manhunts, and some in the media theorize about motives and the last moments of terrorists who commit suicide as law enforcement closes in.

In the *Ultimate* book series, I chronicle the efforts of Judge Raleigh Westlake to capture and secretly put on trial criminals who have escaped punishment. His driving motive is to attain justice for innocent victims. In *Ultimate Truth*, the final book in the trilogy, Judge Westlake pursues a terrorist bomber who has framed an innocent man. And while those books delve into the sometimes-thin line between good and evil, and the conflict between justice and the rule of law, those stories are told from a different perspective, with a nod to the plight of the victims, but not their viewpoint.

In *Ella's Wings*, a victim of a terrorist attack tells you her story, in poignant detail. She could have been attacked in New York, Paris, Beirut, or Orlando, but her story is set in Charlotte, North Carolina, where a terrorist's bomb rips Ella's world apart.

This is her story.

Reader's Guide

Ella's Wings travels a parallel time-frame with *Ultimate Truth*, an interrelated story. If you desire to experience Ella's journey solely through her eyes and voice, I recommend you read this book from cover to cover.

However, there is another option. If you wish to discover events outside of Ella's perspective as they unfold, you might read *Ella's Wings* and *Ultimate Truth* simultaneously. If you choose that path, below is the recommended sequence of chapters.

Ella's Wings	**Ultimate Truth**
1	1-7
2-5	8-14
6	15
7	16
8	17
9	18
10	19
11	20
12	21
13	22
14	23
15	24-34
16	35
17-18	36
19	37
20-23	38-43
24	44-45
25	46
26	47-Epilogue
27-51	

1

The search for survivors.

A flashlight struggles to pierce the smoke hovering in darkness. An outstretched hand beneath a pile of orange bricks and chunks of concrete. An engagement diamond reflects the beam.

Two men in flame-retardant suits and bulky gloves fling bricks with furious energy. The exposed hand leads to an arm. Then a shoulder and a neck and a head. The woman is bruised and battered and bleeding. She is not breathing.

Paddles send a jolt of electricity through her. An electronic beep. A single beep on the monitor. Seconds pass. Another beep. Jagged white lines appear on the black screen. She's lifted onto a stretcher.

Transported by ambulance to a triage unit sheltered in a tent on the asphalt lot of a hospital. Rows of similar tents line the street for almost a mile.

Doctors, nurses, first responders, EMTs, and morticians scurry between cots. Ordering, operating, saving lives. Covering bodies with plastic tarps.

The woman with the battered and broken body recovered beneath the bricks does not yet have a name. For the moment, she is simply labeled patient A-12.

A doctor in sky-blue scrubs and a surgical mask hovers over her. The badge dangling from a neck lanyard identifies him as Viktor Volkov. Through the mask he sucks in the scent of smoke, a whiff of charred skin, the stench of excrement from the dead at the end of the tent. He bends to check her chart. A hurried scrawl contains the diagnosis: "Amputation of upper extremities at SHLDR. ASAP. NF." Necrotizing fasciitis. Flesh-eating bacteria has invaded the woman's arms.

With a gloved thumb he lifts the edge of a bandage. Her arms are black. Bacteria. Burnt skin. Dirt.

Her face is slashed with shrapnel, the glint of glass inside a gash. Her right cheek is torn away. Her right tibia is broken, the ivory bone poking through her skin.

Dr. Volkov lifts each eyelid and examines her pupils with a penlight. "Mydriasis of the right pupil," he whispers to himself. The left pupil is normal and reactive. She probably has increased intracranial pressure—swelling in the brain. A natural consequence of being in the path of a bomb blast, he reminds himself.

A bouncing trip on a gurney to a mobile CT in a trailer outside, where her head is scanned. His hunch is confirmed—her brain is swelling. She will die if he doesn't relieve the pressure.

A nurse holds a computer tablet as Volkov watches a video of the procedure on the internet. He positions a hand drill perpendicular to her skull, ready to penetrate. He hesitates. If he goes too deep, he will enter her frontal lobe, which controls memory and other key functions. He cranks the drill with his right hand, spinning away shreds of her skull. He completes the procedure by fishing a ventricular catheter into A-12's brain.

Volkov straightens up, takes a deep breath.

"Do you know the name of this patient?" he asks the nurse.

She scrolls through a list on her screen. "Not yet identified," she says, shaking her head.

"See if you can find out."

The nurse hustles away.

With a bone saw he slices through her upper arms at the shoulder joint, then bandages the shoulders with white gauze. Perhaps the amputations have removed all of the flesh-eating bacteria. Only time will tell.

He steps back and appraises her, as a mechanic might survey a blown engine. She is approximately 30, athletic build, maybe pretty but it's hard to tell with all the gashes on her face. She reminds him of someone.

Dr. Volkov tosses his mask and his scrubs and his gloves into a bio-waste container and emerges from the triage tent. Gray smoke from the bombing of the sports arena hangs in the air, acrid in his nose. Bits of ash cling to the glossy leaves of oaks and maples and hickories. Clusters of tall pines cradle blackened debris.

Ella's Wings

He bows his head to stretch the muscles of his neck. When he looks up, a single butterfly, its wings orange and black with white dots on the edges, hovers near one side of the canvas tent.

2

I do not remember the explosion. I do not recall the searing flash, or the sound of air splitting, or the fireball that consumed three city blocks.

The gaping hole in my memory starts two days ago and seeps backward for months, maybe longer. What little I know I have pieced together from truncated answers provided by doctors and nurses through tight lips.

Here is the summary. A terrorist bombed the downtown Charlotte arena on August 9, during a country-music concert. The terrorist has not been caught. More than 1,000 people have died. So far. Thousands more are injured.

I am one of those.

I was found on a sidewalk, buried beneath a brick wall, which may be what saved me. My legs are badly burned and shredded by shrapnel. My right tibia had a compound fracture that has been re-set. My arms are gone—missing from the shoulder down on both sides. White gauze covers my shoulders. My legs are swaddled in bandages from hip to ankle. In all, these bandages are my cocoon.

Several of my internal organs were bruised in the blast. My liver is barely functioning. I was in a medically induced coma for five days. Yesterday, I woke up.

A handful of doctors have told me it is a miracle I am alive. Swollen brain, flesh-eating bacteria, heart and breathing stopped. Just some of what I'm going through. My body is a mess, both inside and out. I am attached by wires and plastic tubes to machines that monitor every vital sign with an annoying array of clicks and hisses.

My primary nurse sidles through the sliding glass door of my room in the Critical Care Unit. Her name is Gretchen Fulmer. She is wearing a cloth mask printed with pink and purple flowers.

Ella's Wings

Gretchen adjusts a plastic straw in a clear cup and slips the straw between my lips. My lips grip the straw. The water is cold as it sluices down my raw throat.

A doctor in a white lab coat appears at the foot of my bed without noise, as if he's materialized from my imagination. He has a stethoscope draped around his neck. A blue surgical mask covers his mouth and nose. As he moves to the machine side of my bed, he cradles a computer tablet in his left hand.

"My name is Dr. Viktor Volkov," he says. "I am a reconstructive surgeon." I examine the part of his face I can see. He has hard blue eyes and cropped hair that trends to silver at the tips. A drill sergeant's countenance, I think. He leans over the bed, shines a penlight in my eyes. He swings it back and forth as I blink.

"How do you feel?" he says. His slight accent, maybe Slavic, is thick through the mask.

"I'm tired." I have been asleep for almost a week, but I am utterly exhausted.

"That is to be expected. You have been through a great ordeal." He slips the penlight into the pocket of his coat.

"Water?" I say in a raspy voice.

While nurse Gretchen inserts the straw between my lips again, Dr. Volkov's right hand wanders across his face, stroking stubble at the edges of his mask. I notice things like this. What people do with their hands. His mask has slid to the end of his nose, which is hooked like an eagle's beak. He tugs the mask up. "I have some questions for you."

"Sure," I nod.

"What is your name?" Dr. Volkov asks. The fingers of his right hand are poised over the screen of the tablet.

"Ella Winslow."

"Where do you live?"

"Charlotte, North Carolina."

"What is your address?"

I can't remember my address, the place where I have lived for … how long? "Water," I say to stall. After another sip, I simply shake my head, unable to retrieve this simple piece of information.

"Do you recognize this person?" he says, extending his arm toward a woman who is sitting in a chair next to my bed. She is gowned, gloved and masked.

Even with most of her face covered, I know her. "That's my sister Mattie."

Mattie's cheek bones rise. It is the first time anyone in the room has smiled.

"And do you know this person?" the doctor says, extending his arm toward a woman leaning against the far wall, similarly garbed.

I study her for a moment through blurry eyes. The lower half of her face is covered by a blue mask, and most of her head is covered by a paper hat. Above the mask I see gray, glassy eyes. Beneath the hat a few tight curls are exposed. Her eyes leave me and focus on the floor. She wraps her arms around her torso, as if she is cold. This is a move I recognize.

"That's my mother, Rose Winslow," I say.

The doctor types something into his tablet. "Ms. Winslow, do you remember anything about the night of the explosion?"

I try to pull any memory from that night, but nothing comes. I shake my head. "No."

"What is the last thing you do remember?"

"I'm not sure."

"Why were you at the arena that night? Were you there to see the concert?"

These questions seem irrelevant to my diagnosis or treatment. Why is he asking? What does it matter?

"I can't remember why I was there. Why can't I remember?"

"Trauma can produce amnesia," Dr. Volkov says. "There was a lot of pressure on your brain. The memory loss could be permanent."

I try to contemplate this—the possibility that a large swath of my life may be permanently erased. My memory is just one thing the terrorist stole from me.

"So what happened to my arms?" I swivel my chin between my shoulders. There is nothing where my arms used to be. Empty space.

Dr. Volkov takes a half step away from my bed. "Now is not the time. You need to rest."

"Mattie, mama, do you know what happened to my arms?"

Mattie utters a quiet "no." She looks up at the doctor, begging for explanation.

My mother simply shakes her head. I wonder if she does know.

A flash of pain batters me inside. I gasp. My phantom left hand shoots down to the right side of my abdomen to caress. My face is tight and sore. My scalp feels as if someone pulled out chunks of hair. Recently. The morphine must be wearing off.

As the painkiller ebbs, some clarity returns. Or is this desperation emerging from the murk? My arms are gone, and my legs don't work. Missing memory. I am no longer a whole person. I cannot remember what I look like. My injuries have altered my identity.

"I need a mirror. I want to see my face."

Dr. Volkov's eyes are on me. "You are heavily bandaged, Ms. Winslow. There is little for you to see."

"Then take the bandages off."

"Given the severity of your injuries and the risk of infection, that would be medically imprudent," he says. "You can see we are all wearing masks. For your protection, of course."

What he says makes sense, but … "Take the bandages off so I can see my face," I demand. "I need to see what I look like." My voice has risen to a shrill wail, the sounds coming from me those of an animal whose leg is caught in a steel trap.

Dr. Volkov flattens his left palm against my right shoulder, holding me down.

I try to wriggle out from beneath his hand. In my fury, the beeping cadence of my heart monitor accelerates. "No!" I scream. It is the only way I have to fight back.

With his left hand still pressing me to the pillow, Dr. Volkov reaches his right hand to the machine delivering my medication and pushes a button. In seconds I feel a surge of warmth, and then everything goes gray.

3

Sensations from my missing fingers tease me with what it feels like to scratch an itch, brush my hair, type on a keyboard, make a list. I apply lipstick and fiddle with the buttons of my blouse. I rub cold cream on my face, sweep the back of my hand along the sleeve of an angora sweater, wriggle my fingers into fur-lined gloves. I am certain this is all a horrible nightmare. Then I look to the empty place where my hands used to be.

To pass the time, I make a mental list of things I can no longer do. The Can't Do List plays in my mind like a pesky song:

Can't dress myself, hold a glass, brush my teeth or drive a car; smooth a blanket, hold a book, feed myself, or open a jar; blow my nose, type a letter, or sign my name; wipe my tears, take a pill, or play a game …

Following that is a refrain sung by three women in sleeveless dresses, their arms moving to the music. The words are accompanied by a melody dominated by the high-pitched ringing deposited in my ears by the explosion. It mimics the squeal of a heart monitor when a patient's heart has stopped. Sometimes the squeal is loud, other times subdued. But that ringing is always there.

My hospital room is eerily quiet, except when a medical team scrambles past my glass door, heading to some emergency down the hall. A couple of times a day I hear their hectic footfalls and urgent shouts, watch their arms swing as they race past.

There is a telephone on a table next to my bed. An old handset in black Bakelite with a coiled cord. I imagine it has a harsh, electronic bell. It never rings.

Another emergency erupts. The team bustles past my room. For a few moments I hear the bleat of a machine alarm, then it stops.

Minutes pass. I turn my head to the monitors on the cart next to my bed. The sound is off, but I watch the rhythm of my heart on the black screen. I'm terrified the green line will go flat.

I peer at the call button clipped to my hospital gown. It's a small plastic cylinder with a red button on top. Like a detonator. I wonder if the anonymous terrorist used something like this to set off his bomb. In the snippets of hallway conversation I catch, they call him the arena bomber. Someone without a name has stolen my arms. My hands. My life.

The terrorist is still out there. Maybe here in Charlotte. It's hard to imagine what he might be thinking, difficult to fathom the type of mind that can kill and maim so many people without reason. Maybe he's plotting another attack. The next target could be anything: a school; a night club; a hospital. What type of security does this hospital have? Even if they have some warning about an attack, where could they take us all?

Fear spirals upward. My chest heaves. I scream. The sound raises goose bumps on the flesh of my legs. After the third scream, Gretchen slides open the glass door to my room and stands poised at the machine that dispenses my pain medication.

"No, please don't," I say. "I don't want morphine."

"Then why are you screaming? You're disturbing the other patients."

"I can't push the call button."

She looks down at the useless device and unclips it from my gown, wrapping the white cord into small loops, which she places in the pocket of her lavender smock. Her eyes soften. "I'll find an intercom for you. Maybe we have one that's voice activated. I'm sorry, we didn't think … do you need anything?"

"What type of security does the hospital have?"

"I don't know. There's usually a security guard posted in the lobby. Why are you asking?"

"The bomber is still out there."

"That's true, but they'll catch him soon."

"Will they? How can you be so sure? They didn't know enough to keep him from bombing the arena in the first place."

She looks down at the floor, giving me my answer. Sitting in the lone chair next to my bed, she leans forward, her palms on her knees. "You can't worry about things like that, Ella. You need to focus on your recovery."

"Are you scared, Gretchen?"

"I can't afford to be scared when I have all of you patients to take care of."

"But when you're at a mall, or someplace with a lot of people, don't you get scared?"

"I haven't been anywhere like that since the bombing," she says.

As I listen to her, I realize that terror has varying impacts on people. For me, it's a deep fear the bomber will try again. This black cloud has been with me since I woke up. To someone like Gretchen, maybe it's the avoidance of places where he might strike, the curtailment of her normal routine. And a constant effort to swallow down the fear.

"Can I have some water?" I say this to keep her near. I don't want to be alone right now.

She pours from a tan pitcher into my clear plastic cup, then inserts the long straw. Rather than holding the straw to my lips this time, she places the cup on the table attached to my bed and swings it in front of me. I can't quite reach the straw. The tendons in my neck are tight and inflexible. She nudges the table closer. I grunt and wiggle and thrust, and finally I can grasp the straw between my lips.

After a long drink, I ask, "Gretchen, how long have you been looking after me?"

"Since you came onto the ward."

"Even during my coma?"

"Before."

"Before?"

She nods. "In the triage tent. I assisted Dr. Volkov in relieving the pressure on your brain."

"Okay. Do you know what happened to my arms?" She must know.

Her eyes dart to the ceiling. She is deciding whether to tell me. "You need to ask Dr. Volkov. But I can tell you your arms were amputated." Her eyes narrow above her mask, the top half of a wince perhaps.

"That's obvious. In the explosion?"

"You need to ask Dr. Volkov."

I need to keep her talking. She is the primary source of my medical information. "When I was in a coma, did I say anything?"

"Not a word. Not a sound."

"Nothing?"

"No." Her mouth works beneath her mask. "Frankly, Ella, we didn't think you were going to make it. You were in really bad shape."

She looks over at the heart monitor, as if she's re-living a time when the machine alarms were shrieking.

"How many times did my heart stop?"

"At least once in the ambulance, according to your records. Twice while you were in a coma," she says. "We … well Dr. Volkov, shocked you back with the paddles."

I, of course, remember none of this.

"Do you know how many victims were injured?"

"I'm not sure. Something over seven thousand, I think."

"Do you know how many patients have died after coming to the hospital?"

She sighs, tucks the sheet beneath the mattress. "Let's focus on getting you well." Her eyes dart back behind her facade. Disaster and death are daily occurrences in a nurse's life, and now she busies herself with the knobs and buttons and readouts on the machines next to my bed, making notes on the tablet. When she leaves, the room becomes quiet again. Quiet as a t… I don't dare say it.

At least I'm not alone. There are thousands of people like me out there, in various stages of disrepair and misery, all felled by the same bomber. But I am lonely. My sister and mother live two hours away, so they can't visit every day. I am left to a cadre of nurses and orderlies, who minister to every need. But they are not family.

Dr. Volkov won't let me watch television. He's concerned I might see something that will trigger panic. My eyes have nowhere to go, and I don't want to continually scan the length of my body in its covering of bandages. I do have a window, this one covered by gauzy beige curtains. Through it I can see another wing of the hospital and a patch of sky above. It is the only glimpse I have of a world that is moving on without me. A couple of pigeons cling to the ledge outside, fidgeting and cooing. Sometimes they turn and stare through the glass. I wonder what they see.

Loretta Marvin, my psychiatrist, comes to see me. She is a pleasant woman with curly red hair. Not auburn, but just a shade darker than a candy apple. She speaks with an Irish lilt slightly muffled by her mask. The exposed part of her face is perfect, milky skin. There are times when she is talking and I don't hear her because I am staring at her flawless complexion.

She pulls the plastic chair next to the bed. We talk about things you would expect that a victim in shambles and her psychiatrist would talk about. We avoid discussing the bombing, instead focusing on me, my family history, trying to figure out who I was before. There is a lot of bulky baggage there. A father who committed suicide. A broken marriage. A mother who has remained distant for a decade. And a hole in my memory about one-year wide.

"I don't see how this is helping me," I say as rain pecks at the window.

"This is what we do, Ella. Your mind may be as injured as your body. Trust me. Talking helps."

And so we talk, usually in the afternoons. Dr. Marvin dispenses Zoloft and kind words. Words of solace and encouragement. If she could pour hope into my drip bag, I'm sure she would. I am glad when she arrives, and equally happy when she departs, because I am not ready to undertake the hard work it will take to right my mind.

With rare exception, each encounter I have with a whole, undamaged person leaves me with conflicting emotions. I appreciate the effort to help me crawl my way back, but I am jealous of those who have their limbs. Okay, jealousy is a weak word. I am downright resentful.

Dr. Marvin's perfect skin makes me think of my own damaged face. A face whose current condition I can only imagine, for none of those who come into my room will produce a mirror. I try to conjure my visage. I cannot recall the contours of my face or the shape of my eyes. When I look cross-eyed at my nose, it seems a normal size beneath the bandages. I cannot envision how I might look without hair.

I plead with Gretchen, but she will not let me have a mirror. On Dr. Volkov's orders, she says. Instead, she shows me the picture on my driver's license. The plastic is warped, perhaps from the heat of the explosion. In my driver's license picture I am pretty. Long, dark hair hangs just past my shoulders, parted in the middle. High cheekbones and generous lips. Blue eyes below thick brows. A slender nose.

I feel an itch at my right eyebrow, beneath the bandages. I try to maneuver my right hand to scratch it. Futile. My missing fingers still tingle.

Gretchen feeds me three times a day. She slides a spoon into my wide-open mouth, rarely clicking the metal against my teeth. Her hands smell like the rubber gloves she always wears. Whether she feeds me eggs or oatmeal or cereal or toast, my breakfast always tastes a little like latex.

She cradles the back of my head in her left hand and brushes my teeth with her right. Though she works the brush as far back as she can, my teeth never feel entirely clean. She tips a paper cup filled with mouthwash into my mouth. It takes us awhile to get synchronized on that. I spit into a plastic bowl she holds under my chin. With a paper towel she dabs away the dribbles of escaping mouthwash.

She checks my drip bag, then removes my disposable diaper. She slides a metal bed pan beneath my gown. When I am done, she empties the bed pan, rolls me onto my stomach. She wipes me, then bathes me with a damp sponge.

Maybe this is the hardest part, being forced to let someone else handle my basic hygiene, tasks we learn to do as young children. Routine things I once took for granted are no longer within my grasp.

I add to my Can't Do List: *Can't wear a watch, open a door, put on lipstick, brush my hair, sit on a toilet, wipe myself.*

4

My mother and sister come to visit. Mattie settles into the plastic chair next to my bed, while my mother stands on the other side of the room, arms folded across her chest.

"Why don't you come and sit by my bed, mama?"

"I don't want to sit," she says in her smoker's voice, a hard rake on gravel. Her blue mask slides down her nose when she talks.

"Please." Under ordinary circumstances, I would pat the mattress beside me. Instead, I nod to the vacant spot at the foot of my bed.

"I'm fine right here." She stands beneath the dark television mounted high on the wall and aims her voice toward a distant place.

Mattie teaches English and History at the high school in our hometown. She is pleasant looking, but not pretty. She is shorter than me, on the plump side, with brown, watery eyes and a flaccid face. Her nose borders on bulbous. Her hair is the dun of mouse fur. Even so, she has a full head of it.

"Do you know what today is?" Mattie asks.

Without a television or newspapers, or the ability to scroll a cell phone, I have lost track of the calendar. In my macabre state of mind, I have begun tracking time in relation to the day of the bombing—August 9.

"Thirteen days since D-day," I say.

"Well, yes," Mattie responds. "It's August 22nd." She raises her eyebrows at me. Her mouth might be doing something, but I can't detect it beneath her mask.

I search my memory for the significance of that date, eventually find it. "My birthday," I say. Until now, I'd completely forgotten. In my porous memory, once stolid recollections have sifted through unseen pin holes. "I'm 29 today."

"That's right. Your 29th birthday," Mattie says. She stands up and bounces on her toes Her hands are clasped behind her back. "I got you something," she says, her enthusiasm uncontainable. She whips her hands from behind her back, revealing a pair of calf-length socks. The pattern is gray tabby cat, with dark rubber strips glued to the soles.

I stare at them as they dangle from her plump fingers. "Mattie, you know I can't walk, right?"

"Maybe not now, but soon. Plus, they'll keep your feet warm."

She flips up the end of the bed-sheet and prepares to tug the socks onto my feet. She stops, looks up at me, and blinks a few times. "Ella, I didn't know your feet got burned, too."

"Head to toe," I say. "The doctor says my tennis shoes must have melted onto my feet."

"Is it okay to put these on? I mean, it won't hurt you, will it?"

"No, it will be fine."

She tugs the socks over my toes, inches them up my scarred feet by herself. I certainly can't help her. I feel the callous on her left thumb as it slides over my left ankle bone. It's the first time anyone has touched me without gloves on. She straightens the socks and pats my left foot.

"Have you gotten out of this bed yet?" she says, gripping the side rail with her right hand.

I raise my eyebrows, or at least I think I do. Feeling has not fully returned to my forehead. "No." It should be obvious to her that I am a long way from walking. "I don't think you, or mama, really understand what happened to me."

She stares at me as if I am a defiant student. Crossing her arms over her blouse, she says, "Then help me understand, Ella."

"I could have died, Mattie, probably should have, considering. I lost my arms. My legs are torn up and burned. I may never walk normally. Never. Plus, my liver and my spleen are severely bruised. Nothing works right in what's left of this body. Nothing." There, I've said it. Dr. Marvin has been urging me to talk about it. Maybe this is what she has in mind.

"I know … I know this is hard for you, and even when you leave here it won't be easy, but …"

I cut her off. "Don't say anything about hope," I grumble.

"I wasn't going to. What I was going to say is that we're here to help you. Mama and me." She glances at my mother.

My mother picks up a brown shopping bag and takes a couple of steps toward my bed. "I brought you something for your birthday." She hands the bag to Mattie and retreats to the wall.

From the shopping bag, Mattie extracts a large white box and slips off the lid. She pulls out a wig.

My natural hair color is mahogany. The wig is auburn and cut in a style not worn by anyone I've ever known. It's probably been sitting in my mother's closet for at least two decades because it carries a frosting of dust. My head is still swathed in bandages, and I'm weeks or months away from being able to wear a wig. I wonder if my mother brought it for me, or for her. She's standing against the wall, eyeing the window.

"Why can't you look at me, mama?"

"I am looking at you." She re-directs her eyes to a spot a foot or two above my bed.

"Do I disgust you?"

"No, Ella … you don't disgust me."

"Then why won't you look at me?"

She works her mouth beneath the mask.

"I had a dream last night," I say—a necessary change of topic. "Do you want to hear about it?"

"Sure," my mother says.

"I was at the beach. Down in south Florida. I waded out into the surf and jumped the tiny waves. I swam out into the ocean, pulling through the water with long, powerful strokes. Cupping my hands and swimming with an S stroke, just like daddy taught me. The water was so pretty. Clear and turquoise. I could see twenty feet down. Then I flipped over on my back and looked up at the sky. I just floated on that smooth water, feeling the undulation of the tide, barely moving my arms and legs. It was so peaceful, so beautiful."

"That's nice," my mother says when I pause.

"I don't know how long I floated out there, but when I flipped over on my stomach to swim back in, my arms just disappeared. They were there one minute and gone the next. And of course I started to sink. I was trying to stay afloat by kicking my legs, but it didn't work. I started swallowing water, and when I popped my head up for air the last time, I saw you standing on the beach, staring at me. I yelled for you, begged you to come and save me, but you just stood there. You were looking right at me, and I know you could hear me, but you just stood there. I drowned."

My mother stares at the floor. "It was just a dream," she mutters.

"No, it wasn't just a dream. It was an omen."

"You call it what you want, Ella. You believe what you want to believe. But you remember," she says, pointing a nicotine-stained finger at me, "you're the one who left us. Not the other way around. If you had stayed with your family, none of this would have happened."

"I went away to college, mama. I needed some space." I stare at her for a long time, wanting someone other than Anonymous to blame for my plight.

"I need a cigarette," she says, heading for the door.

"If my heart quit beating, would you even call a nurse?"

She sighs deeply, letting out bad air. "You know, Ella, you're not the only one who has to live with this."

I watch my mother jerk open the sliding door. She doesn't look at me when she leaves.

"She's just upset," Mattie tries to explain.

"Upset about what? I'm the one who should be upset, not her."

Mattie looks down at the floor, deciding whether to concoct an excuse for our mother's behavior. "She's not ready for this, Ella, not yet. I'm working on her. We've been watching videos about caring for people with disabilities."

I start to say something, but she holds up her hand. "I know you'll walk again, Ella. But if we prepare for the worst, then whatever happens, we'll be ready."

"Not even the doctors can fully predict what will happen, Mattie. Surgeries to repair my face, months and months of physical therapy just to see if I can walk again. And if I leave here, daily… no, hourly… care. Forever. Twenty, thirty, fifty years. Are you prepared for that?"

"I am. And if we need help, we'll get it." She says this without hesitation, an unyielding certainty in her eyes. Telling me she'll be there for me. Whatever I need.

I have not really contemplated how my family has been impacted by my injuries. Perhaps misery does love company, but not when it's the company of my mother. It is difficult to know exactly when the rift between us began to form, but the moment of origin is of little consequence, because by the time the explosion took my arms, the chasm was already wide. I did not invite her to my wedding, didn't even tell her I was getting married until after it was over. She did not approve of my marrying Robert, who is twenty years older than me, almost as old as my father would have been if he hadn't killed himself.

"She'll be there for you when you need her most," Mattie says. "We both will."

I have no rebuttal for this, and even if I could manufacture something, it would be designed solely to derail the momentum Mattie is building. I feel a surge coming from her. She's being strong for me because I'm not. To challenge her commitment would only serve to stymie my recovery. She will be there for me. As she stands staring at my feet covered in stupid striped socks, I can see she wants to fix this broken thing. I can see she wants to fix me.

5

Curiosity can be a tricky thing, but I need to know what happened to my arms. Gretchen told me they were amputated, but I don't have details. I don't know why.

Dr. Volkov shows up at 9:37. I know this by the red digits on my bedside clock. I've been preparing myself while Mattie went downstairs to get coffee. She's back, sitting in the chair beside my bed. I look over at her. Dr. Volkov has lifted the mask requirement for my visitors, so I can see Mattie's full face for the first time since I woke up. She nods encouragement.

"What happened to me?" I say before Dr. Volkov even gets to my bedside. It's not really the question I want to ask, but it's a starting point.

He looks up from checking my vitals on the tablet, scratches his maskless chin. He holds my eyes.

"There was a bombing. Downtown. At the arena."

"I know. I mean later. After I was brought to the hospital."

He steps back from my bed. "What do you remember about being brought to the hospital?"

Answering my question with a question is an obvious dodge.

"Nothing. I was in a coma."

"What is the first thing you do remember, when you woke up?"

I turn my head to Mattie, whose mouth is set, her arms resolutely crossed over her chest. "Seeing my sister."

"Yes. Of course. What do you want to know?" Dr. Volkov says.

"Who cut off my arms?"

He does not hesitate this time. "I amputated your upper extremities. It was a necessary procedure to save your life. Your arms were infected with Necrotizing Fasciitis. Flesh-eating bacteria. If I had not performed the amputation, you would have died from infection."

He stares at me, as if he's trying to peer through my skull and into my brain. "I also relieved the intracranial pressure caused by bleeding in your cranium. Without that, you could have suffered severe brain damage, or your vital functions could have ceased."

"So you saved my life?"

He rubs irritated skin on his jaw-line. "Yes. I helped other victims as well."

"Do you know the original meaning of the word 'victim'?" The question comes from Mattie. She tosses this at Dr. Volkov like she is challenging one of her high school students. When he doesn't respond, she answers. "It's Latin. Originally from the fifteenth century, it means a creature killed as a sacrifice to a deity. Later, it came to include a person who is hurt or tortured by another."

"This is torture," I say.

"With the surgeries I will perform, you should soon return to normal."

"Normal? You call this normal?" I rock from side to side, exhibiting the depth of my incapacity. "I'm as helpless as a newborn. Look at me."

"It was a poor choice of words, perhaps." He runs the tips of the fingers of his left hand over his lips, as if to corral other words on the verge of escape.

"How dare you touch your face in front of me. Every time you touch your face, it's an insult to me. I don't have any goddamned hands." I lift my torso from the bed in anger and frustration.

His response is measured. "It might be time to remove the bandages from your face."

He sets his tablet on the counter and approaches me with blunt-tip scissors in his right hand. He snips away the bandages, unwrapping the gauze in a slow twirl.

A coolness descends on my skin like morning mist. With a strong hand on my chin, Dr. Volkov turns my head from side-to-side, studying me as if I am a specimen. I feel his gloved fingers glide across my scalp and trace my cheeks and jawline. He tears open a package and uses sterile gauze to dab away my tears.

"You are healing well, right on schedule," he says. "Skin grafts will be necessary."

"I want to see myself," I say.

"That might not be prudent," Volkov says. "It is too soon. I can show you pictures later."

"Bring me a mirror," I demand, trying to maintain the strength that Mattie has instilled in me.

At some point during my tirade, Gretchen has entered the room. She looks at Dr. Volkov for direction, and he nods. She leaves the room and returns with a small hand mirror, rimmed in pink, and angles it in front of me.

"Oh my god," I whisper.

There is no doubt the creature staring back at me is dead. Its face is pink and chalky. Its lips are pinched and pale. A jagged scar runs from the corner of its mouth to its jaw. Pale patches of stitched skin lie like a ragged quilt on its cheeks and forehead. Its face has been chewed by a malevolent machine. Its head is shaved for burial.

Phantom hands shoot up to caress my damaged face.

"Your scars will fade, Miss Winslow. Some of them may disappear entirely, in time. That is my hope, and my mission."

I cannot meet the eyes of this thing in the mirror. Its face is revolting. When Gretchen pulls the mirror away, I realize the demented bomber has turned me into a creature from a horror movie.

6

When Dr. Volkov shows up to examine me again, I pounce on him. "What did you cut off my arms with?"

"A saw."

"What kind of saw?"

"An oscillating bone saw."

"I want to see it."

His eyes reflect annoyance. "You're not going to stop pestering me until I show you, are you?"

"No."

"Give me a few minutes."

He leaves the room. During this time I engage in my now-equivalent of nervous hand-wringing, curling my socked feet and toes over one another. The nurses have turned on the television, with Dr. Volkov's approval. The sound is barely audible. A female newscaster is talking about the bombing. Blue banners scroll across the bottom of the screen:

2,146 confirmed dead
7,593 injured
FBI press conference imminent

Dr. Volkov returns to my room. "This is a bone saw," he says, presenting it with outstretched arms. "It is battery operated. It has a high-speed motor and an oscillating blade."

"Turn it on. I want to see how it works."

He pauses. "It is very loud," he says in mild rebuttal.

"Turn it on. Please."

He stands next to my bed, pushes the switch with his thumb, rotates the speed dial until the saw emits a high whine.

I watch the metal blade. It oscillates so fast the blade appears stationary, but I can envision it chewing away bone. My bones. The buzz of it makes the skin on the back of my neck crawl. I feel a twinge just below my right shoulder.

"Did you video the procedure?" I ask when he turns off the saw.

"No. It is not something you would want to see," he says with a finality that tells me this discussion is over. He turns toward the door, the saw dangling from one hand.

The scene on the television switches to the press conference. A wooden dais set up on a city street in downtown Charlotte. A man in suit and tie steps to a podium with the blue FBI logo on the front of it.

A banner on the screen identifies the speaker as Special FBI Agent Eric Mullen. I find myself holding my breath.

"Thank you all for coming on such short notice," he says into the array of microphones. "I am pleased to report that we have identified the bomber of the Charlotte arena."

I am transfixed in anticipation. Anonymous has finally been identified.

"The FBI, Homeland Security, ATF and specialists from the US Army, as well as two private genetics testing labs, have been hard at work, sifting through the evidence. As you might imagine," Mullen turns to the hulk of the bombed arena behind him, "this has been a monumental task. But we had to get it right. As you know from previous releases, the bomb was planted in a white delivery van that drove into the underground loading dock of the arena, just behind me. The bomb was made from diesel fuel and fertilizer, and ignited by a cell phone. It was a suicide bomb. And although the bomber himself died in the blast, multiple DNA testing confirms the identity of the bomber. It was former Charlotte Mayor Carmelo Williams."

"Carmelo Williams?" I say. "That can't be."

The media begins hurling questions at the FBI agent. "Please, please, hold your questions for later. We have a special guest. Please welcome the President of the United States."

Our President, Danny Roberts, takes the podium. I have seen him on television on many occasions, but here he is in Charlotte, less than a mile from the hospital where I lay. His face is stoic beneath thick, wavy hair.

"This is a monumental day for law enforcement, from top to bottom," he says, "and for our country. Now this great city, and the entire nation, can truly begin to heal." With his right hand he unbuttons his suit jacket, then places that hand on the lectern, his elbow jutting out.

"All of the credit here goes to the hard, unceasing work put in by a lot of people, including first responders, search and rescue, recovery teams, the FBI, Homeland Security, the US Army, Mecklenburg County Sheriff's Office, Charlotte police, and hundreds of nurses and doctors and other medical professionals who have been caring for our wounded brothers and sisters."

At this I turn to Dr. Volkov, but he has gone.

I had expected that when the bomber was finally identified, I would feel some sense of relief, maybe even jubilation. I would have a face and a name to blame for my plight, for my diminished condition. Some of the nurses and I pondered the identity of the terrorist in the early days of my recovery, and our conclusion was always some jihadist from a foreign country had come to the Queen City, part of a secret cell, and laid waste to a few city blocks and thousands of people.

We could not have been more wrong. I don't understand how the Mayor, a man for whom I voted twice, could have done such a thing. How could he do this to his own people? It occurs to me that maybe this is what victims of a school shooting say when a fellow student carries out a terrorist attack inside their own classroom.

Gretchen comes in to feed me a lunch of vegetable soup, apple sauce, and pudding. Baby food.

"Can you believe the Mayor was the bomber?" I say between spoonfuls.

"It doesn't surprise me one bit that he did it," she says.

"I thought he was a good man," I say.

"He was a former drug dealer, right?" Gretchen says in retort. "I mean, didn't he run for office based on turning his life around—from young thug to community activist, or something like that?"

"I still can't believe our own Mayor was a terrorist."

"They verified it with DNA, Ella."

After Gretchen leaves, the questions dart at me like fireflies in the night. What was his motive? I can't discern one. Maybe a terrorist doesn't need a motive other than to incite terror. But terror is not the predominant emotion I've had since waking up in the hospital. Misery is the right word.

Mayor Carmelo Williams? Part of me wants to muster some evidence that it was not him, but I have nothing. It is damned infuriating that he got off like that, blowing himself up and not having to witness his carnage, avoiding consequences and prison. Now, there is no person for me to curse, or beat with my fists, or spit upon. This isn't right. This isn't justice.

7

Dr. Volkov appears at my bedside early the next morning, holding a pair of blunt-nosed shears. He wordlessly dons vinyl gloves and cuts away the spiral of tape and gauze on my legs, revealing what I have only glimpsed as I stared down the length of my body while the nurses changed my bandages. Today I am sitting up, and I have a full view. Of the scissors snipping away the white gauze. Of one side of Dr. Volkov's face as he bends to the task. Of the salt and pepper hair on the back of his head, a bald spot beginning to emerge just below his crown.

When fully revealed, my legs look like chicken drumsticks left in the oven an hour too long. My skin is marred with curled red scars that resemble dead worms. My muscles are atrophied and drooping. The flesh along my thighs is gray and crinkled and crusty.

Dr. Volkov surveys my legs. He begins at my left hip, tracing a gloved finger down the outside of my leg, along a nerve that no longer feels numb. He tickles the sole of my left foot until I pull my foot back.

"Good," he says.

He repeats the examination on my right leg.

"Can you feel that," he says, flicking his finger along the sole of my right foot.

I shake my head. "No, not really."

He straightens up, fists on his hips. "The nerves in your right leg are less reactive than in your left."

"Why is that?"

"It is possible your right side took the brunt of the explosion," he says. "Or the brick wall that fell on you could have damaged the nerves in your right leg."

He returns to the tablet, tapping and stroking the screen with his fingers. He pulls the tray across and lays the tablet on it, standing next to my shoulder. "Let me show you something."

He scrolls photos of my face, starting with the day I was brought to the emergency tent, moving through them with a quick swipe of his right index finger. The photos are a horrific reminder of the state of my face. I can see a marked improvement since day one, but I cannot imagine how my visage gets much better.

With his right hand Dr. Volkov fingers his chin, as if searching for a beard that used to be there. "Now let's look at your future face."

I nod with a sense of foreboding.

He taps an icon that starts an animated make-over. In the scenes, which dissolve within a few seconds, the swelling subsides. The yellowish skin of healed bruises disappears. My skin grafts, stitched quilt-like across my face, begin to merge until my skin is a consistent peach color. My eyebrows flourish. My hair grows back in.

"You can do that?"

He nods. "With six or seven surgeries."

"Let me see the finished product again," I say.

He taps an icon, and the new me reappears. My hair is dark and lustrous, the color of a wet log. My cheekbones are prominent and flush. My nose is thin, almost regal, and my lips are plump as if full of collagen. This is an improved model if my memory of my driver's license picture is accurate. But the white scar running from the right corner of my lower lip to my chin is still there, faded but not vanished.

"Can you make that scar on my chin disappear?" I can almost feel my index finger tracing its inch-long contour.

"I will endeavor, but it will probably remain. Very faint."

I nod. As the slide show proceeded, I had dreamed of perfection. But I wasn't perfect before, and if the animated images are accurate, I will be beautiful when all is said and done.

"I want to hug you," I say. "For all of your efforts to bring me back."

In response, he kills the power on the tablet, lets it hang by his side. "Your arms will be harder," he says, looking at a place on my hospital bed. "You'll be fitted with prosthetics. Not by me. By a very capable team."

I sense a dilution in his promise of a magic transformation, but something Dr. Marvin told me allows me to dismiss the negative thought before it grows inside.

"When can we start?"

"Next week, but only if you can get out of this bed by then. You'll need to be ambulatory—be able to move and get your blood circulating—to take full advantage of the recovery process." He consults the tablet. "Based on your improving condition and test results, today is your last day in the CCU."

There is an unspoken question on my lips.

"This afternoon you'll be moved to the rehabilitation wing."

"I can't go home?"

"No."

"When can I go home?"

"You cannot walk, Ms. Winslow. You are weeks away, perhaps months." He tucks the tablet computer beneath his arm and leaves without further comment.

I am tired of hospital rooms, of bland walls and windows that only look out upon other colorless structures. I want to feel the sun on my face. I want to hear doves coo in the trees. I want to feel the crunch of leaves beneath my feet. I want the comfort of my own bed.

After Dr. Volkov leaves, I inventory my injuries in case I will have to recite them to a new doctor once I arrive in the rehabilitation wing. My arms are gone. My legs feel like pieces of lumber, rigid and mostly unresponsive. My liver is limping along, barely doing its job. I feel like an animal that has been stalked and mortally wounded, its life-sustaining systems completely wrecked. And left to die in a cave. Each contemplation of my physical condition leaves me sullen, my eyes looking inward. It is too much to absorb, too much to witness.

In preparation for my move to the rehabilitation wing, Gretchen removes the catheter from my left thigh, eases the lead from the heart monitor off my chest. Thus detached, she helps me scoot to the side of the bed, then settles me into a wheelchair.

"How does that feel?"

"I'm good to go."

We emerge into the hallway. "Can we stop by the maternity ward? I'd like to see the newborns."

"We can do that."

Gretchen pushes my chair down a series of hallways, and we take one elevator before we arrive at the maternity ward. The viewing window is low and broad, the glass smudged with finger and nose prints. I count seventeen babies in clear plastic tubs. Their arms and hands and legs and feet are swaddled in white blankets. Pinched pink faces sleep or wail. Utterly helpless.

I have come here to find something, perhaps to gain purpose from these newborns who are aligned like eggs in a carton. I recognize the parallels between these infants and myself. Like them, when I am hungry, I cry out to be fed. I pee and poop in disposable diapers. Until recently, I lay swaddled from head to toe in white. I can escape from my bed only with the aid of others. I am basically helpless.

There are two women in pink scrubs wandering among the bins, cuddling and soothing these babies. I imagine ecstatic parents in rooms down the hall. Perhaps the mothers are sleeping, exhausted from the prolonged process of labor, trying to regain strength between feedings. It's not a feeling I would know.

A young father settles at the window next to me. He taps the glass as if he can garner his child's attention, whose eyes are barely open if at all.

"Which one is yours?" Gretchen asks.

"This row, third from the window," he says. His eyes are puffy but clear.

One of the pink-clad attendants points to the bin, and the father nods. She plucks his child carefully from its nest and brings it to the window. I can't tell if it's a boy or a girl. There are no pink or blue blankets to designate gender, and at this stage their faces and wispy hair all look the same to me. The father lapses into baby talk and wiggles his fingers at his sleeping child. We'd all do it if we could.

I cant my head toward Gretchen. "Are those women nurses or volunteers?"

"Volunteers," she says. "We're stretched too thin to staff the maternity ward with nurses. Except in NICU."

"Do you think I could ...?"

"It's not a good idea," Gretchen says.

"I don't mean now. I mean after I recover. Do you think I could volunteer in the maternity ward?"

I watch the young woman through the window, cradling a child in her arms, swaying slightly from foot to foot. Of course I'll never be able to do that. I am an invalid. *Invalid.* Whether you place the emphasis on the first syllable or the second, it still means the same thing. Not valid. Null and void.

8

My physical therapist introduces himself as Zack, no last name. He has short blond hair and the build of a wrestler. His young face is taut, with a tiny white scar that tugs at his upper lip. He has green eyes that seem ten or fifteen years older than his age, filled with knowledge and understanding.

On our first morning together, Zack moves me to the edge of the bed. I try to sit up, but the muscles of my abdomen and back are so weak that I fall back onto the mattress like a rag doll.

He works my legs up and down, bending my knees and straightening them, watching my face for reactions. I feel the pain in my legs but not the wince on my face as my eyes crinkle and my mouth grimaces at every movement. I only know this because Zack tells me.

"If it hurts, let me know," he says.

"It always hurts," I say.

"Discomfort is fine, but we don't want pain, especially if your nerves are damaged in your right leg. You need to learn the difference." He engages me with his eyes, hazel today, to let me know we are partners in this endeavor.

We work through twice-a-day sessions, Zack twisting and loosening muscles and tendons and ligaments and skin that have been dormant for a long time. He kneads my neck, helping me regain flexibility there. And, on the bed, I do pelvic lifts and leg raises to rebuild the muscles in my abdomen and back.

"Your core is everything," he says. "These muscles have been inactive for a prolonged period, so we have to teach them how to move again and make them strong."

"Okay. Why?"

"Because one day you will leave this place."

"Do you think I'll ever be able to go back to work?" I ask.

"I don't see why not. The fact that you asked that question shows you're motivated to do it."

"I was a software developer, you know."

"You *are* a software developer, Ella."

"Yeah, but I used a keyboard. With my fingers."

He drops my left leg and steps away from me, surveying my bare skin. He opens a jar of cream and rubs it up and down my shins, onto my calves. "So, you'll use voice commands. I think it's time you started using these legs again."

"Right now?"

"You know of a better time?" Zack says. "You're not getting any stronger lying around like you're on vacation or something."

"Some vacation."

Zack lifts me from the bed and plants my legs on the floor. Beside me, he is a stout tree. My right leg is almost as numb as my missing arms. I wobble for a moment, unable to hold out my arms for balance. We stand together on the linoleum floor, watching sixty seconds tick from the wall clock, breathing in unison. Standing without falling is a victory of sorts.

My first step takes the efforts of four people. It isn't actually a step, more of a shuffle. I don't think my socked feet ever leave the floor. Kneeling behind me, Zack nudges my right calf forward, while a new nurse named Heidi supports me at my left shoulder. My sister Mattie supports me on the right. One tentative step. Then two. I am like a skater on ice for the very first time. It takes the four of us almost two minutes to go the twelve feet to the window. Then we slide back to the bed.

"You're making great progress, Ella," Mattie says after Zack departs.

"It's a lot harder than I thought it would be."

She tips the ubiquitous plastic cup and straw to my lips. I take a few sips. I try to keep track of my water intake. Zack and the nurses remind me frequently I need lots of water to re-hydrate my muscles and my skin. A half-gallon per day is my goal, but of course what goes in must come out.

My thighs are cramping with pain beneath the sheet. I shift a few inches. "I thought mama might come visit today."

Mattie sighs, then fiddles with a lock of hair by her ear.

"How long are you going to keep making excuses for her?"

"I'm not. She's just not ready, Ella. I don't know how to explain it."

"I'm her daughter, dammit."

"Yes, in her eyes, the daughter who left."

"Is she still hung up on that?"

Mattie nods. "She's never forgiven you for leaving, not entirely. She feels like you abandoned us after daddy died."

"I went away to college."

"But you didn't come back home after graduation."

"Do you feel like I abandoned you?"

"I did then, but it was a long time ago."

"Why didn't you ever leave?" I ask.

"No reason to. I've got a good job, a comfortable house with no rent. Somebody to cook for me."

I doubt this is the real reason she's stayed, but I don't challenge her. "Look, I don't know when I'm going to get out of here. Dr. Volkov controls that decision. But when I do, I'm going to my house here in Charlotte. I'm not coming back to the farm."

She purses her lips. "You'll have to discuss that with mama."

"It's not up for discussion," I say.

Within a week, I am sliding across my hospital room with only Zack supporting me. I can still barely lift my feet. I don't care. I am walking, or almost walking, and having Zack hold me while we move around the room like drunk dancers makes me forget who I am. At least for a moment.

After a night of bad sleep, Zack pushes my wheelchair down to the Physical Therapy Department. For patients, PT stands for pain and torture. Zack hooks me up to a yellow harness tethered by a white nylon rope to a metal rail on the ceiling. A life vest of sorts. I stumble between parallel rails waist high. The round rails are made of wood, rubbed smooth by patients with hands. When I trip, or my legs slide out from under me, the harness and rope keep me from smacking the floor. My initial goal is to walk the length of the bars without falling. In truth, it is Zack's goal for me. I haven't set any goals for myself. Setting goals will mean thinking about the future, and I can't yet bring myself to contemplate a future in which someone else will decide when the lights can be on in my room, when I can eat, when I can shower, when I can get off the toilet.

Zack's preferred torture is the duck walk, where I have to squat down and waddle along the floor. Sometimes he makes me duck walk ten feet, and on other days I have to cross the entire room before he will let me stop. There is a method to his madness. It's all for my benefit.

Today, I crouch, my feet spread wide, and begin to waddle across the floor. My quadriceps are sore. After a few steps, I teeter and fall onto the linoleum tiles.

"I can't go today," I say from my prone position.

Zack looks at me, his arms crossed, his eyes holding a skeptical sympathy. With a bit of a smile on his face, he says, "If at first you don't succeed …"

"I might get hurt. I don't have anything to break my fall."

"I won't let that happen," Zack says. He retrieves a red helmet from a rack on the wall and buckles it on my head.

I waddle a handful of steps and fall again. I lie on my side on the floor, my breath heaving, and vaguely count the flecks of color in the linoleum squares.

Zack lifts me up as if I am an empty grocery bag and settles me on a padded metal chair. I am 5' 6" tall. My weight used to hover around 130 pounds. Now, I am at 106. I lost about five pounds with each amputated arm, but still.

"What's going on today, Ella?" His eyes study me.

"I don't know. I didn't sleep well last night. My legs hurt. They thrash around all night."

"They're not used to the activity. It's probably your nerve endings healing, the capillaries in your muscles getting bigger from the exercise."

"I'll be better tomorrow. I promise." I try to plead with my eyes, though I don't know what this looks like, coming from a tattered face.

"Okay, we'll double down tomorrow," he says.

I am still having the swimming dream I told my mother about. In each episode, I lose my arms in different ways. In one instance, my arms are shredded by a boat propeller. In another, my arms are sliced off on the razors of an oyster bed. One night, a shark eats my arms, tearing each off at the shoulder, leaving pulpy stumps. The shark version scares me the worst because I never see it coming. Afterward, I lie awake on my bed, my sheets soaked with sweat.

Zack makes me do dozens of toe crunches and toe lifts. I arch my toes to the ceiling and point them at the opposite wall. I stand and roll a tennis ball along the arch of each foot. I twist each foot in clockwise circles, then counterclockwise. He attaches small weights around my ankles to increase resistance and build up strength. When my feet cramp, he massages them and applies a warming salve.

"Why do I have to work so much on my feet?"

"They're your hands now," Zack says.

"Yeah, right." I sputter.

"You'll be surprised what you can learn to do with your feet. You keep practicing, you'll be able to open doors, put on some clothes, maybe even feed yourself."

"You must be joking."

"Do I look like the kind of guy who jokes about something like that?"

He doesn't. I assume the things on my lengthy Can't Do List will always be off limits for me. Zack shows me a series of videos on the internet of women without arms who can do incredible things with their feet. They feed themselves, dress and undress, drive a modified car, cook dinner, open doors. These stark visions, generally void of musical enhancement, capture the grunts and sighs of women accomplishing things I have concluded are impossible. Sometimes, these women introduce themselves on camera, but rarely do they explain how they came to lose their arms. I watch as Sophie from Germany opens a jar of sauerkraut with her feet then, with a standard fork between her toes, heaps sauerkraut into a pot. Elizabeth, who is much older than me, demonstrates how she can shoot an arrow, loading and holding the bow with a steady foot. Laura deftly dresses herself, shrugging on a buttonless blouse hanging from a rod and pulling up elastic-waisted pants with her feet and teeth.

These videos exhibit a power of determination and resilience I can only imagine. Seeing their skills, and how they have coped, is much different than hearing words of encouragement from someone who has all four limbs. I wish someone had showed me these videos weeks ago. Watching them, I am ashamed that I have wallowed in self-pity for so long. I feel a sense of hope that pools tears in my eyes.

On a morning after another shark dream, I turn to Zack and announce: "I don't want to duck walk for you today."

"You're not doing it for me," he says.

"I want something harder," I declare.

He flashes a smile that I know has been waiting for days to emerge. He pulls a foam mat from a stack and centers it on the floor. Then he helps me settle on the mat, on my back. "Okay. Get up and open the door, then go back to your room." He walks to the door, flicks off the lights in the PT room with two fingers of his right hand. Then he grips the doorknob with the fingers of his left hand, pulls opens the door and leaves me alone.

I watch his fingers and catalogue the maneuvers. There is a database in my head of fine digital movements that I hope will translate to the ten digits I still have.

His challenge is a daunting assignment, involving four tasks, two of which I have never accomplished individually. In my heart I feel this is the ultimate test.

First, I have to get off the floor. I twist my body and rise to my knees. I plant my left foot, then push with all my might, using my foot and thigh and abdominal muscles and sheer will to stand up. I wobble. Both legs shake. "I can do this," I whisper to no one. The moment of joy evaporates when I look at the closed door.

I approach the door and its round knob, studying the silver finish that thousands of hands have worn down, revealing a brassy metal beneath. I shuck my socks by placing my right heel just in front of the toes of my left foot, pinch the left sock into the floor, and pull my left foot out of the sock. Then I repeat. I face the door and take a deep breath. Balancing on my right leg, I lean back, raise my left foot and grip the knob with my toes. I rotate my foot to the right, then to the left, toes grasping at the worn metal, but I can't move the knob far enough to release the latch. I hop backward and lower my leg to ease the cramping in my foot. I switch feet, balancing on my left leg and gripping the knob with the toes of my right foot. I get the same result. I can't turn the slick round knob far enough to release the door latch.

I lean my back against the wall, sweat trickling down my nose. The thought that I might fail and have to call for help flickers within me. I can't fail. I conjure the video of Sophie, opening a vacuum-sealed jar of sauerkraut with her feet. Her jaw is clenched. The glass jar is on its side, not upright.

I lean my right shoulder against the wall and, balancing on my left leg, place my right toes on the doorknob. I arch my foot and roll my toes forward and back, the knob like the tennis ball tracing the underside of my foot. I turn the knob away from me, to the left if I were facing the door, and I hear the latch release. I swing the door open and step into an empty hallway. A surge of emotion clogs my throat. It is my first true taste of freedom since the bomb went off.

9

A monarch butterfly flutters outside my hospital window. It hovers at an upper corner, traverses the lower glass as if trying to light on the yellow pansies thriving in a plastic pot near the window. I hear it bump delicately against the window. Tick, tick. Four times. Foiled in its quest for nectar, its orange and black wings carry it off on unseen currents.

Egg, larvae, pupa, butterfly—the monarch's life cycle. I have raised monarchs in a netted enclosure in my backyard. Now is the time they usually migrate along the meandering trail that carries them through Charlotte and down to Mexico.

In our parallel metamorphosis, I am reversing the life cycle—adult to cocooned pupa, swaddled in white bandages until recently. Once I am ready, I will emerge from the hospital, a sleek, caterpillar-like creature.

Mattie visits again on the weekend, bringing with her a picnic of barbeque ribs, cornbread and corn on the cob. She also brings a homemade pecan pie, topped with pecans from last year's crop from the trees in the creek bottom of my mother's farm. Another thing I will never be able to do: pick pecans.

Mattie lays out the food on two blue plastic plates, then settles the plates on the ubiquitous tray attached to a metal arm on my hospital bed. She drags a stool that Dr. Marvin uses over to my bed, positions herself on its padded seat, and picks up a fork.

"Now, how do I do this?" There is an expectant look on her face. Her eyes and mouth are soft and kind. She sees feeding her big sister as a challenge, not a chore.

She is the first person other than the nurses to offer to feed me, but then I have had few visitors.

"Small bites," I say. "Get the piece on the end of the tines, then hold the fork steady, horizontally, in front of my mouth."

She peels rib meat from a bone, cuts it into small chunks, then stabs a piece with the tines. She brings the fork an inch from my mouth. "Close enough?"

I nod, then thrust my head forward, closing my lips around the meat. I slip the chunk into my mouth, then retreat. Like a trout sucking in an insect. The pork is succulent, aromatic. Though I have three meals a day in my room, it's mostly bland food, prepared with delicate stomachs and low-functioning digestive systems in mind.

Mattie puzzles over the cornbread and the corn on the cob, each nearly impossible to fork. "Oh, this is going to be tough."

The cornbread crumbles from Mattie's fingers and spills from my lips. She dabs my mouth with a paper napkin. She presents a cob of corn with her index fingers pressed against the cut ends. I try to take a few nibbles but most of the kernels fall away. We just can't finesse it.

The pecan pie, the filling a mixture of corn syrup, brown sugar, butter and eggs, resuscitates my taste buds. I have two slices, spooned by Mattie. She tilts a foam cup with a plastic straw. I take a long drag of sweet tea.

I lie back against the raised bed, my stomach fuller than it has been in weeks, rumbling with the process of digestion.

"The last time I ate this much was Thanksgiving." I belch. "Excuse me." I can't cover my mouth with my hand, but my brain sends the signal anyway, and I almost expect to see my hand rise. The sensations are still there—the subtle rotation of my left shoulder, the flex in my elbow, my fingers curled to a comma at my lips. I snort at my delusion. Mattie wipes my nose with a clean napkin. We giggle like schoolgirls.

I was not a debutante, but our mother taught us table manners from Emily Post's book, handed down from our grandmother with notations in a neat hand in the margins. We used to practice at dinner. No elbows on the table. Chew with your mouth closed. Don't clink the silverware. Use a napkin and not your sleeve. I can easily comply with most of those rules.

"This is my new reality," I say after the giggling subsides.

"It's all right, Ella. We'll look after you. We'll take care of you."

I eye her, wondering what the "we" really means. "She's still pissed at me for leaving?"

Mattie sighs, gazes through the small window in the wooden door to my room, hoping to be rescued. "I'm not sure," she says. "She hasn't exactly talked about it."

"But?"

"But … she's worried." She stares down at the floor, fiddles two fingers at her chin, deliberating over the words to use. Mattie doesn't want to choose sides. She wants to stay neutral, like Switzerland. She has gained this maturity in my absence, the knowledge that words have real meaning and sometimes can't be taken back.

"My sense is that she recognizes how everything has changed, and she's not sure she's up to the task of taking care of you, of fulfilling your new needs."

"That's a very diplomatic way of putting it," I say. Something rises in my throat, and it's not the food. My heart, no longer monitored by a machine, thrums in my chest like a caged bird. Perhaps it's just the effect of so much sugar. "Mattie, do you think she might see me as an imposition? Maybe even a burden? I mean what parent wants to have to take care of every need of their twenty-nine-year-old daughter?"

Mattie reaches for the plates and begins cleaning up. Without saying a word, she's answered my questions. She stands at the sink, rinsing the dishes.

"When is your next facial surgery?" she asks.

"I don't know." I've had two procedures since I re-learned to walk, each an incremental improvement. "Dr. Volkov hasn't been by in a few days."

She slips the plates into a grocery bag and returns to the bed, sits down near my knees. "I can see a difference," she says, her right thumb smoothing the skin above my eyes. She adjusts the wig on my mostly bald pate.

"Better?" I ask.

"Oh, yes. Absolutely. But different, too."

"Different? What do you mean?"

She pulls a compact from her purse and scooches up next to me on the narrow bed. She angles the mirror so I can see my face.

"Your nose is slimmer. Can you see that? Your nose used to be only slightly more narrow than mine."

I peer at her nose and compare it to the nose in the mirror. Her nose is border-line bulbous; mine is like a sleek arrow that flares at the end.

"And your lips are fuller."

"That's good, right? Full lips?"

"Yes," she says, "but your lips are almost pouty."

"Pull out my driver's license. It's in my wallet in the drawer of the table."

With deft fingers she slides my driver's license from the plastic sleeve and holds it in front of me with her left hand, her right steadying the compact mirror for comparison.

Even through the warped plastic of my driver's license, I can see the difference. My new nose is definitely slimmer, my lips fuller. My eyes have become more elliptical, whereas my eyes in the driver's license photo are rounder.

"I like the changes," I say in an unsettled voice.

Mattie shrugs. "As long as you're okay with him changing your face."

"They're not big changes, right? Maybe that's what he has to work with. There was a lot of damage."

As I stare into the mirror, I convince myself these are the adjustments I would have requested if I'd been undergoing cosmetic surgery. I could be a divorced woman seeking a make-over as I approach that 30-year milestone in life. Sculpting my nose, adding contour to my lips, tightening the skin around my eyes. Still, before changing my face like this, shouldn't Dr. Volkov have asked me?

10

I sit perched on a stool, the filmy white curtains of my window parted, and gaze onto a lawn between the hospital and the parking garage. The view is better here than in the CCU. Life thrives outside. Birds hop among the limbs of an oak tree. Squirrels traverse the edges of the lawn, burying acorns. A stained cement fountain with three tiers spills water to its base, sparkling in fall sunshine. Doctors and nurses and other undamaged people traverse the sidewalk from the parking garage to the building in smooth gaits I can't yet manage.

I catch a glimpse of Dr. Volkov as he navigates the white-washed sidewalk near the garage, dribbling something from a mug into emerald grass. Coffee grounds maybe. He tips the cup as he walks, then glances once into the coffee cup to make sure the litter is fully dispersed.

When he arrives at my hospital room almost two hours later, I charge toward the door.

"Why are you changing my face?" I say in a cracking voice.

He stops a few feet away. "Do you not like your appearance?"

"Well, yes, but that's not the point, is it? You told me you were going to restore my face to normal, or almost normal. You didn't tell me you were going to change it."

"Ms. Winslow," he says, his accent more pronounced now. "I showed you the before and after photographs and images on the tablet. The alterations are clearly depicted in the final version, which you approved. In fact, you seemed ... almost ecstatic."

I do like the changes. He's improving my appearance, at least my face. There's probably not much he can do with the rest of my body.

"Okay. I admit my face looks much better after the last surgery. Now, I need to go home." My throat has regained its full strength, and I declare my intention without a hint of equivocation.

"You are not ready."

"I need to get out of here. This place is slowly killing me."

He ponders this with knuckles pressed beneath his chin. "Do you want me to arrange a wheelchair with a joystick for you?"

"No," I say. "I can walk on my own."

"Have you arranged for nursing care when you leave the hospital? Your extended care will be complicated. You have personal needs you can't accomplish alone."

I have made no such arrangements. There is a shaky presumption my mother may stay with me for a while. Or she may not. I dodge his interrogation. "Why are you keeping me here so long? I'm physically able to go home now. I could check myself out."

"You do not fully understand the challenges you will face. Basic hygiene, cooking meals, entering and leaving rooms and buildings, navigating stairs without hands." He ticks these off the fingers of his left hand with the index finger of his right. "For me to release you, you must meet two conditions. First, you must arrange for suitable after-care. And second, you must be able to walk down the three flights of stairs to the cafeteria, unassisted."

He leaves the room after this pronouncement. As I watch his stiff back retreat into the hall, I have a sudden urge to throw something at him. I can take care of myself already. The list of things I can't do has shrunk considerably. He is holding me in the hospital longer than necessary, but I discern no nefarious motive for him doing so. With my foot, I send the stool wheeling across the room.

For the next few days, I work feverishly with Zack. I lift weights, stretch scarred skin that barely yields, take innumerable soaks in the whirlpool. I duck-walk on cue, and hop up and down a wooden set of three stairs. I spend almost as much time in the PT Department as I do in my room. Between repetitions of leg lifts, I grunt out my frustrations.

"Don't you think I should be let out of here?" I ask Zack.

"I'm not your doctor."

"But your recommendation would carry a lot of weight."

"It's not up to me."

"But I'm ready," I exhale as I raise a padded bar on the quadricep machine, my thighs quaking.

"You're getting close."

My thighs, still not fully recovered from the char and atrophy, are the key to navigating the stairs. With each downward step, each leg will have to take my full weight independently. Without the benefit of arms or handrails. It's my right leg I'm most worried about. The feeling has not fully returned. Much of the time I'm walking on dead wood.

"All right. Let's do one leg at a time," Zack says.

This is no easy trick. I start with my left leg, by far the stronger of the two. I am only supposed to do ten repetitions. As the machine creaks, I count out repetition number twelve.

"Don't strain yourself. Now lift with the right leg."

I complete repetition number seven before my right thigh begins to burn. At least I can feel it. Number eight releases a cascade of sweat down my forehead. At this point, most people would be able to use the leverage of their hands gripping the handles next to the seat. Repetition nine is produced with a clenched jaw and a refusal to acknowledge my quadricep is on fire. I try to remember if this is what my legs felt like when the explosion scorched my jeans to my thighs, but I come up empty. I thrust my back and shoulders into the seat, grit my teeth, and accomplish repetition ten out of sheer will.

I look at Zack. He helps me struggle from the machine. "That's how much I want it," I say between heaving breaths.

Through Mattie, I negotiate an arrangement that my mother will be my primary caretaker once I am released. If she proves unable, or unwilling, we will hire a day nurse to tend to my most urgent needs. The unwilling part is what I worry about most, but I need my mother's agreement for my release.

Unannounced, Dr. Volkov pushes open the door to the PT Department one afternoon. He stands by the door, his arms crossed over his white lab coat, and watches intently as I walk flawlessly between the parallel bars, my head erect, my core engaged. I parade up and down the apparatus several times. Then I stand on one leg for a count of thirty. I hurry over the wooden set of stairs.

I traipse over to him. "Satisfied?" I ask his mirthless face.

"Those aren't real stairs, Ms. Winslow."

"Okay, let's go. I want to do it now."

I pull off my socks, leave them on the floor, and with the dexterous toes of my left foot rotate the round doorknob and exit the PT room into the hallway.

Dr. Volkov follows in my wake, and Zack hangs back only a step. I push the elevator button with my big toe, and together we ride up to the fourth floor.

The stairwell is next to the elevator bay, leading down to the cafeteria on the ground floor. The door to the stairwell has a lever instead of a round knob, and I lean back slightly, lift my left foot to the lever, and tip it down with ease. Then I nudge the door open with my foot.

"I'd like to put a helmet on her head," Zack says. "Just in case."

Dr. Volkov nods his approval.

Zack settles the thin helmet over my wig and buckles the strap beneath my chin. He gives me a wink of encouragement. "You can do this, Ella. You're ready."

I sidle through the steel door, not holding it for my entourage of two. I eye the red-painted rail on my right, reach for it, but of course nothing happens. It's instinct, something I've probably done a thousand times. I stare at the rail for a moment before edging closer so my hip nestles against the rail. A fluorescent light on the landing below casts an eerie glow. I count ten stairs to the landing, half a flight. The stairs are steep. I distribute my weight evenly on each foot. I take a deep breath. Then another.

There is nothing elegant about the first step. I reach down gingerly with my left foot, toes first, and settle my foot on the concrete pad below, my full weight centered over my left leg. I then follow with my right, landing on the same concrete step. I will inch down the 60 steps in this way, like a toddler walking down the stairs for the first time without mommy's guiding hand.

I hear the door close behind me, the shuffle of feet on the landing above. Leaning against the rail, I glance back to see Zack and Dr. Volkov above me. One of them nods encouragement. The other bears a stoic countenance.

I ignore them both. I must do this on my own.

It is an arduous journey, with pauses on each landing to allow my shaking thighs to rest. Though I twice lose my balance, I tilt into the wall of the stairwell and steady myself. Three levels down. The soles of my feet ache with the effort.

When I arrive at the ground floor I push the door lever down, swing the door open, and sidle around it.

I emerge, my face sheened with sweat, to a hallway full of nurses and doctors, their scrubs a riot of color after the dimly lit stairwell. They begin to applaud, and nod, and smile. A few of them pat my back. I realize that all of this has been their journey too, and I have been so selfish not to recognize it. This brings tears to my eyes, and they spill over and run down my cheeks. Because I have nothing to wipe them with, Nurse Gretchen steps toward me and dabs a tissue over my cheeks.

"Thank you. Thanks to all of you," I say. "Everyone has been so great. I could not have gotten to this point without any of you." It is a poor speech, an insufficient show of gratitude, but it is all I have. I turn to Dr. Volkov, who has been standing beside the stairwell door with the expression of a bronze statue.

"Congratulations, Ms. Winslow. I will release you in the morning."

11

I leave the hospital after 51 days. It seems like a lifetime. Dr. Volkov is nowhere in sight. My mother has to sign the discharge papers for me. Zack wheels my chair through the automatic doors, even though I could have walked out by myself. Hospital policy.

I rise from the wheelchair without his aid, careful to engage my core muscles, as Zack has taught me.

"Wow, I can't believe I'm finally getting out of this place," I say as rain splatters beneath the edges of the portico.

"You earned it," he says.

"Couldn't have done it without you."

He nods in acknowledgment. There is no shaking of hands. No hugs. My mother's twelve-year-old Buick pulls up. I sidle onto the passenger seat. Zack reaches across and buckles me in.

"You come back to see me now," he says with a tender hand on my right shoulder.

I'm too choked up to respond.

As I watch Zack retreat into the hospital, I wonder how long I will stay in his memory. Will he remember me for a month? A year? I want him to remember me for forever. I want him to care about what happens to me. As the rain patters against the windshield, it dawns on me that for the past few weeks, primarily Zack has kept me going. Without him, I would probably still be lying in a hospital bed, kicking at the sheets in frustration.

We idle at a stop light. The car radio is off. It is the most quiet I have experienced since I awoke from the coma. The stench of cigarette smoke, embedded in the upholstery and carpet, invades my nostrils.

"You sure you want to go to your place?" my mother breaks the silence.

It is a question she's asked incessantly in our recent telephone conversations, the repetition an argument in itself. After being confined in a hospital with sterile walls and uniformed staff and other patients in various stages of decline that remind me of my own diminished self, I must go home. Not to an apartment with elevators and sliding doors with motion sensors. Not to the childhood home where my mother and sister still live. My home.

"I'm sure."

"It'd be a lot easier on everybody if you'd come back home."

I turn toward her. "You mean easier on you."

"Well of course, but …"

"My home is here, mama. Has been for the past eight years." As I contemplated my release over the past few days, I recalled the day I moved in with Robert Stoudemire. It was in the spring. The pink dogwoods and fuchsia-colored azaleas were in full bloom in the front yard. Their pungent scent filled the air around the front door. Robert carried me over the threshold, even though we weren't yet married. He almost dropped me when he spun to kick the door closed.

But there are still large chunks of missing memory, mostly from the recent past. My grandmother, who died of dementia, could remember as clear as day things that happened decades earlier, but she often couldn't recall whether she'd eaten breakfast that morning. My missing block of recollection seems to start around a year ago.

My mother drives slowly through the mid-morning traffic. She is not eager to arrive at any place where I will be her responsibility. We have not specifically discussed the details of what she will be required to do. I'm fairly certain Mattie has filled her in. I wish Mattie were here, but she has school today and can't get away. My mother and I have not settled on how long she will stay with me, but the arrangement is sufficient to obtain Dr. Volkov's consent.

Hospitals and medical centers line the road for a mile. I ponder how many of the bombing victims are still being treated in those big buildings. How many have died inside those pale concrete walls? How many left the hospital but will never really recover?

I did not seek the company of other patients during my rehabilitation. There were weekly group sessions of victims in a conference room at the hospital, but I never ventured to those meetings. I straddled the proverbial fence, unwilling to spill my misery upon strangers with similar plights, who might view me with pity or jealousy, and I was too selfish to allow empathy for their burdened lives. In the PT room, I'd nod to other patients, men and women, and sometimes children, often with downcast eyes and heads drooping from pain medication or sedatives. I just couldn't engage them.

"You happy to be out of the hospital?" my mother asks. She is trying.

"Sure, mama."

"You don't look happy."

I shrug my shoulders, force a smile. "I don't fully know what to expect."

The problem is I know exactly what to expect. For the rest of my life, somebody else will feed me, bathe me, dress me and wipe me. We will live like conjoined twins, sharing everything except organs and freedom. Unless we can afford home healthcare, I will be at my mother's mercy forever, and mercy is something she has very little of.

One of the things Dr. Marvin has taught me is to recognize my changing moods and halt the slide before it turns into an avalanche. I wish I could say I have healed myself in that regard, but all credit must go to her. It is almost inevitable that when I think of my future, the descent begins. Best for me to take one day at a time and stay in the present, Dr. Marvin counsels—a trite phrase, but it seems to be working.

My mental salve today is trees. From my room in the rehabilitation wing, I could see only one oak tree and one half of a pine. As we drive down glistening streets toward my home, I admire an oak with bark the color of ashes and a graceful set of limbs rising to a beautiful, symmetrical crown of verdant leaves. Pecan, white oak, water oak, hickory, and dogwood in various stages of presentment. Though their limbs will be stripped bare soon, they will sprout leaves when the weather warms and return to their glory. My limbs will not reinvigorate next year.

On my street there is a For Sale sign in the yard of a neighbor whose name I have never known. The lawns are neatly trimmed, except for mine, which is a jungle. In my absence, the azaleas have shot up and now cover a good part of the front windows of my house. The grass is more than a foot tall and runs rampantly across my sidewalk. I will never be able to pull out the mower and mow my yard again. The paint on my house seems more faded, the shingles more rumpled, since I was here last.

Michael Winstead

My car, a white Toyota sedan, sits in the gravel drive of my house, covered in the airborne muck produced by two months of idleness. I vow to wash it as soon as I am settled back in. Then I realize how foolish that vow is.

I see the dilapidated condition of my house and yard as my mother's rebuke of my decision to come home. She could have hired someone to trim the shrubs and mow the lawn, but my unkempt yard is my welcome-home gift. I hope she does not let me fall into similar disrepair.

She unsnaps my seat belt, then steps away from the door. She watches idly as I struggle from the car. I turn my torso, swing my legs to the opening, scooch to the edge of the seat. I plant my feet on the gravel drive and grunt as I extricate myself from the car without hands. I try to keep my face impassive, not wanting to give her a hint that this is difficult for me. Once free, I stride to the brick front porch.

My mother pulls my ring of keys from her purse. The key fob is a triangle of leather with a gold-colored "E" glued to it. I don't remember when or where I got it.

"Which one?" she says.

"The small brass one," I nod.

"This one?"

"No, the next one over. The other way."

Metal clinks together as she slides the key into the lock, turns it to the left. I hear the snap of the bolt pulling back. She fits the same key into the round doorknob, jiggles it, and turns the knob. She pushes the door open with her palm, pulls the key from the lock, and drops my key ring back into her purse. Snaps the purse clasp shut.

The mundane task of opening a locked door has become a fascinating maneuver to me. I make a mental note to hire a handyman to change the round knobs to levers. Maybe I'll install entry locks that operate on voice command, or a retinal scanner.

My house smells of mildew and the dampness of unstirred air. A cloud of dust rises from the couch when I sit on it. My house plants, once vibrant from attention, are shriveled and brown. Crumpled leaves and stems litter the hardwood floors in small circles of decay. Even the cactus has died waiting for me. The curtains have not been opened in months, forming a semi-permanent shroud on the coffin of my home. The absence of sunlight casts a pall in the corners, making the rooms seem small and dank. Dead flies cluster on the windowsill above the kitchen sink. I look at my mother, about to say something, but I hold the thought for another day.

We sit silently in front of the droning television. We watch a series of game shows and talk shows that must be part of my mother's daily routine. In the hospital, the television had become my closest friend. It stayed on from the time I awoke until the nurses turned it off after I had gone to sleep. The babble of voices kept me company like the burble of an aquarium aerator, drowning out the incessant whine of the ghostly bone saw. Now, those same voices keep me from having to make conversation with my mother.

I wander into the kitchen and stare out the window above the sink, framed by turquoise curtains that mimic the color of water in the Caribbean. Outside is my dilapidated butterfly garden, abandoned since the night of the explosion. The netting has been shredded in places by fierce winds. All the butterflies are gone now. I hope they escaped to migrate and did not perish from my lack of care. But I know better.

Two squirrels chatter in the long-limbed live oak in my backyard. As I watch them skitter along the branches, a memory emerges: I was planting bronze-leafed begonias and purple and yellow impatiens last spring. Right there, beneath the spread of the oak tree. Six months ago. I discovered almost a bucketful of forgotten and decaying acorns as I dug with the hand spade in my right glove.

Above the bed of begonias sat a once-white birdhouse with the round door ringed in blue. A sparrow couple birthed a handful of chicks there last spring. As I began to put away my gardening tools, the chirp of a baby sparrow drew my attention to the perch. I thought all the birds had left the nest. I hadn't seen anything fly in or out in days. A scrawny sparrow teetered on the perch, lifting its wings in the dappled light. Then it fell, landing with a soft thud on one of the orange bricks lining the flower bed.

I bent over the bird. Its eyes were glassy. I flicked at it with a gloved finger, but nothing happened. Then the bird opened its beak, exhaled a squeak. And never moved again.

12

On my first night home, as I lie in bed without the company of machine sounds, the darkness envelops me. My thoughts wander to worst-case scenarios. I could get in a car accident and be unable to extricate myself from the burning vehicle. I could fall into a pool and drown. I would be unable to defend myself from an attacker. And though these scenarios are unlikely, perhaps even wildly so, if I am going to die in some unusual way, maybe suicide might be better for everyone in my circle. Yet I can't pull a trigger or tie a noose or slip a plastic bag over my head. The bomber has stolen this from me too.

Dr. Marvin asked me once if I ever "think about suicide." What does that mean? If it flits through your brain like the myriad of impulses you never act upon, is that *thinking about it*?

My father thought about it, and then he did it. With a noose and a hemp rope knotted to a barn rafter in such a way that I, his 17-year-old daughter, found him dangling in the stillness. I still don't know why he did it. He didn't leave a note, and dead people don't explain themselves.

At the time, this singular event consumed me. At home, at school, and everywhere I went I saw his silhouette hanging stiffly in the barn. After I shut my eyes at night, I saw him. I saw him in the morning mist rising from our fields. I saw him when I closed my eyes in the shower.

My father's suicide, and the speculation over his motive, were the talk of our entire town that year. Students whispered about it in the school hallways as I approached. Adult friends of my parents abruptly stopped talking whenever I entered a shop downtown, or the post office, or the convenience store where we gassed up the car. Rarely would I hear them discussing my father's death, but their tight lips and hooded eyes told me.

That's one reason I don't want to return to my childhood home—those stares, sometimes in the form of accusation, as if suicide is a contagious disease spread by the survivors. How would I distinguish those looks from the gawks I'll get because of my empty sleeves?

I roll over in bed and realize I forgot to take my anti-depressant today. I no longer have a nurse to dispense my medication at scheduled intervals. I pad to the guest bedroom in socked feet, wake my mother, and she feeds me a Zoloft.

As she sits on the bed, slipping her hands between her knees, I ask her, "Why did daddy kill himself?"

She looks up at me with creases on her tired face. "Ella, let's not do this tonight. That was twelve years ago."

I am back in bed. My hands are itching. It could be psoriasis. The house is dry, and I have no means of rubbing moisturizing cream on anything. The itch is excruciatingly delicious, the little blisters on my palms and between my fingers begging to be scratched. My fingers are on fire as I intertwine them, rubbing back and worth until the webbing is raw and red. I dig my nails deeply into the flesh of my palm, gouging skin, scraping off the heads of blisters, which weep into my palms. I awaken to empty pajama sleeves.

The next morning, with dew dripping down the kitchen windowpanes, I find a note propped against the sugar bowl, carefully scripted in my mother's hand in blue ink. Written on a pad with a twist of purple wisteria at the top, the note says: "Gone to the grocery store." She signed it "Mother." Inside the "o" she has drawn two eyes over a smiling mouth.

My stomach growls. I didn't eat any supper last night. A form of protest, I guess. I have already grown weary of my mother's presence, though she has probably done nothing to cause that. I want coffee to pull me from sleep, but the pot is empty. Would it matter if the pot were full?

I sit at the kitchen table and wait. Why isn't she back yet? I ask this silently at first, then out loud, though I don't know who I'm talking to. She shouldn't leave me alone in the house. What if there's a fire? How am I supposed to get out? What if somebody breaks in? They could steal something, or I could be raped, or even murdered. How am I supposed to defend myself?

I pace into the living room, looking out the window for signs of her old car, then back to the kitchen, checking the clock as minutes tick by. The window, the clock, and back again. In this state of agitation, I blame my mother for incidents long forgotten. Once, I fell down and bruised my back because my mother forced us to play outside when there was ice on the steps. Happy, our grey terrier, ran away because she whipped him for peeing behind the sofa. She forgot my birthday when I was sixteen.

I hear car tires crunch the driveway gravel. My mother struggles at the door with grocery bags in both arms. She knees her way through the door, sets the bags on the butcher-block counter, and begins putting the groceries away in high cabinets.

"How are you this morning?" she says with her back to me.

I don't answer.

She turns around. "How are you feeling this morning, Ella?"

I sit at the table with hard and bitter eyes, trying to stare a hole right through her. I want retribution for all the awful things she has done to me, and I can think of only one way to get back at her. With steaming eyes, I void my bladder, overflowing the already-saturated incontinent underwear, forming a big puddle on the kitchen tile.

"Ella, what are you doing?" she shouts.

"I peed."

"Why didn't you say you needed to go?"

"You're supposed to change my underwear first thing in the morning."

"I couldn't. You were still asleep."

"You left me alone."

"I had to get groceries."

"You left me alone."

"I was gone less than an hour."

"There could have been a fire."

"I left the back door unlocked, so you could get out."

"You left the door unlocked? I can't believe you did that. Anyone could have come in. You want someone to get me, don't you? You were hoping someone would come in and get me. You want to be rid of me. You want me dead," I scream.

Mother slaps me with an open palm, knocking me from the chair. On the bare skin of my cheek, it sounds like the crack of a gunshot. I fall on my side, into the puddle of urine, soaking my pajama top. I get to my knees, then thrust up to face her.

Ella's Wings

Her arms are rigid at her sides, her lungs heaving, her eyes hard. Her right hand curls and uncurls, as if she is quelling rage. Or preparing to throw a punch.

"Go get in the tub." She says this with the tone of a prison guard, though I've never been to prison, so I don't actually know.

"I can't do it by myself."

She grabs a roll of paper towels and kneels by my puddle, begins sopping up the product of my rebellion. She looks up at me and blinks. Her eyes and mouth have softened a shade. "I'll be there in a minute," she says.

I lie down in the claw-footed tub, still clad in my pajamas. With my toes I flick the lever to engage the drain stop, then inch the faucet handles to the left. The water starts flowing.

My mother has never slapped me before, not that I can remember. My father doled out the discipline in our family, usually with a switch or a belt. Though mother didn't punish Mattie and me physically, she often threatened us with what our father would do to us when he got home. We'd mull that threat all day and watch the clock, waiting for him to come through the door. Before we could say anything in our defense, my mother would tell him what we'd done. His face would change, and he'd slowly unbuckle his belt. My mother, of course, knew she could ruin our entire day with one of her threats. It was almost a relief when my father whipped us.

I am embarrassed by my behavior this morning. My mother did nothing to bring on my bout of anger, and she certainly didn't deserve that outburst. As the steam rises in the tub, my mother appears, her arms crossed over her torso, her hands clamped beneath her upper arms.

"I'm sorry, mama. That was childish."

"To say the least," she says. She takes two steps toward the tub. "Stand up."

Her hands tremble as she slips the plastic buttons through the slits in my pajama top. She peels the soaked top from my shoulders and drops it in the sink with a wet plop. She does the same with the sodden pajama bottoms. She watches as I settle naked back into the tub, resting my head against an air-filled neck cushion affixed to the rolled rim with plastic suction cups.

"Can you turn the water off, too?" she asks.

With my toes I twist the knob for hot to the right, then repeat the maneuver with the cold knob. Now only a trickle of water dribbles from the faucet.

My mother bends down and cinches each knob a smidge until the trickle stops. "Maybe you can do more with those feet than you care to admit."

13

Hospital day. Back again, in a huge room with maybe two thousand other people, for a conference of bombing victims. Doctors and nurses staff a row of white tables set up below the stage. Victims in wheelchairs line the floor in a long chain. Others hobble on canes or walk in halting steps to their seats. Some of the faces are familiar, patients I've seen in the hospital corridors or in the PT room. I scan the line of wheelchairs. I see patients with severe burns on their faces and necks, a woman with both ears and her nose missing, a teenaged boy with his legs amputated at the knee. I am not the most injured victim here. Not even close.

I didn't have to come. The email invitation warned that the event could be emotionally disturbing for some. I spoke to Dr. Marvin about it, and she told me it might be good to assemble with other patients, that it could be an important step forward in my recovery. My mother encouraged me to come, but from her I got a sense she just wanted to get me out of the house. She dropped me off and sped away only after watching me walk through the sliding doors of the lobby.

I climb concrete stairs and settle into a seat about two-thirds up. I draw a few glances. My mother has pinned the long sleeves of my navy-blue dress, so I'm essentially wearing a sack.

From my perch I can see Dr. Volkov. His head is down, his attention focused on the ubiquitous tablet computer, propped on a white table. I don't see nurse Gretchen or Zack. I assume they are working.

The presentation starts with FBI Special Agent Mullen, the one who delivered the news to the world that Mayor Carmelo Williams was the bomber. Our tormentor. Agent Mullen stands behind an oak lectern and tells us that it is rare to be addressing the victims of a terrorist attack, but this is a unique situation for all of us. If we are willing, he can provide us details that have not been released to the public. He asks for a show of hands from anyone who doesn't want to hear details. No one responds. Then, gazing out at us, he also asks that anyone who doesn't want to hear details please say so. There is a moment when I want to object, but then it passes. I guess I am as eager as everyone else to learn why our Mayor inflicted all of this misery and death upon us.

Agent Mullen begins to recite the facts in a monotone, as if reading from a history book about an event none of us witnessed. On the large screen behind him is a video of a white van, taken from the front, as it descends the arena driveway. I've seen it dozens of times on television.

"For those of you who cannot see the screen, it is showing a video of the white delivery van coming down the ramp beneath the arena. The windshield and windows are heavily tinted, so the video doesn't show anything inside the van but a shadow behind the wheel."

The video shows an oblique angle of the driver's side window coming down, and the left elbow of the driver, covered by a dark shirt, resting on the door sill. The video ends when the van passes beneath an overhead camera. You can't tell if the bomber was a man or a woman. You can't tell the bomber's race, or approximate age, or anything else.

This is all we are going to see. My feet tap the concrete step in frustration.

Agent Mullen gives us more details, but I'm tuned out. As I contemplated this event, I found myself wanting a clear explanation of the Mayor's mission, hoping someone might deliver something to help me understand. Something that would explain his reason, his motive. But I, and all the other victims here, have been deprived of that.

"This next bit of information hasn't been released publicly," Agent Mullen says. "You're the first to hear it. The perpetrator acted alone. There were no accomplices. We're sure of that."

Okay. Somewhat reassuring that there's not a terrorist cell planning another attack on us. But I don't feel any great sense of relief.

"I want you to know," Agent Mullen says, "that seeing all of you here inspires me. You are incredibly brave and courageous. You are working to heal. You are working to resume your lives. And I want you to know from the bottom of my heart, that I am truly sorry for what happened to you. Those who survived, and those who didn't. I know that's not enough."

He's right, it isn't enough. Though Agent Mullen seems sincere, his words carry little weight with me. He's in law enforcement, and with the terrorist dead, there is nothing to enforce. The bomber murdered thousands of people and got away with it. He will not endure a trial, or suffer a prison term, or be executed by the government. He will not have to be confronted by any of his victims. He will not have to look at us. Agent Mullen's words are about as consoling as the sheriff who cut my father down from the barn rafter and told me, "I'm sorry for your loss."

A blur of short presentations follow, from specialists in orthopedics, wound care, psychiatry, PTSD therapy, ambulatory medicine, and other topics. Dr. Volkov delivers a video presentation on facial reconstruction surgery and skin grafting. At first the animated image is almost unrecognizable as anything other than a generic victim, alabaster skin and black hair, bruises and slashes of red covering her face. In sequences the computer face morphs into something that resembles normal, with scars disappearing and skin color changing to peach. There is no name attached to the image, but I know it is me.

After the presentations, I wander among the tables set up for individualized consult and advice. I bypass the booth for prosthetics because I have an appointment later, but note several varieties of artificial arms are laid out like jewelry on velvet. There are some with hands, others with pincers, and some with hooks. Steel hooks for hands. I will never wear a hook.

As I pass by these tables, *bizarre* is the only word that fits. Medical professionals lined up like concessionaires at half-time of a football game, offering food and drink to enthusiastic fans. This might sate us, but only temporarily. We need sustenance, sure, but we need to be filled up. We need to be filled with whatever is necessary to remove our unwanted labels: victim; damaged; disabled; maimed.

At Dr. Volkov's table, I wait in a short line while he advises other patients. He glances at me before it is my turn, leans from his chair and flashes an awkward smile, as if I am on a red carpet and somehow more important than the victims who precede me. It might be my imagination, but it appears he rushes the two patients in front of me. When it is my turn, I settle into the padded swivel chair at the side of his table.

After I sit, he examines my face, running his gloved thumbs from between my eyes, separating across my brow, then over my cheek bones and along my jaw line to my chin. While he is doing this, his eyes follow the tracing, not meeting mine directly, as if he is a blind man memorizing the contours of my face with his thumbs.

This makes me feel wanted and uncomfortable all at once. I suppose that a surgeon who enhances breasts and augments the body, who changes piggish noses to slender beauties and imbues terse lips with fullness, who erases scars as if they never existed, probably cannot help but study his work. After all, it is his job to restore people, to make them beautiful. Still, there is something creepy in the way he touches me.

He takes up the stylus and maneuvers it on his computer screen.

"Would you like to be a blonde?" On the computer screen he changes my hair to blonde.

"Or a redhead?"

"I like black just fine." My hair has grown an inch or two, though there is a place on top about the size of a quarter where nothing grows.

He switches my hair color back to black, then shows me the results of my next, and final, surgery. I already have the slender nose and full lips, and my complexion is healing to a natural flesh color, though I'm not there yet. Faint scars imprint my forehead like fossils in ancient stone.

"How confident are you my scars will go away?"

"Ninety-eight percent," he says. "You've made remarkable progress. With new surgical techniques and better skin-tone matching, and if you will diligently follow the recovery protocol I lay out for you, the scars will fade enough that they won't be noticeable with makeup."

I don't have to force a smile. I feel it elevate my cheekbones, raise the corners of my mouth, part my lips. His prognosis produces a smile as easily as if he has drawn it on my computer face.

"You'll call my office when you are ready for the next surgery?"

"I will call."

"Keep using the healing patches I prescribed for you."

"I will, Dr. Volkov." I rise from the chair to make way for the next patient and notice something. "When did you grow the beard?" Salt and pepper whiskers, cropped close, cover the lower half of his face.

He reaches up to stroke the speckled whiskers covering his jaw. "A couple of weeks ago," he says. "Do you like it?"

"It changes your face." I peer at him for a few seconds, studying his face with the same intensity with which he has studied mine.

* * * * *

I head down to the prosthetics lab, where my mother is waiting. As I come within a few feet of her, I smell the acrid smoke that seems to constantly ring her. I wonder if my nose has become more sensitive since my facial surgeries, or if the perfume she spritzes on her clothes is less effective at masking the smoke. She is here only because she has to be.

A technician who introduces himself as Rodney needs to take some measurements. Rodney measures my shoulders and torso, my waist, my legs. He asks me to remove my shoes. He measures my feet, then my toes, to get some idea of the length and thickness of my fingers, he says.

When he is finished with me, Rodney measures my mother's arms and hands too. As he stretches a tailor's tape from her shoulder to her wrist, she flinches.

"Why do you need my measurements?" she says gruffly.

"To help us estimate proportions of limb length," he responds. "I need to measure your inseam, too."

My mother wears an indignant scowl and fixes on the ceiling while Rodney pulls the tape down her inner thigh to her ankle bone.

"There, that wasn't so bad," he says, looping the cloth tape around his fingers.

Rodney reviews the handful of photographs my mother has brought. Pictures of me, most of them at least several years old, showing my bare arms and hands. He enters data into a tablet in small, precise pecks of his index fingers.

Rodney leads us into another room, where the head of the prosthetics lab introduces himself as Dr. Harwell. He talks with his hands plunged into the pockets of his white lab coat, probably a conscious maneuver when he consults with amputees. He explains how they will fabricate the prosthetics to fit me and my special needs. As he describes the process, he scans the results of a battery of tests I was given upon leaving the hospital.

"I won't lie to you," he says, looking alternately at the computer screen and me. "Your new arms will primarily be cosmetic, though you might be able to accomplish some rudimentary tasks with your hands, in time."

"Rudimentary?" I say.

"Simple things like holding a glass of water, or opening a door."

"I can already open a door with my foot. How about typing? Will I be able to type?"

"I'm afraid not." Dr. Harwell shakes his head.

"How about driving?"

"Not with your hands."

"Why not?"

"You will never regain any sensory digital capacity."

"I don't understand that term."

"The brachial-plexus nerves, which run from your spine to your arms, were cut during amputation, so when your brain tries to send a signal to your fingers to pick up a pencil, for example, the signal will run into a roadblock at your shoulders. Think of it as an electric line that stops at the pole outside and doesn't come all the way into your house."

"So the prosthetics won't really help me."

"We're making advances in the technology, but we're not there yet. You're a bilateral shoulder-level amputee, Miss Winslow. That's rare, less than one percent of all cases. For people in your situation, cosmetic limbs are usually the best we can do at present. I'm sorry."

I have been hoping prosthetics would constitute a miracle that would return me to a semblance of who I was before. Dr. Harwell's prognosis confirms I will always be this way. The prosthetics will only fill sleeves.

"I don't want them," I say.

"Ella," my mother rebukes in her scraping voice.

"Mama, he says I won't really be able to use them to do anything. They'll be cosmetic only."

Dr. Harwell holds a sample prosthetic out to me as if it were a gift. "The prosthetics could help you resume a normal life," Dr. Harwell says. "They will cut down on people staring at you, for one thing. And we are making advances, so in time we will be able to make your arms work better. You'll be able to accomplish more tasks on your own."

"Okay."

"It's the right choice, Miss Winslow."

14

I call Dr. Marvin, my psychiatrist, one morning while my mother is out running errands. Mother put Dr. Marvin's number on my new cell phone, and I call her using voice commands.

"Ella, I'm so glad to hear from you. When are you going to come see me for a session?"

I find it odd she can be so cheery when she spends her days listening to people who are depressed or in turmoil. "I don't know. I thought maybe we could talk on the phone."

"Sure, I've got a few minutes until my next appointment. So how are you doing?"

"Fine. I'm doing fine."

"In therapy speak, fine means fucked up, insecure, neurotic and emotional. Are you really doing fine?"

"Exactly," I say.

"You want to talk about what happened that night?" She gets right to it.

"The night of the bombing? I don't remember anything. I must have been outside the arena when it happened, but I don't have a specific recollection that I was there."

"I might be able to help you remember. But it would be best if we meet face to face. Do you think you could come in for an appointment?"

I hesitate, contemplating whether I can endure it. "Are you talking about hypnosis?" I ask.

"Yes. It's sometimes helpful to get to root causes."

"I'm not sure. Let me think about it."

There is a pause on her end, and a deep breath. "You'll make an appointment when you're ready?"

"Sure."

"Are you still taking the medications I prescribed for you?"

"Most of the time."

"Okay. They work best if you take the medication every day, as prescribed."

I remain silent for a time. I know she is right. The anti-depressants make me feel drowsy, but also give me insomnia. I don't feel lifted or happy when I take them.

"So tell me about your days, then."

"Some are good. Some are bad. Mostly, I feel like I'm going sideways."

"What do you mean by that?"

"Well, nothing is really happening. It's like I'm waiting for something to happen."

"What do you think that might be?"

"I don't know. It's just that I feel like this big boulder sunk deep in the earth."

"Interesting. Go on," Dr. Marvin says.

"Well, I used to set goals for myself. Go to college, start a career, get married. But now I feel like all there is ever going to be is one long today. I can't see a future."

I hear a ringing bell. At first, I think it is in my head.

"Sorry, Ella. My next appointment is here. Look, you have to come see me. Soon. How about next Tuesday at three o'clock?"

"I don't know. My mother will have to drive me. I'll have to see what her schedule is."

"We could try a video session instead."

"I don't know. Let me see."

"Ella, please let me help you."

Afterward, reflecting on our conversation, I find the perfect simile. It's like that isn't it? You can't locate it while stammering about and making up excuses, but afterward, with perfect clarity, it comes to you. I am not a boulder lodged in the mud. Not at all. I am like a glacier, moving but a few inches a year. And slowly melting away.

15

Monotony unfolds in front of me like blank newsprint. I rise well after the sun, sit in my pajamas for a prolonged period in the kitchen sipping coffee through a glass straw, then join my mother in the living room to endure her shows. Around noon, she dresses me, usually something simple like a sack dress, which is easy to don and easy to doff, especially without the encumbrance of limbs. Lunch is normally broth, which I also sip through a glass straw. The afternoons I spend on the sofa, watching a series of soap operas, some of which I remember from my childhood. If the weather is nice, I venture into the backyard—though I can't do anything but sit, or stroll around the live oak while it sheds leaves. Dinner is often a protein shake, again imbibed through a straw. Then a bath, my mother dressing me in pajamas for bed. I retire early to stare at the ceiling. Repeat.

After being on my own for years, I am unprepared for a roommate, especially one who constantly hovers over me. In the hospital, I tolerated the ministrations of the nurses and doctors because they eventually moved on to other patients. In my own house, I never have a meal or a trip to the bathroom without the aid of my mother's hand. The air in my home becomes dense and cloying, as if we are trapped in a small cave and forced to breathe each other's exhalations. But only one of us is truly trapped.

Since my mother slapped me, her hands shake most of the time. Some mornings she can't hold a coffee mug without sloshing liquid over the edge. Her hand trembles when she writes out the grocery list.

She uses her unsteady hands as an excuse for not feeding me solid food. "I don't want to stab you with the fork," she explains. "I would never forgive myself."

I've lost four pounds since I left the hospital. I can feel myself getting weaker, becoming less substantial. It's not all in my head, for as I stand on the digital scale each night after my bath, staring down at the black numbers, I have proof that I am melting away like that glacier.

Mattie comes to visit most weekends, bunking on a sofa bed in the room that I turned into a home office years ago. I'm not sure why I need a home office now. I might replace the sofa bed with a real one so Mattie can be comfortable. On those days when Mattie takes over my mother's care duties, I feel myself moving toward normal. My sister's touch is softer, her voice less grating, and when she is necessarily in my personal space, she does not reek of the cigarette smoke my mother constantly carries with her.

Mattie cooks scrambled eggs for breakfast and patiently spoons them into my mouth. Dinner is usually chicken or beef, because Mattie can feed me with steady hands as I lean forward in my chair.

During my nightly bath, as Mattie washes me, I am reminded of our childhood, when we bathed together, splashing as we played with our bathtub toys. Even now, as an adult on naked display to my sister, I am not shy, not embarrassed by my armless torso or the scars that haunt my legs.

As I stand before the mirror, Mattie runs her fingers through my crop of hair.

"What does that feel like?" I ask.

"What?"

"My hair. What does it feel like on your fingers?"

"Soft in most places. A little prickly where it's still short."

"Prickly like a cactus?"

"No, much softer. More like a shoeshine brush. Do you know you have a small bald spot up here?"

I nod. "Dr. Volkov told me that's where he drilled through my skull to relieve fluid on my brain. He says it might grow back on its own, but if it doesn't he can put in hair plugs. I'm hoping my hair gets long enough to cover it soon."

There was a time when I pampered my hands and kept my nails trimmed and polished. I rubbed moisturizer on them daily, twice a day in winter. Now, I would barter my supple hands for the gnarled and arthritic hands of my mother. I long to touch the bristles on my scalp, to run my fingers along the wormlike scars on my legs. To pet a dog.

Michael Winstead

Today is the twelfth anniversary of our father's suicide. I remember it like it was yesterday. It was dusk, the light in our barn muted, when I found him hanging from a barn rafter. An old wooden stool on which he had probably stood when he tied the noose was toppled nearby. I had gone to the barn to get feed for the chickens, and when I saw his feet dangling only two feet off the ground, I ran to him, screaming something indecipherable through the anguish in my throat. I wrapped my arms around his legs and strained to lift him with my thin arms.

"I miss daddy," I say to Mattie, eyeing her in the mirror.

She meets my gaze but says nothing, continuing to rub scar cream on my shoulders.

"You know today is the anniversary of his death? I've asked mama a few times lately why he killed himself, and she just shuts down. Do you have any idea why he did it?"

Something moves across her eyes. If the eyes are the window to the soul, Mattie has just closed and locked her shutters. She puts a cap on the scar cream and replaces it in the bathroom closet.

"Let's talk about something not so gloomy, like when we're going to take you to the hair salon," she says.

My mother wanders in and leans against the door jamb of the bathroom. "That's an excellent idea. How about I schedule an appointment for next Saturday, for the three of us?"

I know she eavesdrops on my conversations with Mattie. She has always been a snooper. I remember when she found my locked diary in a shoe box at the top of our bedroom closet, broke the tiny brass lock, and read my private thoughts. She grounded me over the written confession to myself, when I was seventeen, that I drank too much wine with my high school friends down at the river and let Billy Lambert put his hand down my jeans.

"Do you remember when I used to brush your hair almost every night," my mother says.

"I do. I also remember when you grounded me because I got a pixie cut without your approval."

She emits something between a hrrrmmmph and a phlegmy cough. "You had the prettiest hair in school, and then you cut if all off. Made you look like a boy."

"Long hair was a pain to keep clean."

"You were just being rebellious, Ella. Every girl in school wanted your hair. You inherit your hair from your mother, you know."

When next Saturday rolls around, my mother drives me to the salon. Mattie has not come, begging off because she has to grade papers. I go anyway because I want to see what a professional stylist can do with me.

When I sidle through the door, pungent chemicals greet me. The sharp slap of acetone, nail polish, packets of dye and permanent solution. The blare of hair driers, electric razors, raised voices, a ringing telephone, the blaring television, hand driers, stereo music, and snipping scissors mix into a cacophony that makes me want to cover my ears.

My mother whispers something to the shampoo girl as we walk to the back. The shampoo girl's hair is a long, tangled mass of tendrils died a shade of red that does not exist in nature. Her name tag says "Shania."

"I'm Ella." It seems only right to introduce myself.

"I know. Your mother's been talking about this day for weeks."

She carefully unties the azure scarf from my head, folds it, and lays it on the work-top below the mirror. I settle into a chair covered in faux leather, dyed green. Shania places one hand on my neck and the other on my upper back and tells me to lean back. The rim of the bowl is cool and smooth against my neck. I crane my eyes to meet hers. "Please be careful," I say.

Trepidation slides away as warm water covers my scalp. Kneading fingers massage the taut tendons of my neck, caress the base of my skull and the bumps behind my ears. The coolness of a glob of shampoo on my scalp. Uncalloused fingers spread the shampoo in small circles. A spray of warm water calms the tingle. The jasmine scent of conditioner masks the sharpness of other chemicals. Cool water rinses the conditioner from my hair. Shania pats my damp hair with a soft towel.

When we are done, I cannot pull myself up by gripping the arms of the chair. Shania gently pushes my shoulders from behind until I am erect. Across the aisle, a woman about my age is getting a manicure. I catch her staring at the empty sleeves of my dress, then she looks away.

I turn to Shania with a smile. "You didn't ask me about my missing arms."

"Your mother already told us. I'm so sorry that happened to you."

It occurs to me that of the thousands of women wounded in the bombing, there are probably a handful, maybe more, who had their nails polished and their hair styled in this very shop. I am not a unique visitor. My mother apparently prepped them for my arrival, scars and amputations all.

I wiggle into the stylist's chair. Her name is Harriet and she is my mother's new friend. Harriet's hair is puffed and teased and bleached the color of dry sand.

My mother sits in the reception area in a row of black chairs demarcated by chrome arms, reading a magazine. She occasionally glances at me above the pages.

"You're Rose's daughter, right?"

"Yes, I'm Ella."

"You just relax now, honey. We'll take good care of you."

"I have a bald spot on top," I say because I can think of nothing else.

"We can make that look better."

With my hair in varying lengths but still short everywhere, the styles available are limited. As Harriet stands in front of me, she tilts her head from side to side, conjuring. Her calloused thumb and forefinger grasp my chin and move it up and down, then left and right, while her eyes scan my short crop of hair from all angles. She consults with another stylist, then goes to the table of hair magazines. With dexterous fingers—I still notice hands and fingers with unusual obsession—she flips through the pages, then walks it back to her chair.

"I think this one would be best for you," Harriet says, placing a folded magazine in my lap. On the page, Halle Berry's stunning visage gleams beneath hair swept across her forehead.

"Do I have enough hair for that style cut?"

"I think so. We might be a little short in front, but I can make it work," Harriet says with confidence.

The scissors trim above my ears, then to the back, their sharp snip fading like barking hounds headed for the woods. Short lengths of hair patter on the plastic cape. I strain my eyes to verify that they are indeed short. I don't have enough hair for error.

"Your mama said you were in the hospital quite a while. In a coma for almost a week?"

"Yes," I say.

"What's that like?" Snip. She runs the scissors above my left ear.

"It's like waking up from a long nap, in a way. All of those days have gone by without you."

"Did you dream in the coma?"

I shake my head. A stern hand realigns it.

"Sorry. I do that a lot now, use my head to make gestures."

"I suppose so. It must be hard, honey. I can't imagine."

"It's been a major adjustment. For my mother, too. I lost a good part of my memory, but it's fine." I look across the space, catching my mother's eyes. She is reading me. Perhaps she can hear our conversation.

"Fine really, or fine like you tell somebody because you don't want to say how you're really feeling?"

I remember Dr. Marvin's elaboration on FINE as an acronym and sigh.

"You hang in there, girl."

When Harriet finishes cutting, she uses a soft brush to whisk the hair from my shoulders and neck. She turns the chair so I face the big mirror that spans the length of one wall. Harriet holds a hand mirror so I can see my hair in back.

My bangs barely creep onto my forehead. I look like a boy, but with a neat haircut. She angles the mirror so I can see the bald spot on top is mostly covered.

"It sure is short," I say without thinking.

"You like it?"

"Yeah, I like it." I force a smile.

"It's growing. I can see that. Next time it will be longer and we'll have more options."

My mother pays with cash at the register and leaves a generous tip. I look over her shoulder to see. We leave the salon, and I stand outside on the sidewalk, watching the bustle of people sliding in and out of cars, breezing in and out of stores through glass doors. This is my first foray outside the confines of the hospital or the brick walls of my house since the bombing. I stand by a concrete column, not yet ready to be anything more than an observer. When people pass me, I focus my eyes on my shoes.

The grocery store is next. We pull into a chain grocery store that has a location in my mother's town. I rarely shopped here before, but it is familiar to my mother, and I know she needs that. At the entrance, she wipes down the handle of a cart and pulls a shopping list from her purse. While she pushes the basket, I wander along behind her. We stop in the produce section. She puts several oranges into a plastic bag. Bananas too. None of which I can peel. In the dairy department she pulls a container of cottage cheese from the shelf.

"Get the low-fat kind," I say.

"Since when did you start eating low fat? You hardly eat enough as it is. You need to gain weight. People will think I'm starving you."

It is true. I am down six pounds since leaving the hospital. I wonder if my weight loss is some evidence my liver is failing. My sallow skin is pinking up, and I see no evidence of jaundice in the sclera of my eyes.

"I want low fat," I say, continuing the argument.

"I can pick out groceries without your ordering me."

"You asked me to come along."

"You don't have to order me."

"I'm just telling you what I want."

"I've been buying your groceries long enough to know what you want," she says. She puts the regular cottage cheese in the basket, followed by a low-fat container.

In another aisle, I spot some looping plastic straws. "I want those straws." I nod toward the boxes.

"Those are for kids." She puts them in the basket anyway.

"We need more hand soap," I say.

"We've got plenty at home."

"I don't like the kind you buy."

"Are you serious?" she says in a growl. "What do you care, Ella? I'm the one who uses it, not you."

Before my mother came to live with me, I kept a master list of groceries on a typed sheet of paper on a clipboard, and before every trip to the grocery store, I would take inventory and circle the things I was out of. I miss that routine. I *need* that routine, especially at times like this. And sometimes I forget that I don't need hand soap anymore, or nail polish, or emery boards, or deodorant.

My mother mistakes my silence as pouting. "All right, all right. Is this the brand you like?" She holds up a plastic bottle of hand soap.

"Get what you like," I say.

"You aren't ever going to move on if you're still fretting over hand soap, Ella."

"Maybe it's just wishful thinking."

We walk up the last few aisles in silence, my mother hurrying ahead, me lingering behind. It is a self-imposed penance, I guess. I let her check out alone and slip through the automatic doors with her basket. I walk to the other entrance and go through those automatic doors, relishing their hushed separation at my approach. I think every door in the world should be like these. No knobs, no locks. Parting silently when I approach.

At the car, she puts the groceries in the back seat and opens the front passenger door for me. I sidle onto the bench seat without much grace. She leans in the door opening and pulls the belt across, then snaps the belt into the buckle.

"I'm never going to be normal again, I know that," I say.

She stares down at me. At times, her stare alone can make me tremble.

"Nobody knows it more than I do. But doing stuff like buying hand soap, that makes me feel just a little normal, mama."

She closes my door without fanfare and opens a back door, rummaging through the plastic bags. She reaches over the seat and places a glass jar of expensive hand cream in my lap—the kind I used to sometimes buy myself as a present.

"Thank you," I say with a clogged throat.

"We can use it on your feet," she says.

16

My mother and I reach an unspoken truce. She is no happier caring for me than I am, but I need her to accomplish the simplest, routine tasks of living. I submit, and she relents. At least partially.

On a blustery day that scatters leaves across the pavement, she drives me to the hospital so I can receive my prosthetics. My new arms appear lifelike, but once attached to my shoulder sockets with straps and buckles, they feel lighter than I think they should. The fingers pose in the shape of a comma.

My new arms are a nuisance. The buckles snag my clothes. The limbs frequently clip doorways and the outside corners of walls. The attachment cups hurt my shoulders and chafe my skin.

Dr. Harwell gave me a DVD of the exercises I should do to help my body adjust to the prosthetics. I perform them diligently, twice a day, while my mother monitors. I stand before the full-length mirror in my bedroom and roll and shrug my shoulders until they ache. The arms swing slightly, as if moved by a gentle breeze, but they do not move on my command. Concentrating, I try to send signals to the fake fingers. I strain to create just the slightest sensation. A little movement is all I want. I would be thrilled with a finger twitch or a phantom itch. I will the right hand to move, as if the nerve impulses can somehow leap from my brain directly to the rubber fingers, bypassing all that is dead. They run into the roadblock Dr. Harwell talked about. Despite all the advances in wireless technology, nothing has been invented that will allow me to communicate with dead hands.

To escape the dank cave of my house, I propel myself outside, into the night, and walk the darkened streets of my neighborhood. I wear the arms because I recognize the need to incorporate them into my life, but I cover them with long sleeves to keep people from staring. I walk briskly, waddling in the awkward fashion of a duck on the run. There is no synchronicity between my fake arms and me. The arms and I move in different rhythms, operate at cross-purposes. I turn a sharp corner at a brisk clip, and the right arm swings out and bangs into a steel light pole. I back up and bash the arm against the pole again. To punish the pole or the arm, I can't say which.

These walks become a nightly event for me, even when it's raining. I refuse to allow my mother to come along because I need the solitude, and her offer to accompany me seems disingenuous. I know she would smoke when we walked, and the smell of it repulses me more than it should. She has already insinuated herself into every cranny of my life, has tried to become a surrogate for my missing limbs, and like the prosthetics that constantly hound me, there are times when I simply have to leave my mother in the corner too.

On a clear night that carries the portent of winter, I walk along an unfamiliar street on the edge of my neighborhood. I stop to admire a freshly painted house with a broad concrete porch. The siding is sunflower yellow, the trim eggshell white. The house beams in the night. While I am envisioning a painter's hand spreading paint on the wood clapboards in long, fluid strokes, the wind snatches the wig from my head. I wear the wig occasionally as a sort of disguise, plus it keeps my head warm. The wig tumbles down the street and lodges in the iron grate of a storm drain. I chase it down and stand in the gutter, staring at the clump of auburn hair. I toe it with my shoe, trying to unwedge it, but do not succeed. I am about to kneel down in the gutter and snatch the wig with my teeth when a shadow crosses in front of me. A woman in a dark sweater bends down and picks up my wig.

"Ella is that you?" the woman says, holding my hair in her right hand. "How are you?" She reaches around to hug me.

I lean into her. "I'm fine, Margaret. How are you doing?"

"Okay. Great really," Margaret says. When she glances at my face, she pauses, then quickly recovers. "We miss you at work. When are you coming back?"

"I don't know if I am coming back."

"What do you mean?"

"I'm useless without arms."

"Of course you're not useless, Ella. It will just require some adjustment. That's all. We'll help you."

It is not the first time I have been acutely aware of this chasm in perception of what I can and cannot do. People with all four of their limbs assume that through sheer will and determination, I will re-learn to do everything I could accomplish with arms. They're wrong. That's why they call my condition a *disability.* Lack of ability. In addition to the physical impairment, my determination and enthusiasm for accomplishment have been damaged. I'll admit, however, that I sometimes underestimate what I'm capable of because the effort to get there seems so daunting.

"Let me know when you're coming back, and you can ride in with me." Margaret remembers she is still holding my rescued wig. She moves behind me and settles my hair onto my head, pressing the tape to my pate, adjusting it so the bangs clear my eyes. "There, that's much better."

"Thank you."

"So, do you want to come in for a cup of coffee?" Margaret gestures at the house with fresh paint. "We could talk."

"You live here?"

"Jeff and I bought the house a few months ago," she says. "We've been so busy fixing it up. So busy at work. I've meant to call you a hundred times, you know, now that we're neighbors."

"It's okay, Margaret."

"I've been meaning to call you, Ella. I really have. You want to come in for a minute? Or I could drive you home. It wouldn't be any trouble. We could talk. If you want to. Only if you want to. I mean, losing your arms, that must be terrible. And your hair. I know how that is. My mother had breast cancer. Chemo. Her hair fell completely out. She's fine now. She beat it. Her hair grew back in, eventually."

It is often like this. When people find out about my amputations, they tend to babble. I've known Margaret for three or four years, and though we socialized at work, I would not say we are close. Perhaps she feels guilty that she didn't come visit me in the hospital, though I think she signed the card from the office that came with a pot of yellow pansies. I didn't want visitors when I was in the hospital. Even now, I'm not sure I'm ready to renew old acquaintances.

"I have to go home now," I say, and begin walking away.

"I'll call you, Ella," Margaret shouts after me. "Or you call me. Or come by the office for a visit."

When I return home, my mother is drying her hair. From the hall I watch her swish the brush with one hand, holding the blow dryer in the other. Her hair resembles tightly curled tongues of dark steel. She fluffs and pats, pulling at a few gray strands that have emerged since her last color treatment.

When she's finished with her hair, she detaches my arms. She loops the straps around the wooden clothes rod in my closet, where my benched arms hang, fingers down.

She rubs scar cream on my shoulder stumps, then attaches the healing patches Dr. Volkov prescribed. I stand before a full-length mirror, naked except for my bra and panties. Her hand goes over my right stump, the pressure enough to unbalance me.

"Do you have any feeling there?" she asks, pressing a nail into the flap of skin that covers my right shoulder socket.

I shake my head.

Her hand circles to the top of my shoulder. "How about here?" She's peering at me in the mirror.

I feel the bite of her fingernail and with it a muted optimism that perhaps my shoulder nerves are regenerating, or at least developing sensitivity. "No, I don't feel a thing," I lie.

I'm not sure why I lie to her about something like this. There is no doubt we have become combatants. It's an old feud, one that began sometime before I left for college. My father's death exacerbated the war between my mother and me. A dozen years later, my mother still refuses to tell me why he committed suicide. When you sleep side-by-side with someone for that long, you have to pick up unspoken clues. She has to know. Yet she keeps this a secret. I resent her decision to close that door to me.

My mother has started going to a Baptist church nearby. She says it isn't as friendly as her church back home, that she doesn't agree with the minister's views on everything, but going makes her feel better. It is obvious in her face. She comes back from church with the cloud that is me lifted.

Today, as I sit captive at the kitchen table while she feeds me lunch, she tells me about church. The sermon was focused on redemption. My mother paraphrases a passage from Romans, then one from Ephesians, the blessing of redemption of sinners through Jesus Christ. I am not sure if she includes herself in the mass of sinners. I know she includes me.

"Go to church with me next Sunday," she says as her quivering hand approaches my mouth with a spoonful of oatmeal.

"Mama, I'm not sure I believe anymore. Not with everything that's happened."

"That's when it's most important for you to go, Ella, when you're losing faith."

I relent.

When I walk through the heavy wooden doors, it is the first time I have been in a church, other than for a wedding, since my father died. We sit in a pew near the front, and I settle onto the rose-colored cushion. I object to my mother filling out a new member's card for me. She does it anyway.

When the minister asks if there are any visitors, my mother stands up and pulls me up with her. The minister welcomes me and asks the congregation to remember us in their prayers.

The minister is roughly my age, with neatly trimmed reddish-blonde hair. To me he looks too polished, like he is auditioning for a television show. In the sermon, he speaks sincerely of forgiveness and of the value of family. After that I tune him out.

Since the explosion, I have thought and said many things against God, or whoever is running the show. He, as the omniscient and omnipotent one, is the one who has allowed this to happen to me. God's will, apparently, is to leave me in a disabled state. That's the punishment he inflicted for my sins. If anyone needs absolution, it is Him, not me. It only makes sense that God can sin too, and in my case I think he has an awful lot to atone for. That's my argument, anyway.

I follow along in my mother's Bible and sing from her hymnal. I stand stiffly while the congregation claps with the choir and passes the collection plate. My mother makes up an envelope for me, slips in a bill, and drops it in the plate in my name.

Kneeling at the rail during communion, I let the pastor put a wafer on my tongue.

"Body of Christ," he says. From a paper cup, he spills a swallow of grape juice into my mouth. "Blood of Christ."

Mouth wide open and eyes wide shut. Just like the old and the frail, I have to be helped to my feet. Walking back to the pew, I do not fold my hands in prayer or cup them in submission. I have already submitted quite enough, thank you.

After the service, I shuffle through the front doors with the others to greet the minister outside. He smiles at me and tries to shake my fake hand. My elbow locks, so he pats my shoulders instead and tells me to come back every Sunday.

"I don't think I will," I say, looking directly into his eyes.

"Pardon me?" he says with eyebrows raised.

My mother tugs at my forearm, about to collapse from mortal embarrassment.

"I won't be back." I swing the phony arms. "You see, your wonderful God did this to me."

"Ella!" my mother shouts. She grabs me by the shoulders, spins me around, and ushers me down the concrete steps.

"And don't say he works in mysterious ways," I call over my shoulder. "There's no mystery to this."

I can't say how long such rebellion has been building. It is not the type of venom that can appear overnight. It has been curdling inside of me for a long time. My father's suicide, my divorce, and being the victim of a terrorist attack have all led to this. It feels purifying to spit it out, especially for the effect it has on my mother and the boil it creates among the other church-goers. It puts me in control of something in my life, if only for a minute. My mother escorts me to the car and berates me for my rude and sacrilegious behavior. As I deflect her words, I relish the sweet taste of grape juice on my tongue.

17

The tide of my insurrection quells quickly when my mother refuses to feed me. A forced hunger strike saps my energy within hours. When she opens the refrigerator to fix her own lunch, I catch the door with my foot before it swings shut. I stare at eggs in their carton, at mustard and mayonnaise in lidded jars. A gallon of milk. Sliced cheese, individually wrapped. I tug open the door to the freezer compartment. Frozen fries in a bag, pre-made meals in plastic trays with taut cellophane wrappings. Fish sticks in a box. Standing on a chair, I grasp the knob of a cabinet door with my foot, swing it open. Spaghetti, bags of beans, cans of soup. Crackers and potato chips in plastic bags with reinforced rip strips. I have never carefully examined the packaging to our food. As I stand with the cabinet door open, I realize it would take a monumental effort for me just to open something, never mind the work it would take to cook the food, or then to eat it.

My mother spends much of the afternoon in the kitchen. I sit at the table nearby, my eyes watching every movement. With her hands, she shreds lettuce to make a salad. She wields a peeler on carrots and potatoes. She peppers and salts a roast big enough for four, sets it in a black roasting pan with the vegetables, and slips it into the oven. She wedges a pat of butter into a single roll and wraps it in aluminum foil for later. From a lower cabinet, she pulls out a glass pitcher, drops in three tea bags, and fills the pitcher with water. During her preparations, she doesn't look at me, doesn't say a word. I am a ghost she doesn't want to acknowledge. I don't know which is worse: her silence; or being deprived of food.

She sets the dining room table for one, placing the silverware and cloth napkin with trembling hands. The lone place mat comes from a set Mattie gave me as a housewarming gift years ago. Over the sink, my mother pours tea into a water glass, splashing a little over the side. While she sits at the head of my cherry dining table and eats her dinner, I maneuver a chair from under the table with my foot. Angled toward her, I plop down in the chair and stare at her. Though I am two feet away, my mother refuses to see me.

She scrapes her plate into the trash can, rinses the plate and utensils in the sink, and puts them in the dishwasher. The dishwasher closes with a solid thunk. The salad goes into a plastic bowl with a snap-down lid. She puts the roast and cooked vegetables into a casserole dish with a clear glass top and places the dish on the middle shelf of my refrigerator. My refrigerator. My dishes, my forks, my spoons, my knives. Then she snaps off the lights and goes into the living room to watch television.

I sit in the dark of the kitchen for an interminable time, boiling with resentment. She clearly intends to starve me into obedience. I have not eaten in 24 hours.

I push a chair with casters next to the refrigerator, wiggle into the seat, grip the metal handle with my toes, and tug open the fridge door. In the spotlight of the bulb sits the roast. With much commotion, I raise my legs and sandwich the casserole dish between the soles of my feet. I lift it down from the shelf. The glass lid rattles, but doesn't fall off. I twist the chair around so I can place the container on the counter. I plant my feet on the floor and rest for a minute. A cramp has emerged in the arch of my left foot. To relieve it, I perform some of the stretching exercises I practiced with Zack.

When the cramp subsides, I maneuver the chair to a better angle. With the toes of my right foot, I grasp the knob of the lid and lift it, setting the lid down on the counter with a clatter.

The roast is right there in front of me, puddled juices beginning to congeal. It is a beautiful piece of beef, thick and brown. Potatoes and carrots surround it. Its aroma is still fresh. My stomach growls.

I pull open the silverware drawer and rattle around in the fork slot. With my hip I push the chair into the proper position, step up on it, then step onto the counter. With the open drawer below me, I tip the tines of a fork with my big toe but can't slip the handle between my toes. I'm touching most of the forks, and some of the spoons, with my dirty feet. Even if I manage to slip a fork from the drawer, I can't fathom how I will cut the roast.

I climb down off the counter, almost falling as the chair on casters begins to swivel. I manage to make it to the floor in one piece. I go to the kitchen doorway and peer into the living room. My mother is as fixed as a concrete statue in front of the television. Maybe she will help me if I ask. But as the words form on my lips, I turn away and go back to the kitchen counter.

I position my feet shoulder-width apart, my weight evenly distributed. I bend my knees slightly. Then I lean over and dip my head to the roast and eat. Like a ravenous dog.

I tear at the roast for a few minutes, stripping off a few chunks of meat. The carrots and potatoes are softer, a little easier to chew. I continue on until shreds of roast lodge in spaces between my teeth, until my face is smeared with juice.

When I raise my head I see teeth marks in the potatoes. Juice drips from my chin onto the tile floor. My hunger is not fully sated, but I am done. I sidle to the stove, bend down, and wipe my chin across the towel draped over the handle of the oven, streaking the towel's fruit pattern with brown juice.

When I turn around, my mother is standing in the doorway, her arms across her chest. It is likely she has been standing there for some time. She says nothing, but there is an eerie threat in the set of her mouth.

18

At 6:30 the next morning, the alarm clock next to my bed goes off. The alarm startles me awake and buzzes harshly as I roll away, wishing I could wrap my head in a pillow. Less than a minute later, my mother pushes open the door to my bedroom. She pauses in the doorway. When I don't budge from the bed, she sidles over and punches the alarm off with her right index finger.

"It's high-time you went back to work." Her morning voice is even gruffer than usual, coming from deep in her throat. I smell cigarette smoke on her breath, emanating from her clothes.

"I can't work," I scoff.

"You can obviously feed yourself. You proved that last night. If you can do that, you can go back to work." She stands next to my bed with her hands on her hips.

I have been anticipating this argument since the day I brought the arms home from the hospital. Not a day goes by that I do not think about my old job and the need to validate my existence by doing something productive.

"I'll get you dressed, then drive you in."

"Today? I'm not prepared for this, mama. Besides, they're not ready for me to come back."

"Here's your phone," she says, palming my cell. "Let your boss know you'll be in by nine." She sets the phone on my bedside table, taps a number from my contacts list.

I hear the phone ringing over the speaker.

She remains by my bed in a stolid stance, playing the role of sentinel.

The call goes to voicemail.

I hesitate for a second or two.

"Would you prefer that I leave the message?" she says. She stares me into submission.

"Mr. Strickland," I start, "this is Ella Winslow. I'm coming back to work today. If that's okay. Sorry for the short notice."

It is one thing to sit in your living room all day, scarred and disfigured, with useless artificial limbs making limp company, or to walk briskly through the darkness of unlighted streets. To face your co-workers in a diminished condition is an altogether different challenge. In the past months, they have no doubt toiled late hours, completed projects and met deadlines. They have honed their skills. They have added to their professional reputations. In contrast, I have regressed. Projects and deadlines and even going to the bathroom by myself are now foreign concepts. I am terrified at the prospect of facing them.

After I finish on the toilet, my mother wipes me. It has to be this way, at least for the present, though she's ordered a bidet. A plumber has promised to install it next week. When that happens, it will relieve us of the most discomfiting moments.

Warm water cascades over my head in the shower. She uses the hand wand to clean my crevices thoroughly. With baby shampoo she washes my hair, then dries me off with a burgundy bath sheet. We've searched the internet for a body-sized air dryer, but they are expensive, so we've tabled that purchase for now.

In my bedroom, I stand in front of my dresser. "Maybe we should wait until Mr. Strickland calls back," I say. "I mean, they might not even have a desk for me. It's been four months."

My mother ignores my stalling tactic. She tugs incontinent underwear up my legs, then secures the tabs, smoothing the tape over my protruding hip bones. She cups my breasts in my bra, hooks the double clasp in back. She buckles the arms onto my shoulders and cinches the straps tight.

"Dress, or skirt and blouse?" she asks.

I turn toward the closet. "The purple pants suit?"

"What if you have to go to the bathroom while you're there? Are you going to ask someone to unbutton your pants and then button them back on when you're finished?"

"I don't know, but do you think a skirt or dress would be any easier? This is a big reason why I should not go back to work."

"You're going. That's final. Just hope you don't have to pee for the next ten hours."

Her dark eyes are fixed, her jaw is firm. There is no way I can wriggle out of this.

She pulls a gray muslin dress with black piping from a hanger. It has large black buttons down the front, from the neck to the calf-length hemline, and full-length sleeves. With some difficulty, she manipulates my fake arms and hands and snakes them through the sleeves, then buttons me up. The dress hangs loosely on my frame.

"Makeup," I say.

I sit at my dressing table, mostly unused since my return. With a makeup sponge my mother applies a heavy dose of concealer. Cherry lipstick. A smidgen of rouge brushed on my cheek bones. She dusts on pale gray eye shadow, though she doesn't do my lashes. I look passable, my face in a condition that won't startle anyone at work. When she's done with the makeup, she puts her hands on my shoulders in something of a victory hug. I notice her hands are not shaking now.

"Wig, or no?" she says.

I inspect my hair. It's still short, but ready for display. "No wig," I say.

I stand up and walk to the closet, where I pause, wiggling my toes, the nails adorned with pink polish my mother painted on last week. I slip my feet into low–heeled navy pumps. Inside the house, I have been walking barefoot and in socks, and only on the rare occasion outside do I wear shoes. These heels are only an inch, but I totter during the few steps to the full-length wall mirror.

I appraise myself. I look … different. The dress hangs on me, with few body curves for contour. The makeup is thicker than I'd like, but it covers most of the scars. My hair is neat. The arms hang straight down, as if I am preparing to squeeze into a packed subway car. It has taken us almost two hours of preparation to get to this point.

"Let's go," my mother says.

"What about breakfast?"

She glances at the watch on her left wrist. "We have enough time for a granola bar, maybe oatmeal."

"Granola bar," I say.

She tucks a napkin in my collar and feeds me small bites of a dark chocolate and honey bar with her bare fingers. We have chosen this variety through trial and error because it leaves fewer crumbs. When I am done swallowing, she plucks an oat from my dress front, wipes my mouth with the napkin.

"Coffee?" I ask.

"Oh, I almost forgot," she says. She hurries to the hall closet and returns with a cranberry-colored backpack.

"When did you buy that?"

"A couple of weeks ago. On the internet."

"So, you've been preparing for this day."

She glares at me. "Yes, Ella. Haven't you?"

From the backpack she pulls out two identical plastic bottles, navy with white caps. She fills one with coffee from the pot. In the other she dumps a can of tomato soup.

"You can put these bottles in the microwave," she says with a proud smile. She tightens the screw caps and settles the bottles into the backpack. "And you have a few plastic straws and two glass straws that won't break." She beams at me, holds open the backpack for me to see. "And a couple of extra panties, and some pads in case you have your period."

She half-jogs to my bedroom and comes back with my billfold, cell phone and charger. There is elation in her gait. She drops the wallet into the backpack and stuffs my cell phone and charger into a mesh side pocket. Then she zips it up.

"Okay, let's go."

"You need to brush my teeth."

She looks at her watch again. "No time." She scrabbles around in the backpack and extracts a pack of sugar-free gum. She unwraps a foil stick and offers it to me.

"Mama, you need to brush my teeth. My mouth feels nasty."

"Do you want this or not?"

I nod, and she slides the stick of gum into my mouth.

She has played all of this well because she knows she has the upper hand. In our relationship, the only hand. Without compunction she could refuse to bathe me or change my incontinent underwear. She could haul me to the office without food or money for lunch, if she were so inclined. She could leave my dress unbuttoned in a conspicuous place. But today, she does none of those things.

She pulls up to my office building and scuttles around the front of the car with new-found energy. The passenger door swings open, and she unsnaps the seat belt buckle. When I stand, she loops the straps of my new backpack over my arms and adjusts the straps on my shoulders. I feel like a child heading to school on that first day. Frightened of everything.

"Call me if there's an emergency," she says. "Otherwise, I'll pick you up at five."

19

I stand on the sidewalk in front of my building and watch my mother drive off. For a moment, I think about avenues of escape. I could walk to a bus stop and go somewhere. Anywhere other than here, though I don't know how I would pay the fare. Or I could head to the coffee shop I saw a block back and while away the hours. How long would they let me sit there, sipping my own coffee through a glass straw?

I take a deep breath and exhale a cloud of steam into the frigid air. I slip into the revolving door. After a few seconds I realize I have to turn around, place my back against the brass bar, and walk backward. I proceed through the carpeted lobby adorned with fake trees in concrete planters, then take the elevator to the fourth floor.

Presenting myself at Mr. Strickland's open door, I notice the wood-grained plastic placard attached to the wall, with his name and position printed in white letters. He is now a vice president of the company. With the toe of my shoe, I rap his metal door frame to get his attention. He waves me in and offers me a chair in front of his desk.

"I got your message," he says in a hesitant voice, then adds, "we're glad you're back. We weren't expecting you today."

"Me either," I say. I wonder what preparations he has had to make for my return, the hurried telephone conversations he's had after listening to my announcement.

"So, do you want to go back to coding?"

I shrug my shoulders. "If I can."

"Well, did you have some other position in mind?"

"I'm not sure exactly what I will be able to accomplish."

He looks at me with curious eyes. He wants to ask about my arms. Maybe Margaret has mentioned something to him about my injuries, but maybe she hasn't.

I sigh and stand up, meeting his inquisitive eyes. "Mr. Strickland, both of my arms were amputated at the shoulder. I have two artificial arms and hands, but they're not functional. I want to code, but I'm not sure the best way to get there." I roll my shoulders and the arms sway gently.

His mouth opens for a moment, then closes, like a fish gasping for air. He rubs his forehead with the fingers of his left hand. "I'm sorry, Ella. I didn't know exactly what happened to you. I mean, we knew you were in the hospital and all, but we weren't privy to the details. HIPAA and all that. Have you talked to HR about your disability insurance?"

It's clear what he thinks my chances are.

"I have disability insurance?"

"It's part of the employee benefits package. You should check it out in case … you know."

We stare at each other for several seconds, unsure what's next. When his desk phone rings, he says, "I've got to take this. Head back to your cubicle, and we'll go from there."

I find my cubicle in a condition similar to my house when I returned from the hospital. Dust coats the screen of my dark computer monitor. A wireless ergonomic keyboard with the letters arrayed in an arc sits askew in front of the monitor. To the side of my desktop is a ceramic coffee mug with a faint smudge of red lipstick on the rim. Push pins tacked to the tan fabric walls of the cubicle hold a few pieces of paper: an announcement for the Labor Day picnic; a reminder of the cleaning and trash schedule for our floor; a notice from HR regarding health insurance enrollment in October. All old news. Other than the coffee mug and Devil's Ivy in a terra cotta pot, dangling from the shelf above my desk, my cubicle is devoid of anything personal. In my four-month absence, someone has been watering the ivy, but there are no photographs, no favorite pens, no knickknacks, no personalized stationery or note pads. Am I this sterile, or is there a company policy restricting the display of personal items?

I slip off my pumps and nudge them to the side of my cubicle. With my left foot I pull out the single desk drawer. In it are the usual office supplies, including multi-colored sticky notes, paper clips, a few pens, and a red fluffy duster. I wonder for a moment if I have come to the wrong cubicle. Perhaps this is the desk of someone who has left the company in a hurry, sweeping their personal items into a box with a cupped hand.

Except for the coffee mug. A photograph of a monarch butterfly is wrapped around the mug, its orange wings shimmering. It's undeniably mine. I remember getting the decal affixed to the mug two or three years ago.

I shove the drawer closed and settle into a fabric-covered chair that doesn't seem to fit my sleek outline anymore. After staring at the black eye of my monitor for a minute or two, I use my big toe to punch the power button of the computer beneath my desk. The monitor crackles to life.

Margaret appears at my shoulder. "I heard you were back," she says. She has her hands clasped tightly in front of her. "We're all kind of surprised you're here." Her green eyes are expectant. "But we're happy you're back," she adds. She flips a strand of blonde hair behind her right ear.

"I'm surprised, too."

Her threaded eyebrows arch.

"Long story," I say. "I'll fill you in later. Um, Margaret, did I have stuff on my desk?"

"Stuff?"

"Personal items? You know, pictures or something? I mean, there's only the coffee mug." I spin halfway around in my swivel chair, a gesture intended to convey the barrenness of my cubicle.

She rubs a finger across her lower lip. "Uh, you had a few things."

I wait for an explanation. None is forthcoming. "So what happened to them?"

"Your mother has them."

"My mother? How? When?"

She adopts the posture of the innocent bearer of unwanted news. "She came by about two weeks ago and gathered up your things. There wasn't much. She took them out in a plastic file box."

"You're sure it was my mother?"

"Well, I didn't look at her ID or anything, but Mr. Strickland said she was coming by to gather up your personal possessions, then she showed up with a storage box. That's why we didn't think you were coming back."

I mull this over. Two weeks ago my mother cleaned out my workspace. It's what I would have done if I *weren't* coming back. But this morning she insisted I had to return to work. What changed?

I stand up. "Can you help me with this?" I say, wiggling the backpack.

Margaret helps me shed the backpack, then hangs it on the hook meant for coats. She places my cell phone on the desk next to the keyboard, and the thermos of coffee next to that.

"Can you insert a glass straw in the thermos?" I ask. "Hard to do with my foot."

She silently complies. "What else do you need, Ella?"

"What don't I need?" I say in a half laugh. "Sorry. Let me get settled, and I'll let you know."

Standing in front of me, she puts her palms gingerly on my shoulders. "Welcome back." And then she leaves me alone.

I wiggle back into my chair, eyeing the keyboard and the mouse, trying to figure out how to proceed. My mother's actions are so bewildering that I can't let them go. Not yet. What did my mother do with my personal possessions? And why did she clear out my desk and then force me to come back to work? I will get nothing done until these questions are answered.

I direct my cell phone to call my mother's cell. While the phone rings, I compose my demand, barely realizing I need to balance my outrage with the knowledge that she holds all the cards. Yelling won't help, that's for sure. On the third ring, I take a deep breath to calm myself. The phone picks up. My frustration is barely restrained. I hear her voice. But it is her recorded voice. In her raspy tone she invites me to leave a message.

I decide not to. There's no way to do it right.

I re-focus on the computer monitor. The white arrow awaits my direction. With the mouse on the floor, I maneuver my right foot to click the left button with my big toe and tap the email icon. Once it loads, I see that I have more than three thousand emails that have appeared in my inbox in the past four months. All unopened. With protracted effort and clenching of my toes, I maneuver the scroll button and finally land on the evening of August 9. The day of the bombing.

There are a dozen emails from that date, all time-stamped after six p.m. From this, I assume I must have left the office around six, but my memory of that day is just blank. Not even a blur.

I open an email from Margaret. It's a message about a project we were working on, a software package managing the supply chain for an electric vehicle manufacturer. It's meaningless to me now. Nine other emails are about deadlines on my projects, and one is congratulations for an award our team won for designing software to aid distribution of food, water, and supplies in war-torn Somalia.

The last email is from davlyendowski@gmail.com, and when the cursor lands on the email I get a message of caution that the sender is from outside of our network. The name does not ring a bell. I open it anyway, reasoning that our security measures have scanned the email for viruses, and I won't open any attachments.

The email reads:

> Ella, I left my cell phone at home today, so I'm sending you this email instead of a text. I'm running a little late, so I'll meet you at 8:30, instead of 8, at the usual place. I hope that's okay.
> Love, David ♡

I shove my chair away from the desk and stare at the email, as if it were a rising cobra. *Love, David?*

My eyes go everywhere in search of anything to tell me who David Lyendowski is. I come up with nothing. Not a trace of him anywhere, neither inside my mind nor out. No image, no words, no sounds, no smells. How can that be? Dr. Volkov told me my memory loss might be permanent, but it's hard to fathom I've forgotten everything I once knew about a man who said he loved me.

With my toes I inch the chair closer to the monitor. I read the email again. Perhaps the full meaning of the words escaped me the first time. The email was received at 6:13 p.m. Other than the fact that I must not have read the email because I'd already left work that day, the time has no significance for me. Well, he sent the email about three hours before the bomb went off at the arena at 9:11 p.m. At this realization, my mind whirs out of control with thoughts beyond coincidence. *There can't be any significance to that, can there?*

I study the words. The language is polite. The sentences are grammatically correct and properly punctuated. *The usual place?* So we had a usual place. A restaurant? A bar? The arena?

Using the mouse, I pull up a website for directions and learn that the downtown arena, where I was found under rubble, is more than seven miles from my workplace. Too far to walk. If our usual meeting place was near the arena, or downtown anywhere, I must have driven there or taken the train.

I search my emails and don't find any others from David Lyendowski. I don't find any emails that I may have sent to him. From this I surmise two possibilities. First, the email I just read is the last one David sent me. Second, that because our company email server destroys unsaved emails after thirty days, I must not have saved any of our earlier emails. As I mull this over, sliding my right foot back and forth along the carpet, a third possibility occurs to me. His email of August 9 is the only one either of us sent to the other.

I decide to look him up on social media. For this research, I need to type. I rise from the chair, undulate my hips and roll my shoulders, doing a little dance. The rubber arms begin to sway back and forth in arcs, and as the arms swing up and over the desk, I plop down in the swivel chair. My arms crash onto the keyboard in front of me, making a disturbing racket. I look toward the top of my fabric-walled enclosure, but no one is peering back at me.

My stiff hands lie awkwardly upon the keyboard, facing each other. In their stiffness, they resemble something from an old cartoon, poised in mid-clap. I can drag the hands across the keyboard, but tapping an individual key with one of my fingers is impossible. I feel like a fool.

I bend forward and take a sip of warm coffee. Gripping the glass straw between my lips and teeth, I use it as a stylus and tap the necessary keys to begin searching for David Lyendowski on the internet. I find him first on a professional networking site. His picture reveals a healthy smile, sparkling blue eyes and thinning, reddish-blond hair. He is not particularly handsome, but cute, with a smattering of freckles on the sides of his pale nose. His bio states he is a chemical engineer at a company in the northern suburbs of Charlotte. He graduated from North Carolina State seven years ago. I estimate he is a year younger than I am.

All of this information is gleaned from his profile, and none of it jiggles a recollection. The face of this man is entirely unfamiliar to me. I close my eyes and try to imagine his voice, his smell, the softness of his lips, but the images that pop into my head are from movies or television commercials. Not memories. I realize that I am an unreliable narrator of my own past, that whatever I visualize is as likely a conjuring as it is a memory from my history.

I find him on a social media site and learn that he likes to fish. In his profile picture he is posed next to a large fish that might be a tuna, a faint gold stripe down its middle, its dorsal fin a pale yellow. He is wearing sunglasses and a billed cap and is standing on the deck of a boat called AquaHolic. *Is it his boat?*

I scroll his posts, and there I am. His left arm is around my waist; my right arm is around his. Some third person took our photograph. We are both wearing black-lensed sunglasses and smiling. We appear happy, right? The caption reads: "Ella and me preparing for a hike on the Blue Ridge Parkway." The photograph was posted in late July, about two weeks before his last email.

I study the photograph for clues. I am wearing blue and white striped shorts and a white, sleeveless blouse. I have on short-ankled hiking boots, but no backpack. In my left hand I hold a red water bottle with a strap that slips over my fingers. I am not wearing a hat, and my mahogany hair hangs to my shoulders, gleaming in the sunlight. David is wearing khaki shorts and a khaki camp shirt with lots of pockets. A wide-brimmed hat covers his narrow head, as if he is leading a safari. I joked with him about his hat. This memory comes at me like a lightning bolt, jolting me without warning. It leaves me disoriented, feeling queasy.

I say his name out loud, enunciating slowly. Then just his first name, in a whisper you might use after an intimate moment. I think I hear him whisper my name in return. I stand and whirl in my cubicle, searching for a voice I can't be certain is solely in my head. Staring at our photograph, something overtakes me. Images come streaking at me, too fast to process. Goose bumps march up my legs, my back, and my neck. My bones turn to jelly. I am shaking. I feel pummeled by the fury of invisible fists.

20

There is a huddle of people crowded into my cubicle. I am on the carpeted floor, my legs curled beneath me. My forehead throbs with pain. Margaret kneels over me, dabbing my head with a tissue.

With Margaret's help, I twist off the floor, stand, then lean against my desk. I'm woozy. Everything I see has a double outline to it.

"What happened?" I stammer.

"We heard you scream," Margaret says, looking at the others for confirmation.

"I screamed?"

She nods. "Two or three times. And it looks like you fell and hit your head, maybe on the edge of the desk."

Even now, my phantom right hand shoots toward my forehead to assess the damage. "Am I bleeding?"

"Just a little," Margaret says. She shows me the blood-stained tissue. "But you have a huge goose egg on your forehead. Can you make it to the restroom?"

I nod and stand. My co-workers step back to give me room. Margaret takes a position at my side, wraps her right arm around my shoulders, and steers me down the corridor to the ladies' room.

In the mirror I see the knot, just below the hair-line on the right side of my forehead. The swelling is the color of a ripe tomato, with a blurry one-inch gash in its center. The knot seems to be growing as I gape. I imagine this wound, on a lesser scale, must be similar to the wounds I suffered during the bombing. The bombing. I was re-living it in my cubicle when I apparently fell. I lean against the bathroom counter to steady myself.

"Did I ever mention David Lyendowski to you?" I say.

"No, who is he?"

"A boyfriend, I think."

"I thought you might have a new boyfriend around the end of last summer, but you were pretty cryptic about your relationship."

"Cryptic?"

"You said you wanted to give the relationship some time, to see if it would last, before you introduced him to anybody."

I search her eyes for veracity. I have no reason to believe she would lie to me, but I yearn for some verification that David and I were something more than a photograph on a social media page. It occurs to me that evidence of our relationship probably exists on my old cell phone. My phone was destroyed in the explosion, and I didn't back up my data to the cloud. My cell provider reported weeks ago that my phone "went dark" at 9:11 p.m. on August 9. As did many others, they told me.

"Do you want to go to the emergency room, or an urgent care clinic? That knot looks really nasty." Margaret touches my forehead.

Her touch pulls me out of a hazy attempt to retrieve the visions I was uncovering as I stared at David's picture on my computer. But the memories prove elusive, like a stale dream that leaves you rattled but unable to recall details. I begin to rise from the counter. I stagger. Margaret rights me.

"I'm driving you to urgent care," she says.

"I need to call my mother."

"You can call her on the way."

During the drive, strapped into the front passenger seat of Margaret's car, my head throbs with a regular rhythm. I peer through the side window at buildings and cars and a man on a bicycle, vaguely thinking my eyes must be the gateway to recollection, for until I saw the picture of David and me together, I had no inkling who he was. Then again, his profile photographs did nothing to light my memory, so perhaps my theory is invalid. I close my eyes. Maybe sights are mere distraction, and I can only access my memory bank with my eyes staring into darkness. When I become queasy and dizzy again, I open my eyes and fix on a tan concrete building ahead for the rest of the ride.

The urgent care clinic is in a strip mall that houses a tanning salon, a nail salon, a wine store, an organic grocery store, and a smattering of other retail establishments whose signs flash by me in a blur of color. After

Margaret fills out the intake form, jotting down my answers in a neat script, a physician's assistant with a pert look leads us down a narrow, tiled hallway. We enter an examination room not much larger than my office cubicle. I wriggle onto a padded exam table, and Margaret stands in a near corner, an expression of concern on her face.

The PA, whose name is Sandy, notices my prosthetics when she begins to roll up my left sleeve, preparing to encircle my arm with the blood pressure cuff. "Oh," she says. "Well, I guess we'll just have to skip that step."

After she returns the cuff to a drawer, her gloved fingers gently probe the knot on my forehead. "How did you get this knot?"

"I fell. I think I fainted."

She gives me an ambiguous smile. "Do you have fainting spells?"

"Not before now," I say. I wince as her finger presses my wound. "Will I need stitches?"

"You've had skin grafts on your face," she says. "Were you burned?"

"I was injured in the bombing at the arena," I say.

She nods, then meets my eyes for the first time. "Well, I think butterfly bandages will do the trick. The wound is not very wide. And given what you've been through, I don't want to unnecessarily subject you to more stitches."

"Does she need x-rays, or an MRI, or something? She's been a little dizzy," Margaret explains.

The PA uses a pen light to search my eyes. "Your pupils are reactive. Are you bothered by light or noise?"

"No."

"Have you vomited?"

I shake my head.

The PA turns to Margaret. "I don't think she has a concussion, but you should watch her for 24 hours."

When I emerge from the exam room, I see my mother coming through the glass door of the clinic. She is wearing a dark gray wool coat that hangs below her knees and carrying a caramel-colored leather purse the size of a beach bag. Her left hand pats the steel gray curls behind her left ear, as if she's just come from the beauty salon. That's probably the case. She didn't pick up when I called her from the car, for the second time today. This time I left a message that I was going to urgent care because I fell. She's arrived about 45 minutes later.

"How's your head," she says, rubbing an ungloved thumb near the bump on my forehead.

I pull away from her. "It's fine. No stitches. What took you so long to get here?"

"I just heard your message a few minutes ago. I was at the beauty parlor. Sorry about that."

"You didn't pick up when I called you earlier this morning."

"Did you leave a message?"

She knows I didn't. I can feel my ire rising, threatening to take over. This is not what I want to fight with her about. Certainly not here in the cloistered waiting room of this clinic.

"Let's go outside," I say to my mother. "I need to ask you something." I turn to Margaret. "Can you wait a few minutes, take me back to work?"

Margaret tilts her head to the side. "I don't think that's a good idea. You might have a concussion, and you need to be watched for the next 24 hours. Can't really do that at the office."

I want to deliver a pithy retort, but Margaret is not the one I'm angry at. In the short span of a few hours, she's already become a friend, and I need all the friends I can get.

"You're right," I say. "Thanks for bringing me over here, Margaret. Way beyond the call of duty. I appreciate it." I lean into her in my version of a hug, our shoulders touching.

"Let me get your backpack from my car."

We sidle through the clinic door, and I angle to my mother's Buick, stand waiting at the passenger door to be admitted. Margaret retrieves my backpack, comes over, opens the passenger door and buckles me in. She settles the backpack in the back seat.

"See you tomorrow?"

I nod. "First thing in the morning."

My ally departed, I am now alone with my mother, girding for confrontation. On the drive home, I compose myself and my message. While my wound has been attended to and I've dealt with the throb and shock of my fall, a part of my brain has continued to probe for memories of David. Amid the haze, one thing becomes clear: my mother knows something. But if I just blurt my accusation at her, she will likely install a facade of denial, maybe even destroy the evidence. If there is any evidence.

My mother pulls into the gravel drive of my house. She takes her time getting out of the Buick, hesitates at the trunk as she comes to the passenger side. She eventually swings my door open and unbuckles my seat belt.

Once I am freed, I step in front of her. We are nose to nose. Well, my nose to her forehead, because I'm three or four inches taller. The acrid smell of cigarette smoke emanates from her nostrils and her mouth. It makes my eyes water.

"What did you do with my personal belongings from the office?" I intentionally use a challenging tone because I can't adequately portray menace physically.

She takes in a deep breath, coughs a little. Her smoker's lungs are no longer able to fully inflate. From her purse she pulls a pack of cigarettes she is never without and lights up.

I don't say anything to disrupt her preparations.

She inhales deeply, closing her eyes, holds that breath for several seconds, then turns her head to the side and exhales a blue plume of smoke.

"Let's go inside," she says. She crunches the gravel when she turns away and flicks the burning cigarette onto the drive.

"No. I want you to answer my question."

She is already at the stoop, fiddling in her purse for my house keys. She leaves the front door open for me. I follow and find her in the kitchen, her cell phone in hand. She pushes an icon I can't see, then puts the phone to her left ear.

"It's Rose Winslow," she says in a quiet voice.

I can hear a burble from the person she's talking to, a female voice, but not actual words.

"She's asking about her personal possessions … that's right, from the office … about two weeks ago … went back to work this morning …should I show them to her?"

"Who are you talking to?" I ask.

She glances sideways at me, as if I am an annoyance and not the subject of her conversation. She starts to hand the phone to me, then realizes her mistake. She places the phone on the kitchen table and punches the speaker icon. "It's Dr. Marvin," my mother says. "You know, the psychiatrist you refuse to see."

"How are you, Ella?" Dr. Marvin says in her cheery lilt.

"Okay. I fell. At work. My first day back. I hit my head."

"Are you okay?"

"Just a knot on my forehead. But I'm starting to remember things, Dr. Marvin. I got an email from a man named David Lyendowski. He signed the email Love, David."

"What do you remember about him?" she asks.

"Very little, but I'm wondering if there's something in my belongings from work that might help me remember him. I need to know."

"I see."

In the silence, I imagine her creamy skin and conjure the image of one of her fingers twisting the fire-red curls above her ear, like she sometimes did when we talked in my room at the hospital.

"I think I was with him, on the night of the explosion."

"Rose," Dr. Marvin says, "it's okay to show Ella the things you retrieved from her office, and the other items as well." Her voice is methodical, each word paced and clearly enunciated.

At this I begin to understand. My mother has been keeping secrets, at the instruction of Dr. Marvin. To protect me, I presume, but I'm not ready to ascribe such honorable motives to either of them.

My mother begins to walk from the kitchen. I want to follow her, to see where her secret hiding place is, but Dr. Marvin's voice holds me in place.

"Ella, I have been having regular phone sessions with your mother, and a few with your sister Mattie. Not as patients, *per se*, but to keep me apprised of your emotional state. All so they can help you recover in the best possible way."

"So my mother and sister are spying on me and reporting to you?"

"No, not at all. It's just that you haven't been willing to come see me, or engage in virtual counseling sessions, so I rely on them to monitor the situation. All to protect you. Your mother has already told me what she retrieved from your office, and about some photographs you apparently sent to your sister from your phone."

"What kind of photographs?"

"Of David and you."

"Okay."

"Seeing these photographs may bring back painful memories, Ella. But some happy memories, too, I think. This is one of the reasons I wanted to bring you to the office, so we could explore these things in a controlled setting."

I sit down in one of the swivel chairs at my breakfast table, trying to prepare myself. "I'm ready," I say, even though I'm not convinced this is true.

My mother returns with a plastic file box, sets it on the kitchen table. She removes the wooden bowl of fruit that has anchored the table for the past two months. Oranges and bananas I cannot peel are transferred to the kitchen counter. She begins plucking things from the file box and setting them on the table, one by one: a chartreuse hair scrunchie; a Montblanc pen someone must have given me because I would not have bought such an expensive item for myself; a bottle of Chloe perfume; my gold wedding band from when I was married to Robert, a marriage that ended several years ago; and a packet of folded pages, tied with a sky blue ribbon.

"The rest is just makeup," my mother says, tilting the box so I can see a clutter of lipstick, nail polish, a compact, a hairbrush, etc.

"What are those?" I nod to the bundled pages.

"Letters," she says, but she doesn't move to untie the ribbon. "There are pictures, too. Pictures you sent to Mattie from your phone."

"Ella, how do you feel right now?" Dr. Marvin says.

"Anxious," I say.

"That's perfectly natural, given the circumstances. Are you okay to see the pictures?"

"I am."

"Okay. Rose, show her the pictures. It might be best to show her in chronological order."

My mother wrinkles her mouth, then picks up her phone. While she searches her photo cache, no one says anything. I can hear the seconds tick off the wall clock above the refrigerator, a battery-operated analog clock that must be twenty years old. The refrigerator motor kicks on in a gentle hum.

My mother places the phone in front of me but remains at my shoulder, her right index finger poised in the air. "This is the first one I could find."

It is a photograph of David and me, at night, sitting on a grassy hill somewhere, with fireworks in the background.

"Describe for me what you see," Dr. Marvin says.

"It looks like a Fourth of July photograph of David and me. Possibly taken with a selfie-stick. We're sitting on a blanket. There are red and white firework explosions behind us."

"Do you look happy?"

"We're both smiling."

"Anything else?"

"Our heads are touching. He has his right arm around my shoulders."

"Okay, and do you remember taking that picture, or David taking it?"

I shake my head. "No. But it's obviously me, and him. The caption says: 'Third Date'."

"Ella, do you remember the first or second dates with David?"

I struggle to retrieve something, but nothing emerges. "I don't. Scroll to the next picture, mama." Anticipation is heightened, and I imagine if I still had my real hands, they might be shaking with the surge of adrenaline I'm experiencing.

She swipes her finger across the side arrow and a photograph of David in a dark suit and me in a burgundy cocktail dress appears. We are side-by-side, angled toward each other, probably posed by a professional photographer, but at an event I can neither name nor remember. My hair is up in the back, with curled tresses dangling in front of my ears. There is no caption, but the photo is dated July 17. The next picture is of David and me before our hike on the Blue Ridge Parkway, the same photograph I found on his social media page.

"There's one more," my mother says.

"Ella," Dr. Marvin says, "to prepare you, this photo is from August 9, about twenty minutes before the bombing. And it tells us a lot about your relationship with David."

My mother looks at me with tight lips. "You ready?"

I nod.

With a swipe of her gnarled finger the moment changes. And so does my life. In the photograph, which captures the front of me from my head to my knees, my left arm is extended toward the camera. My hand is fanned open. On my manicured finger is a glittering diamond ring.

"I was engaged?" I glance at the place where my left hand is supposed to be, seeking the corroboration of an engagement ring. It is not there. I have no recollection of David's proposal. Back to the photograph, with the diamond gleaming in the camera flash.

I've been upended, knocked into some other dimension where nothing makes sense. I swivel around in the chair and take in the arrangement of my kitchen. The refrigerator continues its hum, the clock continues its tick. The toaster is in the same place it has always been. The glass front of my center cabinet displays neatly stacked plates and cups.

"Ella, can you hear me?" Dr. Marvin asks.

I don't respond. I can't respond.

"Rose, is she okay?"

"She's holding her breath."

I'm not holding my breath, not intentionally, but my diaphragm has stopped working. I can't feel my heartbeat. Maybe this is what happened when the explosion knocked me flat.

"Rose, if she's not breathing, slap her on the back or something."

I detect panic in Dr. Marvin's voice, even though I'm the one not breathing. My mother begins to pat my back like she's trying to elicit a burp from a just-fed baby. Then she hits me harder, square between the shoulder blades, not unlike the way she slapped my face after I peed on this kitchen floor.

I suck in fresh air and am driven back to that night. David and I are walking, hand-in-hand. The arena is on our right. The thump of music comes from deep within its walls. What materializes is a still photo with sound. Fragments of memories have now coalesced, but they are isolated scenes, not strung together like video.

Another frame emerges. I am kneeling next to a brick wall that separates the arena from the sidewalk. I am tying my shoe, my left shoe. David is standing in the concrete driveway that leads down to the loading dock, a few steps ahead. His face holds kindness. His right hand is extended toward me, beckoning. And then the air shatters.

I watch in horror as David disappears.

21

Contrary to my earlier intentions, I cannot go back to work the next morning. My emotional state, and especially my resolve to work, is as decimated as my body was in the hours after the bombing. My mind is pulp, as if I am in the staggering phase of a bender. I have a fleeting thought that perhaps there is salve there—in strong alcohol—but instead I take two Zoloft and sleep the day away in my darkened room.

In the evening, Mattie calls me. I lie in bed, a sheen of sleep sweat coating my body, talking to her about David.

"Did I mention anything to you about our relationship?"

"You did. After the third date, I think. The one where you sent me the Fourth of July picture. You sounded happy."

I mull this over. Even though my happiness appears to be real, there is little residual evidence of it. Other than the photographs, and my missing engagement ring, there is no tangible proof that I was in a romantic relationship, or in love, or on the verge of marriage.

"What did I say about him?"

"It's not so much what you said, Ella, but your tone. You were effusive. Unguarded. Committed."

"After the third date?"

"If not then, certainly after the charity ball you went to with him in late July."

"What charity?" I ask. I immediately recognize this as a stray question.

"You didn't say."

"Did I call you after he proposed that night?"

There is a pause on the line, as if Mattie is trying out several responses before uttering one. Thinking back, I realize the engagement photograph I sent to her, the diamond gleaming in the flash, was sent only minutes before the bomb went off. I look over at the phone on my nightstand. "Mattie?"

"I was on the phone when …" she trails off.

"When what? When he proposed?"

"No, when …"

It takes me a moment to realize she is crying. "When what, Mattie? When the bomb went off?"

Her answer is a deep, shuddering sob.

"Jesus," I say. "You heard it?"

She only partially regains her composure. Her next words are spoken in stuttering fragments. "I was talking to you. You were walking with David. You handed him the phone. You had to tie your shoe."

"No, that can't be right." The still photograph re-emerges. Me kneeling on the sidewalk next to the arena, both hands knotting my left shoe. David standing on the driveway, his right hand extended to me, a happy and serene smile on his face.

And my phone is at his left ear.

"You were talking to him on my phone," I say.

"Yes." Her response is drawn out, that single word punctuated with wet bubbles.

"You were the last person to talk to him, Mattie. What did he say?"

I hear her take a deep breath, her exhalation throaty, water escaping down a tub drain. "He said …" She trails off, unable to continue.

"What did he say, Mattie?" It has become imperative that I know the last words of my fiancé. Words likely spoken in a cloud of euphoria before the sudden, hopefully painless, end. On my end, I try to recapture those final moments, but all I have are the still photographs with the deep thump of concert music that sounds eerily like a beating heart.

Mattie finally finds the words. She tells me in a stammering, wet sob. "David said, 'congratulations, Mattie. You're going to be an aunt'."

22

They are arrayed around me like inquisitors, only without any menace in their gazes. Mattie sits on the other end of a couch from me, a couch with big, rolled arms and tan chenille cushions designed to soothe. To my right, my mother stretches her arms along the length of a beige club chair with an azure and rose flame-stitch pattern that adds modest color to the room. Dr. Marvin has her legs crossed at the ankle above black pumps, her hands twisting a black pen before her, partially relaxed in a wing chair that gives her the imprimatur of a chief.

"She hasn't spoken a word in three days," my mother says, her gravelly voice tinged with concern.

Dr. Marvin nods. The light curls near her ears bob with acknowledgment. "Since her conversation with you, Mattie."

"Yes," Mattie says, leaning forward with her hands clenched between her jeaned knees. "Since I told her about my conversation with David."

"Ella, can you understand what we are saying?" Dr. Marvin asks. "If so, just nod. You don't need to speak if you don't want to."

I nod.

"Ella, you're probably experiencing shell shock. It's been well-documented in soldiers who have been in battle, and you've been through something just as threatening and disorienting."

She turns to my mother. "What did they say at the emergency room, Rose?"

"Everything seemed normal, physically," she says.

"Normal blood pressure?"

"Yes."

"Did they take an EEG?"

My mother looks puzzled.

"They would have attached leads to her head to scan her brain," Dr. Marvin explains.

"Yes, I saw them do that, and they said the results were normal."

Dr. Marvin has obtained this information while continuing to roll the pen in her fingers with a distinct rhythm. I wonder if it is a sign of anxiety, or if she is using this maneuver as some type of hypnotic device.

"Ella, can you tell me how you're feeling right now?"

My muteness may be a product of shock, or the sense that words offer insufficient solace under the circumstances, but I feel like I swallowed my vocal cords. My throat is empty. All I can do is shake my head.

"It's all right. I'll just talk for a bit, and you can nod or shake your head if I say something you want to comment upon." Dr. Marvin takes a deep breath. "While we were on the phone a few days ago—me, you and your mother—we went through the personal items your mother removed from your office cubicle." Her melodic Irish lilt pauses.

I nod.

"Good. Your memory of that day appears to be intact. And after that, your mother showed you some pictures on her phone, pictures you apparently sent to Mattie and she recently forwarded to your mom. Pictures of you and David."

My mind is affixed to the last photograph, the one with my left hand and a gleaming diamond extended toward the camera. I'm not sure how my memory works any more, but this image seems permanently affixed to the inside of my eyelids. I leave this image for a moment and gaze at Dr. Marvin's creamy skin. I nod.

"And although I'm sure that was a shock for you, finding out you were engaged to David, and seeing the things that you saw, you were still able to speak after that because you had a conversation with Mattie the following evening?"

My attempt to find my voice is akin to an effort to make my phantom fingers work. In both cases, there's an impenetrable roadblock of that brain signal. All I can do is nod.

"Mattie, please recount for me as best you can the exact conversation you had with Ella three evenings ago."

As Mattie speaks, I look beyond Dr. Marvin's office, through the lone window whose blinds are half-drawn, into the twilight. This is not a recap I want to hear, but neither do I attempt to escape. The twinkle of streetlights and the vague sound of automobile traffic invite me outside.

When I hear the last thing Mattie recalls—my fiancé David's final words to the world—something rises from my gut. What emerges are not words, but an animal's mortal wail.

"Ella are you alright?" Dr. Marvin asks.

Mattie's right hand reaches my knee and caresses me through my gingham dress. In the mirror-like reflection of the window I see my face. My eyes are wide, my newly returned eyebrows arched, my lips parted almost an inch.

"What are you trying to say, Ella?" It's Mattie now, her hand still on my leg, trying to rub the words into existence.

I shake my head with exasperation. Mattie leans toward me and dabs a tissue on my cheeks.

"Rose, did you bring David's letters?"

My head swivels to my mother and her huge purse, which she swings from the floor to her lap and digs in with both of her gnarled hands. I have forgotten about the letters. My mother stands and hands the bundle, wrapped in a sky-blue ribbon, to Dr. Marvin.

With speed I don't think I have, I am off the sofa and standing in front of Dr. Marvin, shaking my head vigorously.

"You don't want me to read the letters?"

I nod, then half turn to my mother and thrust my head in her direction as if pointing. I do the same to Mattie.

"Let me see if I understand," Dr. Marvin continues. "If you want me to read the letters, just nod."

I nod. I want to hear David's words through the melodic tones of Dr. Marvin's voice. In some way I want to revive him.

"But you would prefer that Rose and Mattie step outside?"

I nod again. I can't explain why I want to ban them. Perhaps it's because of the intimacy I expect to hear, but also becausc of something else I can't yet define.

Dr. Marvin pauses, shifts in her chair. "Rose, Mattie, would you mind sitting in the waiting room for a bit?"

They trudge out in silence. I try to give them a look of apology, which may not have landed in the absence of words. In a few seconds, we are alone, the room silent, with barely the echo of my mother's muttered objection hanging in the air.

Dr. Marvin unties the blue ribbon. "Ella, would you like to sit? If so, I think I'll join you on the sofa."

I settle against a couch cushion, angling myself in the corner so I am partially facing Dr. Marvin when she sits where Mattie was. Perhaps I only imagine it, but I detect a waft of fragrance when Dr. Marvin unfolds the first letter.

"I'll read these in the order in which you kept them, if that's okay?"

I nod and pull my bare feet from the floor and curl them under me. I do not know what to expect here. I need to hear something positive.

And I do.

Dr. Marvin's voice brings me David's words of love, of future, of discovery and surprise. There are four letters, all hand-written in a script that reminds me of an earlier time when we wrote letters with fountain pens. I am now all but certain that David gave me the Mont Blanc pen that was in my desk at work. His letters are two pages or less. Each sentence is poignant and bonds me to him.

In the final letter, David extolls the happiness he felt when I told him I was pregnant. He writes that he felt no hesitation, no apprehension, when I showed him the three pregnancy-test strips with their undeniable plus marks. He talks of our future together, the three of us. And Dr. Marvin stops short. Her mouth opens for a second, and then she catches herself and closes it. She is supposed to remain composed, serve as my anchor, as I fight my way out of silence.

She lays the last page on my lap. "I think you should read this part, Ella."

My eyes may be too blurry to see the words. I inhale a long breath through my watery throat. A tear drops onto the page, landing next to David's signature. I bend to the letter.

If our child is a boy, I agree with your suggestion to name him Johnny, after your father. And if our child is a girl, I would like to name her Eve. She will be the first of many.

After I read this, I slip back to that night. I don't want to see it again, but I have no choice. Walking along the sidewalk with my fiancé, bending to tie my shoe next to the brick wall. David reaching back for me from the unprotected driveway, a smile on his face and my phone at his ear.

She is there. I can feel her in the womb though she cannot be much larger than a button. As I knot my shoelaces, the bomb goes off.

If I could, my hands would slip down and caress the place where she once harbored. Hot tears stream down my cheeks. An indelible sadness wells in my heart. Her name climbs up my throat and involuntarily escapes my lips: "Eve."

23

The ensuing days are a blur. I take the train to Dr. Marvin's office several times, and we engage in memory recovery sessions. As things come flooding back, present and past meld into a fusion of images. My father's suicide, my divorce from Robert, and David's murder—I am able to call it that now—coalesce as if they all occurred within a week's time. Part of me knows this is not the case, yet in certain moments, I'm unsure whether I'm watching my life movie forwards or backwards.

We parse words: courage; cowardice; fear, anxiety; sadness; terror; anger. All of these apply to me. I am angry that my mother and my sister and the psychiatrist who is supposed to help me heal have kept things from me. Important things. Like my engagement to David. My pregnancy. But Dr. Marvin explains that while I was recovering physically from my injuries and struggling to accept a life without arms, I might not have survived a barrage of more tragic news. And so they hid these things. To protect me.

One resolution I carry from these sessions with Dr. Marvin is that I cannot remain in the past. Focusing on what has happened to me brings only pain. I must somehow push through the grief and plan my future, even if the product of that effort is nothing more than pure imagination.

I return to work one day in the early afternoon, with a singular purpose. I stop in the HR office, where Cindy Morgan explains to me the principal terms of the company's group disability policy.

"In essence," she says, tracing her finger across the computer screen, "you should qualify for disability because you've lost two limbs. It says here that if you lose a hand and a foot, or two feet, or two hands, then you are presumed disabled."

I shrug my shoulders, glance down at my fake hands. "Yes, I've lost two hands. How much are the benefits?"

"Sixty percent of the average of your salary for the two years before you became disabled. After tax."

I run the numbers in my head, comparing the reduced income to my expenses, which are mounting up. The hospital bills, surgeries and prosthetics are not fully covered by my health insurance, and my deductibles are high. "Are the benefits retroactive?"

Cindy scrolls through some pages in my computer file. "I'm pretty sure. You have to file a claim and the administrator will review it for final determination. Is that something you want to do?"

Dr. Marvin has strengthened my mind in the way that Zack strengthened my body. The single word I spoke as I read David's final letter opened gates. With all that has been stolen from me—my unborn child, my future husband, my arms, a large slice of sanity—I must re-take control of my life. This is a first step.

"I'm sure."

"There will be paperwork to sign," she says.

"I can't sign anything with these prosthetics," I say. "Can we do it on-line?"

Cindy stares at me for a second, wrinkles her mouth. "Sure, that will work. Plus, we can give you a small severance if you'll sign a release of liability."

"How much is the severance?"

"Two weeks for each year of employment, so sixteen weeks in all. If we do it this way instead of you resigning, it will help in the event you want to file for unemployment."

I stare past her at a window whose mini-blinds are open enough to see a canopy of bare trees. The sun throws angled slats of light onto the wall. Of all the things I thought about in the hospital and since I've been home, earning money from my disability is not one of them. Still, this is the only way.

"Okay, let's do it."

It is a sad fact that our value is often measured by our ability to work. For years I introduced myself as "Ella Winslow, software developer." I have seen this coming. Developing software *was* my job. Though I have the will, I no longer have the way to accomplish the work. I have become that school-aged child always picked last for softball, stuck in the desert of right field.

When she's finished, Cindy turns her monitor around so I can read the fine print. The conditions of my severance involve me giving up all rights to ever make a claim against the company. Not for wrongful termination, or discrimination, or for rights I have under the Americans with Disabilities Act. I was only vaguely aware I had any rights. The company treated me fairly. Maybe tried harder to make it work than I did. I direct Cindy to sign my name electronically on all of the documents.

I stop by Margaret's workspace for a final goodbye. Though I have not returned to work in almost two months, she seems shocked by my announcement.

"Ella, together we could make this work. The IT department installed voice recognition software on your computer. I'll help you," she says.

"I appreciate everything you've done for me, Margaret, and I really appreciate the offer. But it's not really about the work. I need to move on with my life, whatever that looks like. This job, this place, will keep me in the past."

She nods understanding, wraps her arms around my neck and pulls me into her. "We'll miss you, Ella."

"Can you help me get my stuff, put it in my backpack?"

"Sure."

At my cubicle, the butterfly coffee mug is the only personal item I want to take with me. "You can have the Devil's Ivy," I say, "or toss it in the trash."

I emerge from the office where I worked for eight years into late afternoon sunshine. The cold north air that often travels down from the mountains in winter has been replaced by a moist warmth coming from the Gulf. It feels good on my skin.

I walk to the train station and head north, into the city. The train cars are almost empty. I disembark at the Convention Center station, two blocks from the ruined arena. I want to approach the bombing site on my terms, and not have it thrust upon me.

The only remnant of the arena is a large hole in the ground. The debris has been removed and taken to another place near the airport, where workers are still sifting through the rubble for … well, you know what they are looking for. I walk over to the chain-link fence that surrounds the site and peer at a deep pit that has steel bracing in various places. Workers and equipment move against the backdrop of steep clay walls.

From the location of a concrete driveway heading down into the site, I judge that I am standing in the approximate spot where I was tying my shoe when the bomb was detonated. The brick wall that may have partially protected me is no longer here. I look toward the edge of the driveway, where David was standing with his right arm outstretched.

And then he wasn't.

I kneel, as I remember I did that night. My fake hands dangle near my slip-on pumps that do not have laces. Now, the sun casts waning light between the buildings. That night the sun would have been long gone. This is where Eve died.

I stand and walk back and forth across the driveway because only motion will keep me from doubling over, curling within myself. Dr. Marvin has prepared me for this moment, installing tools that will help me cope. Movement is the tool I now choose. Walking does not stave off the agony, but it distracts me just enough that I do not dart into the street in front of an oncoming bus.

On the sidewalk someone has painted "Pit of Despair" in orange letters. So true.

I find myself scanning the gutter and the dirt beside the sidewalk and the crevices between sidewalk sections for some evidence that I was ever here. Blood, or a piece of shoelace, or my diamond ring. Anything. But I realize what a fool I am, that in the six months since the bombing every inch of this place has been examined and scoured. There is nothing of me left here.

Across the street in a vacant lot is a budding memorial. A curved stone—actually a series of curved pieces of white granite linked together—is being erected in the middle. I suppose the names of the dead will be carved into those stones, and I speculate on which marker David's name will be etched. A temporary plaque describes the contemplated vision, complete with a diagram of the site. I wonder if Eve's name should be etched here, and whether the names of the injured victims will be included.

I am back on the train. I disembark at a stop in the hospital district. I pass the hospital where I stayed for almost two months with barely a glance at its concrete pillars and rows of small windows. The gargantuan buildings and parking decks slowly give way to a tree-lined street with modest structures set back from the road. Some of these buildings are new, the facades constructed of brick, and others are old houses that have been converted to medical offices.

Dr. Volkov's cosmetic surgery practice is housed in a two-story building with a broad front porch, the boards painted gray but void of furniture. The window trim is the color of October sky, Carolina blue. I note the camera eye peering at me from above the door, which opens inward.

There is no receptionist behind the glass, but no sooner have I nudged the door shut with my foot than Dr. Volkov appears in the doorway that leads to the surgical suite. I have been here twice before.

He stands by the door, wiping his hands with a paper towel. He is wearing a red and black flannel shirt and black jeans. His beard has grown in and now covers roughly half his face.

"Ms. Winslow, I am surprised to see you." His eyes today are slate blue, and he fixes on me as if I have interrupted something.

"I just came by to ask you some questions."

"Questions?"

I take two steps toward him, and he slides forward, into the reception area with me. The door with a coded lock clicks shut behind him.

"Sit," he gestures toward the leather reception chairs. "Please."

After sliding onto leather that almost sighs with softness, I turn to him. "Did you know that I was pregnant?"

The startled look on his face tells me the answer. "I did not. When? When you were brought into the hospital?"

"When the bomb exploded."

"I saw no signs of pregnancy when I operated on you. However, with the condition you were in, I wasn't examining you for that purpose."

"I lost the baby that night. Her name was Eve."

"I am sorry for your loss." He says this in a rote tone I presume he has used hundreds of times before. But his eyes stay fixed on mine. "Is there anything else?"

"I had a diamond ring on my left hand. Do you have any idea where that ring might be?"

"I do not. I presume it would have been collected by first responders or by the triage team when you were brought in."

I shake my head. "I've checked with both, and they have no record of it. You didn't see it on my hand when you amputated my arms?"

"I did not. What are you implying?"

I realize my voice has grown an edge to it, but I am not about to apologize. "I'm not implying anything. I just want to know where my ring is. My fiancé gave it to me when he proposed. About twenty minutes before."

"Ah." Dr. Volkov's right hand settles beneath his chin, and his index finger swishes back and forth across his full whiskers.

"Did I have all ten fingers when you operated on me?"

"As I recall, yes. Your medical records should confirm that. Is there anything else?"

I mentally tick off the questions I have been formulating over the past several days. I have exhausted my list. "No. I appreciate your time."

"Well, then. Are you going to schedule your final surgery?"

"Do I need it?"

His eyes, not two feet away, study my face. His fingers graze my forehead, then my cheeks. "I must say you have healed well. How did you get that cut on your forehead?"

"I fell. At work."

"So you're back working. That is good to hear."

"I resigned today. So, no."

"I see." He pauses, as if deciding something. Then, "I have an engagement to get ready for." He stands.

As I am walking down the wooden steps from his office, I hear the deadbolt engage behind me. I stand on the sidewalk out front for a minute or two. The sun has set. Only a tinge of orange light remains on the horizon.

I hear the squeak of brakes as Dr. Volkov's black SUV pulls to a stop at the intersection of his driveway and the street. The driver's window slides down with a hum. He rests his left elbow on the frame, looks over at me. "Can I give you a ride?"

"I thought you had somewhere to be," I say.

"I can spare a few minutes." There is something in his voice. The courtesy seems feigned.

"No. Thank you. I'm going to take the train home."

"A lift to the station, perhaps?"

I see his profile outlined against the last light of the day. His full lips, the slender nose that ends with a tiny downward curve, the prominent forehead. A profile I have seen before. Somewhere.

In response to his offer, I simply shake my head.

He terminates our conversation by closing the window. A memory tries to take shape, but it dissolves with the roar of his engine as he accelerates into the street.

24

In March, I take the train downtown for a hearing in the lawsuit in which I am a plaintiff. A lawsuit about the bombing. I don't understand the specifics, but essentially the victims are suing the owner of the arena and its security company for not ensuring the safety of those in and around the arena. There is a group of people—business invitees they are called—who purchased tickets to the concert. I am in a different group. The innocent bystanders.

In a cold drizzle, I walk up the granite steps and between two-story columns into the courthouse. At the metal detector, I have nothing to empty from my pockets into the plastic bin. Even with a dove gray raincoat draped over me, I pass through security without incident.

The courtroom is ornate and fosters an atmosphere of solemnity, like what you feel when you step into an old-world church. The architecture and the mosaic ceiling draw my eyes. Plush, maroon carpet absorbs my footsteps. The air is warm, or maybe it's just me. A young woman in a navy suit helps me remove my raincoat and drapes it over a chair.

Everyone goes quiet at the bailiff's insistence. A door to the left of the Judge's bench opens, and another bailiff announces we should rise. The Judge's name is Westlake, and he is from Raleigh, but things are happening fast and I'm not sure I hear correctly. From the bench, the Judge looks over the courtroom, which is filled with people wearing gray and black suits.

From my seat at the end of a row of chairs, just behind where the lawyers sit at their table, I look him over, this Judge who will be judging me, or at least my claims and the claims of thousands of other people. He has dark hair peppered with gray at the temples, dark eyes, and a firm set to his jaw. I expect the firm jaw. His eyes, which don't narrow or scowl at anyone, seem kind. He locks on me for a moment, and his lips part just a millimeter. It is a common reaction from people who see an armless woman up close for the first time.

Our lawyer stands up and introduces himself and a handful of other lawyers, who each stand for a second or two when their names are announced. Then the lead lawyer introduces us. There are eight of us. Eight people to represent the thousands of others who have been killed or maimed. It doesn't seem like enough. We are all different, all unique, and I don't feel like I have the *right* to represent anyone else whose life has been ripped apart by the explosion.

Then the lawyer for the defense stands up and introduces himself and about a dozen other lawyers who represent parties whom our lawyers have sued. I've never heard of any of them. Their lawyers outnumber ours. I wonder if this is a bad sign.

The Judge comes down from the bench and pulls over a chair, unzips his robe and drapes it over the back. The court reporter follows with her machine, and when she is finally set up she plops into a chair with rollers just off to the side. The Judge then sits down and faces us.

"Look, this is a preliminary conference, something I would ordinarily hold in chambers, but there are too many of you." He pauses for a moment, trying to find the right words. "I want you all to know, and I'm not judging anyone, not the defendants or their insurance companies or any of the lawyers in this room, that I am only now beginning to truly understand the magnitude of this catastrophe." His eyes settle on me again like he can't avoid it. "I know the numbers of deceased and wounded, but this is an atrocity almost unparalleled in our country, and a magnitude of human devastation and suffering I'm not sure I can fully comprehend. So I want to hear about it, all of it, from every victim who wants to tell it."

Our lawyer begins to speak, but the Judge cuts him off. "Not from counsel. I hear from lawyers all day long. I need to hear it from the victims, and not through some carefully drafted affidavit." His eyes sidetrack to the place where my arms are supposed to be. "Ms. Winslow, I'm not putting you on the spot, but if you're willing to tell me anything, then please, I'm listening."

I lean forward for some unknown reason and look to my left, down the row of other victims and attorneys in gray and black. No one has prepared me for this. No one told me I would need to talk about it. Dr. Marvin has helped me seek courage, but I don't know if I have enough. When I begin speaking, the courtroom is as quiet as a cemetery.

"My name is Ella Winslow. I don't remember the explosion." I glance down at my empty lap.

The Judge leans in, only a few feet separating him from me. His hands are clasped between his knees. I appreciate that. "And your injuries, Ms. Winslow. Can you tell me?" It is a soft voice, a voice I cannot imagine issuing harsh sentences.

My eyes are damp, with tears pooling in the corners. I tilt my head back and sniff, but the tears escape anyway. "I lost both of my arms. I was told a wall fell on me and crushed my arms. My arms were amputated at the hospital. My legs got cut up from flying debris. I had burns and cuts on my neck and face, and the top of my head. I will always have some scars."

The Judge grimaces, unable to find suitable words.

"It's hard, Judge. Until you lose your hands, it's hard to understand everything you can't do."

"Yes, ma'am. Do you have help?"

"Yes, sir. My mother helps. Her and my sister."

His eyes go to the carpet, and he brings his hands together under his chin and closes his eyes, as if trying to imagine me, my life from the explosion to now. I don't see it as pity; I see it as genuine interest.

"Thank you for telling me that," he says.

He moves on, and I sit back in my chair, tears running down my cheeks. No one offers me a tissue.

Two others tell their stories. One is a young boy with traumatic brain injury. He struggles to utter words, each one a burden. But he perseveres, and we all listen. Every day he wakes up and thanks God he is alive, prays to understand why someone would do this to so many people, and prays for the soul of that man. When he speaks about the praying part, his mouth relaxes and the words come more easily. I see how much this soothes him, believing that someone is listening to his prayers. "I will pray for you too, Judge. This must be awfully hard."

A high-school teacher who lost his wife in the bombing has endured seventeen surgeries and four transplants to replace organs that have been decimated by the concussive effects of the explosion. He takes short breaths after every few words, barely getting them out. He is usually on oxygen, he says. We can all hear the wheeze of lungs that don't work right. With other organs failing, he does not expect to live out the year.

No one else wants to talk, and I understand why. It is hard. We aren't exactly reliving it—the explosion or the aftermath—but in those brief moments we are the center of attention. Everyone is focused on us. And we don't like it. Not one bit.

The Judge returns to the high bench, in his shirt sleeves. Each side's lawyers give their view of the claims, and they set deadlines and schedules, but I am done. My mind wanders back to the hours that I must have laid on the sidewalk, bleeding, my baby's life slipping away as sirens wailed. And I imagine the young boy and the teacher are having the same thoughts, remembering their personal tragedies.

I've read about survivors who take years to gather the courage to venture out again. Maybe they venture out in their imaginations, but not in reality. Or they go out physically but keep their minds closed to the evil lurking out there. As I walk out of the courthouse, I think about those others, the ones still imprisoned in the four corners of devastation. Some will never escape.

I walk alone from the courthouse to the victims' memorial. The rain has stopped, though the sky is filled with low-slung clouds. I wander among the curved stones of the memorial, knowing where I am going. I arrive there with my throat clogged and something building within me. I read David's name, now chiseled in the rock. I say it aloud, a sputtering enunciation no stronger than a whisper.

He comes to life in my video, just before the end, reaching back for me with his arm outstretched. I freeze the frame and sit on a bench at the edge of freshly cut grass. Stray blades on the concrete ooze jade stains. I gaze out at the spot where the arena used to be, now a series of pilings rising from the ashes.

I try to conjure the scene the way it was that night, seven months ago.

The arena brick is the hue of a blood orange. The air is thick with humidity. I smell ozone. The hair on both my arms stands up. I hear the distinctive thump of music, the notes not fully contained by the building. The bass is a booming heart.

I am kneeling, my nimble fingers knotting my left shoe. My attention swerves from David to the glittering ring on my left hand. David's face is vibrant with happiness. The ring makes me exuberant with promise. And then he evaporates. I never hear the explosion itself.

I rewind this tape, all of its five or six seconds, holding back the internal surge this produces. Back and forth a few times, each image clear, my perception and senses heightened, until the depictions rearrange themselves and we are walking in the other direction. David's fingers are intertwined in mine. My fingers are bare. No ring, yet. There is a waning light, the day not fully dead. A minor wind tousles my long hair. The sound of car horns and police whistles directing traffic produce a cacophony.

We are on the other side of the driveway, my shoelaces neatly tied, about to head across with a throng of people, until a policeman raises his hand to let a delivery van turn in. A white van, with the name of a beer distributor painted on the side. Through the side window, I see the profile of the driver. He is a bearded man. Dark glasses cover his eyes. His gaze is fixed straight ahead, intent on his course.

This could be the beer delivery van Special Agent Mullen described. The van I have seen on the news a hundred times. The van carrying the bomb.

I rewind this scene a few times, then a dozen. My eyes squeeze shut to focus. And as the images clarify, I see the man driving the van. The man who killed my baby and my fiancé and thousands of people. The man I see driving the van is not the Mayor.

25

How can I be sure? I whisper this to myself throughout the night. My recently recovered memories are unreliable. I am not always able to discern the time-line, to separate what happened months ago from what occurred a decade earlier.

How can I be sure? This question becomes more significant when Dr. Marvin does not answer my call to her cell phone. She is not available to discuss what I'm feeling, to confirm what I remember. In this fog of doubt, terror begins edging in. Because the bomber is still on the loose. Because I have a clear picture of him in my mind. Because I know who he is.

I convince my mother to take me back to the federal courthouse early the next morning. She parks in a handicapped spot and releases me from the car.

"I don't know when I'll get back home, but you don't need to pick me up. I'll take the train and then walk the rest of the way."

She gives me a smile, as if my declaration pleases her. She has no idea what I am about to do. I'm not sure I fully understand it myself.

When I arrive, the courtroom is empty. I ask the bailiff if I can see the Judge. After a few minutes, his law clerk shows me into a conference room behind the courtroom. The Judge comes in with an agitated look on his face.

"Ms. Winslow, this is very unusual, to meet with a party in a case without the attorneys present." His voice is not as calming as it was when he spoke with us yesterday.

"Yes, sir. Your law clerk told me, but this is not about the actual case, Your Honor."

"So, you don't want to talk to me about your injuries, or what happened that night?"

I hesitate because I am unsure what he wants me to say, uncertain which topics might cause him to end our conversation. I have lain awake all night, afraid to close my eyes. My eyes are red-rimmed and puffy.

"Ms. Winslow. I'm willing to listen, but this can't be about your claims in the lawsuit. If it starts to veer in that direction, we'll have to stop. Is that understood?"

"Yes sir," I say.

"Nancy," he calls out, but his law clerk is no longer there. He checks the empty hallway and closes the door. "All right Ms. Winslow, tell me what's weighing on your mind."

Close up, he has a long, faint scar on his right cheek. I wonder if his scar will ever go away, or if it will remain, as mine will, a constant reminder of tragedy. "I see you have some scars, too," I say. "May I ask …"

"I was attacked by a bear."

"I'm sorry. I know how much that must hurt."

He absently rubs the scar with the middle finger of his right hand. "But that's not what you wanted to talk to me about, right?"

"No, sir. Yesterday, in court, you seemed like you really wanted to know if any of us had anything to say. Not many people are willing to listen to me … you know … in my condition."

"In your condition?"

"I had a traumatic brain injury, and I've lost some of my memory." Concern crosses his face, and his fingers fidget. I must be nearing an off-limits topic. "That's just a fact, Judge, but you need to know it, because last night, when I visited the victims' memorial down by the arena, a piece of my memory came back."

The Judge sits back in his chair, his hands gripping the leather arms.

"I saw something that night. The night of the bombing. Something that doesn't fit."

"What do you mean something that doesn't fit?"

"I was on my way to a park, with my fiancé . . ." My voice catches. My newly recovered video of that night swells in my throat. "I saw a van drive down into the loading dock at the arena."

The Judge leans forward, his hands clenched together on the table. His eyes are intense and fixed on me. "What kind of van?"

"A beer distributor van, just like the one the FBI says carried the bomb."

The Judge glances down at the table. His hands are clenched together so tightly his fingers are turning red.

"I saw the driver, or at least the profile of the driver, when he slowed down before going down to the loading dock."

"You saw Carmelo Williams driving the van?" he says.

I shake my head. "It wasn't Carmelo Williams. The driver's skin was too light. I know this is going to sound crazy, sir, but before this happened to me, I was a painter. I study faces so I can paint them from memory. Well, I did once. I don't paint anymore. But the Mayor wasn't driving that van."

For some reason, the Judge's face flushes red. The scar on his cheek remains a vivid white. "Have you told anyone else about this?"

"No, sir."

"How did you get here, by the way, to the courthouse?"

"My mother drove me."

I can tell he is testing me, testing my memory, trying to determine if I'm some crazy woman whom he should immediately dismiss.

"And you haven't told your mother?"

"No sir."

"Or your fiancé?"

"He's dead. He died in the explosion."

"I'm sorry," he says, looking over my head. "You understand, Ms. Winslow, that if you lie to me, even though this is an off-the-record discussion, I can't just erase that knowledge. I'm human. It will likely affect how I view your credibility as your case moves forward."

"I understand that. I've been up all night, replaying it in my mind. Last night at the victims' memorial, looking across the street at the driveway, it started to come back to me. I saw what I saw." I say this with more conviction than I feel, but when I told the Judge the driver of the van was not Carmelo Williams, he didn't roll his eyes, or remind me the Mayor's DNA was found in the van.

"Why are you telling me this? Why not go to the FBI, or the Charlotte police?"

"Because they won't believe me. They've already concluded the Mayor did it. By himself. If I tell them someone else was driving that van, they'll think I'm a crackpot. They might even lock me up for being mentally unstable."

He purses his lips, weighing this information. Judging me. Judging my words the way he judges the actions of criminals. "I don't think you're a crackpot, Ms. Winslow," he says finally. "I can see you're a sincere woman. Are you 100 percent sure you want to tell me this, and 100 percent sure of what you saw?"

"Yes, sir." Two images appear side-by-side in my mind. I compare them. I know the profiles are of the same man.

"All right," he says. "If it wasn't Mayor Williams who drove the van into the loading dock that night, who was it?"

"My doctor."

"And who is your doctor, Ms. Winslow?"

The words come with a bitter taste. My lips tremble as I say his name out loud. "His name is Dr. Volkov. Viktor Volkov."

26

In the aftermath of my revelation, nothing happens. The police do not come to my door. The FBI does not call. The Judge does not follow up to ask for more details.

I'm not sure what I expected, but this absence of contact from law enforcement drives me to the conclusion that I must have misread the Judge. He finds my eyewitness account unreliable. Maybe he even thinks I'm a kook.

Because it makes no sense. Why would a medical doctor who has taken an oath to do no harm set off a bomb, killing and maiming thousands of people? And why is the FBI convinced the Mayor was the bomber and acted alone?

Even though I can't answer these questions, the vision of Volkov's profile behind the wheel of that van is as indelibly etched in my memory as the vision of David disappearing. "Evil" does not adequately describe the man—the animal—who dismembers people and then tries to put them back together. I shiver at the thought of a terrorist touching me, in all the ways he touched me. With his eyes. With his fingers. With his scalpel.

I have not told my mother that I resigned from the software company. In the past few weeks, I've perpetuated the ruse that I'm still working, taking the train and returning at the same time each day. On my way out this morning, with my backpack hanging on my shoulders, my mother asks me what software projects I am working on. When I stammer an answer about a supply chain project, she seems skeptical. I may have told her the same thing last week. I'm not a good liar.

I take the red-line today. It is not my normal route, but I feel tugged to a destination that has been jostling its way to the forefront of my mind. I show up at the house unannounced. The white brick Colonial seems recently washed, standing in stark contrast to the greenery beginning to unfold in the trees.

Mrs. Lyendowski greets me at the black-painted door with her mouth open.

"Hi, I'm Ella Winslow."

"I know who you are," she says. With wet building in her eyes, she hugs me in the doorway. Her hands awkwardly press against my backpack. She ushers me into a neat living room decorated with Queen Anne furniture.

Her husband, David's father Pete, leans against the doorway to another room, his hands thrust into his pockets. "We wondered if you might come" is his only greeting.

I know their names and the address only because I ran an internet search at the library, using one of my glass straws to peck at the keys like a chicken pecking the ground. I take a deep breath. "I don't know what to say. It's all been so chaotic."

Linda Lyendowski cups her right hand on my shoulder. "May I take your backpack and your coat, dear? I'll put them in the coat closet."

"Yes, that would be fine." I recognize they have been waiting for me, waiting for almost eight months to hear from me. "I'm sorry I haven't come sooner." It's an honest attempt at atonement, if inadequate. Given that I am a poignant reminder of what they have lost, a part of me has been frightened to see them, scared to be that person who makes them weep yet again. I sit on the edge of a chair with a firm cushion covered in ecru upholstery.

"Would you like a cup of coffee, or some tea?" Linda asks.

"No, thank you. It's a real chore for me now." I quickly nod at where my arms used to be.

"We are terribly sorry about what happened to you," Linda says. She takes her place in the middle of a three-cushioned sofa and smooths her flower-print dress over her knees.

"David and I were …" I start.

She doesn't avert her gaze. "Engaged," she completes my sentence. "At least, he told us he was going to propose to you that night. I presume you accepted?" Her face is girded against disappointment.

"Yes. Yes, of course. Just before … I had the engagement ring on my finger when the bomb exploded."

"When the terrorist murdered my son," Pete says. This statement is not a correction, but an elucidation. He has moved a few steps toward the sitting area, holding his lips in a grim line. When I look to him in acknowledgment, his eyes veer away into the sunlight streaming through the bay window.

"Yes, we were engaged." I scan their living room. The furniture is reproduction antique. The framed color photographs are from places they may or may not have visited—a serene beach with turquoise waves; a jagged mountain without trees; an isolated desert of sand. These seem to be arranged to provide a view, maybe a distraction, from any vantage point in the room. "Have I been here before?"

Linda nods. "You and David stopped by for a drink just before a charity ball you were going to. Late July, I believe." She turns toward Pete for confirmation.

"This must be hard for you," I say, "seeing me here, David's fiancé, when he is gone."

"Tell us what happened," Pete says. "Please."

His plaintive tone reminds me the family members have fewer facts than the survivors. I felt it too, before I recovered some of my memory. Peering into the black hole where knowledge is supposed to reside is worse than the images that come flooding back.

"I don't remember everything," I say. "But I've been working with a psychiatrist, who has helped me remember some things. It's piecemeal. Sometimes a memory will come back because of a smell, or a noise, or something I can't even define."

Pete comes forward and takes a seat next to his wife. "He was with you, right, when it happened?" He asks this with an unsubtle urgency, a driving need to hear about his son's last moments. I realize now, based on what I saw, it's possible they did not find David's body.

"Yes. We were walking by the arena, near a driveway that leads down to the loading dock."

"I taught my son that when escorting a lady, he should walk on the street side," Linda says. "To protect from cars splashing water on your clothes. Was he on the street side?"

I close my eyes to retrieve that memory. "Yes. He was at first, and then I had to stop and tie my shoe."

"Tie your shoe?" Pete asks.

"Yes, my left shoelaces had become loose, and I knelt down beside a wall to tie it." It is still hard to accept that I was felled by a bomb while doing something so mundane as tying my shoe.

"And where was David?"

"In front of me a few steps, on the driveway."

"Did you tell him your shoe was untied?" Pete asks with some incredulity.

Perhaps he is thinking that if David had knelt to tie my shoe, his son might still be alive. This is beginning to sound like an interrogation, as if I am an accomplice somehow responsible for David's death. I remind myself that Pete's accusatory tone comes from agony that has been building inside of him since he first heard the awful news.

"I was pregnant," I say.

"Pregnant?" Linda says, the word trailing off like the hiss of air escaping a balloon.

"I don't actually remember being pregnant. I know it only because my sister told me. You see, David was on the phone, my phone, talking to my sister Mattie at the time. I couldn't hear what he was saying, but my sister later told me, a few weeks ago. I was pregnant. And ..."

Pete stands up and leaves the room. I cannot tell whether he is upset with me, or if the loss of a son and a grandchild is too much for him to bear. I hear a door slam in the back part of the house.

I turn back to Linda, who is again smoothing her dress in a nervous gesture I am unable to accomplish.

"How far along were you, dear?"

"Not far. I took three at-home pregnancy tests. I don't remember that, either. But David wrote that in a letter he gave me."

"So I was going to be a grandmother." There is a forlorn set to her mouth. She snatches a tissue from a box on the table next to the sofa and dabs it across her eyes.

"Yes," is all I can say at first. "My mother was too. But not now."

"David was our only child," she says.

I don't know if I knew this, but I understand the repercussions for her. She is destined to live out her days without the love of her son, or the laughter and joy of grandchildren.

"Pete hasn't gotten over it," she says, nodding toward the back of the house. "He might not ever get over it."

"I understand. And how about you, Linda?"

She looks at me as if the question is rare. "It's day to day. Better than Pete. I don't know why, exactly, but maybe I need to be strong for him. I have faith this is all part of God's master plan. Although my faith has been severely tested."

I don't know what to say to this, so my eyes wander about the room. I see things I didn't notice before. A gold crucifix is nailed to the wall next to the front door. In the framed photograph of the bald mountain, high up, is a blue-domed church. On the sofa table, on the bottom shelf, lies a black Bible with gold embossed lettering.

I recall David telling me, on the drive to this very house, that his mother went to Mass several times a week. He often attended with her and his father on Sundays, but that had ceased when our romance began to blossom. Instead of being at Mass, he spent his Sunday mornings with me, taking long walks, or lingering over the newspaper, or having brunch in a café that had become our favorite. Sitting here with Linda Lyendowski brings all of this back. I realize she must despise me for taking David away from her. In two different ways.

Her comment about God's master plan threatens to raise my ire. I am reminded of the tirade I threw on the church steps after attending church with my mother. And its aftermath. I rise to leave. This seems like an appropriate juncture. Perhaps I am saving myself from further probing, or even a heated argument. For I cannot fathom, and probably never will, how God's plan can involve the murder of their son and grandchild. The murder of my fiancé and daughter. And my own dismemberment.

So as Linda Lyendowski buttons my coat and loops the straps of my backpack over my shoulders, I do not tell her about the man who murdered her son.

As I scurry away, I realize I forgot to ask them if David has a grave. If he was buried, it's likely in a Catholic cemetery somewhere. I'm not sure how I might find it, but my brief conversation with Linda and Pete has sucked out my remaining energy.

I return home in the mid-afternoon and surprise my mother on the back patio. She is leaning back in a wrought-iron chair whose white paint is chipping away, puffing plumes of blue smoke into the air. From the window, I watch her for a minute before depressing the door lever and heading outside.

"When are you going to quit smoking? I don't appreciate being subjected to your second-hand smoke."

She turns half-way toward me. "Excuse me?"

"I quit my job, which means that you and I will be joined at the hip until one of us dies. It might be me first, but if you don't quit smoking now, it will probably be you. And then I won't have anyone to take care of me. Do it for yourself, or do it for your daughter, but do it. I need you."

In response to my plea, my mother just sighs.

27

I am back to watching shows with my mother, the two of us sitting quietly in my living room. I tend to keep the curtains open now, even though the sun sometimes casts a glare on the television screen. A month or two ago I would have preferred darkness. Perhaps open curtains represent some sort of progress.

In the afternoon, with my mother dozing in the burgundy leather recliner and me curled into a corner of the couch, her soap opera about a dynastic family in California is interrupted by a news bulletin.

A female reporter appears in front of a blue van belonging to a local television station. Her voice brims with urgency. A spring breeze ruffles her blonde bangs.

"I'm standing in front of a farmhouse outside of Charlotte, on Highway 1141. The house is owned by a Charlotte plastic surgeon by the name of Viktor Volkov. We don't know exactly what is going on at this property, but there is a huge operation being conducted here by the FBI and Homeland Security."

"What can you see from your vantage point?" the anchor asks.

"Not much, but the property is swarming with agents. It's something big. We've been told there will be a press conference later this afternoon."

"And this doctor—Viktor Volkov—has he been cooperating with the investigation?"

"We don't know," the reporter says. "We called his medical office earlier, and there's a recorded message that his office is currently closed. We haven't been able to contact him."

I leap from the sofa and hurry to the kitchen, then out the back door onto my brick patio, where I huddle on a wrought iron chair beneath the live oak that anchors my backyard. I wasn't wrong. My conversation with the Judge must have ignited this investigation. I am the reason Dr. Volkov has fled. I reach these conclusions solely out of fear. It has returned with the clamor of a rampaging animal, swirling my thoughts as it eats its way through my mind and down inside.

I had assumed, maybe without justification, that when I disclosed my evidence to a federal judge, the wheels of justice would be set in motion. Dr. Volkov would be apprehended, tried, and put in prison. Instead, he is on the loose. And I cannot help but think that one of his missions is to exact revenge on me. I am the sole witness who can place him in the white van that carried the bomb.

My mother, up from her nap, takes the chair across the brick patio and lights a cigarette. "Ella, you're shaking. What's going on?" she says after exhaling a huge cloud. She comes to stand beside me, holding the cigarette away from me, a curl of smoke rising from it. She bends to my level, so we are eye-to-eye, the way you do when reassuring children.

I blink away an image of Dr. Volkov lurking in shadows. Even in the putrid steam of my mother's cigarette breath, her hand stroking the back of my head offers me some comfort. I glance at the top of the wooden fence encasing my backyard. It is only about six feet high. Certainly no barrier for a man intent on eliminating the key witness to his crime.

I stand abruptly. "Let's go back inside. Please lock all the doors. And make sure the windows are locked, too."

I trail her into each room as she checks the window locks. Only after the curtains in the living room have been drawn, casting us into the sullen darkness that greeted me upon my return from the hospital, do I settle enough to tell her.

"Did you see the news?"

"What news?"

"About Dr. Volkov."

"Your Dr. Volkov?"

I nod vigorously. "I …" My voice becomes a stutter, my brain unable to pluck the right words from all of those colliding inside my head. "There's an investigation," I say finally.

She looks at me with genuine concern, something I have seen little of in recent days. Lately, she inspects me with something akin to a scowl of condemnation. No doubt the effect of my abrupt resignation from work.

"I was at the courthouse. I told the Judge something. I saw Dr. Volkov driving the van. The van with the bomb. The bomb at the arena." Each sentence is punctuated with a shallow draw of breath.

My mother leaves the living room and returns with an amber bottle: my prescription of Paxil. It takes her a minute to unlock the cap. I haven't taken one of these in weeks, but when she offers the yellow pill between her thumb and forefinger, I open my mouth without hesitation.

With a firm hand on my left shoulder, she pushes me to the couch. "You need to calm down, Ella. You're hyperventilating. Do you want to breathe into a paper bag?"

I shake my head. I might need the bag to regulate my breathing, but a bag anywhere near my head right now would propel me into a downward spiral.

"Did you really tell the Judge that?"

I nod. "Yes. I saw him. That night."

"Dr. Volkov?"

"Yes."

"But it was at night. How can you be sure?"

"You don't believe me?"

"Well, it's just that your memory isn't that reliable."

I know this, of course. And before I made my disclosure to the Judge, this is the main battle I fought. How could I be absolutely certain—for that has to be the bar when you make such a serious allegation—that I did in fact see Dr. Volkov driving that van? How could I be certain that it was not a false memory?

The answer is now, as it was then, not so simple. But if my confirmation is not a straight line of connected dots, it's because Dr. Volkov made it that way. As I recounted my numerous visits with him, I realized his face was rarely the same from one encounter to the next. On several occasions, he wore a surgical mask, concealing all but the bridge of his nose and his eyes. Once the mask came off, the lower part of his face was in a constant state of transformation. Clean shaven one day. A thin moustache the next week. A coating of neatly trimmed whiskers after that. A salt and pepper beard. One conclusion I could have drawn is that he changed his look for the simple sake of variety. Boredom, maybe. Another is that he used these various alterations as a form of disguise.

Portrait painters observe proportion. They study shape and shadow and shades of color. They analyze individual facial features to realistically depict the whole image. I used to be an amateur painter. I even took a series of classes to refine my eye and my skills. I claim little talent as an artist, but I at least developed some ability to observe faces.

On the day of the victims' conference, I noted how way Dr. Volkov's salt and pepper beard had changed the way he looked since I'd last seen him at the hospital. Not just the contour of his jaw, or the outline of his lips, but the tint of his skin, the prominence of his cheekbones. In the glaring light of the hospital auditorium, all shadows were removed. The details of his face were laid bare. I noticed a pock mark on his right cheek, in a place that would be covered by a surgical mask. A small pink scar near his hairline would be concealed if he wore a cap.

As I watched him maneuver the imaging program on his computer to enhance my own damaged face, I was reminded of his phenomenal talent for hiding scars. For altering faces. A solid conclusion that leads nowhere in the present, but nestles somewhere in hopes of being discovered later. Later came when I saw his profile while he drove his SUV away from his medical office after our impromptu meeting not so long ago. As I stood on the sidewalk, my view of him through the driver's window was from the same angle that I observed the van the night of the bombing. The gloaming light after sunset was similar. And he was wearing the same beard. Exactly the same.

His questions to me in my early days in the hospital, about what I remembered of the night of the bombing—questions seemingly posed to test my memory—now seem ominous. He could have been asking because he needed to know if I saw him at the wheel of the delivery van. He was trying to discover if I am a witness.

Over the course of the next several days, details of the investigation at Dr. Volkov's farm emerge. A refrigeration truck with a million vials of a lethal virus was parked in his barn. The bodies of two men, both holding visas as Russian diplomats, were discovered in a walk-in freezer in a bunker beneath the barn. Dr. Volkov's medical practice is still closed. He has not been found.

At press conferences, Special Agent Mullen, the FBI agent who came to speak to us at the hospital, is bombarded with questions about Dr. Volkov. Is he a suspect? Does the FBI have any leads on his whereabouts? Is he part of a terrorist cell operating in Charlotte? Agent Mullen refuses to speculate, disclosing only that Dr. Volkov is a person of interest in a foiled terrorist plot to release a deadly virus in our city. There is no mention of my former doctor's involvement in the bombing of the arena, no hint the FBI may have gotten it wrong when it identified Mayor Williams as the lone bomber.

I cannot decide whether Dr. Volkov's role in a thwarted bio-terrorism plot makes him more or less likely to target me. On one hand, his problems are vast, and perhaps I pose no imminent threat to him. On the other, he is a desperate man, and he could come for me as his final salvo.

Dr. Marvin and I have talked often of the fight, flight or freeze response to fear. In my case, fighting would be nearly impossible. Freezing is what I have been doing for the past several months. I have a web session with her, my laptop opened on the kitchen table.

"Can you believe that Dr. Volkov could be involved in something like this?" she asks.

"Yes."

My answer startles her a bit. "You could?"

"You're not in contact with him, are you?" I recognize the question as paranoid, or perhaps even accusatory, but as I have huddled in the dark cave of my house over the past few days, I realize there are a million things I don't know about terrorists. The bare fact throbbing in my mind is that the FBI was unable to link Dr. Volkov to the arena bombing, and for months he has walked freely among us. If a sophisticated organization like that, with all its investigators and technology, was unable to figure it out, how could I possibly understand his full capabilities and talent for deception. As such, in my book, almost everyone is subject to suspicion.

At my question, Dr. Marvin leans back a foot or so from her computer camera. "Ella, of course not. Why would you ask that?" Her eyes, though, have not left me.

I lock gazes with her. "I don't know who to trust."

"You can trust me," she says in a placating voice.

"No offense, but I trusted him, too." I feel the buzz of anxiety plucking at my nerves.

"Well, he fooled us all, didn't he?"

Hers is a natural reaction, I suspect, this presumption of Dr. Volkov's guilt despite the legal presumption of his innocence. I certainly have no doubt, but I know something Dr. Marvin doesn't.

"He was involved in the bombing of the arena," I say.

She does a quick intake of breath, and her left hand goes to the hollow just beneath her neck. Dr. Marvin, who is rarely at a loss for probing or comforting words, is momentarily struck mute. I watch her lips shape and re-shape themselves for a few seconds before she regains her composure and asks the simplest of questions.

"How do you know this?"

I don't immediately respond. Instead, I parse those five words and the way she asked them. There is no disbelief in her tone, but neither is there a wary bent. Her question seems to presume my allegation is true. I study her face to see if she is commencing a subtle interrogation to aid a co-conspirator, or if her concerns are directed at my well-being. Or something else.

"Ella, you have to trust someone."

I know this is true. Despite the times I have placed trust in others and experienced disastrous results, I understand that I cannot treat everyone else is if they are trying to harm me. This is something Dr. Marvin and I have worked on. Still, I trusted Dr. Volkov. I trusted him with re-building my face. I glance to the small window in the upper right corner of my screen and confirm that he did a great job. And yet, I trusted a terrorist.

"I told a judge that I saw Dr. Volkov at the wheel of the van that carried the bomb." I roll my eyes upward, assessing my own words, and am satisfied. Dr. Marvin now knows I am not the only one who holds this key piece of evidence.

"That's good. I'm glad you told someone. How are you dealing with this, Ella?"

Her words shave a layer off my apprehension. "I suspect my revelation may have somehow led the FBI to investigate Dr. Volkov. I feel good about that."

"You should feel very good about that. It sounds like you may have saved the lives of a lot of people."

I have not considered my role in this light. The fear of Dr. Volkov's retaliation has overwhelmed me, almost paralyzed me. "I'm scared of him."

She nods. "That's understandable. But now that law enforcement is onto him, you can feel more secure."

"I don't. He's on the loose. He knows where I live."

"And what do you think would make you feel more secure, Ella?"

"I need to move." A part of me is aware I have been working toward this. Yet uprooting myself again seems like climbing another mountain of devastation.

"If you do move, where would you go?"

"That's the problem," I say.

28

I call my ex-husband. Even though I got the house in the divorce settlement, Robert is still on the mortgage because the bank wouldn't release him. If I want to sell the house, I need his written consent.

The phone lies on the kitchen counter, the speaker on. My mother stands nearby with her arms crossed over her chest.

"Ella, do you know what time it is out here?" Robert says. His voice is groggy.

"It's five o'clock in the morning."

"You woke me up."

"Yeah, sorry about that. I need to sell the house."

"Why?"

"I need to move, and soon."

"Are you in financial trouble or something? Are you current on the mortgage?"

While I was in the hospital, I got behind on the mortgage, but I used a big chunk of my first disability check to catch up. Robert doesn't need to know any of this.

"Does it matter why I'm selling? The house is mine. I can sell whenever I want to. But you know I need your consent."

"How much equity do you think you have?"

I hear the rustle of sheets and a grunt that makes me think he's getting out of bed.

"I don't know. Probably not that much, considering you were behind on the payments when we divorced."

"But house prices are skyrocketing in Charlotte. I've been paying attention to the market over there."

"Why does that matter, Robert?"

"Well, you know, you got a good deal in the divorce. If you have substantial equity, you could throw a little of it my way. To expedite my signature."

"Are you kidding me, Robert? You were delinquent on the mortgage. I paid the past-due amounts. And I've kept up the mortgage for the past five years. This was your debt, not mine. And now you're shaking me down?"

"It's not for me, it's for Malcolm. He's got a lot of college debt to pay down."

Robert has always played my heart this way. He knows I have a soft spot for his son Malcolm. I'm suddenly tired of his tactics.

"You haven't even called to find out how I'm doing, Robert. I am having a hell of a time coming back from my injuries."

"I tried to call you, several times, but I got a message your phone is out of service."

He is telling the truth. My cell phone was lost in the blast, and I have a different number now. I try not to let his modest attempt at redemption deter me from my goal.

"Will you voluntarily sign the papers or not? If you say no, then I'll go to Court and ask a judge to order you to do it."

"What about Malcolm?" His tone has dissolved from strident to a pleading whine.

"I'll consider it after you've signed the paperwork. Are you still at the same address?"

"I haven't moved."

"Is your email still the same?"

"Yes."

"I'm putting he house on the market, and you'll get the paperwork to sign. You'd better do this one thing for me, Robert." I walk away from the kitchen counter. "Hang it up, mama."

"You better not screw my daughter again," my mother says before the line goes dead.

Robert was a chance encounter on an icy night when my car wouldn't start. He provided jumper cables and an opportunity for something different. He bought me expensive presents and took me to dinners at nice restaurants. We vacationed in Mexico and the Caribbean. He owned this three-bedroom house on a quiet street with big trees in the yard, and after we'd been dating about six months, I moved in.

When I told my mother I was going to marry Robert, she responded by saying, "he's almost as old as your father." Then she hung up on me. At the time, Robert was forty-two; I was twenty-two. My mother refused to come to the wedding, and she forbade Mattie from coming. We got married at the courthouse by a magistrate.

Robert and I glided through that first year, idyllic and filled with romance. When I told him on the night of our second anniversary that I wanted to have a child, he resisted.

"We've got Malcolm," he said.

"Malcolm's a wonderful boy," I said, sipping from a glass of Cabernet at our favorite restaurant. "I love him like my own son, but he's not really and truly my child. He didn't come from inside me. He doesn't have my DNA. I don't even know his mother."

"You don't want to know his mother. She's a drug addict. An absolute mess." He signaled the waiter. "Ella, I don't want another child."

We had not talked about this, not specifically, before we got married. During our short engagement, I told Robert I wanted to start a family with him. He said nothing to indicate he was not in agreement. Not until that anniversary dinner.

I don't quite know why I have this fervent longing to have a baby. Sure, it's a natural urge to bear children and nurture then into fine human beings. Maternal instinct. Unconditional love. Based on the way my parents raised Mattie and me, I could easily have concluded I would be an awful mother.

Nevertheless, I persevered. Robert and I argued about it constantly. Vicious arguments that sometimes left me in a rage of tears. He accused me of being naive, said I didn't understand all that was involved in taking care of children, especially while I was trying to climb the corporate ladder.

"I've been in the business world a long time," he would say, "and I know how pregnant women are treated. You can forget about your chances for advancement. Women hit the glass ceiling when they get pregnant."

He might have been right, but I was undeterred. I went off the pill. I didn't tell him. Despite making love three times a week, sometimes more, I still couldn't get pregnant. Under my threat of withholding sex, he begrudgingly went with me to a fertility clinic, where we both got tested. His sperm had low motility. Not so uncommon in a man his age. The doctor prescribed Clomiphene. Robert filled the prescription but refused to take the medication.

So I crushed up the pills and put them in his coffee. And in his eggs. And occasionally in the beer he often had when he got home from work. I was that desperate.

I am not proud of my deception. Perhaps I can't even justify it. As his resistance built, my resolve countered it. I was determined we were going to have a baby, whether he was in favor or not.

I missed my period that February. While Robert was on a five-day business trip to the west coast, I started researching on-line for bassinets, strollers, changing tables, breast pumps. I scrolled through images of onesies and jumpers and cloth balloons. The idea of pregnancy had kindled something in me. I embarked on this new journey with a renewed sense of purpose.

When I picked up Robert at the airport, I could barely contain my excitement. He had just slid behind the wheel and turned the ignition when I blurted it out.

"I think I'm pregnant."

His face went cold. He gnawed his lower lip as he steered the car toward the airport exit. "How could this happen? You're on the pill."

"I went off."

He angled his head toward me and only returned his attention to the road when the tires bumped over the outside lane markers.

"You didn't tell me."

"I wanted it to be a surprise."

"Well, mission accomplished."

"Aren't you excited?"

He didn't say a word, but his face held the look of a condemned man.

I got my period in March. I went back to my gynecologist, by myself, for an explanation. She couldn't find any evidence that I had been pregnant. My hormone levels were normal. She reasoned that perhaps stress had thrown my cycle out of whack.

While putting on my pajamas that night, I studied myself in the mirror. A week earlier, I had rosy cheeks, cheer in my eyes, and a knowing smile on my lips. It had all slipped away, replaced by sullenness and pallor. When Robert came into our bedroom, I told him I wasn't pregnant. He looked away, feigning disappointment. But I could see the slight curl at the corners of his lips. He was happy about it. He had dodged a bullet.

After that, he wore a condom during intercourse. I knew he kept them in the top drawer of his dresser. While he was out of the house, I pulled the packet of condoms out of the box and used a safety pin to pierce each one.

I was too young and naive to understand what this was doing to our marriage, but I wanted with all my being to conceive. I tracked my cycle and took my temperature so I could pinpoint my fertility window. I dragged Robert to a couple's shower for one of my friends at work. I was hoping he would experience their joy, maybe even catch some of it. He didn't. I agreed to watch pornography with him, which excited him and lowered his guard. Still, I didn't get pregnant.

"We are going to have a baby," I said one evening after slipping into bed. "If you don't agree, we're going to stop having sex."

He rolled toward me. "Are you kidding?"

"No, I'm not kidding. I want us to have a baby. I need to have a baby."

"I'm too tired to have this discussion right now." He rolled over, showing me his back.

The next morning, after Malcolm caught the bus to school, I confronted Robert again. He was sitting at the breakfast table in the nook off the kitchen, scanning the newspaper.

I stood across from him. "We're going to have a child, Robert. I'm sick and tired of waiting."

"You're set on this? Dead set on this?" he said, smoothing his striped tie.

"Yes. Absolutely. I'll be ovulating in seven days. I'll fix us a romantic dinner with candles, and we'll have some wine, and then we'll get into bed, and I'll do that thing you like so much."

"There's no talking you out of this?"

"No."

I made arrangements for Malcolm to stay overnight with a friend. It was a Friday, and his friend had the most recent video game console, so it took little persuasion from me. Robert and I would have the house to ourselves.

On the morning of, I kissed Robert as he was heading off to work. I wrapped my arms around his neck. "Be home by seven, okay? I'm fixing lobster. And I've got a nice bottle of Chardonnay."

That night, I kept the candles burning and the lobsters cooling in the refrigerator until well past nine. When Robert didn't come home, I called his cell phone. He didn't pick up. I called his office. The call went to voicemail.

Around eleven p.m., he called me from an airport he refused to identify.

"Did you have an emergency business trip or something?" I asked. "I've been worried about you."

"No, no. I'm okay. It's just that, well, I've been transferred."

"Transferred? You're kidding, right? They transferred you without giving you any notice?"

There was a pause that signaled he was deciding whether to lie to me. "The transfer was at my request, Ella."

"What? We never talked about a transfer … Oh no, Robert, you can't just do that. You can't just move us someplace without telling me."

"You're not coming with us, Ella. We're getting a divorce."

This struck me cold. I'd never thought he would resort to divorce. I stammered a meek response. "We can work this out, Robert."

"It's too late for that. I've got to catch another plane."

"What about Malcolm?"

"He's going to finish out the school year in Charlotte. It's only two weeks. Then he's flying out."

"Flying out where?" I probed.

"Not now, Ella."

"Tell me where you are."

"Not now." The connection clicked off.

The next morning, almost before the sun rose, I was at the house of Malcolm's friend. My polite ringing of the doorbell didn't rouse the family, and only after I pounded my fist on the front door for a minute or more did someone come. It was Malcolm.

"You're making a scene," he said, stepping out onto the stoop.

"I need to talk to you," I said. "About your father."

He rolled his eyes. "I was asleep."

Malcolm didn't call me "mom," but he at least afforded me a modicum of respect. More than I'd gotten from his father last night. "Let's go home. We can talk in the car."

He closed his eyes in a sign of submission. "Let me get my stuff."

"I'll be in the car."

"Did you know your father is transferring?" I said as I pulled away from the curb. My tone was accusatory, as if father and son had conspired to accomplish this.

"He told me yesterday."

"You didn't know before that?"

"Nope." He pulled his legs in, then propped his feet on my dash.

Our conversations had often been like this. I interrogated him with the soft insistence of the step-mother to whom he owed no allegiance, and he gave me standard, terse teenager answers. At 24, I was only eight years older than Malcolm. I remembered when I was his age. In his eyes, I had little gravitas.

"Do you know why he left?"

"Yeah."

"Are you going to tell me?'

"He said not to." He reached over and changed the radio station.

"I think I deserve to know why he left in the middle of the night. With no warning. No discussion."

"He's a douche."

"No argument from me. So why did he leave?"

Malcolm drummed his fingers on the side window, watching the scenery as we glided by.

"Why did your father leave, Malcolm? Please tell me."

He turned to me and pursed his lips, perhaps relishing that he held a valuable secret. Then he blurted it out. "He doesn't want a baby."

"He told you that?"

He shrugged. "Your bedroom walls aren't soundproof, you know."

There was a moment when I wanted to punish Malcolm for the sins of his father. Malcolm was right that his father was a douche. And a selfish asshole. But Malcolm's mother was absent for most of his life. He had the disadvantage of bad parents, one of whose judgment was so impaired that he felt okay leaving his son with the wife he'd just abandoned.

Robert sent a plane ticket for Malcolm. A ticket to Los Angeles, about as far away from Charlotte as you can go within the continental United States. I took Malcolm to the airport, helped him check his bags. I watched him go through security. After he put his shoes back on, leaving his laces untied, he stepped back to the glass that separates the passengers from the rest, found me, and waved. Then he left for his gate. It was not much, but more than his father had given me.

That time seems so distant, the acts of a former me, in a prior lifetime I will never retrieve. As I stand at the bay window, watching my realtor Candace Taylor plant a For Sale sign in my yard, I realize that although this house is mine, it holds no memories that I cannot let go.

The foreboding that Dr. Volkov will find me has abated with the passage of a few days. I have busied myself with things I have to accomplish in preparation for the sale, and once I have a contract, things I need to do before the sale closes.

As I wander through the rooms, I look for signs that my fiancé David was ever here. It is not the first time I have searched, though there are hiding places that are inaccessible to a woman without arms. I find no evidence of him in the obvious spots.

It's possible that before my release from the hospital my mother scrubbed my home of any signs of David's presence, as she did in my cubicle at work.

"Mama, did you find anything of David's that might have been here at the house?" I ask one day at lunch, between slurps of soup.

She looks up from her plate of baked chicken, green beans and mashed potatoes. She takes a sip of iced tea before answering. "I found a pair of men's socks in the dryer. Were those David's?"

"I don't know who else they could have belonged to. What did you do with them?"

"They're in the basket with the cleaning rags."

"Please pack them when we leave."

Within three days, I have two offers on the house. One matches the asking price, and the other is $10,000 lower. I don't ask anything about either of the buyers. I accept the higher offer without hesitation. Candace sends the contract to me via email, and my mother and I go through it, paragraph by paragraph. At the end, I ask her to electronically sign the contract for me in the designated places.

In the butterfly garden out back, the netting is still shredded, but the flowers are full and vibrant. Butterflies dive and dance around my head. There are monarchs, tortoise shells, swallowtails and fritillaries. Powdery wings of bright colors, sucking nectar from perennials I planted with my own hands years ago.

My mother joins me, taking her customary chair. She lights a cigarette. I haven't been counting the number of cancer sticks she smokes each day, but it seems she has curtailed her consumption since my plea.

"You want me to fix a dish of honey?" she asks in her throaty voice.

"That would be nice."

I sit on the stone bench next to a finger bowl filled with honey. Even in my altered state, the butterflies seem to regard me as a fixture there, as permanent and benign as the live oak tree. They have been coming to my garden each year to lay eggs and die. I dip my fake fingers in the honey until they are dripping with it. Then I lie down on the red bricks. From below, the butterflies look different. Their vivid colors set against pale sky give them a mystical, animated appearance.

They soon find the honey and light on my hands. Butter and indigo and fire-orange wings dusted with powdered sugar. As if by silent call, they come in droves, lighting on my forearms, the soft side of my elbows, biceps that have little definition. My rubber arms look as if they are made of fluttering wings. For a brief moment, I wonder if I can fly away.

29

I promised myself it would be a quick goodbye, but when the time comes, I find myself glued to the sidewalk in front of my house. I lean against the brick mailbox whose stick-on numbers are peeling. I sob, streaking eyeliner my mother applied this morning. Hot tears roll down my cheeks.

I did not pick this house, so it is not a place I cherish. But I fought for it. I paid for it. I retreated to it when I left the hospital. I built a home here. And now I have to leave. For my safety, and perhaps the safety of my mother and sister. I add my home to the long list of things Dr. Volkov has taken from me.

As we drive off in my mother's old Buick, I press my face to the passenger window.

"I'm sorry you had to sell the house," my mother says.

"It's all right, mama."

"Maybe things will be better because you're moving back home."

I ignore her remark.

We pass through rolling hills covered by new tract houses on green lots without trees. In less than an hour, we turn onto a highway lined with oaks, which transitions to peach orchards simmering in sun whose intensity raises waves from the pavement. Peach trees give way to cotton and pasture.

We pull off the highway and up a dirt and gravel drive that leads to my mother's house. We pass through a gap in a rusting barbed-wire fence. The pipes of the cattle guard rattle beneath the tires. To me, the racket sounds like the clang of a prison door.

My mother's house sits on a small knoll, surrounded on three sides by pasture. In the back, the yard descends about thirty feet to a slow-moving creek that winds its way beneath broad oaks, pecans and hickory trees. The land, about forty acres, lies outside a small town about halfway between Charlotte and Columbia, South Carolina.

The house I grew up in is a two-bedroom bungalow, one story. White paint peels from the clapboards on the north side, where the weather abuses it most. The bricks of the chimney are smooth from decades of lashing rain. Mortar is missing in places. I remember it as a pretty piece of land, pastoral in the proper light, but the farm and the house have succumbed to the neglect of an owner who is no longer able to maintain it. My father never would have let the house deteriorate into this condition. Despite his ministrations, the farm has succumbed. It now has the bleak appearance of the waiting room just outside death's door.

My mother carries my suitcases into Mattie's bedroom. The small room I shared with my sister until I went away to college eleven years ago has changed some. Posters of teen idols have been replaced by framed art. Above Mattie's desk hangs an enlarged photograph of the Venus de Milo, given to my sister by a fellow teacher who has recently been to Paris. On the wall next to the bed hangs a small landscape I painted, with a gold frame. It is a bucolic view of our farm in its heyday, the outlines of trees and house just a little blurred.

The yellow curtains flanking the single window are new. A mahogany wardrobe covers most of the opposite wall. Mattie and I will share a queen-sized four poster bed shoved in a corner. My armless body takes up less space than a normal person, so hopefully I won't crowd her.

I am given three drawers in Mattie's wardrobe for my folded clothes, and a small span of the clothes rod in the closet. I don't need more than that. I once had a large walk-in closet stuffed with slacks and blouses, business suits and cocktail dresses, and almost fifty pairs of shoes. Most of those clothes, and all but two pairs of the shoes, are packed in boxes I will probably never open again, stacked in a storage warehouse out on the highway. I sit on the queen bed and watch my mother fold and stow my limited wardrobe.

"Does it feel like home, yet?" she asks.

"I'm sure it will, pretty soon."

"Did Mattie tell you about the new rules?"

"Rules?" I haven't expected my mother to exercise her renewed dominance quite so fast.

She nods. "Number one: no one changes the television channel without permission from everyone. Two, you're on your own for lunch, and we take turns making dinner. Since you can't make dinner, we'll have to figure out other chores for you to do. Three, you clean up your own mess. Four, no males in your bedroom. And five, no loud music anytime, unless you want to wear headphones, and no music period after eleven."

"You're kidding right? We're not teenagers, you know."

"What's wrong with rules, Ella? They're for everybody's benefit."

"So you just came up with these when you realized I'd be moving back here?"

"Look, if you're going to be like that, you can just figure out some other place to live. This is my house, and I'm entitled to make rules." She slams a drawer to punctuate her point.

"Okay, mama."

My mother threw an unseen switch the moment we crossed her property line. I can no longer claim ownership of the place where I live, and she is making me regret my decision to sell my house. Now I'm stuck here. Maybe I am safer on this farm, but I may have just stepped into the fiefdom of a tyrant.

I stay in the bedroom the rest of the day. I want to stay clear of my mother so I don't inadvertently violate one of her rules. I am certain there are other, unwritten rules, the breach of which will probably result in some ghastly penalty. She might take away my bathroom privileges or force me to sleep on the floor. From experience, I know she can withhold food without remorse.

Mattie comes home from school and throws her arms around me. "I'm so happy you're here, big sister. It's just like old times."

"Me too," I mumble.

I follow her into the bedroom, where she changes out of her navy dress and into jeans and a t-shirt.

"Do you have enough drawer space?" she asks.

"Sure."

"How about room for hanging clothes? Do you need more? I could move some of my stuff if you do."

"No, it's fine. I don't have much need for fancy clothes these days."

"Which side of the bed do you want?"

"Which side do you usually sleep on?"

"I usually sleep in the middle. But you can have whichever side you want."

"If it's okay with you, I'll take the side next to the wall. Should we pull the bed out a little?"

She brings her index finger to her lips. "I've been thinking about that. That would be better, so you don't have to crawl over me if you need to go to the bathroom or something. You'll need a table on that side, too. Mama! Mama!" she shouts.

My mother comes to the door of our bedroom, drying her hands on a dish towel. "What's with all the yelling?"

"Do we have an extra table in the attic, for that side of the bed?" Mattie points.

"What for?"

"Ella needs a table. Probably a lamp too."

"Now how is she going to turn a lamp on and off?"

"We'll get her one of those touch lamps or something. She can tap it with her toes."

My mother turns to me. "What do you need a lamp for?"

"For reading, maybe."

"Really? You been doing a lot of reading lately, have you?"

"I thought I might." I turn to Mattie. "I've got a nightstand that will work down at the storage warehouse, and a lamp too."

"Excellent," Mattie says. "Let's go get them."

"You should have thought of that earlier," my mother yells after us.

I have retained very little from my earlier life. Necessities only, or items I cannot part with because of sentimental value. I sold most of the furniture, since it was Robert's anyway. I sold my car. I sent the proceeds to Malcolm. I kept a few pieces of furniture I bought before Robert and I got married, and my clothes of course. At the mini-warehouse, Mattie moves the boxes so she can get to the wooden nightstand in the back. She brings it out of the metal shed and into the light.

"It doesn't match your furniture," I say.

"It doesn't matter. Close enough. Where's that lamp?"

"I'm not sure. It's in a box, a tall one."

She shuffles the boxes from one side to the other, reading the labels. "Here's a few boxes of books," she says. "You want me to get these too?"

"Mama said there isn't room."

"We'll make room. Under the bed, or something. You've got to have your books."

I watch her trudge back and forth from the storage shed to her Honda with the nightstand, lamp, and four boxes. When she's finished, we lean against the car.

"That's hard work." She wipes her brow with her sleeve.

"I appreciate you getting some of my things for me."

"Of course. How are you supposed to make yourself at home if all your stuff is in storage? We probably ought to move the rest of it to the attic. You don't have that much. I bet there's room up there."

"Mama said there isn't."

"Yeah, well she says a lot of things."

"Like her rules."

"Her rules?" Mattie gives a dismissive wave.

"She said now that I'm living here, there are five new rules."

"We don't have any rules."

"Don't turn the tv channel without permission," I say. "Clean up your mess, which is next to impossible for me. No boys in our room. Strike that, no males in our room. We take turns making dinner. Again, an impossible task for me unless you both want to starve. And no loud music, or any music after eleven."

"Rose is pulling your chain," Mattie says.

I snort half a laugh. "So she just made all that up so she can remind me she's the boss. Rose is a trip."

"You remember when we first started calling her Rose? I wonder what she'd do if she ever heard us."

"At the very least, that would be rule number six," I say.

It feels good, this renewal of our sisterhood. In only a couple of hours I feel closer to Mattie.

"I went to visit David Lyendowski's parents," I say.

"How did that go?"

I tilt my head side-to-side. "His mother, Linda, was pretty sympathetic towards me. His dad reacted like I was somehow responsible for David's death."

"That's ridiculous."

"He didn't accuse me, not directly, but his tone was kind of like: 'This is all your fault'."

"How could he blame you, of all people? How about blaming the terrorist?"

"He said that, too. But …"

"But what?"

"There's a lot I haven't told you."

The sun has descended to the tree line, casting long shadows against the perimeter of the corrugated steel storage units. As I look around, seeing innumerable places where Dr. Volkov could be lying in wait, I don't feel any safer here than I did in the city.

"Let's get in the car and head back," I say. As we exit the gate and pull up to the highway, I scan the sides of the road. "Dr. Volkov drove the van with the bomb in it down into the loading dock of the Charlotte arena."

Mattie's mouth gapes open, then her eyes narrow with skepticism.

"I guess the Mayor was involved, too," I explain. "His DNA was found in the van. But Dr. Volkov was driving the van. I'm sure of that."

"You're 100 percent sure?"

I nod. "I saw him. I recovered that memory when I was at the victims' memorial, across from the arena. I know you've seen the coverage of what they found at his farm. It seems like he was planning another terrorist attack."

"I'm not the first person you've told about this, am I?"

"No, the fourth. I told the Judge who is presiding over that big lawsuit that I'm part of. And I told Mama, and Dr. Marvin."

"And what did the Judge say?"

"Nothing. But I assume he took it to law enforcement, and that's what led the FBI to go after Dr. Volkov. I don't know that for sure."

"And he hasn't been caught," Mattie says. "Are you scared?"

I nod. "That's the primary reason I sold the house and moved down here."

Mattie pulls onto the two-lane highway, heading back to the farm. "I can't believe it…I mean, I can, given what they found at his farm, but we were standing right next to him on what, a dozen occasions?"

I nod. The memory of all that he has taken from me pushes its way into my throat. I try to stifle my tears, without success.

Mattie pulls the car into a turnout. She wraps her arms around me. She disengages briefly to pull a tissue from a packet in the car console, then dabs my cheeks until I stop sobbing. It feels so good to be loved.

30

It takes little time to re-familiarize myself with the peculiarities of Rose's small house. Three strides from our bedroom to the sole bathroom. The oak floor in the hallway creaks in all the old places. The bathroom door sticks at the top. The toilet seat is loose. The faucets of the bathroom sink are installed incorrectly–hot on the right; cold on the left.

I stumble in there at night, not for a drink of water or to pee, but driven there by a recurring nightmare that raises goose bumps on the back of my neck. It is dark. I am under a crushing load of bricks. My skin feels like it is on fire. My arms are nothing but searing pain. I see Dr. Volkov standing just outside the rubble, the fingers of his right hand stroking his beard, surveying what he has wrought.

In the bathroom, a night light provides a dim glow. I stare into the chipped bathroom mirror. Why did he kill and maim thousands of people? What possible reason could he have for committing such atrocities? My irises stare back at me, telling me I will probably never have answers to these questions. I will never know. I still can't accept that all those deaths and my own amputations are somehow random. There must be a reason.

When Mattie leaves for school each morning, I spend hours on the internet, moving the arrow around with the big toe of my right foot. I was right-handed, and it seems my dominant foot is my right as well. Using voice-activated search, I normally start with a news feed. It is rarely long before I say his name out loud—Viktor Volkov. The usual reports pop up. Most of them are months old. The search of his farm. The discovery of the bio-weapon in the truck in his barn. Nothing linking my doctor to the bombing of the Charlotte arena. Occasionally there will be a follow-up story that says there have been no developments in the search for him.

When the claustrophobia of the house becomes too great, I escape outdoors. The barbed wire fencing marking the boundaries of my mother's farm is in disrepair. The small herd of Angus cattle watch me as I cross a field toward the creek bottom. They neither scamper away nor come closer to inspect me.

I step around a few fire ant mounds and settle against the trunk of an oak tree near the creek, where I stretch out between two huge roots. This is a makeshift throne from my childhood, nestled among long-limbed trees where Mattie and I used to play hide-and-seek. A few split boards from the tree fort our father built remain nailed to the trunk, their surface the color of half-burnt charcoal.

"Home" should be a comforting word, but as I gaze up to my mother's weather-beaten house, it doesn't feel like my home. I'm not sure how to turn it around. Although I have discussed this with Dr. Marvin, I remain unconvinced that a mere shift in my attitude will solve the problem. I reside in a cramped bedroom that, aside from the framed landscape hanging above my side of the bed, will never have my own stamp. The living room couch and curtains my mother has refused to replace hold the stale smell of mildew and old cheese. I am a guest here. A guest who may soon outstay her welcome.

At the top of my tree, a hawk surveys the field for a meal. He waits patiently, then dives for the grass with wings spread wide. He glides on unseen currents, raises his wings as he nears the ground, and with sharp talons catches a mouse.

I have always been fascinated by wings. When I was nine, I built a pair of wings from balsa wood and turkey feathers. I strapped them to my tiny arms with an old leather belt. At a full run, I flapped the wings as fast as I could, trying to take off. When that didn't work, I climbed the ladder to the barn loft. Standing on the edge, fifteen feet off the ground, my legs began to shake. I closed my eyes and pictured a bird gliding gracefully above the treetops. I lifted my arms, holding my wings wide, and jumped. To my astonishment, my tiny body didn't float or glide at all. Instead, I plunged to the ground like a stone. I sprained my ankle.

During my recuperation, I studied birds in take-off and landing positions, the way they soared. I limped into the library and checked out a biography on Orville and Wilbur Wright. I read it seven times. I watched a documentary about the first flight at Kitty Hawk. I struggled to understand the principles of lift.

Once my ankle healed, I began jumping from the barn loft into a pile of hay. Perhaps it was only the power of a child's imagination, but it seemed that once or twice the wind settled for a moment beneath my wings, and I actually flew. Jubilation arose from such successes. I made the wings larger, layering the turkey feathers to create more lift.

One day I sailed beyond the edge of the soft hay pile. I tore a ligament in my left knee. When my father caught me limping about for a second time, he grabbed my wings and burned them in an old barrel.

The barn now holds a foreboding look. It is witness to tragedy. Much of the red paint has worn away, revealing shabby, grey planks. The tin roof is rusting and near collapse. In the wind, the tin groans like the joints of old men. My father would never have let the barn get into this condition, but perhaps it is fitting it has become decrepit in his absence.

I mention it to Rose one day, the way the barn is decaying, and she says she hopes the whole thing will just rot into the ground. That's where my daddy hung himself. When I found him, he was still, the life choked out of him. But I wrapped my arms around his legs anyway, and with all of the strength a seventeen-year-old girl can muster, I tried to hoist him up so the rope would slacken and maybe he could breathe again. I could not hoist the dead weight of my father. His hovering body remained there until the sheriff came to cut him down.

A child does not wish to remember a fallen parent in that way. I prefer to recall happier events, like the times we spent nursing baby calves that appeared miraculously from the void of a cow's hind-end. My father and I watched the mothers lick them clean. We would rub the mothers' tender teats, nibbled raw by hungry calves, with gobs of lanolin ointment. I took photographs of sleek black calves wobbling next to their mamas. And I painted pictures from these photographs, sometimes from the real thing as they lay beneath shadow-casting limbs. My father would hold the photographs next to my painting and claim to be unable to tell the difference. He just knew one day I would a bc a great artist.

For my twelfth birthday, my father gave me a horse. I named her Sugar. She was black all over, except for splotches of white on her forelegs and hind quarters. I fed her apples and carrots and rode her endlessly into the dusk until my father had to ride out in the farm truck and retrieve us.

When Sugar got pregnant she suffered horribly from a bout of colic. As she fidgeted and whinnied on the ground, I suffered too. We had never experienced anything other than the freedom of riding together. When the foal began to emerge, the veterinarian asked my father to take me outside so he could work. My father refused.

"It's her horse, Darwin," he said. "She's raised it as much as anybody. And if something goes wrong, she'll be raising that colt."

I stayed and watched. Perhaps it was not the right decision. Sugar's mane was an awful mess as she twisted about on her side, trying to dispel the foal. Her muscles trembled. She bared her teeth in agony. While my father held her head, I tried to comfort her with soothing words. I squirted syringes of water into her mouth. Her eyes were possessed by dark demons. I had seen that look only once before, when we were out riding and ran across a rattlesnake in our path. It sat coiled and ominous, its forked tongue darting out to taste the smell of us. Sugar had backed away slowly, not rearing or bucking, and taken me to safety.

As the vet worked to turn the foal so that it could come out in the proper position, Sugar's eyes widened in panic. The foal's hooves were tearing her apart inside. She was losing a lot of blood. I knew what that meant.

One of them made it and the other didn't. If you don't say her name, can she really be gone? I held the colt in my arms and wiped its birth coat with an old towel, rubbed my hands across its flanks to quiet quivering muscles. Sweetness drank two bottles of milk before falling asleep, motherless. My father stayed with us in the barn through the night. When my father died, Sweetness and the other horse were sold at auction.

Now, the barn door is secured by a padlock almost as rusted as the roof. Through the crack between the warped doors I can see nothing except a slice of light thrown from a missing board up high. I cajole Rose to open the barn so I can go back in. She says she lost the key to the lock.

"Cut it off with a hacksaw or a bolt cutter," I say.

"No."

I am persistent in my arguments, pelting her over lunch and dinner and baths, and during all the other times each day when we are forced together by the circumstances of my armlessness. I compliment her hair and her pot roast. I cannot explain why I want to go into the barn again. Deep down, I am not prepared to relive anything, to explore wounds scabbed over long ago.

"I thought you were scared to go in there," she says to me in an attempt to quash my plea.

"I'm not scared. Not anymore."

"Have you forgotten what happened in there?"

"I haven't forgotten anything. I'm just better able to handle it now."

Like sand that washes stones smooth on the stream bed, I eventually wear my mother down. One afternoon, I commandeer her attention and force her to miss one of her soap operas, rattling on about the lock on the barn door. She gets up from her lounger with a huff, grabs a key from a hiding place in the kitchen, and marches out to the barn. I follow. She wrestles with the lock until it succumbs. When she pulls on the right-side door, the hinges object with a noise loud enough to evict a barn owl nesting beneath the eaves. With the door open, she refuses to go into the maw with me, not even far enough to flick the switch to see if the lights still work.

Inside, I don't roam far from the wedge of daylight. I take but a few steps before I am standing beneath the ridge beam where the taut rope ended my father's life. I was dismayed at the lack of ceremony when they cut him down. A deputy simply climbed our A-frame ladder, pulled out a pocketknife, and sawed through the rope about a foot above my father's head. It unraveled strand by strand, and as each strand came loose my father dropped an inch or two. No one caught my father when he fell face down in the dirt, his legs curled under him.

We no longer use the barn to harbor our cattle. The odors of musty hay and lathered animals have long ago evaporated. All I can smell now is the stagnant dirt of his suicide. The barn has the stale air of a crypt, a molding air that seems to demand grief from me. I forget about Rose, standing silently behind the door, and kneel in the dirt.

"Why?" I whisper. As if he can hear me. "Why did you do it? What could have tortured you so much that you had to do this?" I don't expect answers, but it has taken me years to muster the courage to ask these questions aloud.

"Ella, come out of there," Rose says, backlit beside the door.

"You know, don't you, mama? You know why he did it. Tell me, and I'll come out." It seems like a well-negotiated compromise to me.

"I'm going to lock this door on you." She begins to swing the door shut. The hinges moan.

Knowing she would lock me in, I scramble to my feet and scurry through the opening. "Why mama?" I say after emerging into sunlight.

"Why what?"

"Why did daddy kill himself?"

She shrugs. "The Sheriff said he was drunk."

"I don't believe you."

"It's in the report, Ella. Why can't you let it go?"

"I tried to let it go. But now that I'm back here, I'm going to see his face every time I look at that barn. His head just hanging down and his eyes all bulged out."

"Stop it," she tells me.

"His neck was all bruised, and his jeans were stained. You know, because he … his muscles let go of everything when he died."

"I don't want to remember him that way. Now stop it."

"I won't. Not until you tell me."

Rose stares at me for a long time. Then she snaps the padlock on the barn door and walks back to the house.

I awake in the morning to a babble of voices. As I approach the kitchen, I hear Rose and Mattie arguing. I creep to a corner of the living room to eavesdrop.

"She asked me yesterday why Johnny killed himself. Again." My mother's voice has turned into a growl, her throat irreparably damaged from smoke and tar.

"What did you tell her?" Mattie asks.

"Said I didn't know why he did it. Said he was drunk."

"Did she believe you?"

"I couldn't tell."

There is silence from the kitchen. I wander in, trying to appear groggy with sleep. I fake a yawn. "Good morning."

Mattie eyes me, a silent question to see what I might have heard.

"What are you guys talking about?"

Nothing from either of them.

"Is there coffee?" I ask.

Rose gets up and pours coffee into my special cup, the insulated one with the glass straw, and sets it down in front of me. She stirs powdered creamer into her own cup until the coffee is the color of soured milk.

"Okay, I heard you talking about daddy's suicide. I can tell by the looks on your faces you're keeping secrets from me. He didn't just decide to kill himself one day. You know something." I take a long sip of coffee.

My mother works her jaw, the muscles bulging.

Mattie's face has gone slack. She's slumped against the counter, as if she needs it for support.

I turn to my mother. "It was us, wasn't it? Me and Mattie? We were too much of a burden for him."

"No," Mattie says. "That's not it. Tell her, mama."

Rose gives Mattie a look that is both appraising and sympathetic, then moves beside Mattie and strokes her hair. "Are you sure?"

Mattie simply nods, tears beginning to pool in her eyes. She seems unable to form words.

My mother stares at me without the sympathy she's just displayed toward my sister. "You've opened a can of worms, you know that? You could have just let it alone." Her gnarled hand goes to her forehead. "Your father committed horrible sins. I guess the only way he knew to pay for his sins was to do what he did."

"What sins?" I keep my eyes on Mattie. She's obviously in turmoil over what my mother is about to say.

"He laid down with Mattie."

At first I don't understand. "What?"

"Don't make this harder than it has to be, Ella." She crosses her arms and grips her biceps. "He took her, you know, in the Biblical sense."

I scramble from my chair. Mattie has fully collapsed onto the kitchen floor. I kneel in front of her. "Is this true?"

All my sister can do is nod.

31

There are no words. All of us are in the grip of high and deep emotion. Mattie is catatonic. Her arms hang limply, her hands unfolded in her lap. Her eyes stare blankly ahead. I assume she is going back there, re-living what our father did to her.

I curl on the floor next to her and whisper hoarsely in her ear. "It'll be okay. It'll be okay." If I could take her in my arms, I might not ever let her go. I realize there may be nothing I can do to bring her solace from the hell she has endured.

Even my mother breaks her normal stoicism. She bends her head, both hands covering her eyes, and begins to sob uncontrollably. Her body heaves and racks. Her sobs scrape upward in her throat.

I need to tell Mattie how sorry I am about what our father did to her, how sorry I am that I've never before said I'm so sorry. I go to the sink and throw up a few swallows of coffee, then dry heave. How could I not have known?

Only after Mattie staggers from the kitchen am I able to compose myself enough to say something to her. I walk into our bedroom, where she's trying to button a rose-colored blouse above a black skirt. Her hands are shaking. Her eyes still hold the vacant look of the shocked survivor.

"You're going to school?" I say.

She turns to me as if I've materialized from thin air. "Of course," she says, "it's Thursday." Her words sound hollow.

"Mattie, you can't go to school. You …" but I stop, realizing it's all she really can do. From experience, I understand that she needs to move. She needs her routine so she can focus on something, anything, other than her trauma.

Mattie stays late at school and misses dinner. When she comes through the front door carrying a bundle of papers, with a harassed look on her face, I attempt to say something, but she waves me off.

"I have to grade these exam papers for my summer school students, and book reports for another teacher who is out sick."

She is gone in an instant. The door to our bedroom closes. The deadbolt latches.

I glance over at my mother. She tries to keep her focus on the television, a nighttime soap opera, but her eyes edge toward me. She blames me for dragging it out of her. I can see it in her crinkled eyes and the tight grip of her mouth, even though she says not a word. It's my fault for unearthing this devastating secret.

At bedtime, Mattie finally unlocks the door, and when I enter the bedroom, she is beneath the covers, her eyes puffy and closed. I slip into my side of the bed and curl against Mattie's back, pressing against her like I used to when we were children and she had a bad dream. I bump my hips against her several times with the specific intention of keeping her from going to sleep.

"Can't you be still?" she mumbles.

"Please tell me this is all a bad dream," I whisper. "Please tell me that didn't happen."

"It happened."

"I can't believe it."

She rolls over to face me, her eyes rimmed in red. "You think I made it up?"

"No. Of course not. I'm sorry it came out that way. It's just so hard to believe that our father could be capable of hurting you so much."

"You don't even know the half of it." She sniffs and wipes her eyes with her pajama sleeve.

"I'm here for you Mattie, if you want to talk about it."

"Do you really want to hear this?"

"Unless it would be too painful to talk about." I offer her this last escape. It's something I've heard Dr. Marvin say a dozen times, and sometimes I take her up on it.

Mattie reaches over and strokes my hair. "I remember when we used to tell each other everything, Ella. You remember how we used to do that?"

"I remember."

She stares at the dark ceiling for a minute or more, steeling herself. "I knew it was wrong, what we were doing out there in the barn. When I started bleeding daddy told me it was natural, that I didn't need to go to the doctor or tell anyone. 'You're a woman now,' he said. 'This is our secret'."

"It *was* a secret, Mattie. I had no clue."

"He told me if I told anyone he'd send me away."

"Away? Like to boarding school?"

"I guess." She takes a moment, perhaps reminiscing, perhaps re-playing our father's words in an effort to discern the specifics of his threat. "I kept quiet because I couldn't stand the idea that I might have to leave. That I might get separated from you."

I meet her eyes, seeing unfathomable pain behind hers. I press my nose against her nose. My voice drops to a whisper. "How did mama find out?"

"She found us in the barn one night. All I heard was mama yelling 'Get off her. Get off her.' She picked up a pitchfork and started to stab him with it, but he ran out the side door. Then she turned on me. 'You ought to be ashamed of yourself, girl. What you've done is a mortal sin. You're going to Hell. You're both going to Hell.' I thought she was going to gig me with the pitchfork like a frog. I was so scared. I started crying. I couldn't stop. Then she told me to get into the house and clean up. And not to let you see me or let on what had happened."

"He's surely damned for what he did," I say. I mean it.

"You know I never looked at him while he was doing it. I was too afraid to see his face. I just kept my eyes shut. But in my nightmares, I sometimes still see him, and he is all red like the Devil. With horns and everything."

For a dozen years, my sister has lived with this terror. I know from experience fear doesn't dissipate on its own. Telling me what happened provides an explanation of our father's suicide. And perhaps it will help Mattie heal. That's probably what Dr. Marvin would say.

Now, Mattie rolls over to sleep. I wonder how I could not have known what our father was doing to her in the barn. How I could have been that naive. I recall that when we were teenagers, I cuddled Mattie in my arms countless times and wiped away nightmare tears. She always gave an innocuous, believable explanation for the nightmares. She was being chased by a wild hog. Or she had fallen into a den of snakes. I was not aware, as I pressed against her back and wrapped my arms around her, that my father had held her in a similar way only hours before.

32

Mattie assumes the nightly duties my mother has been performing. Somehow, this revelation that our father molested Mattie has brought us closer. Mattie bathes me, dries me off, helps me wiggle into adult diapers, brushes my teeth, shaves my legs and pits. After we retire to the bedroom, I sit down at the vanity and its chipped mirror, and she brushes my hair. In contrast to my mother's ministrations, Mattie is gentle, holding my hair between her fingers so the brush won't pull at my scalp.

At times I keep my eyes closed, and at others I watch her hands move about my head, the silver-plated brush winking in the lamplight.

"We're not all that different from each other, Mattie." In the mirror, I watch my mouth utter these words. I want her to understand that although the origins of our independent tragedies are different, the pain we feel is the same, the weight we struggle with is parallel.

"What do you mean?"

"I mean that we've both been through a lot of tragedy."

She pauses in mid-stroke, meets my eyes in the mirror. "I had almost forgotten what daddy did to me," she says. "Almost."

"But that feeling of… I don't know … that it's somehow your fault, that stays with you doesn't it?"

"I don't feel like it's my fault," she says. "I feel tainted. And I feel like other people can see it. Like they just know what happened."

We're not the same. Even though we're both victims. Mattie's shame is immensely different from the fear that still resides deep inside me. The fear that my terrorist is coming for the witness.

While Mattie is teaching summer school, I spend a lot of time listening to audio books, which she checks out from the local library. In our bedroom, I recline in a pink bean-bag chair she retrieved from the attic, which retains the scent of mildew despite her efforts to clean it.

Ella's Wings

I am listening to a book about a family who homesteaded a piece of Alaska wilderness more than fifty miles from the nearest paved road. They cut trees, built a log house, cleared land for animal pens and erected wire fences. They fished for salmon in roaring currents of icy water, ferried food on snowmobiles and fought off angry bears. The writer tells the tale as if the family was never afraid of getting hurt or dying. As if the incessant threat of danger was an accepted condition of their existence.

I pause the book and stand up to stretch my legs. I peer out the bedroom window at the barn and the verdant corner of a pasture whose barbed wire fences are barely hanging on. The sharp banging of a piece of roof tin flapping in the wind makes me flinch.

At times I am able to subdue the terror, but when I catch movement in my peripheral vision, or hear a sound that doesn't belong, the hair on the back of my neck stands up. I think it is him, returning to finish the job. Him, for whom there are no limits.

I run from the bedroom into the living room, where my mother is watching television. I sit on the arm of the sofa closest to her lounger.

She glances at me for a heartbeat or two, then returns her attention to the television.

"Do we have guns in the house?" I ask.

"Yes." She speaks slowly, her eyes focused on the soap opera.

"Where? What do we have?"

"Your father's old revolver in my bedside table. A deer rifle in the hall closet. A shotgun in the truck."

"Are they loaded?"

A commercial interrupts her show, and she uses the remote to turn the volume down.

"The revolver stays loaded. The rifle and the shotgun probably not. Why?"

"Do you know how to shoot? Does Mattie know how to shoot?"

"Ella, what's going on?"

"We're totally isolated out here."

"I wouldn't call it isolated." She picks up a pack of cigarettes and her lighter from the table and heads toward the front porch. "Nobody has bothered us here for 40-plus years."

She means since she married my father and moved into this farmhouse. "Yeah, but things have changed. The world's gotten meaner, and a lot more dangerous."

We're on the porch now, and she settles on a metal chair painted evergreen and lights up. "What are you scared of?"

"Him."

"Dr. Volkov?"

It irks me that she adds "doctor" to my terrorist's name.

"Yes."

She looks out onto the fields. Twenty or so Angus cows linger under the spread of oak trees. "You should talk with Dr. Marvin."

She says this as if we have reached some demarcated line she can't cross. Then I realize she's probably discussed this topic with Dr. Marvin, just like she did my engagement to David and my pregnancy. There must be a list of topics and milestones and ruts marking my road to recovery, and my mother and Mattie and Dr. Marvin have seen the map.

"What day is it? I ask.

"Wednesday."

"No, I mean the date?" Without a job, the calendar has become almost meaningless to me. Days and weeks slide by, inconsequential.

She blows another plume of smoke into the air, and it hovers above us in the sticky air.

"August 9."

One year ago. The day my life changed forever.

I schedule a web session with Dr. Marvin. It's the first time I've spoken with her since I moved out of Charlotte. We spend a minute catching up because it only takes a minute. Other than my switch of abode, nothing has really changed.

"I'm still melting away like a glacier," I say.

"The fact that you acknowledge that might mean you're ready to do something about it."

"Like what?"

"Become more independent. Face your fears rather than shrink from them."

"You've talked to my mother."

"Of course I have, Ella. She's doing her best to help you. She can't do it alone. Neither can you."

"Every time I go outside my anxiety rises. A lot. I feel like I'm a little rabbit or something, waiting for a hawk to swoop down and get me."

"Any particular hawk?"

"Volkov."

"Exactly. Take baby steps. Nothing dramatic. Walk around your farm. When you're comfortable with that, venture out. Maybe Mattie can go with you."

Dr. Marvin's skin is still a flawless ivory. In the light of her office she almost looks like a shimmering portrait.

"I ride into town with my mother sometimes."

"That's good. Do you feel safe when you go into town?"

"Sometimes." I pause, trying to discern the depth of my anxiety. "Maybe I have agoraphobia."

"You don't, not in my opinion. You have a specific fear of a specific man who killed thousands of people and almost killed you. It's natural to be afraid of him."

"Is that supposed to make me feel better?"

"I treat a lot of the bombing victims, Ella. Some of them do have agoraphobia and haven't left their houses at all in the past year. You've progressed much farther than most."

I note that she refers to Volkov as the bomber. "Do you know something about Volkov that I don't? Has there been some development linking him to the bombing?"

She leans forward and smiles at me. "No. I believe you, Ella. You saw what you saw. Your memory is not a hallucination."

This does make me feel better. It's validation I haven't heard from any other source. I carry her words around with me like a mental banner.

For months I have watched Rose fix my meals. I study the way she wields a knife and opens cans and dumps food into pots. How she jiggles the frying pan over the burner so scrambled eggs won't scorch. How she stirs tea with a long wooden spoon. How she maneuvers a fork to her mouth, changing the angle of her wrist so the contents don't spill.

I conclude that the next step toward my emancipation is to learn to feed myself. On an afternoon when my mother is engrossed in the television, I stand on the kitchen ladder and open the silverware drawer with my bare foot. I dig into the utensils, lift the handle of a fork from underneath with my big toe, tilt the fork to the side, then slide it between my big toe and my index toe. I stare down at the fork as if it is treasure I dug from the earth.

My mother comes in then, perhaps alerted by the rattling of metals, and places her fists upon her hips. She says nothing. This feels like the times she caught me taking an extra cookie from the jar on the top shelf, only this time, with one foot engaged, there is no way I can scamper down the kitchen ladder. I lower my foot and place the fork on the counter, re-balance myself on the broad, rubber-covered top step, and descend to the floor. I grasp the fork in my mouth, handle first, and transfer it to the table.

In silence, Rose folds the ladder and sets it against the wall in the utility room. Then she re-opens the silverware drawer and plucks every knife, fork and spoon from the plastic organizer and places them in the dishwasher.

There is no elegance to my eating. I sit on a swivel stool with a high back, perched slightly above the level of my plate. It takes quite a while to get the hang of shifting around without the stool spinning, but I finally learn to grip the fork with the toes of my right foot, cross my right ankle over my left knee, and raise my left knee toward my mouth. I start with slices of chicken and other food that can be easily stabbed with a fork. At first I do not have much flexibility, and the muscles of my butt, legs and feet tire quickly. I resume the exercises Zack taught me, and in a matter of days my muscle endurance and flexibility improve. When my feet cramp, Mattie massages them.

As a next step, I begin to bathe myself. This task is made much easier when Mattie hires a plumber to replace the plastic knobs in our tub-shower with levers. The plumber also installs a shower wand just above the tub faucet, and replaces our toilet with a bidet. We install a dispenser, filled with a no-tears shampoo, that drips shampoo onto my head by triggering an electronic eye. It's only a stop-gap because I can't knead the shampoo into my hair. Once a week, Mattie gives me a thorough hair-washing.

As I learn to do more things on my own, a noticeable change comes over my mother. He eyes narrow less when we talk. Her mouth is not as tight when we argue. I realize she has not relished our forced intimacy either. She talks about taking a trip. She doesn't know where she wants to go. She just wants to go. She has raised two girls, and though she may not have done it right, at least we have survived, she says.

I see in my mother a permanent weariness. It shows in a back that is rounding at the shoulders, in creases at the corners of her eyes and mouth. In the wheezing breath that comes with moderate levels of exertion, though that might be the daily pack of cigarettes she smokes on the front porch. She had a brief rest when Mattie went to college, but after Mattie returned, Rose resumed fixing Mattie's meals, making her bed, laundering her clothes. It's what my mother knows how to do. She has never held a job outside our home.

Through the dexterity of my feet, my life begins to feel somewhat normal, or as normal as I can expect. I remember blowing up at Dr. Harwell because he said artificial limbs might make me normal again. More often than not I leave the arms underneath our queen bed because they will never truly be a part of me. I know what I need to do. It's the same salve I used when I last stood in the spot where the bomb felled me.

With the sun shining brightly in a periwinkle sky, I cross the cattle guard. I stand on the macadam that separates our driveway from the highway, looking up and down the ribbon of gray as if it were a vast river. I examine the silhouettes of men driving pick-ups as they pass. I look beneath their tailgates for the red of activated brake lights. I scan the trees lining the other side of the road, peering into shadows that could be hiding places.

And then I begin to walk. When I arrive at the corner post of our farm, I take a right turn onto a two-lane that winds past a ramshackle house set close to the road. Chickens peck at discarded trash in the yard. Weathered grey clapboards, probably nailed on long before I was born, hang such that the wind surely whistles through the rooms in winter. There is a wire fence around the front yard to corral the chickens. A big Rottweiler watches my approach with black eyes. No mere fence is enough to contain that dog. He charges the fence, scattering the chickens in a blast of clucking, only to be jerked back by a galvanized chain nailed to a tree. I shudder to think what would happen if that chain or his collar ever broke.

Michael Winstead

A rusty tricycle sits near the porch, unused. I sidle to the fence for a closer look, trying to ignore the snarling dog with yellowed canines. A small boy comes out onto the porch and leans against a washing machine. He yells at the dog until it returns to its place of dirt under the tree.

The boy and I stare at each other for a time. He sips from a bottle of orange soda, studying me. He gradually wanders over to the fence.

"I can ride a bike," he says.

"Who rides that tricycle over there," I nod.

"That's my sister's. She can't ride it anymore."

"How come?"

"She's sick in the hospital."

"I'm sorry to hear that. What's your name?"

"Michael. Do you want to see me ride my bike?"

"Sure," I say.

He goes around to the side of the house and returns with a red bicycle with shiny chrome wheels.

"I got it for Christmas. Mom said Santa Claus brought it, but I know it was my pop. I can only ride in the yard. Mom won't let me ride in the road."

Michael makes a circuit of the small yard, dodging the dog and the chickens and the litter of a junked car up on blocks. The dog lays its snout on the ground and watches the little boy make tire tracks in the dirt. After several laps, Michael stops next to the fence again.

The label on the front of his bike reads Huffy. "Who taught you to ride?" I ask.

"My pop. Do you know how to ride a bike?"

"I used to."

"Did you forget how?"

"Well, I didn't forget. I can't ride anymore."

"How come?"

"Because I don't have arms."

He cocks his head and squints up at me, as if he hasn't noticed before. "How come?"

"I was in an accident."

"Oh," he says. "I'll teach you to ride, if you want."

"How old are you?"

"I'll be six and half next month."

I bend down to his level and talk through the wire panes of the fence. "How do you suppose I'd be able to ride a bike without arms or hands?"

He puzzles over this for a moment, shifting his front wheel back and forth in the dirt. "You just ride," he says and takes off around the yard again.

The next time I walk by Michael's house, he waves and brings his bicycle to the fence. As he circles the house, he is wearing a distinct rut in the dirt, though it does nothing to tarnish the appearance of the place. Today he is brave enough to take his hands off the handlebars.

I notice the Rottweiler is gone.

"What happened to your dog?" I ask when Michael stops by the fence.

"Mama shot him."

"Why?"

"He bit me."

"He bit you. Where?"

"Right here." Michael pulls up his pants leg and shows me a circular wound on his calf. Some of the flesh is chewed away, leaving a deep depression and teeth marks on his spindly leg.

"Did it hurt?" I ask.

"Some. I couldn't ride my bike for a week."

As long as he can ride his bike, it doesn't make any difference that he is dirt poor, or his sister is in the hospital, or his dog is dead. Whizzing around in circles, he pedals way too fast for any of this to stick to him.

33

On a morning with heavy dew matting the fields, I test out the new running shoes I bought on the internet. They have Velcro straps instead of laces. Down and back on our packed gravel drive I jog, which is about two hundred yards long. I do not wear the arms, and the rock of my shoulders feels odd with nothing swinging below them.

Mattie and I used to race each other on this driveway. Our skinny legs and arms churned as our father stood at the top of the rise, waiting with a popsicle for the winner. I usually won and had the popsicle between my lips before Mattie finished. But she got a popsicle too.

Today, I manage less than a mile before I have to stop. The muscles of my legs feel energized, quivering beneath my leggings. The scars no longer hamper me. My heaving lungs and pounding heart, however, evidence my lack of fitness.

Mattie is in the vegetable garden back of the barn. She splashes slug bait around squash and spinach and other fall vegetables.

"Should be a good crop if you can keep the slugs away."

She looks over and smiles at me beneath the wide brim of her gardening hat. "Did you go for a run?"

"Barely a mile. I'm so out of shape, it's ridiculous."

"You'll build back up. You always do."

She uncoils the hose and begins to water a row of radishes. The well pump clicks on and emits a low groan.

"Hold the hose for me," I say. I bend to it like a horse to a trough and drink.

Mattie steadies the hose for a few seconds, then raises the nozzle and splashes my face. She douses my hair and my sleeveless shirt. "There, you've had your shower for the day."

She leaves me dripping. I shake my head to wring some of the water out of my hair, long enough now to touch my shoulders. I plop down on a wooden bench and watch her water. Her lips count out fifteen seconds before she moves to the next plant. "Carrots might be ready, soon," she says, as if to encourage them.

This is my world now. It is a drastically truncated version of the life I once knew. Where I had a career, and a house, and a husband, then a fiancé and a baby, now I have rows of vegetables, my sister in a garden apron, a barn where tragedy indelibly altered our lives. I'm not sure how to accept it. But I also know I have no choice.

When Mattie is done, she loops the hose over the metal bracket and stands with her hands on hips in the shade thrown by the barn. She surveys our garden like she might her students while taking a test, appraising each pupil for progress. The sun has already begun to suck out the moisture, turning dirt that was the color of asphalt into a pale grey. Apparently satisfied, she sits next to me on the bench.

"So, what's new at school?" I ask.

"Not much. Same ole, same ole."

"No new cute teachers to talk about?"

Mattie narrows her eyes and scowls.

"What's the matter, you don't like to talk about guys anymore?"

"What's the point?"

"The point is love," I say, nudging her with my shoulder.

"I'm surprised you still hold out hope for that."

I could take this as belittling, but I know she is only trying to keep me grounded. "I must have been in love with David," I say. I still remember little of our months-long romance, except for the horrible last five seconds, permanently imprinted. "Even if it won't ever happen again for me, you could still fall in love, Mattie."

There is a far-off look in her eyes. She snatches a weed from the ground, shakes off the dirt, and flings the weed toward a burn pile. "Love means sex."

There is so much that flows from those words. I infer the rest of what she can't bear to say, as if her thoughts skip across the short space between us. Our father ruined sex for her, and she can't disentangle that from love.

Maybe she'll never get past it. It clouds each breath, every encounter she has with a man. It stymies hopeful thoughts of what a relationship could become.

I lean into her, lay my head on her right shoulder. "You'll meet him one day. Someone for whom sex is an expression of love."

With both palms, she gently straightens my head and stands up. She pounds her fist against the wood siding on the barn three times, then leaves me.

As summer wanes, I retreat into the soliloquy of my own recollections. I sit on shelves of limestone near the creek, my knees up to my chest, trying to dredge up more memories of David. They won't come. I have the photographs I sent to Mattie, of course, and the letters David wrote to me, but aside from that and the five-second video of David's last moments, I have no recollection of my fiancé. It's a cruel addition to my list of injuries. The list of things Volkov stole from me.

Our creek is as low as I have ever seen it, and at times the water seems completely still, as if it is waiting for something to end its stagnation. As a child, I fished the creek with my father many times. He would rig up poles with worms or dough balls, and we would sit on these same rocks and dangle our legs out over deeper water, in search of catfish or sunfish or whatever might bite. Whether we caught fish was secondary. Just being with him was a treat for me.

I remember vividly a morning spent fishing with my father on an unusually cool day in the fall. The mist rose from the water in swirls. With great anticipation, I watched my orange cork bobbing on riffles created by the wind. I stared at the cork so long its rhythms lured me into an almost hypnotic state. Suddenly, the cork was gone. My father yelled my name, and the tip of my rod jerked down, awakening my sense of touch. I pulled back in response, meeting resistance equal to a great stump rooted deeply in the muck. I thought at first my hook was embedded in a submerged tree, but when the line wiggled, I knew I had a fish.

I wonder what goes through the mind of a fish as it battles to free itself of the barb piercing its mouth. I refuse to believe it does not have a strategy of some sort. Of course, it has no idea of the strength or experience of the foe on the rod end of the line, yet its maneuvers seem keenly devised to entangle the line around whatever obstacles are available.

My fish zipped back and forth across the creek, darting under fallen tree limbs. For a time we battled to a stalemate. I might have gained the advantage of a few hard-fought rotations of the reel, dragging the fish a foot or two toward the bank, but then it would strip off a bit of line, and we were again at loggerheads. My tiny muscles wore out before my patience did, and my father took over. He hoisted the fish off the bottom, pulling the rod back and reeling up the slack, until the fish finally broke the surface. Spying us, it gave a final flapping burst, the slap of its tail resounding off the walls of our fogged-in world. My father dragged the spent fish to the bank, and together we lifted it into the net.

It was a carp. My father estimated its weight at eight pounds. I had never before seen a carp up close, and its large, orange scales looked like the armor-plating of some prehistoric creature. As it gasped for breath in the bottom of the net, its mouth pursing, its gill flaps undulating, I realized it was dying. I told my father to throw it back in the creek.

"It's a trash fish," he said. He hurled the carp into the woods behind us. "A fox will get it."

I stood on the bank, my thirteen-year-old body trembling, then went after it. It took me awhile to gather up the slimy fish, but I finally succeeded and brought it back to the bank of the creek, bearing it in my arms as I might a baby doll. My clothes became smeared with fish slime, dirt, and blood. I dropped the fish back into the water and watched for a sign of revival. The fish rolled involuntarily onto its side and began to float down the creek, trailing a finger of red from its gill.

"Will it live?" I asked my father.

"It might."

I had seen death on the farm before, once or twice in the form of a stillborn calve lying motionless in a field. But none of that had been inflicted by my hand. As the carp floated on its side, I had a powerful need to witness its resuscitation. I followed the floating fish along the tangled path on the high bank of the creek. Brambles tore my clothes and scratched my bare arms. The fish bounced off drowned limbs and spun around in swirling eddies. As I followed, the carp floated under the bridge—the highway. The highway was my boundary. I was never to go across the highway. I always obeyed my father's admonition and had never been to the other side of the road unless I was in a car or on the school bus. I knelt down and peered beneath the bridge. There was no bank to walk upon. The dark water seemed deep. The carp floated around a bend.

I could hear my father calling behind me, following my trail through the underbrush, demanding that I come back. Instead, I climbed the embankment, waited for a break in the traffic, and darted across the highway. The embankment on the other side of the road was covered by a blackberry thicket. I tried to wade through the thicket to the creek, to the fish. I picked up a thick stick and fought the brambles. Thorns grabbed my arms and bloodied my skin. I thrashed the blackberry vines and screamed a child's frustration, bringing myself to tears. I hurled the stick at the thicket, scrambled back onto the bridge and peered over the edge, searching the murky water. I could not see the fish. But I knew it was dead. And I had done it.

My father found me clinging to the bridge railing while cars and trucks whizzed behind me. He grabbed my arm.

"You lied to me. The fish is dead." I beat his chest with my small fists, managing to land only a few harmless blows before he snatched me up and carried me back across the road.

He cut a switch from a willow tree with his pocketknife. He made me pull down my underwear and bend over. I held onto the backs of my knees and stared bitterly at the ground as he blistered my behind. I lost count of the number of whacks. When he finished, he dabbed my tears with his handkerchief and carried me in his arms to the house. I blubbered the whole time.

The savage welts on my rear-end kept me sleeping on my stomach for three days. I never fished with my father again.

34

I stride down our gravel drive when the sun has barely emerged above the horizon, mist still hovering in the fields. I need this now, more than ever. I need the fresh air in my lungs and the blood coursing through my body. I need the rhythm of my legs taking me forward.

For me, the beauty of motion lies in the calming of my frazzled mind. Meditation in motion, Dr. Marvin calls it. The soothing effect of steady footfalls on brown pine needles.

As I run in the dappled light beneath pine trees, something flutters by at head height. *Danaus plexippus*—the monarch butterfly. With its broad, orange and black wings, it is a majestic creature.

I follow the monarch to the edge of the woods and a field overgrown with milkweed. The monarch caterpillar feeds on nothing but milkweed, eating enough for the butterfly's full lifetime and southward migration. This field is filled with thousands of monarchs, some clinging to the leaves, raising and lowering their wings to warm their blood. Others weave through the air like a tapestry of color. Their play lifts me, makes me somehow feel lighter. I stay there watching them until the sun reaches its zenith.

* * * * *

My mother picks up a boyfriend. His name is Oscar, and he is a retired high school teacher. He taught Ag or Shop, or maybe both. I vaguely remember him from school, though I took no classes from him.

I accuse Mattie of pairing them up, but she denies it. It seems my mother knew his wife from church, but his wife died of the cancer, as my mother puts it, a few years back.

Oscar is a wrinkled man who has an annoying habit of cracking his knuckles. I don't know whether he performs this deed any place but our house, but he makes an elaborate show of it while he watches television with Rose in our living room. I observe his routine often enough that I memorize it. First, he presses each fist into the opposite palm, pops the middle joint of each finger, then cups the fingers and rolls them back, taking care of the two joints near the end. With his thumb he presses each finger flat against the palm. After that he locks each digit between index finger and thumb, pulling the fingers with some force, until he pops each of the joints where finger meets hand. Then he bends all of the fingers back, one by one. He pulls his thumbs until they crack. Finally, he intertwines his fingers and flexes his hands outward, then twists them until every joint in every finger has been cracked and snapped in every conceivable direction. Sometimes he wrings his hands so fiercely that he pops the joints in his wrists and elbows too. I witness this spectacle almost every day. Rose, of course, doesn't seem to notice.

Oscar slips his hand into Rose's and rubs her knuckles with his thumb. I can't say what he might find interesting about her knobby hands. Both of her hands shake now. At night, as she moves the cigarettes in and out of her mouth on the front porch, the glow of the butt looks like a nervous firefly.

When their heads begin to gravitate toward one another, I am forced to leave the house. I find places to wander, though the milkweed field becomes one of my favorite spots for waiting. Waiting on whatever. I sip from the straw of the water pack on my back, trying to get used to my temporary exile.

Most of the monarchs have headed south, though a few stragglers remain. I venture into the vast field of milkweed. The barbed leaves scrape my calves and thighs. I see dead monarchs on the ground and wonder why they didn't make the journey to Mexico soon enough.

Dr. Marvin's recent words come back to me. A phone call I had with her in which I complained about being exiled from the house so my mother could spend time with her boyfriend alone.

"It bothers you so much, having to leave the house, because that's your anchor. It was your house in Charlotte, now it's your mother's house. You have to have a secure place to just be. A place that's not in your head." At times it irks me that Dr. Marvin's advice consists of my own thoughts repeated back to me in a more eloquent way. But she is right. It is that old feeling of having nothing to hold onto. Perhaps this is my place, a haven for orange and black butterflies, their beauty only temporary, their life cycle so finite, fluttering among prickly weeds farmers try to kill.

Nudging open the front door with my foot, I catch my mother and Oscar kissing on the couch.

"Ella, why don't you knock?" she says, patting her hair and smoothing her skirt. No, she is pulling the hem of her skirt *down.* After an awkward pause, during which we all pretend to watch television, I say, "We need to talk, mama."

Oscar cracks a knuckle or two, then departs. The muffler on his truck growls as he drives off.

My mother goes into the kitchen and rinses coffee cups in the sink.

Not turning around, she says, "I'll pull the shades down in the living room from now on when we want privacy."

"What?"

"Don't come back to the house while the shades are drawn," she says.

"Is this getting serious?"

"He's a nice man."

"Well what about …"

"Johnny? Is that what you were going to say, Ella? Your father's been dead fourteen years now."

"No, it's not him. It's just that, well, you're not a spring chicken anymore."

"I may be old, but I'm not dead yet. Don't put me in the grave before my time."

The window shades stay down longer and longer. I spend more time in the woods by myself. In some ways I am becoming feral, creeping through the trees, making no noise, as if hunting something.

When the first frost hits, I convince Rose to leave the barn door unlocked so I can get out of the wind while she entertains Oscar. I do not want the barn to be my anchor, considering what happened in here, yet I settle into a bale of hay and listen to gusts rattle the tin roof. Half of a cinder block holds the door ajar, providing a wedge of gray light. My eyes dart about the barn. To the spot where he hung himself. To the musty corner where he abused Mattie.

I begin timing how long the shades remain down. I note the time on the kitchen clock when I am evicted from the house and again on my return. These banishments start at twenty minutes and gradually increase to more than an hour. I am convinced Rose is leaving the shades down longer than necessary. To remind me it is still her house. I am only a guest.

When the living room shades go up, I return. I sit alone in front of the silent television. Muted noises come from the direction of my mother's bedroom. I walk down the short hall and put my ear to the door. I hear giggles and other sounds. For reasons I cannot understand, I linger there, bend down and put my eye to the keyhole.

"Why did you pull the shades up if he was still here?" I say after Oscar departs.

"I thought he was going to leave, but he decided to stay."

"I could hear what you were doing in there, you know."

My mother looks away. "Oscar gets a little rambunctious at times."

I notice the rosy glow on her usually pallid cheeks. "Yeah, he's a regular stallion," I say. This fight has been brewing for some time, its tentacles growing from my vulnerabilities. I feel displaced. Adrift. "This is disgusting. My own mother going at it like some nymphomaniac."

"Ella!"

"That's what it looks like to me. You can't even say the word sex when you tell me what daddy did to Mattie. 'In the biblical sense' you said. 'He laid down with her.' But now you're screwing like a teenager."

"Don't you dare compare my relationship with Oscar to what your father did to your sister. You're just jealous because I have a boyfriend."

"He's not your boyfriend. All you do is sit around and watch television, or go in the bedroom and do whatever."

"You couldn't keep your husband happy, Ella."

This bites. I swallow, but the words are out before I can stop them. "Well if your marriage was so great, how come your husband left your bed to fuck your own daughter?"

Ella's Wings

She slaps me hard across the face, stinging my left cheek like a malevolent hornet. I stagger to the side.

"You bitch. That's the second time you've hit me." My voice is quaking. My body is trembling. "If you ever do that again I'll …"

She slaps me again. "You'll do what Ella, hit me back?"

I storm from the house, wanting so badly to slam the door. Wanting so badly to feel the sting of my palm landing on her cheek.

I run down the driveway, hop the cattle guard and cross the highway without slowing. In the fading light of dusk, I stand for a few minutes on the bridge, looking down into the swirling water, where a dead carp once seized my attention. The blackberry thicket guarding the descent to the creek has gone seasonally dormant. I squeeze past the thorns. I have to move. The wind whips brown oak leaves still clinging to branches, rattling them like a baby's toy. I plant my feet carefully on the path as it weaves close to the creek, a creek that slides by without making noise. I can see its surface only when the clouds retreat from the face of the rising moon. I feel the pulse of the creek like I feel the throb of my missing hands.

I don't know how long I run in retreat from Rose's house, but eventually I stop and crouch in the hollow of a massive maple tree. I am shivering—from both the adrenaline coursing through my body and the biting wind.

Perhaps I should not have said that to my mother, but when I replay the argument, I know I got in a really good punch. Rose had to have known what was going on in the barn long before she found them that night. She would have seen changes in my father. She could not have slept side-by-side with him every night and remained completely oblivious to what he was doing. She must have internally questioned why he was suddenly spending all of that time with Mattie in the barn. And she did nothing to stop it.

When I look up again, I see a flame flickering through the trees. It is the only distinguishing mark in the dark woods. I creep towards it and stop just outside the circle where firelight melts dark shadows into gray.

There are two men sitting on camp chairs, warming their hands. And drinking cans of beer. Discarded cans litter the edges of the fire. I see the glint of a gun barrel leaning against a log. Behind them, maybe a hundred feet, is a dark-colored pickup truck.

I don't know precisely where I am. In my fury, I may have run three or four miles from the house. I might have ventured onto state forest land. In the dark, I tell myself I can find my way back on my own. Maybe.

In my haste to escape Rose, I stomped out of the house wearing only a t-shirt, a pair of black leggings, and a light windbreaker. No hat. The icy wind scrapes along the back of my neck.

I take a few steps forward and emerge from the trees. "Can you guys help me?"

One of the men grabs his rifle and swings it toward me.

I cannot hold up my hands to prove I am unarmed.

A flashlight glares in my eyes.

"What are you doing out here?" the other man asks.

I turn my head away from the beam. "I was … it's a long story. I think I'm lost. Can you guys give me a ride home?"

The man with the gun stands and approaches me. He grabs the sleeve of my jacket, as if to pull me fully into the ring of light from the fire, then discovers there is nothing inside. My captor feels the other empty sleeve. He turns to the other man, who has risen from his camp stool.

"Hey, she ain't got no arms."

"What? Let me see." The other man staggers over and squeezes my empty sleeves for confirmation. "Holy shit. Well, at least she won't fight much." He cackles uncontrollably.

"I need a ride home. Please."

The drunkest one jerks my jacket off my shoulders and stands there holding it, perhaps a bit shocked that there is nothing protruding from the short sleeves of my blue t-shirt.

I have never been in this situation before. I am trying to read them. The man fisting my jacket is clearly drunk, barely able to stand without weaving. The one holding the gun, pointed approximately at my knees, is unsteady enough that the rifle barrel wobbles.

"I just need a ride home."

The drunk man grabs my left breast through my t-shirt. I kick his shin, but it's a weak shot. He puts both hands on my shoulders and shoves me to the ground.

I am helpless. One man looms over me. The other points the barrel of his rifle at my mid-section. Terror has wormed its way out of hibernation. My muscles soften into jelly. I wonder if they are going to kill me. Or worse.

The drunk man straddles me, then rips my shirt down the center. He slides his fingers beneath the elastic of my leggings and begins to tug them down.

"Stop it." The voice of a third man comes from the direction of the campfire.

The man on top of me eases his weight to one side, talks over his shoulder. "We were just having a little fun, Rick. Come on man, don't be a spoilsport."

"Let her up." The third man—Rick—is now in view. He is carrying a load of firewood. His eyes are focused on the man on top of me. "Let her up, I said."

When the man hesitates, Rick drops the firewood and shoves him off of me.

The drunkard topples to the ground and says "shit."

I scramble backward a few feet, pushing away, then stand up.

The three of them are silhouettes, backlit by the fire. The man whom Rick pushed stands chin-to-chin with him, as if they are boxers facing off.

Rick bends down, grabs my jacket from the ground, and drapes it over my shoulders.

"I just want a ride," I say.

"We've only got the one vehicle," he says, flicking his head toward the pickup backed into the trees. "Can you find your way back?"

He is a little bigger than the others, but beneath his orange cap, uncertainty invades his eyes. The other two are probably too drunk to drive, and he doesn't want to leave them here in the woods to drive me home. I realize the truck might not even be his.

"I think so."

He walks me across their camp to a sandy, single-track road.

"I could try and call somebody for you, but cell service is bad out here." He points. "Fifty feet up this road is the paved park road. You take it a mile, maybe a mile and a half, and you're back on the county highway."

I nod. "What about them?"

"I'll deal with them. You forget you were ever here. Just get yourself home. All right?"

I turn back toward the campfire. The man who attacked me has picked up his rifle. The butt of the gun rests in his armpit. It would take only a half-second for him to swing it into position.

"You be careful now," he yells. "Wouldn't want anyone to mistake you for a deer." He lifts the rifle barrel a foot.

I examine his face in the flicker of the fire. Beneath his hunting cap, his eyes leer at me. His mouth is a drunken sneer. It is the face of a man who can't predict what he might do in the next few seconds.

"Go," Rick says, putting his palm on my upper back. When I take a step he starts walking back to the campfire, keeping himself between me and the man with the rifle.

I take a deep breath and do what I know how to do. I run. I angle around the front of the truck and plunge into the darkness. Once I reach the pavement, where the footing is more solid, I accelerate up the hill, zigzagging from one edge of the road to the other, making myself a weaving target. I keep my head down and listen for the crack of a rifle. It never comes.

35

I eventually stagger up the gravel drive to Rose's house, feeling like a scared rabbit trying to outrace chasing hounds. As I ran, I dwelled on those men in the woods, and on Volkov, through every labored breath. Twice I had been thrust into the circle of terror, but somehow escaped. Maimed and irreparably damaged, but not dead. Why?

I drag myself up on the front porch and peer through the windows. All of the lights in the living room are off. I cannot see anyone moving about inside.

"Where have you been?" Her voice, cold and throaty, scares me. My mother is sitting in a metal chair against the wall of the porch, bundled in a dark sweater. "What happened to your clothes?"

I am not prepared to tell her the truth. Perhaps I am not ready to face what has happened. "I fell down, near the creek." It is a half-truth. In my escape, I tripped over a cracked piece of pavement and skidded across the macadam. I cannot tell if she accepts this.

"The front door's open," she says.

I stare at her, waiting for an apology. Waiting for some words of sympathy. When nothing comes, I push inside and find Mattie at her desk in our bedroom, grading papers.

She glances up at me and her jaw drops. "Oh my God, what happened Ella?"

"I fell. It looks worse than it is. I want to take a bath. Will you help me?"

"Sure," she says, putting down her work.

Mattie locks the bathroom door and removes my tattered t-shirt. She delicately touches the scrapes on my shoulders, the fingernail scratches above my breasts. She eyes me with a scrutiny that says she doesn't believe I fell.

When I look in the mirror, I see a face with glazed eyes.

We watch the steam rising in the tub. The mirror fogs over, thank goodness. Mattie settles me into the bath. While I soak, she gathers up my clothes.

"What are you going to do with those?" I say.

"What do you want me to do with them?"

"Throw them out. I don't want mama to see them."

"Wasn't she out on the porch when you came in?"

"Yeah, but I don't think she has any idea what happened."

"What did happen, Ella?"

I cannot answer her.

Mattie pulls leaves and twigs from my disheveled hair. She squirts shampoo on my head and gently kneads it in. With a washcloth, she cleans the scrapes and scratches on my body. My skin involuntarily crawls from her touch, unable to distinguish between her caress and the groping of drunken men. She dabs tears from my cheeks.

"You going to be okay?"

"Mama and I had a fight." I stop. I am worried my mother will pry the next bit out of her. "You can't tell her any of this, Mattie. Mama can never know." These words come from quivering lips.

"Just us. I promise," Mattie says, making a gesture sealing the vault.

I search her eyes. I see honesty there. "I ran into some hunters in the woods and they tried to rape me and tore my clothes and …" It spews out of me like vomit.

"What hunters? What woods? Who tried to rape you?"

The breath that escaped my lungs when I fell in the woods comes back now as I heave and sob. My chest feels like it is trying to expel an elephant. "I was mad at mama and ran across the highway and down into the woods and saw two hunters sitting around a campfire and they were drinking and I asked if they could give me a ride home and one of them shoved me down and ripped off my jacket and tore my shirt and squeezed my breast and was pulling off my pants and trying to rape me."

I look down at my naked body. I am suddenly uncomfortable telling this story while I sit naked in the tub. Even with Mattie standing guard. "Help me up," I say.

Mattie towels me off and slips on my terry cloth robe and knots the belt in the front. I sit on the edge of the claw-footed tub and take deep breaths.

"They didn't succeed, did they Ella? I mean, they only tried, right?"

I shake my head. "The third guy, his name was Rick, he stopped the other two before they could … finish."

"What did they look like? Did you recognize any of them?"

"No. I don't know. I can't really describe them. You know, it was dark, and while the guy was on top of me I looked away. I didn't want to … it was dark."

"We should call the police."

"No."

"Why not, Ella?"

"I don't want to go through that. I don't want to press charges and have to face them again and testify and all that mess. I've got enough trouble as it is. I just don't want to … start … something …" I start crying again, drowning the words.

"It's all right, Ella. We can go to the police in the morning."

"That's what you think I should do?" I blubber. My nose is running and I can't wipe it. Mattie does it for me.

"I made the mistake of being quiet once, Ella. I paid a big price for that. I don't think you should make the same mistake."

Though Mattie holds me through the night, I do not sleep well. I'm not sure she ever closes her eyes. Her sadness is my sadness; my tears spill from her eyes. It is not just that my near-rape brings back the pain of our father's deeds. As we lie in bed, her arms around me and my feet intertwined with hers, we re-live it. The brutality. The shock. The pain. The shame. I realize Mattie and I have moved beyond mere empathy. The torment that flows in me flows through her too.

36

The receptionist at the Police Department takes my name. I catch her staring at the empty sleeves of my sweater. When I tell her I want to file charges for attempted rape, she corrects me. "Attempted sexual assault," she says. She seems perturbed that the crime does not fit into one of the neat boxes on her intake form, for she has to write it out.

"Where did this alleged incident happen?" she asks.

"Out in the woods, near Fox Creek. Maybe a mile west of Highway 481."

"Outside the city limits."

"What does that mean?"

"It's not within our jurisdiction. You'll have to file with the sheriff's office."

"Where's that?"

"One block east of the County Courthouse."

She picks up my complaint form and tosses it into a trash can.

"Couldn't you have waited to do that until after I left?"

"Oh, sorry," she says, and goes back to typing.

I glare at her for a time, wondering how long it has taken her to become so calloused to the misery of others. I might have expected this behavior from a man, but I thought all women shared some sort of kinship about these things. Instead, she treats me as if I am a panhandler.

Mattie puts her arm around my shoulder and escorts me outside. We cross the street and angle to the Sheriff's Department. I feel everyone staring at me, and not just because I am armless. They must know what happened in the woods. Somehow, they know.

The deputy in the Sheriff's Department is a young man who seems fresh from high school. His boyish face is deceiving. He is the opposite of the curt police receptionist, exhibiting only professionalism and sympathy for me. He listens to my story without interrupting, making notes on his spiral pad. Whenever I look at him, his face is appropriately solemn.

"Is there anything else you want to add at this point, Miss Winslow?"

"Not that I can think of."

"You sure?"

"Nothing else."

"Okay, then I've got some follow-up questions for you. You ready?" His pen is poised above the pad. "Have you ever seen any of these men before?"

"No."

"Are you certain of that?"

"I'm certain."

"Do you think you would recognize them again if you saw them?"

"I don't know. Maybe. The one who stopped the other two, I might recognize him."

"Do you know any of their names?"

"No, I don't."

"Ella, you mentioned one last night," Mattie interrupts. "You said one of the men called the other one Rick."

"That's right. The one who saved me, they called him Rick."

"Anything other than Rick? A last name maybe?"

"No, I'm sorry."

"Don't be sorry. You've been through a traumatic ordeal. Nonconsensual touching of your breast constitutes assault and battery. Two of your assailants are probably guilty of kidnapping, too.

"Okay."

"Now, I need to ask you some delicate things. If you don't want to answer anything, you just tell me. Okay?" His elbows are on the edge of his desk. His hands fiddle with his pen.

I nod.

"Was there any vaginal penetration?"

"No." I shake my head.

"Are you sure?"

"I'm … pretty sure. He stopped them before they could …" My chest begins to heave again.

"It's okay. Let me know if you need a minute."

I nod, take a deep breath to stave off any further crying. My recollection of what happened last night in the woods is muddled. I don't understand why.

"Was there any oral penetration?"

I think about that for a minute, replaying the events. The ripping of my t-shirt, the man's rough hands at the waistband of my leggings. "No."

"Any anal penetration?"

"No. No penetration. They just attempted. They didn't get very far because the one named Rick stopped them. He had been gathering firewood, and when he saw what the other two were doing, he shoved the drunk guy off of me."

"I understand." He taps his pen against his pad, then leans back in his chair. "This could be kind of tricky," he says.

"What do you mean?"

"It may be difficult to find the guys who did this. I mean, we don't have names, we have only sketchy physical descriptions, and you've already told me you might not be able to identify them because it was dark. This sounds like a one-shot deal. We haven't received any recent reports of anything like this, so we don't have a pattern of other crimes to help us."

"So what are you saying, that I shouldn't pursue this?"

"Not at all. What I'm saying is that you need to know what you're up against. Even if we do find these guys, the prosecution won't be easy. It's probably going to be just your word against theirs. You'll have to testify and go through it all again. Some women can't endure that."

"I can." The strident tone of my voice surprises me.

"It would be very helpful to have physical evidence," he says. "Assuming these guys have been arrested before, we might have their DNA on file."

I think about that. Have they done something criminal before? "I took a bath, but I still have my clothes. If that would be helpful."

"It might. It's not as easy to get DNA off clothes as the crime shows make it seem. And we would need blood samples from you and your sister, and anyone else in your household who might have touched your clothes."

I sense this is the fork in the road. I will have to give a blood sample. Mattie also. And so will my mother. The interview is no longer just about telling this officer what happened to me. It has become mildly invasive. He wants our blood. To rule our DNA out, I understand. But he may want to interview my mother, to learn what propelled me into the woods on a cold night. He is the church-key poised above the can of worms.

I remember my conversation with the Judge at the courthouse in Charlotte. My revelation of what I'd seen that night at the arena. The skepticism shining in his eyes, the doubt in the set of his mouth. The fact that, despite a nationwide manhunt, the terrorist has not been caught.

"How long do I have to file charges?" I ask.

He looks at me with surprise, his mouth turned down at the corners. "Three years," he says. "But evidence tends to disappear over time."

Mattie and I leave the Sheriff's office and wander outside, circling the court square a time or two. Then we sit down on a green, wooden bench. The day has grown warm. Mattie removes my sweater so that my sleeveless shirt is exposed, my armlessness now on full display. People bubble in and out of the courthouse likes ants in a mound. Some of them glance at me—a furtive peek at the disabled woman—but none will meet my eyes. I search the faces of the men in their 20s and 30s.

"Are you sure this is the way you want to go?" Mattie asks.

"What I can't do is file charges and wait and wait and wait while nothing happens."

The next day, with Mattie back in school, I resume my informal surveillance. I sit outside the diner and hardware store, figuring these places provide the best opportunity to spot the men if they come into town. Lots of hunters come from out of town to hunt deer in these forests. During deer season they stretch banners across the main drag welcoming the hunters, and just about every hardware store, gas station and convenience store offers deer corn for sale. The three motels in town fill up with hunters every weekend during deer season. Still, the odds of finding them aren't good.

I hope I can remember their faces, which I saw only by firelight. The menacing eyes—I might remember those, if I can get close enough.

I don't know how police do surveillance, but I find it difficult to be inconspicuous while looking for someone. I stare at faces long and hard when men pass by. I know by the smiles and frowns I get in return that some of them thoroughly misconstrue my intentions. Over the ensuing days, I endure the embarrassment of several false identifications. I never realized how many men wear flannel shirts, jeans and hunting caps. I am walking away from one such encounter when I bump into a man as he leaves the hardware store. I stumble, then right myself.

He doesn't say anything at first. The instant recognition closes his throat. He looks away, stifles a cough. It's him.

"Hello," I say as my mind races. "Remember me?"

"Sure," he says, looking at the ground.

I have not prepared for this. I try to find an approach that won't scare him off. "I'm Ella Winslow. Your name is Rick, right?"

He looks down at his scuffed hunting boots, then glances around to see if there is anyone else within earshot. "You're not going to make trouble for me, are you?"

"Trouble for you? No. You're the one who helped me. If I was going to make trouble for anybody, don't you think it would be the other two?"

"Okay," he says, but he still looks unsure.

"What's your last name?"

He is contemplating whether to tell me, perhaps weighing voluntary disclosure against the odds that I might figure it out anyway. "Lambert," he says finally.

"I went to high school with a Billy Lambert." I reach back into my memory and compare Billy Lambert with the two men who tried to rape me. No match. "You're not related to Billy, are you?"

"He's my older brother."

"How far apart?"

"Three years."

Rick would have been a freshman when I was a senior.

"Look I need to go," he says.

"Okay, okay. I just wanted to thank you for coming to my rescue. I don't know what they would have done to me if you hadn't been there. Well, I do know, and I appreciate you preventing that from happening."

"They're not bad guys, really. They were just drunk."

"One of them held a gun on me. The other one tried to rape me."

He says nothing.

"Being drunk isn't an excuse to assault someone."

"No it's not," he says.

"Do you still go hunting with them?"

"I haven't seen them since that night. They don't live around here, by the way."

"Have you been friends with them long?"

"Look, what are you after? Are you going to file charges or something?"

"I need your help. You're a witness."

"I'm sorry for what they did," he says. His tone is a combination of apology, sympathy and apprehension. He holds my eyes for two or three seconds, never looking down, then walks away.

"You're not the one who needs to apologize," I say to his back. "What if they do it to someone else?"

37

Six days after my encounter with Rick, I discover a white envelope stuck inside the screen on the front door of the house. My name is typed on the outside, but there are no addresses, and no stamp. I did not see the person who delivered it. I lay the envelope on Mattie's desk and cover it with other papers in hopes my mother won't find it. I would open it myself, but my toes are not dexterous enough to manage a letter opener and I, of course, am without a slitting fingernail.

I watch Mattie open the envelope when she gets home from school. There are three pages. The first is a typed letter from Rick Lambert, in which he says he is sorry for what happened, that the hunting trip was all his idea, and if they hadn't been out in the woods drinking that night, none of it would have happened. Even though he was the one who rescued me, he takes responsibility for what happened.

"My friends have written apologies, too," he writes. At the bottom is Rick's signature.

There are two other letters, one page each, both typed. The words in each are apologetic, but the tone is that of men who are sorry they got caught, not truly sorry about what they did. One explains he has a drinking problem and that he'd had a fifth of bourbon that night before turning to beer. The other says he'd had a rough week at work and was blowing off steam, and things got way out of hand.

I parse each letter, the words they use, trying to find meaning between the lines. I am unable to discern which one knelt on top of me and grabbed my breast, though I suspect it was the one with the drinking problem. The other one held a rifle on me. Their explanations are sterile, focused on their misguided reasons, rather than on the terror they instilled in me. Their apologies aren't signed.

"What are you going to do, Ella?"

"I don't know. As far as I can tell, there's no identifying information in here. I still don't know who the two thugs are."

"If you showed these to the deputy, maybe they could question Rick and he'd have to tell them. Or maybe they left fingerprints on the paper or something."

I try to forecast that process, how it would play out for me. How it would play out for Rick—the only one I can identify. The guy who threw another guy off of me and helped me escape through the woods. The thought of filing criminal charges revives a sense of power, but there is an undercurrent of something else, something that makes me shiver.

I nestle against Mattie's back during the night, but I cannot sleep. When I revealed to the Judge who I saw at the wheel of the delivery van, I did it in part to bring some justice to other victims. Thousands of them were under the illusion that the terrorist was dead. What I revealed would hurt nobody other than Volkov, who deserved the severest punishment imaginable. But my sexual assault has but one victim—me. And I can easily fathom, if not predict, the damage that could be inflicted on Rick if I were to pursue criminal charges.

The next morning, I sit once again across the desk from the deputy sheriff who interviewed me.

"Is there any update," I say.

"Well, Miss Winslow, without a filed complaint, we haven't started investigating. Is that something you want to do now—file a complaint."

"Let me ask you something. The guy who prevented the other two guys from going through with it, could he face charges, too?"

"Not sure. That would be up to the Solicitor." He peruses the notes in his spiral notebook. "If we can identify this guy Rick, and he won't cooperate, he could potentially be prosecuted for obstruction of justice."

The deputy studies me, tapping his pen on the blotter. "Do you know something you're not telling me Miss Winslow?"

"It's just … I don't want him to be prosecuted. I've spent a lot of time thinking about this over the past few weeks, and I don't think he's guilty of anything, other than choosing loser friends."

"This is a hard decision, Miss Winslow." He looks at me in a sympathetic way.

I start to get up from the chair in front of his desk, but think of another question. "Does the Sheriff's Department keep records of suicides?"

"Probably. Why?"

"My father committed suicide. Almost thirteen years ago."

"Last name Winslow?"

I nod. "John Winslow."

He taps some keys on his computer. "John Winslow, date of birth 10/26/65?"

"That's him."

"He had an arrest for DUI back in 1997," the deputy says as he scans his screen. "Pleaded out. Deferred adjudication, so he didn't serve time. Oh, here it is. Deceased by suicide 11-10-09."

"Is there a paper file?"

"No file number. So there wasn't an inquest. The coroner might have some records. A death certificate at least."

I catch myself gnawing my lower lip. "Hey, is suicide a crime in South Carolina?"

The deputy shakes his head. "Not suicide. But any person who assists someone in committing suicide is guilty of a felony."

"Okay." I get up to leave. The deputy eyes me, as if I have something important to tell him. "Thank you for your time," I say.

As I stand on the steps to the Sheriff's Office, my nerves are jangled because the deputy mentioned assisted suicide. In my darkest moments, in the early days after I woke up in the hospital, suicide had crossed my mind. It's not something I could have done on my own. I'd never thought about recruiting someone to assist, and even thinking about it now seems inane. I did not survive the bombing and Volkov's menace simply to turn around and do myself in, with or without help. I did not escape those men in the woods only to kill myself.

I run home from town, picking up the pace a little as I navigate the narrow strip of grass beside the highway. Sweat pours from me even though the air is cool. Once I crest the rise in front of our house, I feel refreshed, as if I have emerged from a long bout of fever.

38

At the cemetery where my father is buried. I barrel up the steep hill with legs churning and lungs gasping and collapse in a heap on the ground. His gravestone is the only one in the plot, with space left for three more.

Settling my back against his headstone, my father's grave suddenly seems like a sad place to be. The grass is matted and withered. The vase I used to fill with fresh flowers on holidays and his birthday is chipped and mottled with dirt. The gray granite gravestone lists his name, the date of his birth, the date of his death, and nothing more. Absent are phrases like "loving father" or "faithful husband," because my mother couldn't bring herself to honor him with platitudes. I am surprised she didn't cremate him, but perhaps something in her upbringing equates cremation to Hell's fires, and she couldn't go that far. Despite what he'd done, I guess she wasn't ready to banish him to eternal damnation.

From my perch on the hill, I see a few neighboring farms, laid out in a patchwork quilt of green pine forests and yellowed, dormant pastures. The roads are empty, save for a solitary vehicle whose presence I detect only from the plume of dust it spews behind. A hawk lights on a branch nearby, its wings barely fluttering as it lands.

My fury at what he did to Mattie is only slightly subdued. When I think of my father my teeth grind together, my jaw gets tight, and bitterness wells within. As I sit on his grave, my rancor rises in intensity like the whine of Volkov's bone saw. My father's unforgivable behavior and suicide have left us an empty family. We have lost something fundamental, something the three survivors have been unable to substitute for.

I stand up and kick his headstone with the toes of my shoes, then stomp on the place where I imagine his head would be. I jump up and down on his grave. For a few moments, I am a human pogo stick.

"How could you do this to us?" I shout loud enough to scare off the hawk.

Dr. Marvin says I have to forgive him. That I can't move on until I do that. Only recently have I told her that he molested Mattie. I will never forget how he whipped me savagely with a willow switch. More than once. Forgiveness seems unattainable. Dr. Marvin reminds me forgiveness is for me, not for him.

The indelible image of him hanging from a rope in the barn pushes to the forefront of my mind like a bully. The rope was made of unbleached hemp the color of straw. His neck was encircled by a hangman's noose, knotted six times. The other end of the rope had been thrown over a blackened rafter fifteen or so feet in the air, then tied off to a metal hook embedded in a post on the barn wall.

I remember some of this from thirteen years earlier. The rest is clear from the photographs the coroner recently showed me. The coroner didn't want to answer my questions, especially the one hardest for me to ask.

"Did he die instantly?"

The bearded coroner tilted his head down, then responded with his eyes peering above his steel-rimmed glasses.

"No," with a slight shake of his head.

"Can you explain that?"

He looked at me across the expanse of a metal desk, color photographs of the suicide scene arrayed before him. "Are you sure you want to know this? Sometimes it's better not to know the details."

"I'm sure."

He sighs, clearly reluctant to discuss a file that has been closed for more than a decade. Even for a relative.

"In most cases, when someone hangs themselves, the body weight pulling against the knot will separate the vertebrae in the person's neck, and they die instantly." He uses his finger to cull a photograph from the array. He holds it up for me to see. "In this case, the knot was positioned so that your father's neck didn't break. Instead, the knot constricted his carotid artery and strangled him." He points to the knot, positioned in front of my father's left ear.

"Strangled him?"

"Cut off the blood flow to his brain. He didn't die instantly. It would have taken a few minutes, I'm sorry to say."

"The Sheriff told me at the time he smelled alcohol on my father."

"We checked his blood. Routine. His blood-alcohol level was about double the legal limit if he'd been driving. He was drunk ma'am. And he had Oxycontin in his system. The good news is that the combination of alcohol and opiates would have suppressed pain. He probably didn't suffer."

Standing on top of his grave, peering down as if I can see through six feet of dirt and the lid of the metal coffin, I wonder if my father did suffer. Was he even conscious? If so, I suspect he felt something as he dangled from the rope. If not pain, maybe he felt fear of the inescapable end. He must have been consumed with guilt.

I can't stay here any longer. I tromp down the hill and, once on the flat, I pick up my pace and run over the bridge that spans the creek filled with dank water and down a sand road between towering pines, across the dormant field of milkweed, the butterflies long gone, wintering in Mexico. I reach a pace where the dopamine takes over and my breath becomes raspy and intense. Tears stream from my eyes. I keep going, through the woods on a path that doesn't really exist, weaving between pine trees on a bed of brown needles.

39

I am planted in the hallway of my mother's house, staring at the attic hatch, when Mattie comes home from school on a Thursday afternoon.

"What are you looking at?" she asks.

"I'm just wondering what all is still up there."

She settles a stack of papers on the desk in our room, then returns to the hall. "Let's find out." She pulls the chain and the door swings down. Then she unfolds the wooden stairs.

I wish for an attic like the ones in the movies, a grand space of treasures and heirlooms and mysteries. Our attic is cramped and not big enough to stand up in, with yellow insulation stuffed between the ceiling beams. The storage area itself is tiny, the boxes resting on splintered plywood, such that a misstep might send us plunging through the ceiling.

Mattie finds my old paintings leaning against a post, encased in garbage bags to keep the dust off. She pulls out a landscape I painted when I was fifteen, a depiction of our gravel drive leading off into a mist of pine trees. I study my work in the dim light of the attic bulb. It is an interesting rendering only because the cattle guard and the border fence are absent, as if I obliterated something that hemmed me in. Mattie sets the landscape aside and pulls out another painting.

"Oh, I remember this one," she says, holding up an unframed canvas, crisscrossed with slashes.

"How could anyone forget," I say.

It is my last painting, a portrait of my mother. I painted it a few months after my father hung himself in the barn. She could not sit patiently and kept turning her head to see what I was drawing. I worked hard to find the woman beneath that face. I studied her brow, the hollows beneath her eyes, the minute crevasses and shadows surrounding her lips. I detailed her philtrum— the depression between her nose and upper lip. I drew and redrew the slope of her nose. I knew even before she got up from the sitting that the portrait was only half-finished. Long after she had left me I stared at my mother's eyes on canvas, blank eyes from which I could not draw emotion. To me, her eyes looked like false rumors, with nothing on the other side. Over the course of the next few days, I repeatedly changed her eyes, painted and repainted them, always leaving them dark and vacant. In a state I could describe as either sleep-deprived or an out-of-mind experience, I finished the painting. In her left eye I painted the image of my father, handsome and robust. In her other eye I painted his limp, lifeless body, hanging from the hemp rope.

When I unveiled the finished portrait, she stared for a long time at the painting without comment. Her lips replicated the grim line I had captured on the portrait. Her real eyes seethed. "That's what you think of me?" she said finally.

Her tone flattened me. In my eighteen-year-old eyes, I thought I had captured all of her. I stammered a reply. "That's what I think you see most of the time."

"What do you mean by that?"

"You look right through us, Mattie and me. When you look at us, you only see him."

While I was at school, my mother took a knife to the portrait. She slashed the canvas in every direction. She left it shredded on the easel in my bedroom. When I came home from school and discovered she'd slashed the portrait, I said nothing to her. She had made her statement. The last word belonged to Rose, as it always did. I packed up the slashed portrait, and my paints and brushes and easel, and stashed them in the attic.

My fingers have not touched my brushes since.

From a moldering cardboard box in the attic, Mattie unearths our high-school yearbooks. The hard covers are purple, with gold ink. We sit on the plywood decking, Mattie and me, as she thumbs through the pages of my senior book. The photographs of long-haired cherubic teenagers remind me how much I have been through in the dozen years since graduation. My senior photo holds some innocence, though I am fairly certain I lost most of it the year before, when I'd stood in the barn trying to release my dead father from the hangman's noose.

In Mattie's senior book she scans rows of student portraits, tapping Rick Lambert's photograph with a bent index finger.

"That's him, right?" she says.

I bend my head to the page and study his photograph in the dim light. Of course, he's changed. His hair is shorter now. The angular features of his nose and cheeks have filled out. Yet, there's no doubt this boy became the man who saved me from being raped.

"What do you remember about him?" I ask.

"He played football. He was in 4-H, too." Mattie flips to the sports team photographs. Rick kneels on one knee in his football uniform on an emerald field, his hand poised on a purple helmet. The number 48, emblazoned on his jersey in gold, seems to cover his entire upper body. In the photograph of the 4-H club, Mattie stands on the left end of the front row, her hands cupped in front of a tan jumper. Rick Lambert is in the back, a broad smile showing perfect teeth. He is half a head taller than all the girls.

"Is he married?" I ask.

"I don't think so. I think he got married soon after high school, then divorced."

"Kids?"

"Not that I know of, but I haven't really kept up with him."

"You could check if you wanted to, right? To see if he has school-aged kids?" I assume Mattie has access to the files of all the kids in the district.

She leans away from me, slips her hands behind her on the ceiling joists. "Where is all this going?"

I don't look at her.

"Ella?"

"I'm just interested in finding out who he is. He wrote me an apology, and he got the other two guys to write apologies, too. I didn't ask him to do that."

It takes several days to compose the letter. I sit at Mattie's desk, speaking words into a foam-covered microphone. The software program garbles some of my words, so I correct them by angling my neck to tap my laptop keys with a glass stylus clenched between my teeth. After I re-read the letter, I wind up deleting whole sentences, entire paragraphs. In some sense, my complicated feelings for this man I barely know prove ineffable. I think of giving up, of taking the easy road. Dr. Marvin's words remind me I have to face the past to embrace the future. She believes I did so when I went to the Judge and told him I had seen Volkov at the wheel of the van that delivered the bomb. Even so, Volkov and his deeds are not fully behind me.

When I show Mattie the letter, she stares at me with my eyes. "You can't send this to him."

"I just want Rick to understand how much I appreciate what he did."

"You mean because he did what any normal-thinking man would have done?"

"Mattie, I don't know how to explain this. People aren't that predictable. Look at Volkov. A doctor sworn to do no harm killed thousands of people. Then he worked to save some of the survivors. Rick could have joined in with his buddies, but he didn't. That means something to me."

"So this is just a thank-you note?"

"I want him to know I respect him. He was very courageous."

"You were almost raped."

"Yes, and he stopped it."

Our verbal argument ceases but we continue with scowls, each of us straining to furrow our brows until our eyes become mere slits.

Even if I knew Rick Lambert's email address, that mode of communication seems an inferior medium for the sentiment I want to convey. I retrieve the Mont Blanc pen David gave me from the drawer of my bedside table. In a shop on the town square, I purchase ochre-colored stationery. With my toes I nudge the clear plastic cover from the box and inch an unblemished first page onto Mattie's desk. I take up the pen between the big toe and index toe of my right foot. I am unable to complete even the first sentence before I have to put the pen down and flex my cramping foot. I examine my work. The letters are of different sizes. The loops are irregular. In places, the ink is smeared. My scrawl is indecipherable.

I convince Mattie to pen the letter for me. Her left hand moves across the stationery with a fluid rhythm, the letters tight and bold. She writes in a script I could never manage, even when I had fingers. When she finishes, she sets the pen down and assumes the tight-lipped countenance of our mother in judgment.

"Read it back to me."

She does so, in a voice that soon loses its harshness. When I hear my own words, I begin to understand the cathartic effect composing this missive has brought to me.

"I was so scared," Mattie reads. "You can't possibly understand what it feels like to be that vulnerable. On the ground, with one man on top of me and the other pointing the barrel of his rifle at me. He was an infinite weight. I was trapped. Be raped or die. Those were my only two choices. Until you appeared."

When she finishes, I exhale from deep within.

Mattie stares at me for a moment. Her eyes are brighter. "How do you want to sign it?"

I conjure my toes stumbling across the page with a wobbling pen, ruining Mattie's penmanship, which almost has the look of calligraphy. "You do it for me," I say.

"Of course. But do you want me to put 'Sincerely,' or 'Very truly yours,' or what?"

I mull these options, but neither fits. One is too business-like; the other sounds like something I might have used in a letter to David. Even though I hold Rick in high esteem, "truly yours" goes too far.

"Just sign it Ella," I say.

40

Two days after I mail my letter to Rick, I am in the lobby of our post office. As I wait by the bronze boxes, I scan the cork bulletin board. I remember as a child staring open-mouthed at the wanted posters tacked here. Now, there are no posters of criminals wanted by the FBI.

Given my difficulty in opening our bronze box with a key between my teeth, the staff accommodates me and brings our mail to the counter. Today, there is nothing but bills and solicitations. The gray-haired woman at the counter stuffs a packet wrapped with a rubber band into my cranberry backpack.

"What happened to the wanted posters?" I ask.

"We haven't put those up for years. But we do have a binder. Not sure if it's kept up to date, though."

She scrabbles around behind the counter, searching in alcoves I cannot see. She finally produces a black binder with laminated pages. She flips it open on the counter. "Looking for anyone in particular?" she asks.

"No. Yes. Viktor Vidal." I spell it for her.

The first page is not him. The second one is. She turns the binder 180 degrees so I can see the poster. There are two recent head shots of him. In one he is clean-shaven, similar to the face I recall when he finally doffed his mask in my hospital room. The other photograph shows a bearded Vidal, the visage the same he had during our last meeting in his office. And the man I saw driving the van on August 9.

I read the summary description. He is wanted for Conspiracy to Kill U.S. Nationals; Conspiracy to Use Weapons of Mass Destruction Against U.S. Nationals. He was born in Russia. He is 56 years old. He is an American citizen. There is nothing about his suspected whereabouts. There is no information about the search the FBI has conducted.

Visiting the post office becomes a daily ritual for me. When I approach the counter, I no longer ask to see the binder of wanted posters. Two weeks go by, then three, with no mail from Rick. Several times each day I check for an envelope inside our screen door.

"I'll bet he's stunned," I explain to Mattie. "He just doesn't know how to respond."

Mattie's explanation is simple and pragmatic. "Nothing is expected to follow a thank-you note."

"That was more than just a thank-you note."

After three weeks without a response from Rick, I ask Mattie to pen a second letter. She does so with minimal resistance.

Dear Rick,

I'm sorry if my letter surprised you. That was not my intention. This whole experience has been an emotional roller coaster for me. Since the bombing, I haven't encountered anyone who has been willing to see me as a person. You do. You showed that with what you did out in the forest that night. I appreciate that more than you know. Please write me back.

Ella

Rick finally responds, via email. It has been almost three months since my assault, and 31 days since I sent him my first, purging letter.

> Sorry for not responding sooner. I've been out of town a lot lately. I meant to write before now. I'm glad I was there that night in the woods. I don't really know what would have happened, but I'm glad you've gotten past it. Best of luck.
>
> Rick

I show the email to Mattie. After reading it over my shoulder, she shrugs. "I guess that's the end of it, then."

"I need to see him again," I say.

"Why?"

"I don't know. I just do."

"Ella, are you sure you're not taking this too far?"

"Maybe."

"I don't want you to get hurt."

"Nothing can hurt me more than I already have been."

Alone in our bedroom at night, Mattie and I talk about Rick. We are aware that voices carry far in a cramped house with wooden floors, so we whisper beneath the covers. Is Rick a responsible person? Is he gentle? Would he be a good father? Would he be good in bed?

Without Mattie's knowledge, I draft an email to Rick naming a time we can meet at a café across from the courthouse. Before I send it, a twinge of guilt causes me to open David's final email to me. David's words are less mysterious than when I read them that first time at work, months after he proposed to me. I have read David's hand-written letters so many times I've left toe smudges on the stationery. Even so, I still don't remember much about David. We must have been passionate about our relationship. About our future. I know we must have been elated at the prospect of starting a family together. Even though the memories of this short romance aren't there, I want that again.

I send Rick the email.

I sit at a window table at the café half an hour before I expect Rick to show. Through a glass straw, I sip a double latte the barista has poured into my insulated cup. The day has turned gray and cold. I watch pedestrians scurrying along the sidewalk, some wearing scarves, others clenching their coats to their necks, leaning into the stiff breeze.

I am wearing black wool tights and a running top whose sleeves my mother has stitched closed on the ancient Singer we found in the attic. I'm also wearing a sleeveless down jacket in canary yellow. My mother's arthritic hands were barely able to complete the task of altering my blouses and shirts to fit an armless woman, but she persevered. She did a nice job, though the shirts hang loosely on my gaunt frame.

It's not her fault. In the last six months, I have lost another five pounds. I attribute my weight loss to all the running I've been doing and my distaste for the laborious task of feeding myself with my feet. I suspect, however, there's a medical reason I'm losing weight. It probably has something to do with my liver. I eye my reflection in the café window and see hollow cheeks and a flaxen complexion.

I watch the café clock tick past 4 p.m., the suggested time of our rendezvous. No sign of Rick. I drink the last of my coffee, which has grown tepid. I start to feel jittery. I'm uncertain whether this is from the surge of caffeine or the growing realization that I've been stood up. At 4:45 I go to the counter, which is staffed by a girl of high-school age who has a case of uncontrolled acne dotting her cheeks.

"Can you put my cup in the mesh pocket and help me put on my backpack?"

"Sure," she says. She follows me back to my table.

When my backpack is strapped on, I tell her to take the $5 bill in the top zippered pocket as a tip.

"I've been waiting for somebody," I say over my shoulder. "I guess he got held up. But if he comes by later, please tell him Ella waited for him for almost an hour. He's tall, with dark hair. His name is Rick."

Leaving this message makes the situation seem less embarrassing, as if Rick got caught up in something important and his failure to show is supported by a reasonable explanation.

I run home in a de-energized state. My stomach feels hollow and full of acid. I'm trying to shake off the sting of Rick's rudeness. If he wasn't going to come, he could have at least let me know. I realize as I'm trudging up our gravel drive that he doesn't have my cell phone number. I burst through the front door and hustle through the living room to my bedroom to check my laptop. No email from Rick.

I bear this frustration alone, for I have not told Mattie or my mother that I was supposed to meet Rick this afternoon. Mattie thinks I have accepted Rick's email as our final communication. As I curl up against her in bed, it is all I can do to refrain from telling her the truth.

I have erotic dreams about Rick. Vivid dreams of entangled legs and naked torsos and kissing and licking and rising passion. These are dreams

I don't tell Mattie about. It has been a long time since I've had erotic dreams. I don't fight them. On the contrary, I encourage the dreams with late-night snacks that include jalapeno peppers and other food that stirs my stomach. These dreams awaken something in me. Something that has been asleep during the involuntary celibacy I have endured since the bombing almost eighteen months ago.

One morning I stay in bed long after Mattie leaves for school, and I listen for a time to ensure Rose has left the house, too. A Rick dream is still fresh within me. In this dream, I had arms and hands and I wrapped both around him. I can still feel the goosebumps on my skin.

I have contemplated often the manner in which such a thing can be done. All the possibilities seem to require hands. With my feet I slide my right arm from beneath the bed and lift it to the sheet. I roll over on my stomach, and position the hand so the rigid rubber fingers press against me through the fabric of my panties. I recognize the irony of it, this plastic appendage I never think of as my own flesh, snug between my legs. But it is Rick's hand there, and the momentum of lust soon takes over. His attention is solely on me, and his fingers work magic. Almost before I start, I discover myself sputtering and wheezing into the pillow, trying to recover from the surging wash.

I feel blissfully relaxed, then greedy. I do it again, slower this time. It is still Rick's face I see. We are at the edge of a pine forest. Monarchs dance around us, their fluttering wings matching our synchronized movements. This time lasts longer, tingles almost indefinitely. When I am through, I roll onto my back and nudge the arm gently to the floor. I fall asleep and awaken to Rose's footfalls in the hall.

41

Mattie has been eating dinner out lately.

One night, as she's slipping pink pajama bottoms over my legs, I ask her about it.

"Are you not eating with us because watching me eat with my feet, dropping food on the table and all over myself, disgusts you?"

"No, it's not that. Not at all, Ella. Just having dinner with friends."

"Friends …" A thought strikes me. "I wonder if I should invite Rick over for dinner, show him that I can cook a meal. What do you think?"

She stops buttoning my pajama top. "I thought that was over, Ella."

"I haven't met anybody since David," I say. "I can't just huddle in this bedroom while the world passes me by. Look at me. How many more opportunities do you think I might get?"

She sighs, wipes my face with a damp cloth. She sweeps a brush through my hair, which descends just below my shoulders now. My lustrous mahogany hair frames my face and covers the faint scars on my forehead. I admit that having or not having hair shouldn't change me. But it does. Or at least my confidence in myself.

Mattie tries to tug the brush through a tangle.

"Ouch," I say. My left hand makes a phantom move toward my scalp.

"Sorry." She puts the brush down and studies me in the mirror.

"What's the matter?" I ask.

"Nothing."

I can tell she wants to say something more, but she remains quiet as we crawl into bed.

"Rick is really handsome, don't you think?" I say, snuggling up to her back.

She wiggles her body in response.

"All right, I know you've got school tomorrow, so I'll let you get some sleep. We can talk about this in the morning."

I lie awake most of the night, making plans. If I approach Rick in person, he's less likely to ignore my dinner invitation, I conclude. I think about what to cook. Something I can manage. Perhaps steak on the grill. He raises cattle, so he has to like steak. I'll need to practice turning the steak with a fork between my toes. Or, I could have him grill the steak while I cook vegetables and heat up some sourdough rolls. I should buy some beer. I wonder what kind he likes. And I'll have to make sure Mattie and my mother are out of the house.

When I wake the next morning to sunlight streaming through our window, Mattie has already left for school. I have a fuzzy, sleep-deprived feeling in my body. I step to the dressing table and plop down on the upholstered stool in front of the mirror to get a better look at myself.

There are unfolded pages lined up on the dressing table. Mattie has laid out my letters to Rick, the ones I sent and the ones I didn't. I begin to read the pages, some of the words disappearing in the folds.

"Dear Mattie:" … "My dearest Rick," … "I long to" … "Love, your special one" … "Love, Rick."

These are not my letters. I try to blink the words away, as if I'm in the middle of a dream whose outcome I can alter. My heart is beating at the speed of a hummingbird's wings. To take a Paxil would require my mother's assistance. I'm not going to ask her. Not yet.

I calm myself enough to read the letters again, slowly this time. I am the mother reading for the fifteenth time the last letter she received from her soldier son. She knows he is dead, but in the re-reading there is some vague and distant hope for his resuscitation, or the belief that someone might have misidentified the body.

The letters are undated, but there is no way to misread this evidence. When I finish, I bend my neck, snatch a page between my teeth and try to shred it, shaking my head vigorously. I jump up and down. My feet thud on the oak floor. I wail for the death of a fledgling relationship and the culmination of a lifetime of shit.

At the noise, my mother comes to the door. "Ella, what's the matter?"

"I need a Paxil. Please."

When Mattie returns from school, it is almost dusk. I note she's an hour later than usual. And I know why. I'm standing at her driver's door when she cuts the ignition. She eyes me through the glass, obviously girding for this confrontation. She finally opens the door and sidles out.

"How could you?" My voice is loud enough to carry across our misty fields.

She says nothing, but wraps her arms around me from behind and interlocks her hands in the middle of my chest.

I buck against her restraint. "No, no, no, no, no. You can't do this."

She remains silent, just holds onto me.

I knock her with the side of my head and kick her shins like a donkey. She proves a stolid post and takes the brunt of all of me. When I am completely worn out, she unlocks her hands and strokes the back of my head.

"I'm sorry," she says. "I didn't know how else to tell you."

I shake away from her and stomp down the gravel drive. I don't feel the sting of the rocks on my bare feet. I veer down the fence line toward the creek. A murder of crows in the oak trees mock me. I scream at them until they fly off.

Mattie follows me at some distance. I guess she is afraid of what I might do to myself. After I settle onto one of the rocks that overlooks the creek, she comes down to the edge of the water. She stops a few feet away.

"How long?" I ask.

"Since the beginning."

"Since I wrote the first letter?"

She folds her arms across her chest. "Right after he got it, he came to the school one afternoon. I talked to him in the parking lot. He asked me to please make you stop writing to him. I think he was afraid you were going to file the assault charges or something. He just wanted it to be over."

"What did you tell him?"

She digs the toe of her shoe in the dirt. "I told him I couldn't stop you from contacting him."

"But he wrote me back. He sent that email to me."

"We both wrote it," Mattie says.

I think about this. She and Rick were together some place, constructing the language of an email designed to stop me from pestering Rick.

"Did you know I invited him for coffee at the café?"

She's looking across the water of the creek. "He told me."

"Do you know why he didn't show?"

"We agreed if he went it would only encourage you. I didn't want you to get hurt. Neither of us did."

This is only part of the story. Mattie's perfidy goes much deeper. "So the whole time I was trying to get him interested in me, you weren't just dissuading him, you were plotting to steal him away from me?"

"It wasn't like that, Ella. I was trying to protect you, and then it became something else. I didn't want it to happen this way."

"You didn't? So what happened that you and Rick suddenly fell in love?"

She turns to face me now. "I don't really know. I mean, I knew him when we were both in 4-H. We just got to talking after school. One thing led to another. He's a really nice, guy Ella. Don't I deserve that?"

This throws a switch. I swallow the biting remark forming in my throat and opt for something else. "You're in love with him."

She nods two or three times, looking down.

"Why didn't you tell me before?"

"I wanted to protect you."

This is the umpteenth time I've heard this explanation from Mattie, or my mother, or Dr. Marvin. Though it might be true, it doesn't take away the sting.

"Does mama know?" I ask.

Mattie nods her head again.

"How long?"

"She found the letters a few days ago."

"She didn't say anything to me."

"I asked her not to," Mattie says.

That explains the look my mother gave me this morning, as she was holding the Paxil in front of my mouth, with her hand trembling. She knew Mattie and Rick had started a romantic relationship. In her twisted way, maybe she was trying to express sympathy. As I stare at Mattie, her outline barely visible in the gloaming, it strikes me that in the wake of her selfish betrayal, my mother is all I have to hold onto.

42

During the next few weeks, I wander like a boat ripped from its mooring. I sleep on the sofa in the living room, which disrupts our family dynamic in countless ways. This is my attempt to distance myself from Mattie. I take my meals at odd times so that I am rarely in the house when she is there. Truth is, she's been spending a lot of time somewhere else. I have my suspicions.

On a mid-week afternoon when Mattie should be in her classroom grading papers or preparing tomorrow's lesson plan, I don my running shoes and head to the high school. Mattie's car is not in the teacher parking lot, so I go to the visitors' desk inside.

"Hi, I'm Ella Winslow. I was just wondering if my sister Mattie is still in her classroom."

A volunteer with a white bouffant checks a register under the counter. "No, she's already left for the day."

I spin on my heels and head out. The temperature is comfortable, and I soon find a steady pace as I traverse the narrow shoulder on the edge of the pavement. I have to dodge a wide mirror on a pickup truck whose driver veers too close to the solid white line. He seems engrossed in his phone and doesn't notice me.

From town, which is built on the banks of the broad creek that also winds through our property, the terrain rises a hundred or two hundred feet in a series of rolling hills. I climb these hills as I churn toward a destination where I feel all but certain I will find my sister.

I cover almost six miles before I turn onto the farm-to-market road whose asphalt is pocked from the burden of heavily laden trucks. Over the next rise, I see it. A white farmhouse sitting on a bare knoll, not a single tree concealing it. The house has a green metal roof covering its sprawl.

Near the front door sits Mattie's tan Honda. Next to it is a gray pickup truck I recognize. This is Rick's house.

The anger and resentment have been building since the morning Mattie left their love letters for me to find. My confrontation when she returned to the house that afternoon only left me wanting more. My venom is not yet spent.

Dr. Marvin often tells me that under stress people will either fight, freeze or flee. Were I an able-bodied woman, this might be the moment I storm the farmhouse with my father's shotgun in hand and end three lives. But that's where my reality finds its boundaries. I am not able-bodied. I cannot exact vengeance in the way most people can.

Freezing is not an option for me. I have done that a few times, usually with disastrous consequences. I froze when my father committed suicide. I froze when Robert became cold and distant. I froze in the face of Mattie's treachery. Now she has Rick. I have no one.

So I flee. Down the country road weaving between the trees beneath a full moon that lights my way like I am on a track under stadium lights. As I run, the green eyes of small animals peer at me from roadside ditches. A buck watches my approach from a dip in the road, his majestic antlers rising above his head like a regal crown, until the slap of my footfalls reach him and he leaps the ditch and into the woods. As if I, without hands to hold a rifle or a shotgun or a bow, am somehow a threat to him.

There is a boldness building within me as I plunge headlong into the night. Maybe it's merely recklessness, but I have a sense that my lifetime allotment of tragedy has expired. I'm not sure what can be done to me that has not already been inflicted. Fear evaporates before it can form. I move with an effortless gait through the countryside as dew begins to build on the pasture grasses and roosters start to crow even before the sun's first rays crest the horizon.

The slip-slap of my running shoes echoes off trees shrouded in fog. My breath is even, just beneath labored. My leg muscles have found a rhythm such that the movement seems so natural I may not be able to stop. This is where I find my peace. An undefined space, neither inside me nor without. Maybe the only place.

My backpack bouncing against my shoulders reminds me that I am almost out of water. I run into town. We still have outdoor water fountains on the courthouse square, and I fill my camel back at one whose stainless-steel bowl looks clean. I take a long drink through the curving plastic tube whose tip is always poised near my mouth. I look around. I am not ready to go home.

My body, or something inside, continues to demand motion. I walk briskly past storefronts on empty sidewalks. The drug store is closed. The coffee shop where I was supposed to meet Rick is open, with a smattering of early customers. This place now holds a bitter taste for me, so I don't go in.

In the middle of a block of brick buildings that have been turned into offices for lawyers and accountants and other professionals, a woman unlocks the deadbolt on her front door. I recognize her and stop.

"Belinda Nunez?" I say.

She turns toward me with the momentary shock of someone who thought they were alone. "Ella," she says too loudly, as if I've lost my hearing. "Wow, it's been a long time." She tilts backward and sizes me up. She lets the door swing shut, then puts her hands on my shoulders and shakes me. "So, how are you?"

"I'm great," I say.

"That's wonderful to hear. What are you doing in town? Are you living here now?"

"Yep. Same place. How about you?"

"I've been back for about three months now. This is my office," she says, pointing to the gold lettering with CPA at the end.

"Are you married?"

"Divorced," she says. "That's why I moved back. And you?"

"Divorced, too."

"Really?" She says this as if she's found a kindred sister. "Men are the worst, aren't they?"

"Women are sometimes too," I say, referring to my sister. Belinda doesn't understand, and I don't offer to explain.

"Hey, we should get together for a drink."

"I don't drink. Well I don't drink alcohol. It's a liver thing."

"Well, coffee then. After tax season is over," she says.

She puts her finger to her lips, obviously pondering whether to ask me something.

"I heard you were injured. I should have called you, Ella. Or something. I just didn't know what to say."

I shrug. "Nobody does."

"You lost your arms."

"Yes. They were amputated by a doctor who …" I am teetering between finishing this sentence with: "saved my life" or "killed thousands of people." I do neither.

"Do you have someone to help you? I mean, it must be …"

In initial encounters with me, most people stumble over their words when they ask about my injuries, or how I accomplish life's simplest tasks. They usually try to express sympathy without slipping down the road to pity. Sometimes they stop in mid-sentence.

"I can do most things with my feet. I feed myself and bathe myself. My mother helps me a lot. Sometimes it's hard to get dressed."

"You eat with your feet? That's cool."

"Cool? You think it's cool?"

"Hey, you've learned to get by. So you're a little different. Do you really want to be like everybody else?"

"Every single day."

Belinda and I meet at the Townhouse restaurant for dinner on the Friday night after April 15. It is the first time I have been out to a restaurant since the night of the bombing, 20 months ago. Mama buys me a new dress, with long sleeves, and takes me down to her beauty parlor so I can have my hair done and get a pedicure. I feel like I'm getting ready for prom. I wear sandals because it's easier to slip them on and off. My toes do look fabulous. The arms dangle like broken limbs after an ice storm.

With two margaritas in her, Belinda tells me about her divorce.

"He cheated on me with four or five different women," Belinda says. "All younger and thinner versions of me. After the second or third one, I don't remember which. I started cheating on him."

"Younger and thinner versions of him?"

She takes a long sip of her margarita and dabs froth from her upper lip with a napkin. "Hell, no. He was an egotistical corporate lawyer without an ounce of tenderness. I went for the opposite. First, I had an affair with an artist. That lasted about six months, until he came to me to pay his rent. I got rid of him. Then I had a brief, but very torrid affair, with a personal trainer from my gym." She points an index finger at me. "That's the guy you really want if it's just for sex."

Our food arrives. I've ordered a vegetable plate, and the waiter offloads small dishes of carrots, lima beans, and corn, plus a larger dish of apple sauce. All things I can eat with a spoon.

The waiter sets a huge chef salad in front of Belinda. She adds some vinaigrette from a plastic cup on the side, then rakes it in with her fork.

"Are you going to feed yourself, or do you want me to help?" Belinda asks.

Even though I've been feeding myself for the better part of a year, my technique has flaws. When I'm done with a meal, my place at the table is often littered with food. At home I wear a plastic bib because some portion of my meal usually winds up on my shirt front.

"Are you sure you're willing to feed me?"

She shrugs. "Why not?" She moves her chair next to me. With the spoon in her right hand, we quickly develop a smooth rhythm. Before long, all of my dishes are empty, which rarely happens because I usually quit in frustration before the meal is done.

I sip tea from a glass straw while she digs into her salad.

Afterward, Belinda and I sit in front of my house in her Tesla, listening to music. We talk about the cruelties of our ex-husbands and the dark places both of us have been.

"Throwing myself into work ultimately got me through the divorce," she says.

"I did the same thing. Do you like being a CPA?"

"Yeah. It's been good to me. Numbers are refreshing," she says. "They never lie, unless the people who record them do. I used a spreadsheet to keep track of all the times my husband cheated on me. Fifty-two times in eight years, that I know of."

"That seems like a lot."

"Those are just the times I was able to trace his credit card receipts or unusual cash withdrawals that I couldn't support with marital or home purchases. It was probably more." She stares off through the windshield. "You know, I did everything I could to keep him at home. God, listen to this. I can't even believe I'm telling you this." She grips the steering wheel and giggles her way into courage. "One time I confronted him, and I said, 'Look, if you're going to keep this up, just bring her home, and we'll have a threesome'."

"Did you go through with it?"

"No. I might have, but he chickened out. Can you believe I was that desperate?"

"You wanted to hold onto something," I say. "I truly understand that." I am thinking of David, his arm stretching across the driveway for me. If I had reached up and grabbed his hand, he would have pulled me up from the walk, tugged me from behind the brick wall. I would have vanished with him.

"Yeah, but it's still sad," she says. "I really surprised myself by how low I would go. I even thought of killing myself. It was during the worst part of our marriage, before I filed for divorce. I just wanted that SOB to come home and find me swinging from the ceiling fan in the den. I couldn't find any rope anywhere, so I started pulling all the laces out of his shoes. By the time I got 'em all out, I was too tired to tie them together."

I look at her in the darkness of the car. "Do you think you would have really done it?"

"No. I just wanted him to notice me, that's all."

"Yeah, I understand that," I say.

It is well after midnight when I go inside. My mother has left the door unlocked for me. Mattie is still out. I bet I know where. I struggle to undress myself but give up after a few minutes of fumbling the buttons with my toes. I push my mother's door open with my hip and go into her bedroom.

"Mama?" I say softly.

"I'm awake."

"Can you help me get undressed?"

She sits upright on the edge of her bed and turns on the table lamp. Then she unbuttons my dress and helps me slip into my pajamas.

"How was your night?"

"We had a good time. I forgot how much fun it can be to go out with a friend. And Belinda fed me so I didn't have to do it myself."

"Good. Go to bed now." She coughs, deep and wracking.

"Mama, are you okay?"

She wipes her mouth with her sleeve. There is a smear of blood on her nightgown. "Mama, you're coughing up blood."

She eyes me for a few seconds, then gazes off in the distance. "I know."

"How long has this been going on?"

"Three or four weeks."

"Three or four weeks? Have you been to the doctor?"

"Yes, I went to the doctor." Her voice is wet and thick.

"And?"

"You know what it is, Ella. I knew before the doctor told me."

"Lung cancer?" I ask.

She nods. "Stage 4. Four B. No surprise to me. I've been smoking since I was fifteen."

"That means …" I sit there with my mouth agape, trying to sort the ramifications.

"It's spread. Pretty much everywhere."

I climb into bed with her and listen to her breathing. The wet, blood-filled draw of breath by lungs that can barely inflate. I realize now that my lifetime allotment of tragedy has not run out. The latest tragedy is my mother. The person on whom I have come to rely to do the things impossible for an armless woman to accomplish. I stay with her until she goes to sleep.

Back in my bedroom, Mattie is still absent. I sit on the floor and slide my mother's portrait from beneath my bed. I study the painting, slashed through her face and eyes. I almost expect to see blood oozing from these wounds. I finally push the painting back under the bed. I vow to throw it in the trash tomorrow.

43

In the morning, Mattie is not in the bed next to me. I need to tell her about mama's cancer. We need to discuss how to care for her. My phone is on the nightstand. I command it to call Mattie. I hear the ringing through the speaker phone, and a millisecond later another ringing. I follow the sound into the kitchen, where Mattie is standing with a cup of coffee in her right hand. She is wearing jeans and a white blouse. The same outfit she was wearing when she left the house last night. Her phone is on the counter. With her left hand she taps a button on her phone. The ringing stops. She appraises me as if I am the one who didn't come home last night.

And then I see it. On her left hand. A sparkling diamond.

"You got engaged?"

"Rick asked me last night."

"That was fast."

She doesn't move from the counter. The ten feet between us serve as a meager buffer. "No faster than you and David. I guess you get to a certain point, and you just know." Her face is aglow, her eyes brighter than I've seen them in a long time.

"Mama has lung cancer," I announce. I watch the air hiss out of Mattie's jubilation.

"What?"

"She told me last night. It's bad."

My mother shuffles into the kitchen, wiping her mouth with a damp washcloth. She stops by the table, observes the looks on both our faces. She turns to me. "You told her, I guess." Her voice, deeper and more gravelly than usual, struggles to get out.

"Yes, mama." I rise and scoot her usual chair from beneath the table with my left foot.

Mattie helps her sit, even though our mother has not yet weakened enough to require assistance. Mattie pours coffee into mama's favorite mug. Her right hand doesn't leave mama's shoulder.

"Lung cancer?" Mattie asks. She gulps, like this is an unfathomable diagnosis.

"Stage 4B."

"Okay."

"Metastasized." Mama stumbles over the word. "Spread into my other organs."

"When did you find out, mama?"

"Couple of weeks ago."

"Why didn't you tell us?" Mattie asks.

She shrugs. "What difference would it make?"

"We can help you. Take you to treatments. All that." Mattie looks at me for cooperation.

Mama takes a sip of coffee, sputtering a bit when she swallows. "I've decided not to get treatment."

Mattie starts to protest, but my mother holds up her left palm.

"It's everywhere," she says. "Treatment might get me a couple more months, but it would be miserable. I'd have to spend too much time at the hospital. Too much time away from you girls. I'd lose all my hair and be throwing up all the time," she says. "I don't want that."

I'm not surprised. Lying awake in bed, I had a few hours to absorb my mother's diagnosis. Without meaning to sound detached, I have reached a tenuous state of acceptance. I know all too well her feeling of helplessness. I know too well the futility of denial.

Mattie leans in toward mama. Her eyes are brimming with tears. "You have to fight."

My mother's head swings back and forth, her eyes downcast. "This is how I want it." She swipes her damp washcloth across Mattie's cheeks, then sweeps Mattie's bangs from her forehead. "Now show me that ring."

With tears running down her cheeks, Mattie stretches her fingers out before us.

From a few feet away, I study her diamond. It is smaller than the engagement ring David gave me. I'm almost certain. My sole reference for comparison is the photograph I sent to Mattie.

"It's beautiful, Mattie. Have you set a date?" mama asks.

"Not yet. Rick just proposed last night. I haven't even started thinking about a wedding date. Discovering that you're sick, I just don't know."

Mama coughs. When she pulls the washcloth from her mouth, it's speckled with blood.

In the ensuing days, after making sure my mother is comfortable in her recliner and that the television is tuned to the right station, I retreat to the vegetable garden Mattie planted. I sit between the rows, trying to pull milkweed with a contraption that's supposed to get the whole root. Most of the time the root simply breaks a few inches below the soil. As I'm maneuvering the tines into the dirt, a dun-colored cottontail approaches the chicken-wire fence surrounding our garden. The fence is two feet high, low enough for me to step over. The rabbit pauses on the outside, surveying our lush vegetables. With little effort, it hops the fence.

"Hey, get out of here," I shout.

The rabbit freezes next to a row of carrots with lush leaves.

Only when I drop the weed puller and stomp toward the cottontail does it run back to the fence, leap over, and scurry away.

"The rabbits are about to eat up the whole garden," I announce at lunch.

Mattie doesn't respond. Her eyes are glued to a bridal magazine. "Do you like this dress?" she points.

"What are we going to do about the rabbits?"

"The rabbits?"

"They're eating our garden to the nubs."

She turns toward our mother, then looks back at me with exasperation. "Ella, with all that's going on—the wedding, mama's cancer—you're worried about rabbits eating a few vegetables?"

For the first time since the bombing, I can worry about things like rabbits. When it might rain. How much fertilizer to use on the radishes. Whether the car needs an oil change. How many calves our cows might produce this summer. I have yearned for this. Something that approaches normal.

I see from her open mouth that Mattie is eager to escape it.

I accompany my mother and sister to a bridal shop on a Saturday afternoon. Mattie selects a white gown with a flowing train, similar to one she has seen in a magazine. It is an expensive dress, but it is the only wedding my mother will ever help plan, so despite its price tag she eagerly hands the woman behind the cash register her credit card.

I watch the seamstress gather the gown and delicately insert the pins so they do not prick my sister's skin. The seamstress doesn't realize how thick my sister's skin actually is. She gathers the bodice, then the hem that looks a bit like the gauzy silk of a monarch's cocoon.

Once the seamstress has measured Mattie and my mother, she turns her attention to me.

"I think your dress will be sleeveless," she says after a thorough examination.

"She's going to wear artificial limbs," Mattie says.

"No, I'm not." I say this with conviction, even though I haven't completely decided.

"Then how will you hold a bouquet?"

"Not with fake hands, that's for sure."

Mattie starts to retort, but my mother puts her hand on my sister's shoulder.

For a moment, I ponder whether I even want to be part of a wedding in which my sister will marry the man I once pursued. Whether I want to stand next to her during the ceremony. Then my eyes land on my mother, sitting in an upholstered chair of red velvet. Her face exudes exhaustion. She wants nothing else out of life than to see one of her daughters walk down the aisle.

I turn toward my sister. "I'll wear the arms if that's what you want."

The rabbits continue to prove pesky. While Mattie is at school, my mother and I drive to the feed store in the dilapidated gray farm truck.

"What's the best way to get rid of rabbits?" I ask the man behind the counter.

"Poison them. It's the only way." His lower lip protrudes, packed with snuff.

"What about a repellant, or something?"

"We carry a repellant for deer and rabbits, but the first rain will wash it away. It doesn't work anyway."

"What if I trap them and take them off somewhere?"

"They'll probably come back. Poison's over there," he points to an aisle nearby.

My mother and I find the poison. There's a picture of a grayish-brown rabbit on the label, with a bold red circle surrounding the animal, and a slash through its body. I look at my mother.

"I don't want to kill the rabbits," I say. "I just can't."

She nods in understanding. "Let's get a couple of traps, then."

I'm not sure why my mother joins me in the fight against the rabbits. Of course, I can't set the traps alone. I suspect the work takes her mind off her disease. She's not the type to dwell on it. Not the type to talk about her misery.

We bait two metal cage traps with carrots and food scraps. If effective, these traps will capture rabbits, but not kill them. We'll have to take them somewhere and set them free.

In the morning, just after sunrise, I coax my mother from bed. She rises with bone-tired weariness. A gray pallor has taken over her skin—the result of failing lungs that struggle to provide oxygen. When she trudges to the living room, her chest wracks with a wheezing cough. She looks out the front window at the fog in the fields and rubs her hands up and down her arms. She wraps herself in a long coat our father once wore.

On our walk to the garden, our lower pants legs become wet with dew. She stops for a moment to catch a breath, leans against the side of the barn with one hand on her chest. She rests there for a minute, maybe two. She looks back at the house, then at the weathered boards of the barn.

"Once I'm gone," she says in a rasp I can barely discern, "tear this damned barn down." Then she pulls out a cigarette from the pack in her coat pocket and lights up. She takes a long drag and spews a cloud of smoke, followed by a sputtering cough she tries to cover with her coat sleeve. She takes another puff, then drops the cigarette in the dirt and grinds it with her boot heel.

I stoop to peer into a metal trap and discover a frightened cottontail's black eyes looking back at me furtively through the wire of the cage. The second trap also has a rabbit occupant.

With a grunt my mother lifts each trap into the bed of our farm truck. In the process, she wheezes like she's breathing through a wet sack. With steady hands and a fixed gaze, she drives us several miles to the state forest, navigating past the tables where our family used to have Sunday afternoon picnics. Back when we were a family.

She stops at a pullout where a trail begins, the dirt rutted with vehicle tires. On the weekends, hikers and bikers fill these woods. Today, the forest is mostly ours.

She fumbles the traps out of the pickup and sets them next to the trail. Then she pulls up the u-shaped catch that secures the metal door. The first cottontail hops a few feet into the underbrush, then freezes, staring at us as if trying to memorize our faces. The second rabbit, frightened by the clang of metal against metal, scurries into the forest.

After our excursion, my mother has to spend three days in the hospital because she can't stop coughing up blood. I stay at her bedside from morning until night. As I watch her sleeping beneath a clear plastic mask that fogs with each breath, I remind myself she stood guard over me when I was in a coma for five days.

On day three, her eyes blink open and she sees me sitting next to the bed. At first there is a startled look on her face. Perhaps she has been expecting that Mattie would be here. With a wiggle of her fingers she beckons me closer. She lifts the mask from her face and says in a voice only slightly cleared of coarseness, "Mattie needs to have her wedding ASAP."

From her face and dark eyes that look past me, I see that she knows. Maybe she doesn't know the exact day she will pass, but she knows that day is coming. Imminently. She wants it to be over, but not before she can hear Mattie say her vows.

Home from the hospital, mama exists in a haze of drugs that control her cough and dull the pain that is slowly creeping into every corner of her being. Most of her sentences are followed by moans and short exhalations of breath. She has stopped smoking. Finally.

Rick and Mattie are forced to settle for wedding on a Thursday afternoon because all of the prime dates in the near future are already booked. A chauffeured town car drives mama, Mattie and me to the church. With the minimal strength she has left, mama helps Mattie gather her dress so the taffeta hem doesn't drag in the dirt.

The walls of the small country church are made of blue granite, with countless chisel marks on the stones. The newly stained wooden front doors are ornamented with wrought iron and wreaths of white lilies.

Inside, there are fifteen pews in a center row, with aisles down both sides. When the music starts, the pews are less than half-filled.

During the ceremony, as I stand at my sister's shoulder, cupping a bouquet of white orchids with rubber hands that have been bent into place by my mother, I stare at the stained-glass window behind the pulpit. The last time I visited a church I stormed out in a wave of rebellion, which led to my mother forcing me into a brief hunger strike. I promised her that today my exit would not be so dramatic.

I try not to look at Mattie, or at Rick, though he does look handsome in a black suit with a red tie. Every now and then I steal a peek at my sister, but only when her attention is on the minister or her new husband. When the rings and vows are exchanged, I fix my eyes on the cedar beams above the chapel.

After Mattie and Rick duck into the backseat of the town car as bird seed rains down on them, my mother and I settle on the bench seat of her Buick. Her hands are rigid on the wheel, at 10 and 2. She eases the gear shift to drive, and we head off at the approximate speed of a stalking cat. Before we even leave the parking lot, she gasps against a flare of organ pain.

"I need you to drive," she says through clenched teeth.

I have been practicing in our driveway. Not on real roads with traffic. Nevertheless, her grimace tells me this is the only way.

She unlatches my seatbelt and I slide out of the car, then over to the driver's side door. My mother struggles from the car and leans against the rear fender, smearing a bit of dust on the bodice of her pink gown. She throws her head back to gain breath.

"Should I call an ambulance?"

She shakes me off and eases her way around the back of the car with her left hand braced on the trunk.

I slide behind the steering wheel and slip off my right shoe, which has been dyed pink.

"Can you buckle the seat belt for me?"

Mama reaches over, pulls the belt across, and snaps it into the buckle. With her help, I am able to position my hands on the wheel, just above the cross bar, though gripping the plastic in my fingers is impossible. With gentle pressure on the wheel and by rocking my shoulders, I can steer the car. Sharp turns are unpredictable.

I have been making a mental list of the modifications I will need before I can drive her car with minimal risk: push-button starter; shoulder belts that automatically engage and disengage; keyless entry; a special steering wheel with a protruding knob that I can grasp with my foot; gears on the steering column. Today, I'll have to make do. I do hope for a driverless car someday. If that ever becomes reality.

She puts the car in gear with her left hand, leaves it on the shifter as if it is the knob of a cane. What I wouldn't give right now to cover her hand with mine.

As we creep down the road, I rotate my torso to adjust the wheel and keep the car between the lines. When we near a stop sign, I stomp the brake with my left foot. We jerk to a halt. "Sorry."

"It's okay. Just go slow." Her words are separated by sharp and short inhalations.

I ease the gas pedal down, and we move down the highway. It is harder than I thought to keep the car straight, but with no oncoming traffic, I have the luxury of two lanes to keep us out of the ditches. As our speed increases, I look down at the dials. We are going 33 miles per hour on a road with a speed limit of 55.

In the distance, a pickup that might be black or dark blue pulls onto the road, coming in our direction. It is towing an empty flat-bed trailer. I try to ease our car to the right, but I'm not confident enough in my steering to hold the tires steady on the edge of the pavement, so our car weaves back and forth. Finally, I hit the brake and stop the car with the left fender in about the middle of the road.

The driver of the pickup stares at me as he passes close. He's wearing a green gimme cap and dark sunglasses. With his left hand he gives me the one-fingered salute. He probably figures I'm drunk.

"Asshole," my mother yells at the windshield. This sends her into a coughing fit that leaves droplets of blood on the glass and mars the lower part of her dress. She tries to wipe the blood away with a napkin from the door pocket but only succeeds at smearing the blood.

"Mama, do we need to go to the hospital?"

"No. I want to go to the cemetery."

At this hour, with dusk descending, we are the only visitors in the cemetery. It is an ancient property, designed with narrow dirt tracks knifing at right angles through the rows of plots, probably constructed when horse-drawn wagons led funeral processions. I stop the car and step on the parking brake. Mama slides the gearshift up to "P."

Once out of the car, she stands on an empty plot next to my father's grave, staring down as if she's deciding whether to accept this space. The smell of cut grass pervades the air.

She points a bony finger at the spot where her gravestone might soon be placed.

"I want my headstone the same size and color of his," she says. She coughs from a deep place and bends over to stay it. When she straightens up, she says, "Ella, please put something nice on there. 'Loving mother' or something like that. If you can bring yourself to."

"Sure, mama."

She turns to her deceased husband. "Johnny, I'll forgive you if you forgive me. We need to settle that now if I'm going to be laid right next to you for eternity." She cocks her head, as if listening for his reply.

I break the silence. "Why do you need his forgiveness, mama? After what he did to Mattie?"

First she turns her head to me, then her body follows, a monumental effort on a final ounce of strength. Her mouth quivers as she forms the words. "Because I killed him." She offers no further explanation, but trudges back to the car.

With this in mind, I head toward home. I steal glances at my mother as we glide by pastures whose grass bows in the steady breeze, wondering where her utterance came from, wondering about its veracity. The rumble of the tires over the steel cattle guard announces we have arrived at our driveway. I heave a sigh of relief. I park in the carport, only slightly askew. From my sister's wedding to a perilous trip with me behind the wheel to my mother's declaration as she stared down at my father's grave, it has been a trying afternoon.

In the passenger seat, my mother's head lolls to the left, almost touching my shoulder. I jostle her. She does not respond. I put my ear to her nose because that's what I've seen people do on television. No sound emerges from her nostrils. I can't check her pulse. I straighten up and gaze at her waxen face, then my own face in the mirror. Tears spill from my eyes.

44

My mother's death reminds me no one gets out alive. Whether the journey ends in a dark hole or we continue onward in some transmogrified state, we all face the inevitable moment when the pulse of life simply stops. My own moment came at the hands of a maniac disguised as a re-builder of faces and a purveyor of hope, whose bomb and its aftermath stopped my heart a handful of times. On at least two occasions, Volkov shocked me back to life. Why? This man who wielded his power to end and then restore my life is still out there. Somewhere.

My mother lies in a cherry coffin in a black dress my father bought her way back when. Her neck is adorned with a string of costume pearls. As I stand looking down at her, with Mattie at my side, I hear her raspy voice issue its final words: *Because I killed him.*

Mattie has been home from her honeymoon for two days. An ebullience marks her with a rosy glow, giving her a protective sheen that has kept tears from her eyes. She peers into the coffin with a soft smile, her lips parted slightly, and slides her finger across our mother's brow. She leans in, touches her lips gently to our mother's pale right cheek. "Goodbye mama."

It is all I can do to restrain myself from asking Mattie about our mother's final statement. I've endlessly dissected those four words and analyzed the expression on the face that uttered them as she confronted her final moments. My mother's lips had returned to a grim line soon afterward, their color almost as pale as the oxygen-deprived skin surrounding them, but in her countenance was not an ounce of doubt or insincerity.

Whatever she meant was not some joke. In her confession, was she alluding to the long and almost indecipherable chain of events that led my father to molest Mattie and, ultimately, to commit suicide? Was that her guilt? Or was my mother confessing to actual murder?

It is only after my mother has been covered with dirt and Mattie and I are cleaning up a monumental pile of dishes in the kitchen that I can bring myself to broach it.

"We went to the cemetery after your wedding," I say, as if reminiscing some happy moment.

Mattie's eyes dance around their sockets. "The cemetery?"

"She knew she was dying, I guess. As we were standing by daddy's grave, she asked him to forgive her."

Mattie stops drying the serving dish in her left hand. Her eyes adopt that protective glaze of happier, more recent memories. "Oh." After the pause, her right hand resumes its duty with the dish towel.

"Why do you think mama would need him to forgive her?" It is the last question I asked her. I don't want Mattie to know what she said in response. Not yet.

"I have no idea." She settles the serving dish on the counter and picks up a glass pitcher that a few minutes ago held sweet tea.

"I mean, I can understand why she would want to forgive him before she died, but why would she need forgiveness?"

"I don't know, Ella. You were there. Did she say anything else?"

I turn so I can fully see her face. The rosy hue has disappeared, and her lips bear a tight grimace, as if she is stifling physical pain.

"Mama said, 'Because I killed him'."

There is a sharp uptake of breath from my sister, a momentary pause in the movement of her hands. She fumbles the glass pitcher. She catches it before it tumbles to the floor. Her reaction is that of a person who long ago buried a dark secret and is forced to watch in horror as it's unearthed.

"What do you think she meant by that?" I ask.

Mattie remains quiet, her eyes downcast to the pitcher, rubbing at a water spot that isn't there.

"Mattie?"

She straightens herself. "I'm not talking to you about this on the night of our mother's funeral." She bangs the pitcher down on the counter to punctuate her point, then leaves the kitchen.

I hear the front door creak and the screen door groan. From the living room window I watch as she gets in her car and drives off in a swirl of dust. I glance back at the kitchen and the mountainous stacks of dirty dishes.

*****

Belinda Nunez comes by on Sunday morning. At the funeral she suggested we should spend more time together. I know she is worried about me, concerned about how I will get along now that my mother's hands are no longer available, and my sister is fully ensconced in her new life as Mrs. Mattie Lambert.

I show Belinda into the kitchen, where I use my toes to make her a cup of coffee from the one cup I bought the morning after my mother died. While my mother was alive, I recognized her as the chief of our little tribe, deferring to her even when she acted as despot, because I had proved myself incapable of true insurrection. A one-cup coffee maker was my first purchase, followed by paper plates and a slew of microwavable meals to ease my new duties as sole cook and bottle washer.

"The kitchen looks as neat and clean as when your mother was alive," Belinda, says, holding the steaming mug in her palms.

"It took a few days for me to wash and put everything away after the reception."

"Days? Where was Mattie?"

I think about this. The truth will open too many pathways. "Settling in with her new husband," I say.

"Maybe the next time I should stay and help."

I lean toward her. "I don't want our friendship to be based on my needs. I can take care of myself. I just have to be patient."

Belinda and I step outside onto the porch, then wander down to the front pasture as if it lures us. The monarch butterflies have reached South Carolina on their southward journey to Mexico. In the last several months, with my mother barely hanging on and Mattie consumed with wedding plans, milkweed has proliferated in our front field. I don't know if the monarchs will be here more than a day or two, but the milkweed provides a place to lay eggs and nourishment for the caterpillars. Through the night the monarchs can nest in the tall pines bordering our field.

As we stand among the milkweed and Johnson grass, the monarchs flutter around us in a kaleidoscope of wings, orange with black veins and white spots at the tips. It feels like I'm part of an animated fairy tale.

"You used to raise butterflies, as I remember," Belinda says, her eyes scanning the tapestry in the sky.

"That was a long time ago. I used to buy caterpillars from a catalogue. I had three or four generations a year, and the ones that are born in the late summer will usually migrate to Mexico for the winter."

"We should go."

"Go where?"

"To Mexico. To see the monarchs," she says.

"I'm not easy to travel with," I say. "I'm a lot of work."

"So?"

This strikes me as a strange retort. Up to now, I have assumed the only people willing to endure the burden that is me must come from family or hired caretakers. Perhaps it has been way too long since I had a true friend.

As the cloud of monarchs grows, grackles begin diving into the swarm from nearby trees. Though the monarchs' milkweed diet makes most birds that ingest monarchs sick, these grackles must be young. They have not yet learned their lesson. With feathers the oily black of evil, the birds snatch monarchs in their beaks, sometimes eating them on the wing, sometimes settling in the nearby trees before consuming their meal.

I yell "hey, hey, hey" at the grackles, as if that will deter their attack. Belinda joins in, waving her arms and yelling along with me. Through our efforts, maybe we save a butterfly or two. From the trees the grackles croak back at us, sounding like the hinge of a rusty gate.

"I haven't been anywhere since the bombing," I say. "I can't even fathom how to prepare for a vacation far from home."

"Ella, I know you're not going to just sit here in your mother's house day after day, for the rest of your life," she says in an admonishing tone. "I would think that with everything that has happened here, you'd want to get away."

"The cows need me."

"Hire some help."

I wrinkle up my mouth.

As the sun rises to its zenith, Belinda and I retire to the porch and sit on the glider with sweaty glasses of iced tea.

"Let me run something by you," I say.

Belinda nods. "Okay."

"On the day my mother died, we were up at the cemetery, at my father's grave, and she asked my father for forgiveness. When I questioned her about it, she said she killed him. I didn't take this literally, but there are some things about his death that don't add up."

"The coroner declared his death a suicide, right?"

"He did. But he has some pictures, which I saw a few months ago. The noose around my father's neck was tied and arranged in such a way that when he stepped off the stool, it didn't break his neck. Instead, the noose strangled him."

"That's macabre. But it sounds like he just didn't adjust it right."

"My father was an expert with knots. He was a boy scout and knew how to tie every knot imaginable. He taught me quite a few. So, if he was going to commit suicide, he would have known how to tie a noose that would end it quickly."

Belinda taps the toes of one tennis shoe on the concrete porch. "Seems like you're reaching. Just because he knew how to tie boy scout knots doesn't make him an expert in tying a noose. Plus, how careful do you expect him to be, under the circumstances?"

"Maybe," I say.

"That's not much to go on."

Belinda doesn't know our father molested Mattie. I'm not going to tell her. That's a deep secret I have to keep. Maybe for Mattie. Maybe for me. I realize, as the glider squeaks back and forth, I have sought Belinda's opinion without a willingness to divulge this key fact that fully explains my father's motivation to kill himself.

I need to change the topic. "Let's go to Mexico to see the monarchs."

45

On a Saturday morning with a cold rain spitting on the tarmac, Belinda and I board a plane in Columbia. We stop in Atlanta before heading to Mexico City. In making the reservations, I made sure to secure the window seat, even though the things I hope to see vanish almost instantly as we top low-slung clouds and rivulets of water sweep across our plastic window.

At the immigration station in the airport in Mexico City, Belinda slides my passport across the wooden counter to a man in a khaki uniform. He examines the recent passport photograph, his eyes flicking to my face, but asks me no questions. Outside, as Belinda hales a cab, young children hustle me, trying to sell me gum and small wood carvings of animals and warm bottles of orange soda and already-tarnished jewelry that might hold authentic or fake turquoise stones. Belinda shoos them away, shouting "no dinero" until they scurry toward a couple emerging from the baggage claim.

That evening, we meet Maria Sanchez in the lobby of our hotel. She is a friend Belinda met while they were in college together in Texas. Maria now works for the geology department at a university here, studying volcanoes. She will serve as *de facto* guide on our trip to the Monarch Butterfly Biosphere Reserve in Michoacan.

We settle at a table in the restaurant, which has a floor of beautiful red, brown and black ceramic tile. Maria and Belinda order margaritas. With my liver perpetually in jeopardy, I opt for a bottle of tangerine soda. When the food comes, Belinda asks if I want her to feed me.

"No, thanks." I grasp the metal fork between my toes and maneuver a piece of skirt steak into my mouth.

Maria watches me. "You are very adroit at eating in that way," she says.

I dip my head to my foot and swallow a bite of charro beans.

"If it is not too personal, how did you come to lose your arms?"

"A bomb," I say. "The terrorist attack in Charlotte two years ago."

She nods, as if in her country terrorist bombings are a common occurrence. "Belinda tells me you have been interested in the butterflies for a long time."

"Since I was young. I used to raise them. And you?" I ask.

"I have seen them many times when I am studying the volcanoes. They are beautiful and curious also, no?"

"Yes, very beautiful."

The next morning we drive to the Reserve. We refuse the option to be led on horseback up the path to where the butterflies are nesting. Instead, we opt to walk. For Belinda, who holds some extra pounds of winter weight, the journey proves taxing. All the running I have been doing has strengthened my legs and my lungs, and as I move along with her, I offer encouragement, to which she responds with glares. Her hair is stringy with sweat. The diminished oxygen in the air at almost 9,000 feet leaves her heaving.

We stop at an overlook to rest. Eyeing a panorama that stretches a hundred miles in three directions, I cannot help but feel lighter. I have spent so much time during the past two years rolling in the muck of my own diminished world. Looking back on it, I can justify some of my self-absorption, but perhaps I overdid it. I can forgive myself for roiling in a state of helplessness that may accompany all victims. What I cannot forgive is how much time I wasted trying to convince myself the future holds nothing for me.

When we resume our ascent, Belinda slips her fingers beneath one strap of my backpack. I lean into the hill, pulling her along like a plough horse pulling a wagon laden with bales of hay.

Maria is the first to spot orange and black wings, fluttering in the dappled sunlight amid the pines and oyamel firs. Her announcement produces murmurs of glee from our fellow travelers, spoken in five or six different languages. Isolated monarchs turn into clusters, and then clouds of them weaving above us on unseen air currents.

We slow our pace, and Belinda takes out her cell phone and begins taking pictures. A butterfly colony clinging to an oyamel branch. A lone butterfly hovering about my head. Two monarchs perched on the hindquarters of a dappled brown horse.

We all need somewhere we feel safe and secure, if not happy. Perhaps when I was younger, in the years before my father's death, the farm on which I now live was that safe harbor. His death tainted that for me. I can no longer gaze at the cows grazing the pasture or pass the barn as I run down the driveway without also feeling the pall of his death. I cannot shake the sensation, more pronounced on nights when I cannot sleep, that he is still hovering in that barn. And was his death the suicide I have always been led to believe? Or was it a desperate killing by my mother and sister? This unanswered question—perhaps forever unanswerable now—leaves me with an unsettled feeling as I move about my mother's farm.

As I watch the butterflies dance, they imbue me with a tiny bit of magic. This cannot be, and never will be, a place where mayhem or terrorist acts will be perpetrated. It cannot be a place where men rape or kill. Even if among these tourists there were a person capable of such evil, he or she could not, beneath this sky of fluttering orange and black wings, carry out heinous crimes. Volkov could not exist here, at least not for very long.

If my mother were with me, she would probably point a gnarled finger at the monarchs and the halcyon atmosphere they produce and proclaim as she billowed a plume of gray cigarette smoke that what we see is evidence of divinity. In this place, with the monarchs lifting me, I might not argue with her.

We stay for an hour, then two, lost in transformation, in the same way a favorite movie obliterates all of the cares and worries in a blackened theater. The three of us talk little. Words are of minimal value here, and I know that even though Belinda is taking dozens of pictures with her phone, the things I will remember about this place cannot be retained as pixels. The warmth of the sun on my cheeks, dappling through branches of fir. The slight breeze that tousles the hair behind my ears. The beating of wings that sound like the crinkle of thousands of wax paper sheets. The simple peacefulness which descends upon me. None of this can be captured.

The parade of monarchs slackens as the yolk of sun breaks on the mountain peaks to the west. The monarchs drop into the trees. There may be hundreds of them in a single cluster, clinging to the pine branches, clinging to each other. Cold blooded, they will be almost paralyzed until the late morning sun peeks over the eastern ring of mountains and warms their wings again.

On the way up I read the plastic placards detailing the monarch migration and life cycle. I know that every single one of the monarchs I am seeing now will be dead before the end of winter. It will be the grandchildren of these butterflies that migrate north when winter ends, through an intuition or genetic history that no scientist has ever cracked.

In the hotel near the entrance to the Monarch Reserve, I shiver in my bed, as if whatever I gained today is escaping through my pores and exhalations. My mind has become more settled. The message is clear. Though I am at peace now, I cannot take this place with me. I have to create my own idyll.

46

As Mattie and I drift apart, I realize that my mother was our unlikely tether. Now snipped, I see Mattie rarely, usually one or two Sundays a month when she invites me over for dinner after she and Rick get home from church. Mattie is not as good a cook as our mother, but she fries chicken and makes pot roast far better than I ever will.

"It looks like you've lost weight," she says to me over her shoulder as she lifts the lid on the slow cooker on the counter. The aroma of roast wafts across the kitchen.

She's probably right, but I've stopped weighing myself. My weight seems an inconsequential concern.

"Maybe you're running too much."

"I need it." Running has become an almost daily affair for me. In fact, it has become a priority, something that gives me an hour or two of joy, a break in the routine that has sunk beneath mundane. I have been wondering, as I soak my legs in Epsom salts in the tub at night, how I ever had time for a career, how I had time to even think about starting a family. The daily demands of bathing and feeding myself, washing my clothes, weeding the garden, looking after our cows, keeping the house passably clean, and the other necessities of my life consume all of my time.

Mattie sidles over. "Are you eating enough?"

She sounds like our mother, without the croaking voice. "Two meals a day. Sometimes three."

"What do you eat? Soup?"

I shrug. "Soup is easy."

She twists her hands against her apron and stares out the window above the sink. The deciduous trees are barren. A brcczc scatters rust and orange leaves across their unkempt side yard. "I kind of miss not having you around," she says.

"You've got Rick."

"Yeah, Rick's good. But you know, well, it's just not the same as being with your sister."

I give a muffled snort. "Has the romance worn off already?"

"What makes you say that?"

I tilt my head toward my right shoulder. From necessity, I have developed gestures that don't involve hands or arms, creating a limited dictionary of body language that may or may not accurately convey my intentions. As I stare at Mattie, a part of me is gratified that perhaps her marriage has lost some of its splendor.

Mattie traces the outside seam of her jeans with her right index finger. "Rick and I want to have a baby, but I can't get pregnant." There is a noticeable tremble in her lower lip.

"Mattie? What do you mean you can't get pregnant?"

"I just can't. So …"

Rick bursts into the kitchen, gripping the sides of the door frame with each hand. "You ask her yet?" he says.

"Rick, we're talking here. Go away." Mattie tries to wave him away with a wooden spoon.

"You didn't ask her, did you?"

"Ask me what?" I say.

"I was getting around to it, Rick. It's not something you just blurt out."

"She's your sister."

"Not even to your sister," Mattie says.

"Okay, I'll do it." Rick pulls out the adjacent chair at the kitchen table and sits on it backward. He locks my eyes with his. The expectant look he holds is nothing like the look of fear when I first saw him by firelight that night in the woods. "Ella, we want you to carry our baby."

"You what?" I sputter. I look to Mattie for explanation, but Rick holds the floor.

"Mattie can't get pregnant. We want you to have our baby."

I swallow. My mind is in tornadic swirl. *They* want *me* to have their baby? The potential repercussions will not settle for some time. I look at Mattie. She's leaning against the counter, her arms crossed over chest. She offers no words.

I turn back to Rick. "You mean like a surrogate?"

"Not exactly. We want your eggs and your womb."

"Rick! You don't have to say it like that." Mattie has found the courage to participate.

"Okay, maybe that was blunt. But it's true." He turns to me. "We want … well, I'll impregnate you."

"You mean artificial insemination?"

"No," he shakes his head. "We can't afford AI. Mattie's insurance won't pay for it. I don't have health insurance. It would have to be the usual way."

"The usual way?" I say. "You mean you want to sleep with me?"

"Uh-huh," Rick nods.

"You want me to have your baby?"

"That's what I said, didn't I?"

My mind has settled a bit, but the full panoply of consequences will take a long time to digest. I've wanted a child since Robert and I got married. And I obviously wanted to have a baby with David. In a way, this new opportunity to become a mother is a gift. A chance to nurture a little human being. To teach, to care, to hold.

As I sit in their kitchen, scanning their expectant faces, I recognize this is a different scenario. They want me to carry *their* baby.

Holding Mattie's eyes, I say, "you're okay with your new husband having sex with me?"

Mattie closes her eyes, skips a beat, then nods.

So there it is. My sister, who married the man I had convinced myself was interested in me, is now asking me to sleep with her husband. Of the two daughters of Johnny and Rose Duncan, only the one maimed in a terrorist bombing can bear children.

"Why can't you get pregnant?"

"It's medically complicated." She angles her head toward Rick, a gesticulation I've understood for many years. She's signaling me that Rick doesn't know everything, and this isn't the time or place for him to find out. They both peer at me in anticipation.

"I need to think about it," I say.

Dinner is an uncomfortable affair. Rick, perhaps even more than Mattie, wants an answer, but Mattie is withholding information that I have deemed necessary to my decision. Well, perhaps not necessary, but I've discovered I hold some leverage now, and I want to know why Mattie can't get pregnant. I convince myself this should be part of the bargain.

After dinner, I leave in my mother's car. I've had it modified so I can steer with my left foot on a rotating disk next to the brake pedal. This convenience has expanded my range, given me additional freedom and made me safer. As I climb the narrow driveway to my house, I am awash in euphoria.

Mattie, however, is a wreck. Over the years, we talked so often about having children—three or four apiece was the goal—I am certain discovering she is infertile has devastated her to an almost-unimaginable degree. Without a child, she may always feel empty. I think that's why she stole Rick from me. Yet the prospect of having a baby boosts me like nothing I've felt since I discovered I was engaged to David Lyendowski. David wanted me to be his wife. To bear his children. Mattie wants me to have sex with her husband. She wants him to fertilize *my* eggs.

After class one day, Mattie comes over at my invitation—as if she needs an invitation. I greet her at the front door. A north wind carries a chill and rattles the few leaves still clinging to the trees. The sun casts a wan light behind purpling clouds that threaten rain. She settles into her favorite chair at the kitchen table. Her arms are wrapped about her shoulders, as if she is cold. Or in need of protection.

"Have you decided?" Her right leg crosses her left at the knee, and her right foot pumps the air.

"I need to know why you can't get pregnant."

"You *need* to know?"

"Yes."

She seems unconvinced.

"If I'm going to carry your and Rick's baby, I deserve to know. You're asking a lot of me."

She lets out a snort, uncrosses her arms. "I need a drink. A glass of wine at least." She goes to the refrigerator, finds an unfinished bottle of Chablis that has been there at least since mama's funeral, and pours herself a big glass.

"Maybe you deserve to know," she says after settling back in the vinyl chair. Her right hand is twisting her wedding ring. "Mama had me sterilized," she blurts. "After daddy raped me."

I had conjured a number of possible reasons for Mattie's infertility, but this is worse than I imagined. I look at the set of her mouth, which remains a tight, thin line even after she takes a double swallow of wine. She's not embellishing here. She didn't say this for dramatic effect. As I linger upon the final moments before the funeral director closed my mother's casket, the slight smile on Mattie's face that I presumed was the afterglow of her honeymoon, I realize that my mother's death may have in some macabre way brought satisfaction to Mattie. Retribution for a dastardly deed, perhaps.

"When did you find out?"

Mattie's foot is pumping again. "Officially, a month ago. I had a CT scan, and it showed my tubes have been tied. But I suspected something a few years back."

"Only a few years back? Didn't your period stop, like ten years ago?"

She shakes her head. "Nope. Still getting my period, even now."

"How could she have done that without your consent, Mattie?"

"After she discovered what daddy was doing to me, she took me to her gynecologist, ostensibly to see if our father had gotten me pregnant. Somehow, she convinced the doctor to tie my tubes. Without my knowledge. And afterward, as a teenaged girl who was still having her period, I didn't really notice any changes. Plus …"

This revelation has emboldened her. In her strident tone and the firm set of her jaw is something akin to defiance. Or maybe anger.

"I've kept this secret for a long time. I thought I was protecting our parents, maybe even protecting myself, but I'm at the point now, with both of them gone, that I don't give a shit anymore about protecting them."

She drains her wine glass, goes to the refrigerator and pours another. "You asked me after mama's funeral if I knew what she meant when she said she killed daddy. I do know. I know exactly what happened." Another big swig of wine, which is serving as truth serum. "She killed him. I helped her."

"You helped her?"

"I did. Want to know how?"

"Well …"

Having adopted this procedure of declaration followed by explanation, Mattie doesn't wait for encouragement. Now that she's started down this road, she needs this expurgation like a person needs to vomit a meal of contaminated meat.

"He didn't hang himself. We did it for him. After we got back from the doctor's office, he was out in the barn. Mostly drunk, it seemed. I think he was scared shitless of mama. Scared of where we might have gone. Scared of what she might have told people. She coaxed him to eat some supper, and she crushed up some pain pills from the prescription the doctor gave me, and put them in his food. Half an hour later, he was out."

"Where was I all this time?"

"Asleep. Mama gave you a sedative in your tea."

I search my memory and find no sign that I knew anything was amiss. I was as ignorant of their plot as I was of what my father had been doing with Mattie out in the barn. My mother drugged me. Perhaps I should feel outrage, but I don't. I want to hear the rest of the story.

"Who tied the noose?"

Mattie raises her hand. "Easy instructions on the internet."

"So you what, carried him out to the barn while he was stoned?"

She takes another deep swallow of wine. The skin of her throat is mottled red. "Mama grabbed his arms, and I grabbed his feet, and we carried him out there, put the noose around his neck, and balanced him on an old farm stool. The stool's still in the barn."

"And then what?" even though I know perfectly well what happened next.

"He woke up. Not wide awake, but enough to know what was happening. He was standing on the stool and said, 'what are you doing'?"

Not what I expected. "What did you say?"

"Nothing, I kind of went inside myself. I wasn't expecting him to be awake. The whole thing took on a different cast for me with him staring at me like that."

"What did mama do?"

Mattie smiles, running her finger around the rim of her wine glass. "You know how after you've had a confrontation or something, and you're away from it for a while, you suddenly think of the perfect thing you wanted to say? Mama had it ready, like she'd rehearsed it."

"What did she say?"

"She said, 'Johnny, what you've done is a mortal sin. You have two choices here. You can go down to the Sheriff's office and turn yourself in, tell him what you've done to your daughter. They won't kill you, probably, but you'll serve a long time in prison as a child molester. There's no telling what the prisoners will do to you. Or you can kick that stool out from under you and end it. If you don't decide in 60 seconds, I'll decide for you."

"And then what?" I ask.

"Mama grabbed my hand and pulled me out of the barn. I'd never seen her act so strong. She made me swear that I would never, ever tell anyone about this. Especially you. Then she sent me back to the house."

"And then what?"

"She went back inside the barn. Closed the barn door."

"Did he kick the stool over, or did she?"

"Based on what she told you at the cemetery the day she died, I presume she did it."

For a moment I ponder the cunning and gall of which my mother had been capable, then my mind veers in another direction. "That's why you stayed here all that time. Stayed with mama. You had that secret together."

She shrugs. "Maybe so. Now you know why I can't get pregnant. And all the sordid details surrounding it."

While she talked, I had been transporting myself back to that night in the barn, trying to convert Mattie's recount into images. I could see my father on the stool, his hooded eyes staring down at them in terror. My mother, her arms probably crossed, uttering to my father in her gravelly voice what amounted to a death sentence. Fourteen-year-old Mattie at the peak of her strength, conscripted by our mother into this plot, but never trying to desert. I notice my bare toes have curled.

"So, are you going to be our surrogate?"

Thinking about Mattie's request, I am imbued with an emotion I can compare only to the moment you hear a favorite song, rendered perfectly, coming at you when you need it most.

My chest shudders. I can't shake what she's just told me. But I respect my sister for telling me. I go to Mattie and kiss her on the cheek. In a voice beginning to crack I answer her.

"Absolutely."

47

Truth is, I'm not doing this solely for Mattie. Having a child is something I have yearned for so long I can't remember when the yearning first started. I was born to be a mother. Robert's recalcitrance notwithstanding. Eve's murder doesn't change any of that.

As I sit by myself sipping coffee through a glass straw, I have not really fathomed how I will handle this without arms. The pregnancy itself is not what disturbs me. But how will I hold my baby to my breast? How will I change a diaper? How will I warm a bottle and cuddle my child as I slip the nipple between its lips? How will I strap my baby into a stroller? Or a car seat?

I find myself hesitating in response to Rick's request "to set up a meeting to discuss how he will inseminate me." His words. Clinical. Probably scripted by Mattie. I have begun referring to this prospect, internally only, as "the tryst." Though our purpose is congruent, my sister's and my perspectives of what her husband and I are about to do could not be more disparate.

At our next Sunday dinner, Mattie and Rick and I settle on the protocol whereby Rick will get me pregnant. "Protocol" is Mattie's word. I understand why she refers to it in that way, trying to make it sound like a medical procedure, rather than something lascivious that her husband and sister are about to do.

From a kitchen drawer she pulls out a white box.

"It's an electronic fertility monitor," she says, "so we can track your fertility window. It's …"

"I know what a fertility window is, Mattie. I used a kit when Robert and I were trying to get pregnant."

"Good. Then you know it works. We need to pinpoint the window so we don't have to do this more than once."

Her eyes bore into mine, an admonition to get it right the first time. She doesn't want me, or her husband, to actually enjoy it. I wonder if she will be standing by the bedside while it happens.

When it is time, Rick comes over and picks me up in his truck. He holds open the front door of my house as I exit, and does the same with the passenger door of his truck as I slide onto the bench seat. From the driver's side, he pulls my shoulder strap across and buckles me in.

"You're wearing your arms," he says. His breath smells of spearmint gum.

"I thought it might make it easier for you."

"Okay." There is a nervousness in his words, an extra beat of laughter.

On the short drive over, he asks me about my trip to Mexico. I do my best to explain to him what I saw and heard and felt as I watched the monarchs shimmering against the azure sky, but from his responses I sense he is only being polite. Or maybe I'm at a loss to explain the experience adequately. I feel transformed. How do you make someone understand that?

"Mattie's at the movies," Rick says as he slips the key in his front door.

"You sure?" I look around.

He nods. "Yeah."

"She's not hiding in a closet or something, is she?"

"No, she's gone."

A white linen tablecloth covers the dining room table. On it is the good china Rick and Mattie received as wedding gifts. Two silver candlesticks I gave them stand in the middle of the table. Rick lights the red candles with a kitchen match.

"Whose idea was this?" I say. "The tablecloth, the candles?"

"Mine."

"Did you set it up before or after Mattie left for the movies?"

"After."

This set-up is not consistent with Mattie's protocol, which she carefully memorialized in an email she sent me two days ago. "She wouldn't like this."

But I do.

Rick pours himself a glass of red wine and me a club soda, with a wedge of lime and a straw. I take a long sip.

"Ella, would you like some music?" Rick says as he stands next to a bookshelf filled with vinyl records.

"Are you a collector? Not many people have old records."

"I like the sound of vinyl. What type of music do you like? I don't even know what kind of music you listen to and all."

Music is not mentioned in Mattie's protocol, either as allowed or prohibited. I sidle over to the rows of records and, with some effort, raise my right hand and point a rubber finger at a jazz album from an artist Robert and I used to listen to.

Rick pops it into the player.

While I sit in a soft, leather chair, Rick prepares dinner. He brings out a dozen chilled oysters on the half-shell and sets the platter at one end of the table.

"I've researched oysters on the internet," he says. "They contain a lot of zinc, which helps boost sperm count." He shrugs.

"It might be a little late," I say.

"Oh, I've been eating oysters several times a week for the last month. I drive down to a seafood shop in Columbia to get them. Plus, I like them."

He feeds me three oysters, with a tiny fork that looks like a triton. He slides the rest into his mouth from the shells. Then he removes the plate of discards and busies himself in the kitchen.

With instrumental jazz filling the living room, I peruse the spines of a few books I presume Mattie has placed there. There are classics from English and American authors, a few Oprah Book Club selections, and two books on pregnancy. Did Mattie buy these when she was trying to get pregnant? Or does she intend to use them to manage me?

Rick appears at the doorway and asks if I'm okay. His smile has loosened. I see an entirely different man from the one I saw by the flickering light of a campfire a little more than a year ago. Then, I was petrified, completely unable to protect myself, preparing to be raped by two drunks. Who could have predicted that encounter would lead to this? I wonder if Rick ever thinks about that night, whether he marvels at the serendipity of circumstances that aimed him at me, who may soon be carrying his child, and to my sister, who carries his love.

Dinner is grilled snapper, mashed potatoes and steamed asparagus. Although I could feed myself with my feet, I let Rick feed me with a spoon. As I chew my food, he poises a spoonful in mid-air, watching me. I am enjoying myself, the soft music, the scent of romance from the candles. Rick is a handsome man. And, I see now, an attentive one. Into my mind sneaks the thought that all this could be permanent if only … I dismiss the maverick suggestion. I have already decided it is not the love of a man I want. I don't want to do anything that will hurt Mattie. I am not stealing her husband.

After dinner, with the dishes cleared away, we sit side-by-side on the maroon leather couch. Rick keeps his hands pressed between his knees.

"We, Mattie and me, we really appreciate what you're doing."

"You're welcome. It's special for me, too."

"You have really pretty hair," he says.

"Thank you. I like yours too."

He self-consciously ruffles his own hair. "I don't really know how to go about this," he says.

"You've done fine so far."

He smiles and leans over and kisses me on the lips. "How's that?"

"Very nice."

He kisses me again, more urgently this time. This is definitely not in the protocol. It has been more than two years since a man kissed me, and just as in the dreams I had when I saw Rick as my rescuing knight, his kisses stir something inside me. I kiss him back, leaning into him. After a few minutes, Rick leads me into the bedroom.

The only light is from a small lamp on Mattie's dressing table—the same table on which she once arranged her and Rick's love letters for me to find. The dim light leaves shadows everywhere and plenty of fodder for the imagination.

Rick shucks his clothes, except for his underwear, and slides under the sheets.

I remain at the foot of the bed. "You're going to have to undress me."

"Oh, I forgot about that."

He moves to the foot of the mattress on his knees. He unbuttons my burgundy blouse from the top to the bottom, his fingers grazing my cleavage, my abdomen, then a spot a few inches below my navel. My breath has shallowed. He slides the blouse carefully from each arm, as if my appendages are rose petals he doesn't want to disturb.

He peels my black skirt over my hips and lets it drop to the floor. I kick off my shoes and am standing before him in a white bra and panties edged with lace.

He clears his throat.

"Kiss me again," I say.

He leans in and kisses me, unclasping my bra at the same time. It is an awkward, one-person embrace. Closing his eyes, he kisses my earlobes, then down the left side of my neck. He spends a few seconds nibbling at the hollow of my collar bone. I watch him the whole time, feeling my body come alive, my nerves abuzz.

I have anticipated a semi-clinical undertaking void of passion, with impregnation as the only goal. But Rick is giving me more than that. He is making me feel good, making me feel womanly. Releasing sensations I didn't know were still possible. I suck air between my lips when he slides his tongue across my navel. He slips off my panties.

"Do you need any lubricant?" he asks. His face is upturned, his eyes searching mine.

"You've already taken care of that."

He picks me up and lays me on the bed, adjusting a pillow beneath my head. My arms are stiff noodles at my sides. He slips off his boxer shorts. Then he crawls onto the bed and gently lowers himself.

Burying his face in my neck, he eases inside of me. I gasp, then stifle another gasp. It has been far too long. My arms want to wrap themselves around his neck and pull him in. My fingers want to stroke the back of his head. Instead, I wrap my legs around him. I lose track of minutes as he rocks on top of me. Each thrust unleashes pleasure deep inside. I had forgotten what this feels like, how this can obliterate everything else. The rest of the world doesn't matter as the tingle builds and builds.

As his tempo increases, Rick's breath becomes ragged and raspy. I buck with him. He is almost there. "Wait," I beg.

"What?"

"Hold off, just a few more seconds."

He pushes himself up on his hands and looks at me, puzzled. Sweat beads his forehead.

"Are you thinking about me, or are you thinking about her?" I ask.

He clenches his eyes and thrusts harder. "You."

"Me?"

"You."

"Me?"

"Yes, you. God, you."

He plunges himself as deep as my body will let him go and shudders. My head goes back and I arch my back and release in a series of guttural moans, gasping for oxygen as a long-forgotten rush washes through me. Rick collapses on top of me. His arms envelop me. We lay still for a minute, maybe two.

"Move off me," I whisper.

He pushes up on his hands. "I want to go again. You know, to make sure." His eyes hold an innocent earnestness.

This is an enticing suggestion. My brain is aglow. My heartbeat still elevated. I feel the thump in my chest, different from the way it pounds when I kick hard at the end of a long run. I have felt nothing like this in…I don't know how long. The part of me that craves attention and passion and the orgasmic wave wants to submit.

As I study his eyes and the beads of sweat on his upper lip, damp bangs matted to his forehead, I see that this romp has been better than he anticipated. Through no fault of her own, sex is forever tainted for Mattie. She is unable to segregate the pleasure produced by her husband from the indelible physical and emotional damage left by our father's molestation.

"It wouldn't be fair to Mattie," I say. "Based on what I saw and heard and felt, once is enough. I need to get my legs up."

He looks at me for a moment, a combination of arousal and rejection and marital fidelity fighting on his face. He slides his hands beneath my thighs, lifts me up as if I am no heavier than a cat, and slides two pillows beneath my buttocks.

He gazes down at my vulva. "That was really nice, Ella. Are you sure you don't want to go again? Just for insurance?"

I put my knees together. "Mattie doesn't do this for you, does she?"

He remains silent for a long time. "Every once in a while," he says as if the words burn coming out. "But not that often."

"I understand."

"Why is that? Do you think it's me?"

Mattie hasn't told him. I don't fault her for that. It's a secret she kept from me for a dozen years, a secret whose signs were all over the place if I'd simply looked. Still, it's not my place to inform her husband.

"No, it's not you. I promise."

He gives me that stare of someone who is mulling another, incisive question, who wants to suggest I simply signal him if he guesses the real reason so I haven't actually spilled the beans. Then it passes. He looks at his watch. "Mattie said she'd be back at ten."

I lie there for a few minutes more, and then I roll off the bed so Rick can dress me. My panties first, then my bra and blouse and skirt. He takes me home in silence.

I stand beneath the shower, the water like warm rain cascading over my head and trickling down my body. I am not trying to wash anything off. I am attempting to hold onto a feeling that is slowly seeping away. I sense this may be the last time for me, that the confluence of circumstances that led my sister to ask me, or allow me, to have sex with her husband will come less frequently than the appearance of Halley's Comet.

I slip my head around the shower curtain and glance at the phone resting on the toilet tank. "Call Mattie."

The phone rings three times, and on the fourth ring Mattie steps into the bathroom. Her arms are crossed over her chest. She settles against the sink counter with something akin to a frowning curiosity on her lips.

"Well?"

It's an ambiguous question that could serve as an invitation for me to tell her everything about my evening with her husband in intricate detail. It would probably come from me in an effusive gush, which is not what she would want to hear. Instead, I focus on the only thing she needs to know.

"It was probably successful."

She leans there for a bit, examining her shoes, then reaches down and plucks a piece of lint near the hem of her navy dress with white polka dots.

"How was the movie?"

"Good, I guess. I zoned out for parts of it."

"Did you fall asleep or something?"

"No. You know, just wondering about you guys." She carries the look of the cuckold, a melancholy countenance, as if in granting permission for her husband to have sex with me she has opened a door she can never close.

"Come here," I say. When she does, I lean from the shower and plant a kiss on her forehead. "I can tell you this, Mattie. Rick loves you very much. He wonders why you don't want to have sex with him. Maybe you should find a way to tell him."

She takes a step back and tilts her head down, two rivulets of shower water snaking down her brow.

48

I buy a baby on-line. She is made of vinyl and has dark brown hair and life-like green eyes whose lids lift and close. She has four limbs, though her fingers are almost as stiff as mine. She weighs less than four pounds, so she's lighter than my baby will be.

I practice wrapping and taping a diaper around her tiny bottom. From a package I pull baby wipes with my toes, awkwardly mashing them into places I'll have to wipe to keep her clean. This is going to be a problem, because I can't hold her little legs up in the air while I clean her crevices with a wipe gripped awkwardly between my toes.

I wrap her in a pink onesie with tiny silver snaps I cannot secure. Another problem. I slide a yarn cap over her head, pulling down the edges with my toes, only jabbing her delicate little eyes twice. Lying down on the floor, my calves propped upon a chair seat to make a trough to hold her, I cuddle her to my left breast as if she is taking my milk.

Back on the internet, I buy a harness that will slip over my neck and hold her securely to my chest while she suckles. I buy a breast pump and several one-piece pajamas without buttons or snaps.

Belinda and I meet at a nail salon so I can get a pedicure. Only while using my feet to caress practice baby do I realize how unsightly my feet have become. The running has repeatedly mashed my toes in the toe box and given my nails a yellowish cast. The pedicurist massages my feet, removes old and dead skin from my soles, and paints my nails with a pink that should be soothing to my child. Belinda gets all twenty of her digits polished and painted in fire engine red.

I lean my head toward Belinda. "It worked," I say. "I'm pregnant." She is the only one I've told. Not even Mattie knows for sure.

From the stylist's chair, she tilts her head a few inches in my direction. "You've been to the doctor?"

"Not yet. At-home tests. But three straight positives." It is the same number of positives I had for Eve.

"Are you ready for this?" she asks, as chemical scents waft around us.

"I'm working on it. It's awkward. I'm realizing how much I will be unable to do once the baby is born."

"Maybe Mattie will hire a nanny," Belinda says.

I haven't thought of that. I have assumed Mattie and I will handle the myriad of significant tasks necessary to care for a baby. At Belinda's comment, a part of me deflates.

"I doubt they have money for a nanny," I say.

She gazes at me with dubious eyes. I can see she is weighing the depth of our friendship against the blunt reality of reminding me of the difficulties facing me as primary care-giver for an infant. She's wondering if she should pick a side. Her eyes retreat to her half-painted toes. "I'm sure you'll figure it out."

"What is that supposed to mean?"

She blows air upward, ruffling her bangs. "Well, you're having this baby for your sister, right? Doesn't a surrogate's role usually end once the baby is born?"

I shift in my vinyl seat. The pedicurist grabs my left ankle to still the foot she's trying to paint.

Belinda is looking at me, her threaded eyebrows raised, the corners of her mouth upturned in a sympathetic smile that conveys she's surprised I haven't recognized this.

"I'm not just a surrogate, Belinda." I look down at my abdomen, which has not yet begun to expand into a new shape. "I'm this baby's mother."

When I return from an eight-mile run the following Saturday, Mattie is waiting for me on the front porch.

"It's official. I'm pregnant," I say, making sure our eyes meet.

"Are you sure?" Mattie is bouncing on her toes, her arms extended toward me.

"Yes."

She hugs me, then releases my sweaty torso. "Shouldn't we go to the doctor to confirm?"

"We can."

"When?"

"I'll call and make an appointment."

We go into the living room, where I collapse with a sigh on the sofa.

Mattie's hand caresses my armless right shoulder. "Are you eating enough?"

"Yes, Mattie."

"Are you getting enough sleep?"

"Seven hours, every night."

"Do you talk to my baby? What do you say?"

I do talk to our baby, but the messages are as much to assure myself that I can do this as they are to impart anything to this child. "It will all be okay," I find myself uttering several times a day as I look down at my abdomen, which hasn't bulged a bit.

"Are you getting enough iron? The books say you need lots of iron. To avoid anemia."

I rise from the couch—my mother's old striped couch that I have not had the gumption to replace—and trek to the kitchen, where I pour myself a cup of water from the faucet. Mattie follows me into the kitchen, as if some accident might befall me if she is not on watch.

I sit at the kitchen table. The pill organizer that contains my pre-natal vitamins and supplements lies in front of me. I flip up the plastic lid for Saturday, dump the five pills onto a salad plate, and pluck them one at a time with my teeth, swallowing each with a sip of water from my ubiquitous plastic cup with the glass straw.

"Maybe you should move in with us, Ella. It must be awfully difficult taking care of yourself and everything. Without help."

In her offer I detect the spark of an argument. In the few months I have lived alone since the death of our mother, Mattie has expressed little concern about the difficulties I face. Until now, she's seemed satisfied that I have learned to take care of myself in passable fashion. In fact, I have. Necessity being the mother of invention, I have learned to do all sorts of things that I once found impossible. In the wake of our mother's death, I rearranged her kitchen so the daily items are in the lower cabinets, which I can reach with my feet without having to climb onto a chair or onto the countertop. I have expanded my cooking regimen and can fry a steak on the old gas stove. I bathe and dress myself. I drive. I can shop.

With an infant, however, I am untested. Mattie has issued an unsubtle challenge. She doesn't think I can handle this. And though I have the opportunity to spit something back about how she's only concerned about me because I now carry our baby, I let it slide. "Come with me."

I lead her to our old bedroom, which I have converted into a nursery. A high school student assembled the crib, leaving off the lower legs so the mattress rests almost on the floor. He also helped modify the changing table so that the plastic pad where the baby will lie is on the bottom, with the top shelf arranged with diapers and wipes and powder and rash cream. Not until I watched him unpacking the boxes I bought on the internet did I realize that baby furniture is made for adults, at a level so they don't have to bend over to minister to their child. Lowering the baby furniture closer to the floor seems safer for the baby. And more convenient for me.

This morning, practice baby is swaddled in a soft pink pajama dress adorned with unicorns in yellow, blue and white, her feet sporting tiny socks that took me almost an hour to pull up over her toes with my own. I lower myself to the floor and slip off my shoes. I squirt some foot sanitizer onto my left instep, then spread the gel onto my toes, between my toes, and over the soles of both feet.

"Do you smell that," I say looking up at Mattie from my perch on the floor.

"The alcohol from the sanitizer?"

"No. This baby needs to be changed."

With only a little effort I unlatch the crib side. The crib hardware has been modified so the slatted side can be swung out on hinges like a door. With one foot beneath the baby's head and the other curled under her knees, I lift her from the crib mattress and, holding her aloft, spin on my haunches and set her gently on the pad for the changing table. I do this smoothly, without jostling or dropping her.

I look up at Mattie, who is observing me, her arms crossed under her breasts as if watching one of her students taking a make-up test. Her lips do not form a smile, but a soft-lipped skepticism. She slides one shoe forward a few inches on the carpet, then back to its original position.

I have practiced this dozens and dozens of times. From all the running, my legs are strong, and substituting them for arms to lift the baby is not a chore. My core muscles, however, were not strong enough initially to hold the baby aloft for more than a few seconds. So I do daily sets of crunches, leg lifts, pelvic tilts, sit-ups and trunk curls until the muscles of my abdomen quiver and burn. I practice lifting and setting down a gallon-jug of milk.

I slide the lower hem of her pajamas up to my practice baby's stomach, revealing a diaper whose tape is secure, though somewhat askew. I maneuver my feet and toes to peel off the tape, then slip the diaper from the baby's behind and legs, dropping the diaper deftly into a foot-pedal stainless trash can. Then I lift the baby's legs with my left foot and wipe her with an infused wipe wedged between the painted toes of my right foot.

"There's no poop, so how do you know you're getting it all?" Mattie says in a challenging tone.

"I lost my arms, not my sight, Mattie."

"What if you drop her, or him? What if there's a fire? How will you bathe my baby?"

Despite Mattie's protestations, I have become proficient, if not adept, at changing and bathing and feeding practice baby. Yet we both know there are a thousand variables with which I will be confronted once our child is born. I want to show my sister—need to show her—that I can do this. If she is not satisfied, I am worried she will insist I move in with her and Rick, or hire the nanny Belinda mentioned.

"Maybe we should sell this house," Mattie says now, swiveling her head as if she is appraising its value on the spot.

Our mother has a will in which she bestowed all of her property to her two daughters in equal shares. It has not occurred to me, until Mattie makes this suggestion, that the house is not mine to live in as I please.

"We could use the money to hire a nanny." Her segue is indiscreet, her conclusion no surprise.

"I'll buy your half of the house," I say.

"With what?" she sputters.

I roll the hem of practice baby's pajamas back down to her knees. "My disability payments."

"Why would you want to do that, Ella?"

"Because I need a place of my own. I thought this was it." I wrinkle my mouth at her. I am not certain this is where I want to live permanently, but I add this to the argument because I need some ammunition.

"This is not about the house. Not really, is it?"

I push myself up from the floor because I have begun to feel like one of her students, Mattie looming over me with an authoritative stare. Her tone has sunk to disciplinary. I stand and stretch myself out, rising on my toes, then settle to my normal height, a few inches taller than she.

"Then what is it about, Mattie?"

She spins away, then stops at the doorway and turns back to me. "You act like this baby is yours."

"Well I …" I stop because she's right. I have been thinking of the baby as mine, not as a gift to my sister and her husband. I haven't wanted to contemplate exactly how I plan to go from the woman whose eggs have been fertilized into a growing child within her, to someone with the mere title of "Aunt."

She points an accusing finger at me. "We should have had an attorney draw up a contract. I told Rick that. This has gotten more than awkward."

"I'm your sister, Mattie. Not just your surrogate." Our defiant postures are reminiscent of our confrontation over Rick when I discovered their love letters lined up on the dressing table. She stole Rick from me. I wonder if she thinks I might steal this child from her as retaliation.

"We have to work this out," I say. Hot tears pool in my eyes as I silently recount what I have lost: my father; my mother; ex-husband Robert; Malcolm; my fiancé David; and my baby Eve. I can't lose Mattie too.

After a pause, Mattie steps forward. Her arms encircle me, pulling me in. I hear the sobs working their way up her throat, feel the shudder in her chest. She's suffered losses, too. Our father. Our mother. Almost me.

Through our tears, we reach an unspoken truce. Yet so much remains unsettled.

49

On a murky morning with spring fog cloaking our pastures, Mattie and I meet at the doctor's office for the first ultrasound. Mattie wants to drive me, but I insist on driving myself. I angle into a space away from other cars in the parking lot, and my mother's car sputters to a stop with a rattle.

I am scheduled to see Dr. Julian Anderson, an OB/Gyn I've never met. Mattie researched him on the internet and got several recommendations from teachers at the high school. Dr. Anderson is probably forty, with a tight head of dark curls beginning to gray at the temples. He maneuvers the wand over the cold jelly on my stomach as I watch the screen reveal vague shades of black and white. Eventually he finds our child. I cannot hear a heartbeat.

"Why can't I hear a heartbeat?" I say, tension in my throat.

"It's a little too early, Ms. Winslow. Nothing to be alarmed about," Dr. Anderson says. He takes some measurements. "I'd estimate about six weeks," he says through his mask.

"Ella thinks it's a girl," Mattie says. "Can you tell the sex this early? My research indicates we can't determine gender until three or four months."

"That's right," Dr. Anderson says. "It's too early for gender determination. But both mother and child look healthy."

Cleaned up and with my clothes back on, Mattie and I stare at the sonogram they have printed for us, squinting at the fuzzy confirmation of life not much larger than a kidney bean. Dr. Anderson knocks, then re-enters the exam room. He has taken off his mask, and his lips purse as he reads something on his tablet computer.

"What do you see that you're not telling us about?" I say.

He seems startled, both at my interruption and my insistent tone. He turns to me, his pleated blue mask dangling from one ear strap, and peruses me as if trying to detect something his science may not reveal. "The embryo appears fine," he says. "It's you I'm concerned about."

"I'm as healthy as a horse," I say. But then a grainy image of my horse Sweetness in agony flicks through my brain, and I remember what happened to her right after we pulled Sugar out of her.

"I've just now had a chance to look over your medical records from your doctors in Charlotte. In going over your latest lab results, I see an area of concern."

"My liver?"

He nods. "Your liver enzymes are way above normal. You may or may not know this, but by the time you reach full term, you will probably have 50% more than your pre-pregnancy blood volume. Your liver will have to process all of that blood. For you and the baby. We'll have to watch you carefully, and test your liver function every two weeks or so."

"But I'm not jaundiced."

"No, not at present." He pauses and looks me over, his eyes scanning my armless torso. "I was stationed in a hospital in a war zone in Afghanistan for a year," he says. "I saw a lot of injuries from explosions, mostly mines and IEDs. Excuse me for the blunt question, but did you lose your arms from the blast?"

"No, my arms were amputated in the hospital. I was told I had a flesh-eating bacterial infection."

He rubs his right palm across his chin. "We know very little about the long-term damage to blast victims, but the impact of the shock waves and the shrapnel can last years. Maybe even be permanent."

"I've been told as much."

"Your gall bladder may be impaired as well. That's normally not a concern, except during pregnancy. The liver and gall bladder have to work together. Does the baby's father know about your health issues?"

Mattie interjects. "We know about her liver. The gall bladder issue is new."

The doctor gives us both a puzzled look.

"Her husband is the baby's father," I say. "I'm the surrogate." There, I've said it. "And her sister." I nod at Mattie. "It's all consensual, even if it's a little complicated. Is the baby at risk?"

"No, not at the moment, but we have to keep a watchful eye on you. If you have any bleeding, abnormal urine discharge, or any pain, you let us know immediately."

When I step from the exam room into the tiled corridor, a tall man in a white coat dodges past me. He pauses at the door of a room at the end of the hall. In the florescent lights, his face is brightly lit. His salt and pepper hair is closely cropped, his face covered in a three-day growth of beard. As he glances back at me over a beak nose, he reminds me of Volkov. My tormentor. The man who killed my baby. The man who vaporized my fiancé. The terrorist who has yet to be caught.

I feel a spasm on my right side, just beneath the rib cage. I bend to that side to relieve the pain.

"Ella, what's the matter?" It's Mattie, her mouth ajar, her left hand steadying my shoulder.

"Ms. Winslow, are you alright?" Dr. Anderson asks.

As it rises into my throat, I swallow the pain back down. I nod my head. "Just a little tired. That's all."

On the way to my car, I lean against Mattie. I let her settle me into the front seat.

"Are you okay to drive?" she asks, her hand atop the driver's door.

I take a couple of deep breaths to calm myself. To steady my stomach. I feel it coming, like the rumble of a mini-volcano. Then I bend toward the asphalt and vomit. Mattie dances back but isn't quick enough. I splatter one of her shoes.

50

Fear. It has been a looming presence since I recognized Volkov as the man who drove the white van beneath the arena. I have successfully subdued the fear at times. But now it has decided to emerge from hibernation. While I am pregnant. Its malevolence is rampaging within me, alongside a burgeoning life now the size of an avocado.

It was not morning sickness that caused me to vomit in the parking lot that morning. I haven't had a bout of it, ever. To deal with the omnipresent sense of dread, I have taken to the roads, trying to gain dominion. Dr. Marvin says this is better than sitting around the house all day.

Over cracked asphalt and packed dirt and pine needle paths I move with the swiftness of deer. If I cannot face it, cannot fight it, I must flee it. For me. For the baby. For surely if I do not defeat fear, our baby will be adversely affected, perhaps emerging from my womb riddled with paranoia and terror.

When I return from a six-mile run through the coolness of narrow paths beneath towering yellow pines, I do not stop at the cattle guard as I usually do, but instead leap over the pipes and push up the tight hill to my house. Everything is pulsing. My lungs, my blood, my rounding abdomen. I finish on the grassy edge where the yard is invading the rocky driveway and stretch upward and back to give myself that extra sip of air.

That's when I feel the first flutter. It's subtle. No more than the flicker of a butterfly's wings. But it's there. A foot perhaps. Or an elbow. I cannot press my hand there to feel the movement or to reassure. Instead I parade across the yard, my shoes dampening with dew, my head thrown back and my mouth wide as if I am trying to drink it all in. There are tears, too. Mixed with the sweat and the grime from a jaunt in the woods.

In the distance, I hear the rattle of the cattle guard. Tires over galvanized steel pipes. An incoming car. Not one that I recognize. A dark sedan snakes up the driveway, neither cautiously nor aggressively. Tinted windows reflect the sun. Blocking my view inside.

As I watch, the anonymous driver parks behind my mother's car. With the engine still on, the tinted driver's window rolls down. Behind it is a man with hair far more pepper than salt, his face lined but tan, gold-rimmed sunglasses covering his eyes. He turns to me as if he has a message to deliver.

"Ms. Winslow," the man says.

The voice is strong. A voice not to be ignored.

"I'm Judge Westlake." He plucks the sunglasses from his face.

Recognition comes slowly, perhaps because he's not in a black robe sitting atop a wooden bench in a regal courtroom. Instead, he's wearing a denim shirt with a slightly frayed left collar. It looks like him. But what if it's not?

"If you have a few minutes, I'd like to talk to you."

I nod, expel the breath I've apparently been holding. He unfolds himself from his Mercedes and ranges above the top. I didn't remember him being quite so tall. But it is the Judge. He still has a faint, whitish scar on his right cheek. Confirmation.

"Have you been out running?" he asks, leaning against the fender with the tips of his fingers politely tucked in the front pockets of a pair of black jeans.

"Yes. I run almost every day."

"Me, too," he says. "In fact, I'm heading down to Charleston to run a 10k tomorrow."

"You race?"

He purses his lips. "That's up for debate. I do okay in my age group, but I wouldn't really call it racing."

He swivels around, taking in the house and the barn and the pastures that hold our small herd of cattle, grazing in the morning sun. "Looks like a peaceful place. Would you prefer to talk out here or …?"

"Oh, sorry," I say, still a bit off-balance. "How about on the porch?"

I mount the concrete steps. He follows. Since my mother's death, I have added two putty-colored plastic chairs to the porch furniture.

"May I sit here?" he asks, pointing to the glider. The padded seat of the porch glider is covered with yellow pollen.

"Sure. It's kind of dirty, though."

He begins to swipe away yellow gunk that has congealed with moisture on the vinyl pad of the glider. The pollen is mostly smearing, so he picks up the cushion and flips it over. That side is marred with dark stains.

He sidles over to one of the putty chairs instead. "Here is just fine."

I settle in the other chair, a round metal table between us. As I wait for him to announce the purpose of this strange visit, I see cobwebs in the upper corners of the porch, the beginnings of a papery nest for red wasps.

"Sorry for the mess, I … my mother died a few months ago. I haven't hired a housekeeper to help me."

He holds up a hand. "I'm an intruder here," he says. "Don't apologize. I live alone, so I know how it can be." He palms the plastic arms of the chair. His gaze returns to the fields. His mouth softens.

"I've been presiding over settlement negotiations in the lawsuits that you and the other victims have filed," he starts.

I remember his admonitions to me the day we sat in his conference room, before I told him I had seen Volkov driving the white van. "The lawsuit, are we supposed to be talking about that?"

"It's settled," he says. "The documentation is almost done. All of the victims, including you, will be compensated for your injuries. Maybe not enough, but substantial sums of money."

"I see. That sounds like good news."

"Yes, I think so. But that's not why I came here." He pauses then, swinging his sunglasses across the denim covering his thigh.

There can be only one other reason he's here. "This is about Volkov," I say.

He nods. "You're probably wondering what I did with the information you provided me during our meeting that day," he says. "Very valuable information." His eyes appear to be in contemplation of something in the distance. A cloud or a tree line. Or a memory, perhaps.

"I did wonder, for a while. I was a little surprised I didn't hear from the FBI or the police. Or somebody."

He turns to me. "This is highly confidential," he starts. "You can't disclose this to anyone." He measures me, his eyes drilling in. "Agreed?"

I nod. "Yes. Yes of course."

"I won't go into specifics, but you should know that Dr. Viktor Volkov is gone. He is no longer a threat to you. Or to anyone else."

What does that mean? Should I ask for details? Can I trust what he says enough to erase my fear forever?

"I wanted to inform you earlier. I suspect not knowing anything about him has been more than trying. Beyond difficult."

I gulp. "Yes. I'm still deathly afraid of him."

"That's the nature of terror. It lingers long after the act. Long after the terrorist is gone. But Volkov is gone."

"You're sure?" I say. "Because I'm about four months pregnant. It would help to be certain I'm bringing a new life into a world without someone like him lurking around the corner."

He looks me over, perhaps for confirmation of my pregnancy. "I'm positive. You have nothing to fear from him."

He says this as if issuing a final edict in his courtroom. Yet, I still have doubts.

"How can I be certain?"

"Volkov told me a story, Ms. Winslow. About his sister. That's really why I'm here."

"His sister?"

"Volkov was born in Russia. I don't know if you knew that. He had a sister who was born without arms. A birth defect. He said she was quite adept at caring for herself. Even so, he smothered her with a pillow. He was thirteen at the time."

"Oh my God." I don't know what to think. Except that if he was capable of murdering his sister as a young teenager, he is capable of anything.

"When Homeland Security raided his farm, which you probably saw on the news, they found old pictures of a young woman without arms." The Judge holds out his cell phone. On the screen is a photograph of a photograph. An old color photograph, creased on one side. A girl in her late teens. Black hair. Ice-blue eyes. Slender nose. Full lips. Armless.

She could be my twin.

Her image propels me from the chair. I scurry down the porch steps and into the front yard, hustling back and forth across the lawn. If I move with speed, maybe none of this will stick to me. I pivot and gyrate as if I'm dodging raindrops.

When I realize he's watching me, I stop. I take a deep breath. A sob goes down with it. I peer back at the Judge, who is standing on the edge of the porch, his hands at his sides. He comes down the steps and places his left hand flat at the top of my back.

"Are you okay, Ms. Winslow?"

I nod. But I'm not okay. Maybe I'm safe from Volkov, but the ramifications of what the Judge just told me will be with me forever. I understand it now. He re-shaped my eyes. He thinned my nose. He added fullness to my lips. Volkov remade me in the image of his sister.

The Judge's right hand dabs a white handkerchief beneath my eyes.

"I'll stand here for as long as you need me to," he says.

51

Rick sits atop a blue bulldozer. The smoke coming from its diesel engine is the dusky gray of a dove's wings. Before us lies the rubble of the old barn. Faded boards and rusted tin and stones from the rubble foundation litter the bare dirt. In this state, it looks nothing like the place in which my father raped my sister. It looks nothing like the chamber where he stood on a rickety three-legged stool, peering down at his executioners.

She hasn't said so, but I know Mattie has told Rick what happened in there. I can see it in the way he wields the bucket of the dozer, smashing Mattie's prison into splinters.

Once Rick clears the sheets of tin that formed the barn roof, Mattie and I light gas-soaked rags. I hold the flaming rag in my cupped fake hand and touch it to splinters of wood. I fling it away and scurry back from the first flames as the tinder begins to crackle and spit.

Mattie pulls me to her chest, her arms draped over my shoulders, her chin planted to the side of my neck.

"We should have done this years ago," she says.

"I know. It feels so cleansing."

In due time, the barn is nothing but a pile of char, with swirls of smoke drifting into an azure sky. Rick maneuvers the dozer, making the pile smaller, scraping the dirt clean and smooth. When the fire burns itself out, he douses the remains with the hose, scoops them into the dozer bucket, and buries them out of sight.

Mattie and I settle into roles unmarred by labels. She no longer nags me incessantly about my diet, or the runs that have gotten shorter and less intense, or the fact that when the wind shifts I am standing in the flow of smoke. She does not ask if I am taking my pre-natal vitamins or my iron supplements. She trusts me to tell her if my liver spasms, or if anything else is awry on the inside.

On the cleared site where the barn once stood, Mattie and Rick and I plant milkweed and zinnias and Mexican sunflower. We drape a loose canopy of black netting upon corner poles of three-inch PVC, which Rick and Mattie spray paint hunter green.

I spend most mornings and evenings in the butterfly garden, which is flourishing with flowers. The summer monarchs come and lay their tiny white eggs. The new generation emerges as gray-white larva with jet black heads. They eat nothing but milkweed until they grow into jade caterpillars two inches long. I watch the miracle of dozens of caterpillars spinning cocoons.

In month nine, I wander out to the butterfly garden in my pajamas and slippers as the sun breaches the eastern tree-line. I have temporarily abandoned running because my abdomen precedes me by nearly a foot, and the back pain has become so intense that not even Mattie's back rubs can quell it. I settle my haunches on the concrete bench that Rick has placed next to a white plastic fountain, from which a cherub spills water from an intricately molded can into a shallow dish.

A bevy of young butterflies already are exploring the habitat, hiding in the foliage, sipping nectar. I reach out to touch a translucent chrysalis with the index finger of my rubber hand. The soft womb vibrates from the gyrations of the butterfly inside. I can see the tightly wrapped orange and black wings. I hear the faint split of the chrysalis. The monarch's dual wings are tiny, its abdomen distended with fluid. It takes about twelve minutes for it to fully emerge.

I feel warm fluid running down my legs, dampening my pajamas. It's the release I've been anticipating for days. With effort, I wrestle my cell phone from the pocket of my pajama top.

"Call Mattie," I instruct.

Even though she is in class, she picks up on the second ring.

"It's time," I say.

"Your water broke?"

"Yes. It's time."

I waddle back to the house and stand in the shower for a few minutes. Then I slip on a pair of maternity panties three sizes larger than before I was pregnant. Using my special clothes rack, I don a sunflower yellow dress, slipping it over my head and arms with ease. It fits me like a tent.

I sit on the couch, the overnight bag Mattie and I packed three weeks ago at my feet. The first contraction hits me. It's not a mind-scrambler, but it catches me off-guard and snatches my breath. Then Mattie is here.

At the hospital, my liver fills me with sharp pains. This is what Dr. Anderson warned me about. I have developed red splotches on my face, signs my liver is deteriorating. I have disguised the splotches with base makeup. Because I don't want Mattie to know.

Mattie is sitting in a green vinyl chair next to the bed, watching my every movement. It would be futile for her to hold my hand.

As I lie in bed with uterine contractions alternating with liver spasms, sweat pops out on my face and beads my makeup. A nurse wipes my face with a cold, white cloth. She stares at the revealed red splotches, then locks eyes with me for about five seconds.

I shake my head in a silent plea for her discretion.

With a glance at Mattie, the nurse goes between my legs. She wiggles her fingers into me.

"You're dilated two centimeters," she says.

"That's good, right?" Mattie asks.

"Early enough for an epidural," the nurse says.

A doctor in blue scrubs and a paper hat rolls me onto my side and admonishes me to be still. I feel a pinch as something slides into my lower back and hear the scritch of medical tape being unrolled. I feel the press of it being applied to my skin. Then the doctor gently rolls me back over.

After the medicine surges up my spine, the pain of my liver and uterine contractions tapers to a mere annoyance. For the most part.

The nurse attaches leads to my chest and my abdomen. I turn to watch the rhythmic lines of the monitors tracking my pulse. And the baby's.

As I pored over the pregnancy books Mattie delivered to the house within days after Dr. Anderson confirmed I was pregnant, I inhaled the information as if it were sustenance itself. I wanted to know everything about every aspect of being pregnant. Every risk factor. Every predictable pang, whether physical, mental or emotional. When I needed to dig deeper, the internet gave me an abundance of information. I read OB/Gyn blogs. Hospital websites. Clinical studies on liver anomalies in pregnant women, preeclampsia, gestational diabetes. And even though I was willingly consuming this information, it began to overwhelm me. The mystery and magic of pregnancy and childbirth began to take on a sterile, clinical cast.

And so, when Dr. Anderson asked during the ultrasound in month five if I wanted to know the gender of the baby, I said "no."

"I do," Mattie responded.

I gave her what I hoped was an imploring look. "Let's leave it a mystery, Mattie. Just this one thing."

"It's a big thing, Ella."

"Knowing won't change anything, though. I certainly don't need to know the baby's gender to birth this child. Neither do you."

So Mattie relented. Not without some post-decision griping and churlish words. But I am convinced, as I lie here in a state of waiting, that Mattie does not know the gender of her child.

After seven hours, I am dilated only four centimeters. This baby does not want to come out. I cannot blame it, although staying inside of me much longer isn't really an option. I talk to the baby silently, urging it to find the path, assuring it that life outside will be perfectly fine. As if this will somehow encourage the baby to descend. The epidural drugs have made my mind into muck.

I suppose it is inevitable that in the throes of labor and contractions and the occasional side-splitting knife of pain the epidural fails to diminish, I would go back. Under the influence of painkillers, the whine of the bone saw returns. The scream works its way from my subconscious into my ears, as if Volkov is standing in the hallway revving up the saw. I know he's not. But still.

And then I am walking along a sidewalk, stopping to tie my shoe next to a brick wall. The fiancé whose face I still cannot conjure without a photograph beckons to me across the driveway. My tiny Eve and the womb I was creating to protect her have caused me to kneel, rather than lift my foot to the wall, so that I can tie up a loose lace. And survive. Eve was the real hero that day. Nobody knows that but me.

When I begin labor for real, one of the heart monitors emits an erratic beeping. The nurse makes Mattie leave.

"That's my baby in there," she protests all the way to the door.

Dr. Anderson's face appears, only his eyes exposed above his mask and below his paper cap.

"The baby is in distress," he says. Or I think he says. At this point, the amalgam of medication, pain, spasms, bleating monitors and resurrected fear leaves me in an addled state.

"I need to perform a C-section," he says. This I hear clearly, for it triggers in me something akin to a blaring red siren. Complications may include blood clots, sepsis, injury to my bladder or intestines, amniotic fluid embolism, and other risks I am too exhausted to enumerate.

"Your liver can't stand the stress. If we wait much longer, you might experience permanent liver damage. Or liver failure." He is holding a scalpel aloft. I see the glint of steel as his hand lowers toward my belly.

"If it's me or the baby," I whisper, "save the baby."

He holds my eyes for a second, then nods.

I hear screams. For several anesthesia-laden moments, I am convinced the screaming is coming from me. But then my eyes begin to clear, and I see the nurse is holding a bundle in a white blanket. That's where the screams are coming from.

Dr. Anderson appears noiselessly on the opposite side of my bed, bends his head toward me. "We almost lost you, Miss Winslow. Your heart stopped beating."

Yes, it did. Somehow, I am aware that for several moments I was dead. Not the first time. I swallow this down. "Thank you for saving both of us," I say.

He grips my fake arm and gives it a shake. "You're a fighter. Incredibly strong," he says. "Your son is lucky to have a mother like you."

"Son?" I say.

"He needs to be fed," the nurse says, lowering the bundle to my chest.

Mattie takes Dr. Anderson's place at my right side. She bends and twists my rubber arms and hands into a position akin to a cradle, what real arms can do. This little boy with clenched eyes and hen-pecked cheeks and wisps of dark hair curling from beneath his blue and white striped knit hat rolls toward me. He locks onto my left nipple. The screams immediately cease.

I feel the milk flowing from my breast into him as he slurps. He needs this from me. I need so much more from him.

AUTHOR'S NOTE

This book would not have been possible without the incredible courage of dozens of armless people, who have generously shared snippets of their lives, including moments of failure. I cannot express enough my gratitude and awe for each of them, and all of them as a group. The challenges they face in a single day exceed those most of us face in a lifetime.

Over the two decades it took to write this story, Ella's tone progressed from depressing to hopeful to elated as I began to understand Ella Winslow and appreciate the capabilities of amputees. I have watched double amputees drive cars, cook, eat with chopsticks, fly a plane, shoot a bow and arrow, play a cello. In the description of her life and its challenges, I have undoubtedly underestimated all that amputees can accomplish. For that, I apologize. The failing is mine alone, and a product of my own limitations and ignorance. I encourage all readers to spend some time watching the wondrous feats these able-bodied people can accomplish. I promise you will be amazed.

OTHER BOOKS BY MICHAEL WINSTEAD

Ultimate Verdict – A Legal Thriller
Ultimate Deception - The Secret Tribunal
Ultimate Truth - The Final Installment

ABOUT THE AUTHOR

Michael Winstead is a veteran of courtroom battles. He has tried dozens of cases and argued many appeals in our state and federal courts. He is intrigued by the judicial system and how it affects the human condition, frequently altering lives in unforeseen and irreversible ways.

The author of the Ultimate Verdict trilogy, his novels examine the motives and purposes that drive people to commit horrible and evil crimes. His books also portray the devastating impact that violence has on victims, their families, and the judicial system at large.

Winstead lives and writes fiction in the mountains of North Carolina and on the first coast of Florida.

You can contact the author at michaelwinstead.com.

www.ingramcontent.com/pod-product-compliance
Lightning Source LLC
LaVergne TN
LVHW020705110826
845149LV00012B/2111

9780999242124